CHARLIE RESPONSE

Joseph Meece

Grace & Peace
Be With You

Joseph
Meece

Faithful Life Publishers
North Fort Myers, FL
FaithfulLifePublishers.com

Charlie Response

© 2013 Joseph Meece
ISBN: 978-1-63073-003-1

Published and printed by:
Faithful Life Publishers
3335 Galaxy Way
North Fort Myers, FL   33903

888.720.0950

www.FaithfulLifePublishers.com
info@FLPublishers.com

19 18 17 16 15 14 13   1 2 3 4 5

I dedicate this book to my loving family and to my Lord and Savior, Jesus Christ, without Whom, nothing is possible.

CHARLIE RESPONSE
ACKNOWLEDGEMENTS

I wish to acknowledge the many people that helped make this book possible.

Thank you to my lovely wife for her patience and understanding. She answered me patiently every time I asked how to spell a word or how a phrase sounded. Any other woman might have killed me.

To my late mother, who told me to write this book, thank you for always believing in me. I wish you were still here to enjoy this with me.

To my former Division Officer, Commander Bohannan, thank you for sending me a copy of my own manuscript when my computer crashed and I did not have a back-up copy. You really saved me and I learned a valuable lesson. Thanks also for your critique and guidance, both in and out of the Navy.

Thank you to my VA doctors, Dr. K and Dr. Cook, for your encouragement over the years and your faith in my writing.

Thank you to all the magazines that have published my articles— HOG Magazine, Full Throttle Magazine, Go Far Magazine, and of course, Katie of Kruising with Katie. I also want to thank the many people on Katie's forum, Kruising with Katie, who encouraged me throughout this process.

Thank you to the employees of Harley-Davidson of Ft. Myers, #1 Cycle Center of Centre Hall, and Apple Harley-Davidson in Duncansville. I talked to all of you about different things in the book and about the different models of Harley-Davidson motorcycles. I give you thanks for your input and your time.

Thank you to the city of Ft. Myers, Florida for having your Downtown Bike Nights in the winter months. I totally enjoy them and met many riders there. It was there that I saw a member of the Christian Motorcycle Association witness to a biker about our Lord and Savior. It was very moving when I saw a gray haired biker fall to his knees and ask our Savior for forgiveness of his sins and asked Jesus Christ into his heart.

Thank you to my editor and the staff at Faithful Life Publishers. Without your help, this book would never have made it this far.

Thank you to all my friends, whether in life or in church, throughout the years for standing by me.

To all the pastors I have had throughout my life, thank you, for without your teaching I would never have learned about my Savior, Jesus Christ. Thank you, Pastor Strange and Pastor Christine, my current pastors. Pastor Fred Ruby, who helped guide me in prayer in the directions I should take while writing this novel. Without your guidance, I do not know what I would have done. Thank you.

Finally, but most importantly, I want to thank my Lord and Savior, Jesus Christ. Words cannot fully express how grateful I am that You count me as one of Your own. Without You, nothing in my life makes sense and this book would not be possible.

CHARLIE RESPONSE
CHAPTER ONE

Jacob's broad muscles strained as he finished unloading the last of the Silver Queen sweet corn from his buckboard trailer. He and his young bride, Rebecca, were getting their wares ready for the big Belleville Sale, a local farmer's market and livestock auction. Just married the year before, Jacob and Rebecca were in the beginning stages of making a fine life for themselves within the Amish community. Rebecca was happy, loving the life of an Amish homemaker. Jacob turned to her and said, "I'll head back and get the load of Red Haven peaches; then I can help you with the customers."

She grinned at him and replied, "Hurry back; I love it when you have free time to spend with me, even in work." Rebecca turned back to getting the produce ready for customers.

Jacob lightly held the reigns and thought about the many ways that the Lord had blessed him. He had a caring and beautiful wife that adored him; a farm that had produced an abundant crop this year; and a talent for woodworking that had many people in the area calling him for special projects.

Jacob took off his straw hat to wipe the sweat from his brow, thanking God for the light breeze that fanned his thick, brown hair. It was only 8 a.m., but the needle on the thermometer had already reached the eighty degree mark. Jacob knew he would have to water his Morgan horse as he loaded the peaches onto the trailer, before heading back to the sale grounds.

• • • • • • • • • • •

Hugh Lamadeleine, a truck driver from Ontario, Canada, walked into the office at Interforest Lumber Company to pick up his paperwork. Interforest Lumber Company was located in Shade Gap, Pennsylvania, a small rural community of about a hundred people. As he filled out the proper forms, the dispatcher walked over and asked, "Would you mind going a little out of your way to pick up an extra load for a bit of extra money?"

Hugh replied, "Of course, I wouldn't mind at all. Money is what keeps the truck on the road, after all."

"Good. You would be helping me out quite a bit. They are out of this wood up in Perth, Canada, where this load is heading, but they already have some cut at the Allensville Planning Mill. I'll give you an extra $250 for your trouble."

"Sounds like a good deal to me," exclaimed Hugh.

Hugh walked around his trailer, making sure all the straps were tight, and then climbed into the cab of his two year old Volvo truck. Home sweet home for several weeks at a time, his truck was outfitted much like a tiny house with a bed, microwave, television, and small refrigerator. He logged the start time into his log book, as well as his computer. Sending the information to his company via e-mail, he noticed that his wife, Martha, had sent him a message, telling him that she was praying for his safe travels and that the church was praying for him, as well.

Hugh put the address for the Allensville Planning Mill into his GPS and headed out, traveling on Route 522 North. The quaint Welcome to Shade Gap sign passed from his view as he shifted gears and headed up the ridge. He turned on his CB radio and sent out a radio check for Snow Fox, but there was no response. Hugh figured he must be the only one on the road for now. So he turned on the radio looking for some music to keep him company, but the only station he could find was Froggy 98, a country station from Altoona.

. . . .

A slight, misty fog hovered over part of Lake Raystown Resort, making the boats tied to trees on shore just barely visible. The smell of bacon hung in the air from several cabins and campfires. People lingered over their breakfast in this neck of the woods, before gearing up for life on the lake. Swimming, boating, fishing, and hiking were the order of the day for most people visiting the 32 mile long lake. The area even had its own legendary myth, a creature much like the Loch Ness monster, which brought photographers here, cameras in hand. Life in this place was idyllic; the worst that happened in this beautiful oasis were skinned knees from running on slippery rocks.

Joseph Daniels, known to his friends as Joey D, stepped out of his cabin, stretched in the morning sun, and said, "Honey, it's beautiful out here this morning. I'll get the Beast uncovered for our ride." The Beast, as it was affectionately known, was a Harley-Davidson Electra Glide Ultra Limited. He lifted the cover, squinting from the sun glaring off the shining 103 cubic inch motor. As he walked around the back of the bike, he wiped the dust off the Pennsylvania license plate that read USN RET. He rolled up the cover and took it into the cabin.

Joey D and his wife, Kelly, came out ready for their ride to the Belleville Sale, dressed in jeans and lightweight t-shirts. He tossed his leather riding jacket and gloves on the seat of the Beast. Meanwhile, Kelly dropped her keys on the front seat of the pickup truck which was their chase vehicle. She had made this ride many times; but since they planned on going to the sale, she decided to bring the truck to carry their purchases. She knew having the truck along was also a good idea in case a bike broke down and needed to be hauled back to the cabins.

They walked over to a small cluster of people standing by the row of motorcycles in the parking lot. Kelly greeted her friend, Hope, and asked how she and her husband, Sam, had slept. Samuel and Hope Adams had made the long ride from Mississippi to Pennsylvania to meet the group, arriving the previous evening. Sam looked up from polishing the chrome on his Ultra Glide, and grimaced when he said, "Well, I slept like a rock, but I don't think the ache in my shoulders will ever go away. Ouch!" The small group laughed; they all knew that feeling.

Terry Miller, who rode his Screaming Eagle Ultra Glide over from Maryland, said, "I just got off the phone with my wife. She says to have a great ride today and she can't wait to get here tomorrow. Personally, I can't wait until she sees this place. This is one of our best meeting places ever. We'll definitely have to come here again." The others murmured their agreement, and then started to plan the day. Terry bent down to tighten the screw of the license plate on his bike, which read 1ST CLAS.

Mark Brown and his wife, Paula, came out of their cabin and strolled over to join the group. All of them were dressed similarly, wearing jeans, t-shirts, riding jackets, and gloves, much of which had the Harley-Davidson logo on them. As Mark climbed on his Screaming Eagle Road Glide and Paula stood next to her Screaming Eagle Street Glide, Joey D addressed everyone, "Today, I will be in the lead and Kelly will follow in the truck. All of us, including Kelly, have CB radios, so we can communicate with each other as we go along on the ride. We will stay on channel 1, because we are number one!" Here a few chuckles interrupted him.

"But also remember to use hand signals," he continued. "We'll be leaving the resort and making a right turn onto Route 994. Watch out for the sharp turns and also for deer in the fog this morning. After a while, we'll turn left and go into the town of Todd. Again, watch out for deer on this road. We'll head towards Cassville, then turn onto Route 829. Those with GPS will find this easy. It's going to be a nice ride. After Cassville, we will go past the towns of Calvin and Colfax. And no, Calvin isn't named after the famous John Calvin. We'll then cross over a mountain. After we come off the mountain, please be careful after we cross the bridge going over the Juniata River, because there we cross railroad tracks. We'll make a right on Route 22 East. In Mill Creek, at the traffic light we make another left on Route 655 towards Belleville. Are there any questions? No? Then let's ride and keep it safe out there."

There was a general rumble as everyone started to get their gear ready to go. Joey D raised his hand and called for a few moments of silence, "Okay, let's gather around for prayer. Heavenly Father, we gather this morning to give thanks for a beautiful morning and a restful night's sleep. We praise Thee for all that You have given us. We humbly request that You extend traveling mercies upon us today as we ride. Please be with us and with our family and friends. Bless our country and our troops. In Jesus name, we pray, Amen."

Sam said, "Amen, let's roll." The Harley-Davidson motorcycles came to life with their signature sound as they pulled away—potato, potato, potato.

• • • • • • • • • • •

Sweat rolled down his arms as Jacob finished loading the rest of the peaches onto his buckboard trailer. He absently wondered how many would brave the heat and humidity to come to the sale. He knew that his fellow Amish would all be there, but how many English would come today? The Amish people belong to tight-knit communities. Most Amish families have a heritage belonging to the German or Swiss-German countries, so they call non-Amish people that live in this country the English.

As Jacob headed back, he saw other buggies heading to the sale. In the still of the early morning, it was already a busy day for all of them. Jacob raised his hand and waved to his friends as they trotted by.

· · · · · · · · · · ·

Jacob began to unload the trailer full of peaches as soon as he got back to the sales stands. His father, Jeb, walked over and said, "Jacob, everything looks fine. It's going to be a good day. There will be many English here today. You should go back and get some of your woodwork. I think some of your rocking chairs, gun cabinets, and wood carvings would sell today. Hurry home and get them. Your mother can help Rebecca if it gets too busy."

Jacob pulled Rebecca aside and explained, "Father wants me to bring some of my wood workings. No matter what, this will be my last trip back to the farm for the day. When I return, I'll be here for good."

"I love you, Jacob. Be very careful. The English will soon be out on the roads in their cars," whispered Rebecca as she squeezed his hand.

Her soft brown eyes followed him as he walked away saying, "I will."

Many Amish men are great wood workers, and Jacob was counted as one of them. People throughout Big Valley called Jacob Peachey Wood Working for special projects. He quickly loaded two rocking chairs, two benches with carvings of deer, a gun cabinet with beautiful nature carvings on it, and some smaller wood carvings into his trailer. As Jacob turned his horse down the lane and in the direction of the Belleville Sale, he whistled a tune trying to match the birds singing in the trees. He smiled to himself as he said, "Sure hope I won't have to bring any of this back home with me.

. . . .

As they pulled up to a stop sign in Cassville, Joey D let the others catch up and asked, "Are you all enjoying this ride so far?" Several of the group nodded in the affirmative or gave thumbs-up. "I know of a great back road called Beavertown Road. I hear that it's all twists and turns. It would be a great road to check out on the way back. What do you all think?"

"Sounds like a good plan!" responded Mark. "The scenery is great here, but I would love to go a little more off the beaten path."

"All right then, let's ride, people!" They pulled away from the stop sign with a roar. Sam's voice came over the CB radio commenting on the fact that a small town as Cassville had such a large new car dealership. They headed onto Route 829 and up into the glorious heights of the mountains.

After they had ridden for some time, Joey D pulled into a sightseeing turn off. He pointed down into the valley, saying, "That's a sand plant down there. Sand that came from there was used to make the glass for the Hubble telescope. We'll pass by some of the digging." Several of the riders got their cameras out of their saddle bags and took photos of the picturesque valley below. After a brief rest period and drinks from their water bottles, they climbed back onto the bikes. Making it safely over the railroad tracks, they pointed the motorcycles eastbound on Route 22.

Descending down into Big Valley, the small assembly of roaring motorcycles wound their way through rolling hills and carefully laid out farms. Amish horse and buggies clip clopped along the roads, adding to the historic feel of the area.

Carefully, they pulled into the parking lot of the Belleville Sale, crowded with cars, trucks, and Amish buggies. They slowly maneuvered their motorcycles between and around people, careful not to hit anyone.

Inside the sale area were many different kinds of people; children running to keep up with their families, people with cameras rudely trying to capture photographs of the shy Amish people, adults trying to haggle a better deal from a vendor, and people from all walks of life just sauntering and sight-seeing. The Belleville Sale is part livestock sale, part produce sale, and part flea market; making every direction you look something interesting to see.

"Let's head over to where they sell the livestock. It would be pretty amazing to see how that process works. I just kind of want to see the animals, too," said Joey D.

Kelly chuckled as she commented, "He always did want to be a farmer. Never really grew out of it, I guess." And so the group of friends went off to see the farmers unloading the livestock that were to be sold later that day.

• • • • • • • • • • •

Hugh pulled his big Volvo into the Allensville Planning Mill and was directed toward the loading docks. As he climbed down out of his big rig, a man approached him. "Hey there, I'm Tom. We'll take care of getting you loaded. Why don't you go get something to eat while you wait? This should take us about thirty minutes."

Hugh replied, "Thanks, Tom. Is there any place you'd recommend for getting a quick bite?"

Walking the two blocks to the restaurant that Tom had pointed him toward, Hugh noticed the savory aroma wafting through the air and his stomach rumbled. He noticed two Amish buggies parked outside. He went inside and ordered the Amish Special and a cup of coffee.

After eating, Hugh walked back to his truck feeling the wonderful effects of a great meal. *Amish cooking sure is good—and filling*, he thought to himself. When he returned to the mill, Tom showed him where the scales were to have his truck reweighed.

Once all the legalities were taken care of, Hugh was given the green light to go. He made his entry into his log book and his laptop computer. He pulled out onto the road and went through the gears, gathering speed on his way to Belleville. When he got closer to town, he noticed that traffic was much heavier than normal. The Belleville Sale had swelled the amount of traffic to many times its normal amount. Also, the horse and buggies going along on the road were much slower than the usual speed of cars and trucks. He would have to keep a watchful eye on the road.

Hugh picked up his cell phone to call his wife. "Hi, Martha. I'm going to be running a bit late. I picked up my load in Shade Gap, but they asked me to pick up an extra load in Allensville. They are having a big flea market or something nearby that is backing up traffic a little, but I should be back in Perth tomorrow afternoon and home by evening," Hugh said, as he reached over to pick up a map that had fallen onto the floor. "Yeah, I'd love to grill some steaks when I get there. Of course, I'll be careful. I'll call you later. Love you, sweetheart." He hung up and put his cell phone back in its place on the passenger seat.

• • • • • • • • • • • •

While the men were looking at the livestock, Kelly, Paula, and Hope decided to check out the fresh farm produce at the sale. They picked out some corn and peaches from Jacob and Rebecca Peachey's stand. "This corn will be great tonight with some grilled hamburgers, and fresh peaches with some ice cream will just hit the spot for dessert, don't you think?" Kelly asked of her companions.

The girls nodded in agreement, while Paula replied, "That sounds great!"

Kelly handed Rebecca the correct amount of change, as she told her what beautiful produce they had at their stand. She explained that she and her husband lived just outside of Shade Gap and were here visiting Lake Raystown on a motorcycle trip with their friends. "These are my friends, Paula and Hope," she commented to Rebecca. "Our husbands are off looking at the livestock. They all served in the Navy together and we've all been friends ever since." While Rebecca bagged the corn and peaches for her, Kelly continued, "This whole area is beautiful and the lake is so relaxing; I wish there was a rocking chair on the porch at our cabin. You wouldn't happen to know if any of the stands here at the sale have any products like that, do you?"

Rebecca smiled as she replied, "My husband, Jacob, makes handcrafted rocking chairs. He actually just went back to pick up a load of his woodworking. If you're going to be around a while, come back by here in a little bit to see what a fine craftsman he is."

"My husband's birthday is tomorrow. That would make a great present for him. I'll be back around pretty soon," Kelly happily informed Rebecca.

The ladies met back up with the men just moments later. Sam asked Hope if she was ready to get back on the road. The idea had been tossed around by the men to ride the Beavertown Road back towards the cabin and take Joey D and Kelly's pontoon boat out on the lake. "I think I'm going to stick around for a little while longer, if that's alright with you," Kelly informed Joey D.

Hope added, "I think I'll stay with her. I wouldn't mind looking around a bit more."

"Call us when you get back and we'll swing around and pick you up on the boat," agreed Joey D.

"I will. Ride safely. Take it easy on the Beast," she cautioned as she reached up to kiss him good-bye. "I love you." After general good-byes all around, the men and Paula took off on their ride back to the cabin to spend the rest of the afternoon on the Daniels' 27 foot Premier pontoon boat.

· · · · · · · · · · · ·

Having loaded as much as he could into his trailer, Jacob headed back to the sale grounds. He drove carefully over the top of a small hill. There was an orange triangle and flashing light on the back of his trailer to caution other drivers that he had a slow moving vehicle. Still, he kept a watchful eye on both the road and his horse.

Hugh was multi-tasking as he drove down the road; listening to both the CB and the radio, talking on his cell phone, and checking e-mails on his laptop computer. He called his wife back, just moments after he ended his previous call with her. "Honey, they're playing our song on the radio, *Eighteen Wheels and a Dozen Roses.*" He took a quick glance at his laptop screen, and then looked back up at the road in front of him. He saw a hill and increased his speed.

Joey D reached for his CB radio, "Everyone watch out for buggies. We're going up a small hill and you never know what's on the other side. Decrease speed."

Sam and Terry both responded, "Roger, copy that."

As Hugh crested the top of the hill, he glanced down at the screen on his laptop and said to Martha on his cell phone, "Yes, that's a great picture of our grandson." He looked back up just in time to see Jacob's buggy. Hugh's cell phone fell to the floor as he shouted, "LOOK OUT!"

Yanking the wheel hard to the left, Hugh was completely surprised by the motorcycles headed straight for him. Slamming on his brakes, Hugh cut the wheel to the right and headed into the cornfield. However, as Hugh bounced around trying to control his rig, his trailer had other ideas about staying on the road. The jack-knifed trailer torpedoed toward the other occupants of the road, like a windshield wiper scraping a bug off your window.

The back of the trailer slammed into Jacob's buggy, leaving his broken body lying among the ruins of his now shattered woodworking.

Like most experienced cyclists, Joey D's group was riding in staggered formation. Due to their years of experience and many motorcycle safety classes, they each did their best maneuvers to escape the impending danger.

Joey D hit his brakes and swerved to avoid the trailer, but his saddlebag clipped it, which resulted in a low-side fall where he hit Jacob's buggy.

Sam, riding opposite behind Joey D, let out a scream and applied both brakes, leaning to the left. His bike slammed into the truck and the tires ran over Sam's Ultra Glide.

Because Terry was riding using the two second rule that he had learned in the Harley-Davidson Rider's Edge Class, he had more time to brake efficiently. However, as he swerved he hit Joey D's bike, which launched him over the handlebars in a high-side fall, hitting the horse's belly with his head.

Mark saw everything happening in front of him and tried to execute a quick stop with both brakes. He had to lay the bike down and slide underneath the trailer to avoid hitting it.

Using every bit of knowledge that she had learned in the Motorcycle Safety Foundation Basic Course and the Harley-Davidson Rider's Edge Experience Riders Course, Paula was able to perform a perfect quick stop. Keeping her bike upright, she was able to avoid the horrible accident. Immediately, Paula retrieved her mobile phone and called 911 to report the accident.

Paula, being a retired US Navy Hospital Corpsman and Chambersburg Paramedic, was trained to handle situations just like this—but these were her friends! Before panic could set in, Paula swiftly went to check on her four riding buddies. She determined they were all in bad shape. Joey D, Sam, Terry, and Mark were all unconscious, but it looked as if Terry and Mark fared better than the others. Mark was wavering between different levels of unconsciousness. She went to check on Jacob, who was screaming, "Help me!"

The call came across the scanners of Big Valley, "Charlie Response! A tractor trailer truck hit four motorcycles and an Amish buggy one and a half miles outside of Belleville on Route 655. There are serious injuries to at least five people. Send engines, rescue, and ALS Units from Belleville, Allensville, and Reedsville to respond. Paramedic on the scene, requesting multiple life flights to be on standby."

When the Belleville Fire Chief arrived at the scene, he called in to dispatch requesting that everyone responding switch to the alternate channel for communications. He ordered four life flight helicopters and extra manpower to assist with the landing zones. He let dispatch know that there was a field at the scene which could be used for landing the helicopters and passed along the readings from his GPS to be sent to the chopper pilots. Then he stood silently shaking his head, praying for all involved in the carnage he saw before him. Living in this peaceful area, he had never seen such a horrible sight.

Paula took a quick second to call Kelly to tell her about the accident, "Yes, it's really bad, Kelly. I need you girls to get here as quick as you can, but watch for emergency vehicles. We don't want to slow them down from getting here. The boys need help quickly."

Kelly started trembling, and Hope said, "What's going on?"

As Kelly explained everything to Hope, Rebecca started to feel faint. She knew instinctively that Jacob was involved, too. She yelled for Jeb to take her to her husband. "You can ride with me! Come on!" urged Kelly.

Paula showed the Belleville Chief her paramedic badge and explained to the Bellville EMS Chief what she had witnessed. She assured the medics that she had not touched the victims, but offered to help in any way she could. She was checked out for shock; but when it was determined that she was fine, she was sent to help the EMTs that were working on the young Amish man lying on the side of the road.

The Chief set up the command center and then let the emergency medical people do their jobs. The helicopters were on their way. The choppers from State College and Altoona would be the first to arrive, with ones from Hagerstown, Maryland and Johnstown, Pennsylvania arriving shortly after. Word of mouth in Amish communities worked almost as fast as telephones in other areas. As a result, people were already starting to gather to see what was happening in their small rural neighborhood. When the Chief looked toward the crowd of on-lookers, he grimaced. He would have a problem getting emergency vehicles through, if he did not take care of this problem immediately.

Cars, trucks, and buggies lined the road. Kelly only got so far with the truck before she, Hope, and Rebecca started running. When they were a little closer to the scene, they were stopped by a fireman as he said, "Sorry, ladies. Only emergency personnel allowed." Kelly explained that their husbands were the ones in the accident. He quickly called the Chief, who sent Paula to her friends to give them information and comfort them. He showed Paula an area that he was assigning to them to wait for more information.

With the first two life flight helicopters arriving at the same time, there was a bit of a scramble to get them both landed safely. Luckily, the field was large enough for both to land and the fire fighters directed them in with the skill of professional airport workers. As soon as they were able, the life flight crew came over to load Sam, with his already attached IVs, into the chopper. As expedient as it came in, it was off again. A man in the crowd of by-standers commented to his wife, "That reminded me of a dust-off helicopter in Vietnam. They came out of nowhere and left in a flash."

Joey D was soon loaded up in the helicopter from Altoona. He also had advance life support equipment hooked up to him. When Kelly started running for her husband, screaming, Fire police stopped her, saying that they were taking everyone to Penn State Hershey Medical Center and that she should go there.

Fearing that he had a broken neck, Terry was prepped with a cervical collar. Badly banged up and in serious condition, he was carefully loaded into the third life flight helicopter.

Finally, the life flight from Johnstown arrived. As the medics were attending to Mark to get him ready for the flight, it was decided that Jacob needed the flight more urgently than he did. So they settled Mark into an ambulance for the trip to the hospital in Hershey.

Being thoughtful of others, Kelly asked a fireman how Rebecca would get to Hershey Medical Center, since she obviously would not have a car. He explained, "The Amish people rely on neighbors that have vehicles to help them out. Somehow, they always seem to manage to get by."

As Kelly walked back to join the group, she heard Rebecca filling in all the details for Jeb. They watched as Jacob was being loaded into the helicopter and Jeb said, "Rebecca, we must take the time right now to pray for everyone involved." He bowed his head as he continued, "Father, please take care of Jacob and everyone else in the accident. Guide the hands and minds of everyone on the medical staff. We give thanks for all those who came out today. Please bless them all. Father, let Thy will be done, in the name of Jesus Christ, Amen."

Kelly informed the small gathering of worried friends that she knew the way to Hershey Medical Center. She invited Jeb and Rebecca to ride with her in the truck. While Rebecca turned to others to assure they would take care of their stand at the sale, Jeb gratefully accepted, "God bless you, child! Thank you so much. Yes, we would like that. I can give you some money for your trouble."

Kelly responded with, "No. That's not necessary at all. We all just need to be there for each other today."

Before they left, Kelly and Hope loaded Paula's bike into the back of the truck with the Rampage Power Lift Ramp. They all climbed into Kelly's Dodge together and set off east toward Hershey. Her mind burdened with so much worry, Kelly wondered if she would be able to keep her focus on the road. However, what Kelly did not know, was that many strangers were on their knees joining her in prayer for safety in the hands of God.

· · · · · · · · · · ·

Just one week prior to the accident, Penn State Hershey ran their Mass Casualties drill. This time the drama was for real. Four life flight helicopters were coming in and the hospital was in organized chaos getting prepared. Emergency room technicians were quickly getting everything in order. Doctors, nurses, x-ray technicians, and surgeons were paged to come to the emergency room. Doctors who had the day off were put on stand-by, just in case. The blood bank was also put on notice.

Shortly, the hospital started receiving calls from the in-coming helicopters. Flight nurses informed the hospital of the patient's statistics and vital signs. Pilots gave the hospital the estimated time of arrival (ETA).

Throughout the flight, people with scanners could listen in on the conversations between the helicopters and the hospital. Local churches started prayer chains for everyone, including the emergency workers. The air waves still filled the air with vital information that was being sent to the emergency room. The doctors had prepared a battle plan for how they were going to treat everyone, even before the first patient arrived. Thanks to modern technology, everyone was informed early on and could implement a quick response.

· · · · · · · · · · ·

At the scene of the accident, Pennsylvania State Police spoke to Hugh and the other witnesses, as well. They administered a field sobriety test which Hugh passed. They then pulled the information from the semi truck's onboard computer which recorded the speed of the large truck at the time of the accident. At that time, Pennsylvania had a new law about cell phone usage while driving. Did typing on a laptop computer fall under the *no texting while driving* law?

After the Police took pictures and measurements of skid marks and the placement of different vehicles, it was time for the fire companies to start cleaning up the accident scene. While they gathered up the twisted metal and wood, the police called the local towing companies. Regular rollback tow trucks could handle the motorcycles, but the truck and trailer required that a heavy duty wrecker be called in. Runk's Towing from James Creek, near Lake Raystown, was called to move the big rig, because he had a heavy duty tow truck made just for eighteen wheelers.

As she was driving, it occurred to Kelly that Terry's wife, Heidi, knew nothing of the dreadful circumstances. "Hope, I think one of us should get in touch with Heidi and let her know what's going on."

Hope tried to contact Heidi at her home and on her cell phone, but there was no answer. "Try calling her at work. She can't take her cell phone in the building while she is working," instructed Kelly.

Hope called the office and Heidi answered, "Hello. T-Comm, Heidi speaking."

"Heidi, this is Hope."

"Hi dear, how are things? I can't wait until my vacation starts tomorrow and I see you all," replied Heidi.

"Heidi, stop talking. I have to tell you something." Hope began to whimper, but quickly regained her composure and continued, "Sweetie, the boys were in an accident outside of Belleville. An eighteen wheeler swerved to miss a horse and buggy and came into the boy's path."

Heidi stifled a small scream, as people in the office looked at her and wondered what was going on. She started crying softly. Hope continued, "Listen, Joey D and Sam are hurt extremely badly and Terry and Mark are also in serious condition. Terry missed the truck, but was thrown over the handlebars and landed head first into the side of the horse. Right now, he has no feeling in his legs! Everyone was life flighted to Penn State Hershey Medical Center. You need to get there as soon as you can! We're on our way there now."

Like the others in the group, Heidi had joined the Navy as a Cryptologic Technician, but she went to college while she was in the Navy and then became a U.S. Naval Intelligence Officer. She retired as a Lt. Commander. She then went to work at the National Security Agency in research. It was during Terry's tour of duty at the Agency that they met. He fell head over heels for Heidi, a tall, blonde, green eyed lady, who loved the outdoors and sports. Eventually, she became one of the big bosses at T-Comm with the rank of GS-14, all while working on her PHD from the University of Maryland in Applied Physics. Terry, with the rank of GS-11, also worked at the Agency in Tech Control, while at the same time working on his Masters in electrical engineering from University of Maryland.

All the college degrees and work related awards just did not seem to matter now. The love of her life, Terry, was hurt and she, momentarily, did not know what to do. First, she called her staff to her office to let them know what happened. Then she called her boss, who told her to take as much time off as she needed. She went home and grabbed her overnight bag, which was always ready, in case of a work related emergency. She never dreamed the emergency would be something like this. Quickly, she was on I-81 headed north towards Harrisburg, where she would catch Route 322 toward Hershey. Her Lincoln MKZ was made for the interstate. She was making up for lost time by traveling at a high rate of speed. She wondered if she would even beat Kelly and Hope there.

• • • • • • • • • • •

Hugh called Martha to let her know what happened, then told her he would call her back after he reported the accident to his trucking company. She said she would pray for him and the injured people. "I'm so glad that you weren't hurt in the accident," Martha told Hugh, "I love you, please come home as soon as you can."

Hugh called the trucking company and reported the accident, as required by law. He was concerned for those in the accident and began to pray for their safe recovery. Being a Christian, Hugh also prayed for forgiveness.

A Pennsylvania State police officer asked him step over to the command center to answer some more questions, so Hugh walked over to where there were. The police officer then told Hugh to turn around and put his hands on the car. They frisked him, put him in handcuffs, read him his rights, and placed him under arrest. The on-lookers were stunned—they do not usually arrest people for getting into an accident, do they? A low murmur was heard as the crowd asked the question of each other. Hugh had to ask why he was being arrested. The arresting officer informed him that they had discovered three outstanding warrants from York County. All three were for hit and run accidents involving a tractor trailer. One of these accidents had produced a fatality.

"N-n-not possible!" stammered Hugh. "I've never been in an accident in forty two years of driving! This must be a mistake!" The thought briefly crossed his mind that he was being blamed because he was from Canada and they needed a scapegoat.

Hugh was taken to Lewistown Hospital to have blood work done to check for alcohol or drugs in his system. From there they took him to the Pennsylvania State Police Headquarters for further questioning.

The funny thing about rumors is how quickly they can start. People throughout Big Valley immediately started telling tall tales about a rogue killer truck driver killing anywhere from four to eight people. A fire fighter, taking off his turn out gear, confronted one person who was telling another that eight people were killed. "You really know a lot about what happened, don't you?"

"Yes. I saw the whole thing," the man assured him.

"That's funny! There weren't even eight people involved in the accident!" the firefighter snarled. "And as of right now—no one is dead. The best thing you could do is to spend your time praying for those injured in the accident, instead of spreading ridiculous rumors. I'm an EMT and I definitely know what happened. You, on the other hand, know nothing."

"Can you tell us who was in the accident?"

"You know I can't release information like that yet," the firefighter commented as he walked towards another officer who was being questioned by a reporter for WTAJ TV10.

CHARLIE RESPONSE
CHAPTER TWO

They checked in at the Emergency Room's front desk and were shown into a waiting room where medical personnel would soon talk to them. No one at the front desk had any information about the condition of their loved ones. Heidi arrived at the hospital and wanted answers that no one could give her. It was very frustrating for all of them and they felt so helpless.

When Kelly, Hope, and Paula saw that Heidi had arrived, they ran down the hall and embraced her in a group hug, crying. They all started talking at once, telling her what had happened. They walked back into the waiting room as Paula described Hugh's truck hitting the Amish buggy. Hearing her words, Rebecca could not hold back the tears from flowing down her cheeks.

"Oh my, Rebecca! I'm so sorry, that was really thoughtless of me. Please don't cry. This is Terry's wife, Heidi. Heidi, this is Jacob's wife, Rebecca. Her father-in-law, Jeb, is down the hall. She's the wife of the young Amish man whose buggy was hit by the truck."

Heidi pulled Rebecca into an embrace, saying, "Oh dear, I'm so sorry about your husband."

"Thank you very much," sniffled Rebecca. Jeb came back with some coffee for Rebecca and she introduced him to Heidi.

Jeb asked the small group of women if they would like him to pray for everyone. "Please do! We all need it so much!" they answered.

Jeb picked up his King James Bible and turned to James, chapter 5. He read verses 13 through 16. "*Is any among you afflicted? Let him pray. Is any merry? Let him sing psalms. Is any sick among you? Let him call for the elders of the church; and let them pray over him, anointing him with oil in the name of the Lord; And the prayer of faith shall save the sick, and the Lord shall raise him up; and if he have committed sins, they shall be forgiven him. Confess your faults one to another, and pray one for another, that ye may be healed. The effectual, fervent prayer of a righteous man availeth much."*

Jeb then turned to Mark 2:17 and read, *"When Jesus heard it, he saith unto them, They that are whole have no need of the physician, but they that are sick. I came not to call the righteous, but sinners to repentance."*

Jeb continued on with Matthew 10:7-8; *"And as ye go, preach, saying, The kingdom of heaven is at hand. Heal the sick, cleanse the lepers, raise the dead, cast out devils; freely ye have received, freely give."*

Everyone said, "Amen."

Jeb offered up prayer to the Lord. "Lord, our Father, we pray for Thy healing powers in the physicians hands, as our loved ones are in the emergency room. We pray for our young Jacob. We also pray for our English friends, Joey D, Sam, Terry, and Mark. We ask for your spiritual guidance as we wait here. We also pray for the truck driver. We don't know his name, but you do, Lord. We pray that he will be able to forgive himself, because there is nothing to forgive. It was an accident. We pray for his family as they must be worried, too. Father, we pray for others in this waiting room. They too have loved ones that they are worried about and are in need of your healing powers. Amen."

Other people in the waiting room thanked Jeb for his prayer, saying it brought a feeling of comfort to them and gave them some hope. A woman, whose son was in emergency surgery, said to Jeb, "Sir, you're truly a man of God. The Lord sent you here today to be with us. We're sorry that your son was hurt. We'll include him and the other men in our prayers, too. Thank you!"

An angry looking woman, sitting in the corner, started mumbling to herself and cursing. "Excuse me," commented Kelly, "please watch your language, Miss. We're Christians and don't appreciate anyone taking our Lord's name in vain. There are also children here who shouldn't be subjected to that kind of language."

"I would say the children should not be subjected to your myths about God!" sneered the angry woman, crossing her arms.

"Well, this is America. We have the right to worship as we please; just like you have the freedom not to worship, if that is what you choose," stated Kelly. "Our husbands and some of us women served in the military and took an oath to support and defend these rights, including yours."

The woman got out of her chair as she claimed, "That must be the reason your husbands were in the accident; they were being punished for killing women and children!" As she headed for the exit, she turned and spat on Kelly and Rebecca. Anticipating trouble, the medical secretary had called for hospital security and they came running.

The women talked about having the lady arrested for simple assault charges, but Jeb interjected, "Is that what Jesus would do?" He continued, "We are supposed to forgive this woman for she is unclean. She needs spiritual guidance. Jesus taught that if she will not accept, then we are to wipe the dust off our feet and move on."

When asked for her name, the angry woman replied, "Sunshine. Just Sunshine." When the security officer asked for her address she answered, "I'm from the great state of California. Hopefully soon, our liberal politics and way of life and beliefs will spread across the United States and people like you will be silenced for good! With the president we have now, hopefully we can turn America into the United Socialist States of America!"

The security officer asked Jeb, Rebecca, Kelly, Paula, Heidi, and Hope to go to the meditation room to ease the tension. Paula argued, "Why should we be the ones to go? We did nothing wrong. We prayed and read some Bible verses. Other people in the waiting room were happy and comforted by the words of God. The only one who's upset is this lady, Sunshine."

Hope interrupted saying, "Of course, we'll be happy to go. We don't want to cause any trouble." As Hope and her friends were moving into the meditation room down the hall, they could hear Sunshine still complaining.

"We can't get in to see a doctor because these ladies' husbands are taking up the entire emergency room. It's not fair! I've been sitting here for over two hours waiting to be seen. I know I broke my finger on the roller coaster at Hershey Park. My lawyer will be hearing about this and the cruel punishment I was subjected to while waiting—having to listen to prayers and be around you murderers of women and children!"

"I don't know why anyone would name her Sunshine!" griped one of the security officers.

A young Latino man, wearing a hospital shirt, walked over to Sunshine. She looked at him and said, "Hola."

"Here in Pennsylvania, we speak English." He continued, "My name is Jose. Let me take a look at your finger." Jose looked at her finger and asked her to look out the window. As she turned her head, he pulled her finger and snapped it back into place. He wrapped it with two tongue depressors and some tape. "I believe your finger will be fine now," he smiled at her. "Don't worry about payment. Since you waited such a long time, it's on the house."

Just then a nurse came to Jose and said, "Jose, your wife and new baby boy are doing fantastic. Would you like to take a look at him as soon as we have him all cleaned up?"

Jose was obviously excited that he had a new son and announced it to anyone who would listen to him. Sunshine, with obvious disdain, grumbled, "Why are you so excited? As a doctor, you must see babies all the time."

"I never said I was a doctor," stated Jose.

"But you are wearing a hospital shirt."

Jose replied, "Of course, I am. I just came from the farm and my shirt was filthy. I bought this shirt in the gift shop."

Sunshine snapped, "Are you telling me a common farm hand set my finger?"

"I'm not a common farm hand. I own my own farm!" Jose proudly announced. "I've set many fingers from the days when I worked in the fields. My grandfather came to Texas on a work visa and then moved to the Chambersburg area. My dad worked on farms and I worked in the fields until I joined the Army. In fact, I still serve in the Army Reserves. I saved my re-enlistment bonus money and invested it. When I got out, I had enough for the down payment on my farm." He looked at her in disapproval, "So this country that you put down, gave me the opportunity to own my farm. That would never happen in Mexico. So, God bless America!"

When Sunshine ranted at him that she would sue him and then she would own his farm, Jose replied, "That's funny, lady. I never claimed to be a doctor, you just assumed I was. As for your liberal views, they are way off base. Political correctness is hurting the minorities. Most people assume that we all came across the border illegally. Most came here legally with work visas and became U.S. citizens. We've done every type of menial job just to get the American Dream we all hear about. You liberals also always talk about saving the planet, all while flying around in jets and driving big SUVs. That girl you spit on is Amish. The Amish are truly green. They don't drive cars; they don't even have electricity. Mostly they stick to themselves and stay away from the world. It was an honor just to listen to the man pray. Listen to them singing in there. Those Amish people have probably never heard a recorded song from an iPod, but they are singing the songs on it."

The song was from the Methodist Hymnal. "This is my song," Jose said to Sunshine. "Listen to this part of the song; my country's skies are bluer than the ocean. And sunlight beams on cloverleaf and pine. But other lands have sunlight too, and clover. And skies are everywhere as blue as mine. Oh hear my song, Thou God of all the nations. A song of peace for their land and for mine."

Jose commented, "Ms. California Sunshine, they aren't singing about what country is better or which race is better, are they? I think you need to do a little soul searching and start showing compassion toward your fellow man. They are singing a song that teaches us to love everyone, no matter where they live. The song teaches that no person or country is better than the next. That's another thing church teaches us, compassion for our fellow man. Something you aren't showing." He smiled as he said, "Please think about what I've said, okay? I'm going to go take a look at my new boy! I'm a new father!!"

In the meditation room, they sang another song—How Great Thou Art. By the time they got to the words, *then sings my soul, my Savior God to Thee*, everyone was standing outside the door singing with them. Even the hospital security guard started humming. A revival was happening in the Penn State Hershey Medical Center's waiting room. How fitting that the next song they sang was Victory in Jesus!

• • • • • • • • • • •

The amazing thing about people is how resilient we are; how we all have a different way of coping with a crisis; and how, no matter who we are, the first thing we, as human beings, do is surround ourselves with other people who care.

Black Amish buggies filled the road to the Peachey farm. Everyone came to pray and be supportive for Sarah, Jeb's wife. Even though she worried, Sarah believed that the Lord's loving hands would protect her family. The women brought an abundance of food to feed all those who came to pray with Sarah. While the adults were inside, the older girls watched the children playing outside. Everyone waited anxiously for some news from town.

Cars pulled into the parking lot at the Belleville Fire Station. Emergency personnel from Reedsville, Allensville, and Belleville Fire Departments came for grief counseling. County social workers came to counsel the responders as requested. Pulling their chairs into a circle, everyone shared their thoughts and feelings about the accident and things they had seen that day. For some, it would be difficult to turn off their thoughts, and most would have nightmares or trouble sleeping. Talking with others in their profession helped a lot. Most people remember the victims; but no one ever thinks about what the first responders go through, after they cleaned everything up and went home.

· · · · · · · · · · · ·

For hours, the Pennsylvania State Police questioned Hugh. Then, they said they would be back shortly. They left him sitting in the tiny, sparsely furnished room most of the afternoon. Finally, another officer came in and asked, "Are you thirsty? How does some food and a drink sound to you?"

"Thank you. That would be much appreciated," replied Hugh.

"Then admit to the three accidents in York County. Tell us what you know about them. Tell us about today."

Hugh shook his head and sighed. Apparently, they thought they could back him into a corner. He sighed as he said, "Today, I was talking on the cell phone to my wife and glanced away from the road for a split second as I rounded the top of a hill. A horse and buggy was on the road. I swerved to miss it and noticed the group of motorcycles coming straight at me. I continued to drive my rig off the road to avoid hitting anyone. Unfortunately, I ended up hitting everyone." Hugh looked around the room at the various officers and continued, "As for the accidents in York County—I've said it once, I'll say it a thousand times—I've never had an accident in York County! This has been my first accident in 42 years of driving a big rig truck."

"Hugh, make it easier on yourself. We have the truck number from four different witnesses. They all said it was a Volvo truck with side numbers 6969 on it. You have a Volvo truck with the numbers 6969 on your side door. We can cut you a deal and make this easier on you," advised the officer to his right.

Hugh thought a minute and asked, "When did these accidents happen?"

"Three years ago, this past January."

Hugh laughed and said, "I guess you don't check with your State Department too much, do you? My wife, Martha, and I have been spending our winters in Bokeelia, Florida for the past five years. We stay there from January 2 until April 2 every year. I take my truck down and drive local routes hauling livestock to and from the Okeechobee stock yards."

The interviewing officer smirked and said, "How long did it take you to think that one up, Mr. Lamadeleine?

Hugh looked around the room in obvious frustration, "I believe I've said all I'm going to say, gentlemen. I want my court appointed lawyer now."

· · · · · · · · · · ·

The doctor smiled as she walked into the meditation room and asked, "Is there a Peachey family here?"

"Yes," both Jeb and Rebecca answered at the same time. They stood up and took a step toward the doctor, but she waved them back into their seats.

"Good evening, I am the emergency room physician that was assigned to Jacob. I want to give you an update of his injuries and what we are doing to help him. First off, I wanted to tell you he's going to be alright." She smiled kindly at them and carried on, "Right now, Jacob is in stable condition. None of his injuries are life threatening in any way."

"Oh, praise God! Thank you, Jesus!" breathed Rebecca.

The doctor continued to explain, "He's going to be okay, but he does have quite a few injuries. He has a broken nose and a dislocated jaw, both of which have been reset. He also has broken a bone in his left arm and dislocated that same shoulder. The four ribs that he cracked are going to be a bit painful until they are healed, but as he will be on pain medicine for quite a while, that shouldn't bother him too terribly much," she stopped speaking and shuffled her papers for a few seconds. "We have already set the shoulder and the arm, but he also has a badly broken ankle which will require surgery. We'll probably take care of that tomorrow. Minor cut and bruises round out the remainder of his injuries. He looks a mess, but from what I hear, it could have been so much worse. Oh, he also has a concussion which we will be keeping an eye on tonight. A few days after the surgery on his ankle, he'll be transferred to a rehabilitation center near your home." She smiled again, "Do you have any questions for me?"

"When can we see him?"

"As soon as we get him settled into a room, you can see him," the doctor replied. "He was a lucky guy; it could have gone very badly for him."

Rebecca looked up with tears in her eyes and softly stated, "It wasn't luck; it was the hand of God."

More than a few hearts skipped a beat when the next doctor came through the doorway of the meditation room. "Is there a Paula Brown here?" asked the kindly looking doctor.

Paula opened her mouth to answer him, but no sound would come out. She raised her hand, instead. The other girls gathered around Paula and Hope held her hand as they waited for the news—good or bad.

"Mrs. Brown, your husband is doing fine and wanted me to come out and give you an update. But first, he wants to know how bad his bike is," chuckled the shaggy, gray haired physician.

"WHAT?!? He's asking about his bike?"

The doctor's blue eyes sparkled as he said, "A true biker. I see it all the time. Mark has a concussion, but no other head injuries. We did an MRI and found nothing else wrong. It's a true testament to the benefits of wearing a helmet. His left ankle is going to need surgery and he has a bad case of road rash on his left calf, which we've cleaned out and taken care of. Once we get him into a room you can go see him, but he wants you to check on his bike first."

Paula reached over and hugged him, kissing him on the cheek. "Thank you so much for taking care of my husband."

"It was my pleasure," he reassured her.

Paula turned to the other girls, "I'm sorry for being so happy, but I know that Joey D, Sam, and Terry will be fine, too. I'm sure their doctors will be here in just a few moments." Joyful hugs were passed around the whole group and the rest of the girls assured her that they were just as happy for her good news.

A third doctor came in and cleared his throat to get their attention, "Is there someone here for Terry Miller?"

Heidi took a few steps toward him and announced, "That would be me. I'm Terry's wife and these are our friends."

"Mrs. Miller we feared that your husband had broken his neck, so we sent him for x-rays and also an MRI. I'm happy to say that they both came back negative. He does have some swelling that's causing him not to have any movement. We're very hopeful that this will pass with time as the swelling goes down. We're still checking him for other injuries and he's in and out of consciousness. I'm sorry, but this is the best I can tell you for now. I don't want to seem rude, but I really must get back to your husband. I can assure you that he's in the best of hands."

Paula held tight to his hand and tearfully said, "Thank you, Doctor. Please, just remember this man is my whole life." He squeezed her hand and hurried away.

After talking about all the doctors had told them, they sat down in the padded chairs huddled around Kelly and Hope. Constant, silent prayers were being offered up as they waited.

It seemed liked hours; time passed so slowly. The hospital chaplain came and sat with them. He offered prayer for them. A tired looking doctor came in with a nurse, asking if anyone was there for Joseph Daniels. Kelly stood up and said that he was her husband.

"Can you all excuse us for a while, please?" he announced to the worried group.

Kelly requested that they all stay and said, "We're all friends here. We've all been friends for over twenty years. You can say anything in front of them."

The doctor sat down and took a deep breath. "I don't know how to begin, so I'll just be frank with you. Your husband is in serious condition. Right now, he's in a coma."

Kelly let out a small gasp and waited, gripping the edge of her chair so tight her knuckles were white.

"We believe that he'll come out of it, but the next 48 hours are going to be critical. His skull is fractured and there's massive swelling on his brain. We may have to do emergency surgery to relieve this swelling. We're doing another MRI right now. Mr. Daniels also has quite a list of other injuries, including a fractured eye socket, cheek bone, nose, right arm, both legs, and some ribs. The ribs have punctured his lungs and he's on a machine to help him breathe right now. If you have any family, I would suggest you call them to come. In the meantime, the chaplain is here to help you out with anything you might need. If you're a praying woman, you might want to talk to God right now; your husband needs a miracle." With that, he rushed back into the emergency room.

• • • • • • • • • • •

The Boatswain pipe blew, then came the announcement on the ship's intercom—"Attention on the USS George Bush. Will Lieutenant Terry Miller report to the Wardroom to meet with the Commanding Officer?"

The USS George Bush CVN-77 was the US Navy's newest nuclear aircraft carrier. At this time, it was at Pier 12 Norfolk Naval Base, in Norfolk, Virginia, and Lt. Terry J. Miller Jr. was the ship's Division Officer for the Cryptologic Technicians. He always wanted to follow in his parent's footsteps and had succeeded beyond his wildest dreams. A graduate of the U.S. Naval Academy, he was now a Plank Owner of the USS George Bush, meaning he was part of the ship's first crew.

He knocked on the door of the Wardroom. The Skipper ordered, "Enter."

"Lt. Miller reporting as ordered, Sir."

The Commanding Officer said, "Have a seat, Lieutenant. The ship's chaplain is here to talk to you. We're sad to inform you that your father was in a motorcycle accident in Pennsylvania and is in bad condition. The hospital informed the Red Cross, and they, in turn, informed us. As of now, you are on emergency leave. We can get by since we are at pier side."

The Lieutenant asked the condition of his dad. The chaplain replied, "All we can say is there are head injuries and, right now, they think he might have a broken neck. I'm sorry, but that's all we can tell you."

"Thank you, Sir. How long do I have off?"

The CO informed him that he had thirty days; if he needed more, just call the ship. If things went well and he did not need the full thirty days, he was to come back to the ship early. He then reminded him to keep everyone informed.

Terry went to his work place, the Ships Signals Exploitation Space (SSES). He gave his men the details. They asked him if there was anything that they could do for him. His Division Chief said to keep in contact and let everyone know what was happening. Being the smallest division on the ship, everyone was close. When something happened to someone's family, it was like something happened to everyone's family.

TJ went to his stateroom, got his motorcycle tour pack to carry his clothes in, and packed everything he would need for an extended leave. He was already wearing his naval working uniform with a pair of boots. He carefully placed his dress summer white uniform into his bag, just in case he needed it. TJ grabbed his helmet, leather jacket, and high visibility vest, which was required for riding on the military base. He walked down the hall a short distance before quickly turning around and heading back. He realized he had forgotten his iPhone and laptop. He packed them into his bag and headed out of the room.

TJ walked to the Quarterdeck of the ship and told his friend, Lt. Jg. John Beam, who was on duty as the Officer of the Day (OOD), why he was leaving. Jim said, "Fair winds, my friend. My prayers are with you and your family. Travel safely."

TJ saluted the OOD and walked down the brow a few feet before turning toward the aft of the ship and saluting the American flag. He picked up his bag and walked down the pier to the parking lot. Spotting his motorcycle from behind, he saw the word SPOOK on the vanity plate that he just recently received and chuckled to himself. TJ loaded up the leather saddlebags on his Harley-Davidson Heritage Softail. He joined the Navy like his parents and he rode a Harley like them, too. Coming from a biking family, he felt the motto painted on each side of his gas tank said it all, *Khai Zhive Baik!,* which is Ukranian for *Long Live the Bike!"*

TJ dialed his mother's number on his cell phone to let her know that he was on his way. "Hey Mom, I just wanted to let you know that I'm leaving now. How's Dad doing?"

"The doctor said that your father might be okay with time. We just don't know everything yet," murmured Heidi to her son.

"Okay. I should be there in about five or six hours, depending on the traffic. I'm riding my bike so I can get there quicker." TJ paused for a few seconds while he listened to his mother, "Of course, I'll be careful. Remember I'm the ship's motorcycle safety officer? See you soon, Mom. Love you."

TJ made one more quick call to his girlfriend to let her know what was going on. "Hello, this is Lt. Miller; may I please speak to Ensign Sally Morgan?"

"Hi, TJ. What's up?"

"I'm sorry, Sally. I have to break our date tonight." TJ went on to tell her the reason. Sally offered to take time off and go with him. "That's alright. I might need you to come down later on. Maybe you can come for the weekend. Would that work out?" They decided that she would take off Friday and meet him there Thursday evening.

With his last minute phone calls out of the way, TJ put his phone on vibrate and stuffed it in his leather jacket's pocket. He swung his leg over the seat, settled his helmet on his head, and pulled out of the parking lot heading toward I-64. It was going to be a long ride.

· · · · · · · · · · · ·

"Is someone here from the Adams family?"

Hope shakily stood up and started to shake harder. Paula put her arm around Hope to steady her.

"Please, sit down, Mrs. Adams," he kindly instructed her. She looked up at him and noticed the chaplain was by his side. She could hardly breathe; she knew it, the bad news was about to come.

"Mrs. Adams, let me start off by saying that your husband is in grave condition. We're doing all we can for him. At this moment, we have him on life support while we assess all of his injuries."

Hope was shaking so badly, she thought she was going to pass out. Paula pushed her head between her knees and called to Kelly to get a glass of cold water. When she finally settled down, the doctor continued, "Mrs. Adams, your husband has massive head trauma. The fact that he had his helmet on is probably the only reason he's still alive. We're also dealing with broken legs, broken ribs, internal bleeding, and a punctured lung. For now, I'm sorry, but this is all I can tell you. The chaplain is here to talk to you. If there's anything you need, let him know. I'm sorry to rush off, but I need to get back to your husband."

The chaplain spoke, "Is there any family that you need to contact? I can call them for you."

Hope responded through her tears, "I have two sons in the Navy. My youngest son, Frank, is assigned to the USS Ronald Reagan CVN-76 in San Diego, California. He's a Cryptologic Technician Seaman in the Operations Department. My other son, Sammy, is a US Navy Seal in Little Creek, Virginia. He's a Petty Officer First Class." She then gave him all the information he needed to contact her sons. The hospital's chaplain told her he would contact the Red Cross as he had for Mrs. Miller and they would contact the sailor's command.

A nurse came over and asked Hope if she needed something to help calm her down. Hope sniffed and said, "No, thank you. I have my friends here. Knowing that God is in control is my greatest comfort. I'll be alright."

The chaplain came back into the room to talk to Rebecca. He told her he contacted some people in the Belleville area. They would be going to the Peachey farm to fill them in on the day's events. "Thank you so much for your kindness," Rebecca said quietly. "I was just sitting here worrying and praying about how to get the word to Jacob's mother. It's just one more answer to my prayers."

On Channel 10, the CBS Station from Altoona, the 6 o'clock news came on. The accident was the lead story. Luckily, the women and Jeb did not see it, for their eyes were closed while they brought their burdens and blessings to God.

· · · · · · · · · · · ·

"Frank the Crank, come here!" When the sailor appeared, the Petty Officer said, "You've completed your mess duties onboard the USS Ronald Reagan. Congratulations, sailor! Now you can head back to your division and carry out your spook duties. Just don't forget that for ninety days you worked with us normal sailors. Seaman Adams, you're a good worker and a good sailor. You'll go far in this man's navy. I'll be seeing you around. Good luck in your division and thanks for your good work."

Seaman Frank Adams knocked on the vault door of SSES. Chief Rich Balorous opened the door saying, "Hey, look who's here, our Mess Crank! What brings you back to the real world?"

Frank answered, "I was told that I'm now officially assigned back to the Division! This is the happiest day I've had in months! Nothing can destroy being back!"

The combination lock for the door opened and Lt. Commander Tom Brown joined them. He asked Chief Balorous to speak with him privately and they departed into the communications room. Lt. Commander Brown filled the Chief in on what he had just learned about Seaman Adam's father. Frank was then called into the room.

The Lt. Commander said, "There's no easy way to say this— Frank, your dad was in a motorcycle accident in Pennsylvania. He was life-flighted to Penn State Hershey Medical Center and he's in grave condition. Your mother wasn't in the accident. They were on vacation with friends. The Red Cross contacted us and said your mother is okay, but is in shock right now and finding it hard to talk. The Red Cross is also contacting your brother. You're being sent home on emergency leave. You have fifteen minutes to pack and be back here. We're going to drive you to pick up a navy hop that's flying to Norfolk. From there, my wife's sister will pick you up at NAS Norfolk and drive you to the airport, from there you'll fly into Harrisburg. As of this moment, you are on thirty days emergency leave. This leave can be upgraded or, if needed, you could have a hardship transfer, but we'll leave that for down the road."

Frank hurried back to SSES with his sea bag full of both navy and civilian clothes. He was wearing his dress uniform. The Lt. Commander said, "On pay day, take your emergency leave papers to Mechanicsburg Navy Depot and they'll pay you. In the meantime, the Navy takes care of our own. Here is some money from the men in Division. Don't bother asking who gave how much and how to pay it back; it's a gift. Remember to be there for your mom and dad. Take care, sailor; here is the Chief's and my cell phone numbers. Keep us informed about what is happening."

Frank said, "Thank you, everyone!" And he hurried out the door.

Petty Officer Samuel Adams had his boat crew out for training. He heard that the croakers were running and they decided to get some boat handling skills in. In reality, they were fishing by an abandoned light house near Oyster, Virginia. They spent the afternoon fishing and catching a lot of croakers and flounder. When the petty officer decided they had enough, they headed back to the base with over 200 fish. The helmsman led the rigid inflatable boat up to the dock. A man came running up to them yelling, "Sammy, the Skipper wants to see you ASAP!"

Sammy turned to the crew and joked, "It isn't the first time I've been in trouble and it won't be the last. Take the fish over to the chow hall and see if they can fry them up for supper. Also take care of the boat and stow the gear. Thanks. Talk to y'all later."

Sammy knocked at the lieutenant's door and was told to enter. Inside he found not just his Division Officer, but the entire chain of command. *Wow, I must be in real trouble this time.*

After the Navy Chaplain talked to him about his father, the Captain told him they had found some chopper pilots who needed flight time. They would be flying him into Mechanicsburg Navy Depot, outside of Harrisburg. A duty driver would take him the rest of the way to the hospital. "Get back to your barracks and pack quickly. Your flight is waiting for you, sailor. We'll let your men know what's going on." The Captain's eyes sparkled with laughter as he added sarcastically, "Also, we invited ourselves to your fish fry. I didn't think you would mind."

. . . .

Kelly thought about telling the devastating news to her children. Her daughter, Tracy, was a farmer's wife and ran a busy daycare center out of her home. Her husband, Rich, worked for Grove Manufacturing outside of Chambersburg, PA. They had sixty head of cattle and 200 acres of farmland. Rich also served in the Army Reserves in the Stryker Brigade in Huntingdon, PA. They had a little girl named Peggy Sue, whom Kelly loved to spoil, and Tracy was six months pregnant.

Joey D and Kelly's son, Todd, worked at JLG Manufacturing outside of Fort Littleton, PA. He also served in the U.S. Navy Reserves as a Cryptologic Technician Interpreter. He went to Navy School to learn Chinese. He lived on the family farm and helped Joey D with the work of the small 150 acre farm. They had four Morgan horses, mainly for riding and pulling a sleigh in the winter and 100 alpacas, whose fur they sold to be made into fleece and yarn. They farmed the rest of the land, growing corn and wheat. Todd was married to a nice girl named Bobbie Jo. They met when they were both in Navy Class A School and now they had an eight year old son named Joseph. Bobbie Jo grew up in the south, but loved her life up in the ridges of Pennsylvania. Kelly slowly tapped the numbers on her cellphone, dreading making these phone calls to her family, but desperately needing their support.

CHARLIE RESPONSE
CHAPTER THREE

The Chaplain came back later to speak to everyone. He offered prayers and guidance for them. He said that it would be a few hours before anyone would be able to visit their loved ones. They should think about going to get something to eat and arrange for hotel rooms for the night.

"How could we possibly think about eating and sleeping at a time like this?" moaned Kelly.

Smiling at her, the chaplain answered, "I know it's hard, but I also know that your husbands would want you to stay well. You need to eat to maintain your strength. You need to sleep to keep rested in case you are needed later." He paused to let it sink in. "I know that you're mostly Navy families. Don't you remember on the ship when we would be told to take advantage of down times; to eat and sleep whenever we get the chance? I know this because after ten years in the enlisted ranks, I became an officer, a Navy Chaplain, and then retired as a Navy Lieutenant Commander. Well, the same goes here."

A handsome sailor entered the room in his dress white uniform, completely decked out with all his ribbons and medals, including the Seal Team Trident. People could not help but stare at him; he was an impressive sight.

"Mom, how is Dad?" he spoke in a deep bass voice.

Hope whirled around and gasped, "Sammy, you're here! How did you get here so fast?"

He told her the details of his travel arrangements and added that his brother would be arriving soon, as well. Sometimes, the perks of being a Navy Seal were pretty great. Hope filled him in on the information they had gotten so far from the staff at the hospital.

As they were talking, Kelly's family came in. She introduced them to those who did not know them. Todd said, "Mom, I don't want to be rude, but all I want to know is how dad is—then, how everyone else is. After all of that, I want to know what happened! Everyone here is an experienced rider. Stuff like this shouldn't happen to experienced riders!"

Kelly answered his questions the best she could.

A nurse came into the room and announced, "Excuse me. I am one of the emergency room's nurses. My name is Jean Kough. I'm working a double shift tonight, so I'll be your contact person throughout the night. I'm to reiterate what the chaplain told you—go get something to eat! Nothing is going to change in the amount of time that will take. It's going to be a long night and I won't have updates for you for a while; so my advice would be to get a hotel room, unless you live close-by. I'm sorry that I don't have any updates for you at this time." She stopped and looked around the crowded room. "Please go eat. I have cellphone numbers. I'll call if anything changes."

Sammy addressed the group, "People, I know of a place down the road we can go. I'm sure that Jeb and Rebecca will approve of it. It's a nice family restaurant called Kreider Dairy Farm Family Restaurant. It's on Briarcrest Square Road. One of my shipmates recommended it to me before I left. I'm guessing that he knows the family or something, since his last name was Kreider. Since most of us belong to Harley Owners Group, we can use our benefits and get a reduced rate at the Best Western. I figure with our H.O.G. discount, military discount, and possible group discount we should get a much reduced rate. After eating and getting a hotel room, we can come back here. Does that sound like a good plan to everyone?"

Everyone agreed and headed out to eat and get lodging.

• • • • • • • • • • •

Back at the state police barracks, Hugh was worried. Not only was he from out of state, he was from out of country! He worried what would happen to him and his wife, Martha. He worried how his truck payments would be made if he went to jail or prison. Then, he wondered about all the people involved in the accident. He wondered how badly they were hurt. He was all alone in the interrogation room.

He had requested a court appointed lawyer and none came. He had asked for some food and a drink and received neither. He got up to walk around the room, but was light headed and his hands were shaking. After thirty more minutes another police officer came in to check on him. He saw him lying on the floor and he called for backup. They called the dispatcher to send an ambulance.

A female paramedic came in and did an exam on Hugh. While talking to the police officers, she took his blood sugar. Hugh was having a low blood sugar attack due to his stress, diabetes, and lack of food in his system. He had eaten breakfast and an early lunch, but he had not had any food or anything to drink in over ten hours! She treated him with IVs and some orange juice when he was able to drink it. Finally, he started coming around.

Hugh's court appointed lawyer finally arrived and angrily scolded the police sergeant that it was unacceptable behavior not to feed a person who had diabetes. The lawyer threatened that he would be going after the department in a lawsuit, because of their neglect towards his client.

"How was I supposed to know he had diabetes?" argued the sergeant.

"Well, I don't know—maybe check his Medic-alert bracelet? Isn't that one of their functions— to alert the paramedics or police of his condition? Just by seeing it on his wrist, you should have checked it," lectured the lawyer.

Hugh finally came around and was more alert. The medic gave him some more orange juice and commented that his dinner was being brought in momentarily. Hugh exclaimed, "It's about time!"

His lawyer angrily pointed out, "About time? I'd say it's a little too late."

• • • • • • • • • • •

TJ was tired of fighting the interstate traffic, so he checked on the map and found that Route 15 would take him around the bigger cities and right into Harrisburg. From there, he could take Route 322 to Hershey. Pulling over in Fredricksburg for fuel and a quick meal, he called his mother to see if anything had changed. Then quick as a flash, he was back on the road again.

In a rush to get to his parents, TJ had been traveling at a high rate of speed, averaging around eighty miles per hour. The music coming out of the speakers between his handlebars was quite loud to compensate for the noise of the rumble of his bike. As he neared Quantico Marine Corps Base heading for the Maryland state line, TJ looked in his side mirror and saw the flashing lights behind him. He quickly pulled his Harley over to the side of the road and waited for the police officer.

"License and registration, please."

TJ said, "I have to get it out of my wallet."

"Oh, I'm really going to give it to you now. You boys from Quantico think you can come into my town and act like you own it. If there is one thing I hate as much as bikers, it's a Marine, Captain Miller," sneered the police officer.

TJ responded, "Sorry officer, but I'm not a Captain. I'm a lieutenant in the Navy. I'm stationed in Norfolk onboard the USS George Bush. I'm on emergency leave because my father and his friends were hit by a truck driver in Pennsylvania. They were life flighted to a hospital in Hershey, Pennsylvania. I'm on my way there now. See my uniform says US NAVY, not USMC. Now may I please have my ticket so I can be on my way?"

The policeman gave him the $175 ticket and told him to pay it in cash or he would arrest him. TJ paid the fine and went on his way, more conscientious of his speed. He made a mental note to make sure to let his CO know the police officer's name so the Navy could bring charges against him for harassment, not just on him, but for Marines too.

• • • • • • • • • • •

The hospital chaplain contacted Jackie Yoder, the Assistant Fire Chief in Belleville. "Ms. Yoder, I was hoping that you could get word to the Jacob Peachey family about his condition."

"Oh, my goodness, of course I will. Please tell me how he and the others are," Jackie answered.

He explained the condition of Jacob and the others, and told her that Rebecca and Jeb would possibly be staying several nights at the Best Western Hotel. Jackie asked him if Jeb wanted his wife, Sarah, there. The chaplain responded that he did not know.

"I think it would be a good idea if I drive her down. I know where she lives and I'll bet she's worrying about Jacob, Rebecca, and Jeb," Jackie said. The chaplain agreed and Sarah went to ask Sarah if she would like a ride to the hospital.

The Peachey farmhouse was crowded when Jackie knocked on the door. She found Sarah in the kitchen helping to fix food for all the people who came to comfort her. They greeted each other warmly; everyone knew everyone in this small community. Sarah was grateful to Jackie for the offer of a ride to her family. The men in the group assured her they would take care of things on both Jacob's and Jeb's farms. Meanwhile, the women packed a small box with some food for the trip.

· · · · · · · · · · · ·

After they had put in their orders with the waitress, Kelly asked Sammy how his hitch in the Navy was going. Sammy replied that he had not expected to enjoy it as much as he did.

"What were you doing earlier today?" asked Heidi.

Sammy chuckled as he said, "We had a down day, so I thought I'd do some small boat training and maybe some scuba diving with the men. So off we went, but when we saw the amount of croakers and flounders near the shore, we got out the fishing poles and went fishing. We headed back after we had caught about a hundred or so. It was when we got back that I was told to go to the CO's office. I thought I was in big trouble."

As the waitress brought them their drinks, Rebecca asked what Sammy did in the Navy. He explained, "I'm a Navy Seal, which is in the Special Forces of the Navy. We have to go through 42 weeks of intense training, then more special training after that. At any time we can be booted out or we can quit, if it's too hard for us. Some people call us modern day ninjas, but I prefer the nickname the Elite of the Fleet. We're trained to protect shipping lanes and we have special training to save lives. People mistakenly think of us as killers, but most of our missions are saving lives or just taking pictures of things."

At that time, a boy about twelve years old interrupted them, "Hey mister, are you a real life Navy Seal?" With Sammy's affirmative nod he continued, "Would you mind taking a picture with me on my cellphone?"

"I'll be glad to do that for you, if you don't mind chopping me off from my nose up. I can't have my picture floating around on Facebook. Well, don't I feel just like a celebrity now!" Sammy smiled as the boy's mother snapped the picture and the boy thanked him, grinning from ear to ear.

"Who are those people?" a patron asked his waitress.

The waitress replied that they were the families of the people in the big motorcycle accident down in Belleville. He walked over to them and shook Sammy's hand and said, "Thank you for your service. Your country is proud of you and your fellow shipmates. I'm sorry about your unfortunate circumstances right now. We'll be praying for you. My family and I are here on vacation; I'm a pastor from Maine. To show you that Americans still care, we've picked up your bill."

"Thank you, but you don't have to do that, Sir," exclaimed Sammy.

The man assured him, "I know I don't, but I want to. We'll be on our way now. God bless you all."

Jeb looked confused and asked Sammy, "Does that happen a lot to you?"

Sammy laughed and said, "That's funny, because it's the first time here in America that has ever happened to me. When I was in Perth, Australia, they treated all sailors like that. Here in America, it's a different story. There were hotels, restaurants, and nightclubs on Virginia Beach that didn't allow sailors to go inside. I remember a story Dad told of coming back from an Indian Ocean cruise. He was thirsty for a milk shake and stopped at a fast food restaurant. When he came out, he saw signs all through Norfolk that read *Dog's and Sailors keep off the grass!* Dad was upset about that.

"I went to a certain retail chain to do some Christmas shopping while in my Naval Working Uniform and was told to leave. I went to the papers and a TV station to let them know what happened to me and others in the military. They contacted the national headquarters of the store and were told that it's not store policy; but the only reason a military person would be kicked out of the store. would be if he was recruiting inside the store. We get treated better in other countries than inside our own country in some places. This has happened to other military men too, but on the internet Snoopes says it has never happened. They only quote what the corporate office said about it. They didn't investigate it themselves; no one has. But I know firsthand, it's true!"

Kelly added, "I remember all the stories Joey D told us of how he was treated in Perth, Darwin, and Sydney, Australia. He said they were his favorite places on earth. I met him in Perth one time and couldn't believe how friendly the people were and still are."

Paula noticed how quiet Hope was and asked her what was wrong. It was a few seconds before Hope answered, "Sam always wanted to go back. He dreamed about all of us going back and riding our bikes around Australia. He said he wanted to start in Darwin and ride south to Perth. We could spend some time in Perth, and then ride the southern coast to Sydney. After that, we would head north to go fishing and diving on the Great Barrier Reef." She bit her lip as she stared down at her plate and then quietly said, "Now he might never be able to even ride again, let alone take his dream ride." Her face crumpled as tears ran down her cheeks.

Paula put her arms around her friend and hugged her as she reassured her, "Honey, you have to keep your faith in God. We all have lived a great life and seen much more than the average person on this earth ever has. Remember, the boys said they wanted to ride all fifty states before we go to Australia and Europe. There's so much we just don't know yet; don't get so down on things. You just have to keep the faith. God always has a plan for us. I believe that with everything I am. We spread the Gospel everywhere we go. God wants to use us for His glory. Just keep praying, Hope."

Rebecca could not believe how much they all had traveled. This was the farthest she had traveled in a long time. She had never seen the ocean; the largest body of water she had seen was the Juniata River. Kelly suggested that they all get together on their pontoon boat on Lake Raystown for the day sometime. Rebecca smiled, as she looked for approval from Jeb.

Kelly noticed and went on, "Jeb, this would be fun for everyone. We all can get together. We can bring some food and have a cookout on an island. We have enough fishing poles that we can all go fishing. We have an inner tube that we pull behind the boat. You can get in it, ride, and have some fun."

Jeb nodded, "Some of the children use inner tubes on the river when it's high. They have a lot of fun, but I doubt it could happen this year."

"I know it can't happen this year, but maybe we can get together as a small group and get together next summer. We'll just wait and see," agreed Kelly.

Sammy announced, "I guess it's time for us to go get hotel rooms and then get back to the hospital. No news is good news, but maybe one of us will be able to see someone."

The ladies at the front desk of the hotel were discussing the details of the accident, which they had seen on the evening news. Sammy cleared his throat, as he felt they might be upsetting some of the ladies.

"I'm sorry, did I say something wrong?" asked one of the ladies.

"Absolutely not, miss. But we're all family members of those *poor people* in the *horrible accident* and we need to trouble you for some rooms. Thank you for your sympathy though. Your prayers would be welcomed, as well." Only Sammy could get away with scolding someone, while at the same time being entirely charming. The clerk apologized and asked how many rooms they needed.

Sammy did a quick count and had a brief discussion with his mother before telling the clerk that they needed six rooms. He negotiated a good price, taking advantage of discounts for H.O.G members and military personnel, as well as getting a large group discount. The clerk handed out the keycards and gave them directions to their rooms. The rooms were nice and everyone was pleased with them.

Sammy went back to the front desk and asked if they had any toothbrushes and toothpaste. The clerk gave him enough for everyone. He went room to room, handing them out, telling everyone that they should be getting back to the hospital soon.

As soon as they had returned to the hospital, a doctor came out and asked for Paula Brown. As Paula stood up, the doctor walked over to her. "As you know about your husband's injuries, I'm just giving you an update on them. He does have a concussion, but we don't think there will be anything wrong in the future. His road rash has been cleaned up and bandaged. That's going to hurt for quite a while until it heals. We went ahead and did the surgery on his left ankle. He came through just fine. We're still keeping an eye on his neck. Right now, he's being taken from the recovery room to his private room. I'll send a nurse out to show you the way." Paula grasped his hand and thanked him over and over.

Paula cried, as the other women hugged her. They prayed together, thanking God for answering their prayers and praising Him. Kelly pulled her aside and said that they would always be there for her should she need them. The nurse appeared in the doorway and Paula exclaimed, "Praise God! To God be all the glory!" And she followed the nurse out of the room.

Rebecca asked Kelly, "Does she have any children?"

Suddenly there was silence in the room. Sammy stared down at his hands and tears came to his eyes. He quickly walked away from everyone. Hope quietly told Rebecca the story.

"You know that all of us are military. We all served as Cryptologic Technicians, which is a fancy way of saying classified naval communications. We've all been friends for over 25 years. Our children are all friends, too. Even when we weren't stationed together, we would write back and forth, as would our children. Most of the time, we were all together at Norfolk Naval Base, but the guys were quite often on different ships. I think our families would be together as friends, even if our husbands didn't serve together.

"Mark and Paula had a son, Luke, who went to the Naval Academy, just like Heidi and Terry's son, TJ. He was a wide receiver on the Naval Academy football team. He was so good that he got the nickname Luke

Skywalker, because of the way he could jump high and catch the ball. People thought he would play professional football after his required tour in the military.

"Instead of becoming a Naval Officer, he became a Marine Officer and was sent to Afghanistan. One day, he and his men were pinned down and they called in for help. Help came in the form of an eight man Seal Team, which provided cover for the 75 Marines to get out of the tight spot they were in and advance to another position. As they were moving, they noticed some children playing in the area. Lt. Luke Brown went running towards the children to save them, because he saw what he believed to be an IED near them. An IED is any type of homemade bomb, typically used by terrorists. As Luke got nearer, he saw a person with a cell phone and believed that he was going to use it to blow up the IED. He threw his body on IED as it went off. He saved the lives of all the children, as well as the lives of the other Marines near him; but he sacrificed his own life. Luke was a true hero!

"A member of that Seal Team ran and rescued the children and the Marines. As they were moving to safety, the Seal stayed behind to lay down covering fire. This action saved the lives of the children, the Marines, and his fellow Seal Team members. That particular Seal was awarded the Silver Star for his actions on that day. That Silver Star winner is right over there, Petty Officer Sammy Adams. Lt. Luke Brown's family is still waiting for whatever medal will be awarded their son for saving the children. Luke was the only child the Brown's had. That day, Sammy watched his best friend die in front of him while saving the lives of children. A true American hero!"

There was not a dry eye in the room. Rebecca looked at Sammy in admiration. Hope said, "Sammy doesn't like to talk about that day. It was the day he lost the best part of his childhood. So, let's not say any more about it." Other people in the waiting room looked at the Seal hero and thought of the family of another hero. They all knew they were in the same room as our nation's finest.

Another nurse came in to escort Jeb and Rebecca to Jacob's room. Rebecca was warned that Jacob's face was very swollen. She was told not to be worry, that it was normal and would take several days for the swelling to go down.

Even though Jacob was groggy, he was very happy to see them. He could not open his mouth since it was wired shut. The nurse told Rebecca not to hug him since he had broken ribs. She then told her that the operation on his ankle would be the next afternoon. As they were talking, there was a sound at the doorway. Jeb and Rebecca turned and were surprised to see Sarah looking at her son with tears of joy running down her face. After Sarah assured herself that Jacob would be alright, she told them that Jackie had driven her to the hospital and was in the waiting room with the others. Jeb commented on the kindness of so many people and that they needed to remember to thank them all.

Later when talking to Jacob, Jeb asked him if he could remember anything from the accident. Jacob wrote on a pad of paper that he only remembered loading up the trailer and leaving the farm, then waking up in the hospital. Sarah pointed out, "Maybe that's a blessing. You just concentrate on getting better."

· · · · · · · · · · · ·

A man answered the ringing phone in the naval office, saying, "Hello, CO speaking."

"Sir, this is Petty Officer Adams. I thought I'd give you an update on my father's condition. He has massive head trauma, broken ribs which punctured a lung, internal bleeding, crushed legs, and is on life support right now."

The Commanding Officer replied, "I'm sorry to hear this, Petty Officer. I called the hospital and was given the same report. There is some summer training going on a Fort Indiantown Gap which is about ten miles from you. Your brother is being flown there. A duty driver will bring him to the hospital."

The Commanding Officer spoke briefly to someone in the room with him, then continued, "Adams, I hate to see you and your brother waste all of your leave, so I'm working out the details to have your brother assigned temporary additional duty orders to me. I'm still working on it, but both of you would be training some Army Reservist on how to interact with the Navy and the Seal Team. I think it would be great training for them, but also great for us. Your brother will be on TAD orders assigned to me and the both of you can work as long as you feel needed up there. You won't be charged leave. This way, you and Frank can use it in the future. For now, your primary job is to be with your Dad and Mother. You hear me, sailor?"

Sammy replied, "Yes, Sir!"

"Okay good. This might take a few days. Your brother will provide Combat Cryptologic Support to you. Just in case you need the emergency leave later, you'll still have it on the books. You leave everything to me for now. Your brother should be landing in about an hour," the CO explained.

Sammy said, "Thank you, Sir! I really appreciate all this."

• • • • • • • • • • •

Still at the police station, Hugh's lawyer informed him that the company Hugh worked for was sending another truck to pick up his load. Unfortunately, Hugh's truck and trailer had been taken to the impound lot. They discussed the fact that the police were bringing Hugh up on other charges that could cause him to lose his CDL license. They claimed he should not be driving professionally, because of his uncontrollably high blood sugar. Hugh dropped his head into his hands and wondered, *Is this ever going to be over? It's getting ridiculous.*

Hugh's lawyer had a meeting with the DA and argued that he did not belong in the jail with hardened criminals. He tried to make the point that Hugh was an upstanding person with no criminal history.

"He just caused the accident that resulted in several people having to fight for their lives," replied the DA.

"That's not criminal," argued the lawyer.

"No, it's not criminal," acknowledged the DA. "But he is also a suspect in three different cases of hit and run, one of which resulted in a death. That's called vehicular homicide and it is criminal."

• • • • • • • • • • •

TJ pulled his bike into the parking lot and ran to the emergency room waiting room and yelled, "Mom, how's Dad?" People looked up from their magazines to see who was yelling.

Heidi ran over to him and he grabbed her up in a hug. She exclaimed, "Honey, how did you get here so fast?"

"I would have been here sooner, but there was a cop trying to get his quota for the day and he gave me a ticket. What about Dad?"

Just then the doctor came into the room and requested to speak to the Miller family. TJ spoke up, "I'm his son and this is my mother, Heidi." The doctor suggested they go into another room for privacy.

Heidi objected, "I think we can stay in here. Whatever you tell me, I'll have to repeat anyway. Whatever you have to say can be said in front of our friends."

The doctor began, "Okay then, Mr. Miller suffered a spinal injury. We did an MRI and found no fractures. However, he has no feeling in his lower extremities. Mr. Miller's team of doctors believes this is most likely a temporary condition due to swelling. Since I last spoke with you, we discovered that he also dislocated his shoulder. We put that back into place. He also has two cracked ribs. Due to his protective gear, his road rash is pretty minimal. We're going to let you see him now. Try not to be alarmed by the tubes and monitors. He'll be able to talk to you for a bit, but don't stay too long. He needs to rest. After seeing him, you should head on over to your hotel and get some sleep."

Seaman Frank Adams came into the waiting room and ran right into Hope's waiting arms. Sammy was there to greet him, too. Hope said, "Frank, your father's in bad shape. It doesn't look good. He really needs prayers."

Frank responded, "I know, Mom. The guys back on the USS Reagan are praying for them all. The Reagan's Chaplain, Commander Dave Dubbs, said he would have prayer for them during his evening prayer on the ship tonight. I also want to say thank you, Brother, for looking out for me and getting me here so fast!"

Sammy smiled, "Little brother, sorry to burst your bubble, but I did nothing. That was all my Skipper's doing; he's the one who looked out for you. There are some things we need to talk about, but we can do that later."

A doctor came in to talk to the Adams family. He sat down with them and stated, "I felt I should come give you an update, but nothing has changed. In fact, his blood pressure has fallen dangerously low and we're worried about that. He's in a coma and we have him on life support. I talked it over with his team of doctors and we all agree that you should come into the ICU to see him. Please try to be positive and cheerful. We find that sometimes this is the best medicine. Just talk to him. Tell him you love him and are praying for him. Talk to him about motorcycle rides you've taken, or ones that you're planning on taking. You can even read him the newspaper. The main thing is to remain positive!"

As they headed to the room, Hope sniffled, "Sammy, I don't know if I can do this. Your father means so much to me. He's my soul mate. We're supposed to grow old together."

Sammy took her aside, "Mom, you have to straighten up. You're acting like he passed away and he hasn't. You can still grow old together." Hope took a deep breath and nodded her head.

As they went into the room, they were surprised by the amount of tubes and wires attached to him. Hope steeled her resolve and announced to her husband, "Attention on deck, sailor! This is your wife here! I want you to get better, so we can grow old together. We have so many places to go and many more motorcycle rides to take. You hear me, sailor? Your sons are here. Sammy is here from Norfolk and Frank flew in from California."

Both of them said, "Hello, Dad!"

Hope continued on, "Everyone else is in the waiting room, waiting for you to come home. So you get better, shipmate!"

Sammy sang a Seal Team style running cadence for his dad,

Hey, hey, Navy.

World's finest Navy.

Pick up your Sea Bag and run with me.

55

"Dad, you have to get well. We have to do that ride down the Blue Ridge Parkway, just you and me."

Frank walked over and said to his father, "Dad, I finally finished mess cranking. I just got assigned back to my Division today, before I flew here to be with you. Next month I take the Petty Officer's exam. I believe I'll make it since I have two years of college. I'm signed up for some more classes on the Navy's College Afloat program. Over the years, I hope to get my BS in Computer Science. Then, I'll go to OCS (Officers Candidate School) and become a Naval Officer. Just think about how much I could boss Sammy around then!"

The nurse popped her head in and said, "Just five more minutes. You can see him again tomorrow." So, reluctantly, Hope, Sammy, and Frank said their good-byes and left the room.

Back in the waiting room, Kelly braced herself as the doctor came to speak to her and the kids. He began, "Let me say first of all, at the moment there isn't much change in Mr. Daniels' condition. Due to the trauma, he's still in a coma. We believe that, with time, he'll come out of it on his own. We did discover there was a fracture in his skull. We need to do surgery to relieve some of the pressure in his brain cavity or it could be fatal. During the surgery, we'll have a team of doctors take care of other problems, such as his fractured eye socket and cheek bone. We have set some of his other fractures already. We'll be prepping him for surgery in a few minutes."

The doctor paused and asked if there were any questions so far, then continued, "We'll also take care of the leg that is broken in two places during this surgery. We want to get as much taken care of in one surgery as possible. It's less traumatic. I can take you back to see him now, but only for a few moments."

The Daniels' went in, each kissing his good hand. Kelly said a quick prayer, "Father, I come unto You in the name of my Savior, Jesus Christ. I humbly request that You be with the doctors as they perform surgery on my husband. Let the healing hands of these physicians be guided by You. Father, in the name of Jesus, please take care of my husband. He has suffered so much in his life. You say if we have the faith of a mustard seed we can move mountains. Father, I have enough faith to say, Your will be done. Please watch over him. In the name of Jesus Christ, our Savior, Amen."

"It's going to be an extremely long night; you really should go get some rest now. There's nothing you can do here anyway. The surgery is going to take several hours. I'll call your cell phone as soon as we're finished in the operating room. Write your number down on this paper, please," instructed the doctor, handing her a small notebook.

"Please call, no matter what the time is. I probably won't be able to sleep anyway," responded Kelly.

The doctor smiled, knowing what a long night it would be for Kelly, and answered, "Of course, I will. If I'm able, I'll try to have a nurse call you with updates as well."

Since Kelly's children both lived fairly close, they decided to head home and come back in the morning. Tracy told her to call them as soon as she had any word at all from the hospital and Kelly agreed.

Everyone else headed over to the hotel and gathered in the lobby. They made plans to eat breakfast together in the morning. Sammy suggested that they pray together before going to their rooms for the night.

TJ took charge and said, "While we were in the waiting room I was reading my Bible and these passages helped me. I'll read them for everyone. Matthew 8:24-26; *And, behold, there arose a great tempest in the sea, insomuch that the ship was covered with the waves; but He was asleep. And his disciples came to him, and awoke him, saying, Lord, save us; we perish. And He saith unto them, Why are ye fearful, O ye of little faith? Then he arose, and rebuked the winds and the sea; and there was a great calm.* Now I'll read from Matthew 17:20-21; *And Jesus said unto them, Because of your unbelief: for verily I say unto you, If ye have faith as a grain of mustard seed, ye shall say unto this mountain, Remove from here to yonder place; and it shall remove; and nothing shall be impossible unto you. Howbeit, this kind goeth not out but by prayer and fasting."*

TJ looked up from his Bible and continued, "Since we're all sailors, most of us have experienced the wrath of the sea. We can all tell stories of some of the most terrible storms. Jesus was telling us not only are there storms at sea, but also within our own lives. Jesus told the disciples they had lost their faith and become afraid. If Christ's disciples could lose faith, how are we any different? Jesus rebuked the wind and the sea and He can rebuke any storms we have in our personal lives, too. We must have faith, as Jesus said, and trust in our Lord and Savior. Let's pray together, both for our loved ones and for ourselves, that we remain faithful."

Everyone in the small circle took the hand of the one next to them. TJ looked at Sammy and nodded. Sammy prayed, "Father, in the name of our Savior, Jesus Christ, we come to you this evening. We humbly acknowledge that You are the Great Physician. Only through You will we be able to accomplish great things. We ask that You will be guiding the hands of the doctors tonight. We lift up the names of Jacob, Joey D, Terry, Sam, and Mark. Please be with them, that their recovery might glorify You. We also pray for ourselves tonight, that we may keep the faith in our times of trouble, and that we will trust You enough to continually say *Thy will be done*. In the name of Jesus Christ we pray, Amen."

Sammy said to TJ, "The verses you just read reminded me of the story Dad would tell us about when he was on his first aircraft carrier, the USS America, where he met Joey D, Terry, and Mark. Dad said off the coast of North Carolina, they ran into a category four hurricane. The hurricane didn't make landfall, but they sent all the ships out of Norfolk and Charleston Navy bases, just in case. He said that hurricane was really something! Dad said they were rocking and rolling so badly that people were getting sick. Can you imagine? Getting sick on an aircraft carrier! For three days they were in heavy seas. I remember him saying the ship had millions of dollars of damage—the catwalk below flight deck was destroyed, three aircraft were washed overboard, even the Golden Anchor was lost in the storm."

Rebecca interrupted, "A golden anchor on a ship? Why?"

Sammy explained, "The Navy gives the Golden Anchor Award to the best re-enlistment ship in each class of ship in the fleet. It isn't really gold; it's just painted that way. The USS America won it that year, as well as a few years before that. Dad joked that people re-enlisted to get off the ship, but in reality, they re-enlisted to stay onboard—it was that great of a ship and the officers and crew worked really well as a team."

Kelly tiredly rubbed the back of her neck and murmured, "I hate to break this up, but I'm exhausted. It's been a long, horrible day and tomorrow will probably be just as difficult. I need to get some sleep before they call me later tonight." Everyone agreed to go to their rooms and try to rest. It had indeed been a long day—one that none of them would ever forget.

CHARLIE RESPONSE
CHAPTER FOUR

Sammy woke up Frank and asked him if he wanted to go running with him. Frank asked from under the pillow, "What time is it?"

"Time to get up! It's 0500 and half the day has gone by. Be quiet so we don't wake Mom," responded Sammy.

Decked out in shorts, t-shirts, and running shoes, they headed out and saw Jeb and Rebecca outside sitting on chairs. They said good morning and asked if they wanted to go running with them. Rebecca asked how far they were going. Sammy replied, "Only a short run this morning, probably around three miles."

Jeb chuckled and said, "I'll decline on that. Have fun on your run."

"Thanks. After we get back and take showers, we're going to get some breakfast. You're going to eat with us, aren't you?" asked Sammy.

"Sure we are," responded Jeb.

Half a mile into the run Sammy said, "Frank, I thought you were going to try to get back into BUDS."

Frank answered his brother's question, "I am, just as soon as the doctors clear me."

"Is your knee going to hold out?"

"Of course. That's why I had the surgery done six months ago," replied Frank. "How about calling out some cadences for this run, brother?"

Sammy called out,

"Hey, hey, Navy.

World's finest Navy.

Get off your ships and follow me.

We are the sons of UDT."

Frank repeated each line after Sammy. They adjusted their pace to match the rhythm of the cadence. They sang a cadence for each branch of the service.

As they finished up their second lap around, TJ came out to see who was calling cadence. "Why didn't you boys wake me up? How far have you gone so far?" he called to them.

Frank answered, "Around two miles."

"Well, I'm planning on running this morning, too," said TJ.

Sammy turned to Frank, "Oh well, Brother, I guess we are running some more." And off they went.

Down the road a bit, Sammy started singing cadence again,

"Wake up Navy,

We've been up

Since half pass five.

We have been running

That's no jive.

Running and swimming

All day long.

That's what makes a tadpole strong."

About a mile into the run Sammy asked, "Hey TJ, are you keeping up with us?"

TJ laughed and answered, "Just running and singing all morning long. I'm going to PT until this depression is gone."

After a few more blocks, they saw three policemen by a Dunkin Donuts laughing at them for singing while they were running. Sammy said in a soft voice, "Listen up, you two. Let's sing this one real good and loud."

"Hey, hey, policemen,

protecting and serving policemen.

Lay down your doughnuts and run with me.

We are the sons of UDT."

One officer yelled at them to stop. He asked what they were running from. TJ thought, *Here I go again, more trouble from local cops.* He explained that they were in town because their fathers had been in a motorcycle accident. The Dairy Township Police Sergeant exclaimed, "Oh, okay. You're the Navy boys staying at the Best Western. My wife works the desk there. I'm so sorry about your dads."

Sammy apologized, "Hey, I didn't mean anything about the doughnut remark. I was just having some fun while running. I'm sorry."

The sergeant laughed and said, "No reason to be sorry, we were actually eating doughnuts. What you don't know is, I'm a retired Gunners mate and also a member of Team 3. These other guys were Army MPs in the Airborne Rangers. Are you guys going to be in town for a while?"

"Yes, we were told it could be quite a while."

"Why don't we all run together tomorrow morning then?" offered the sergeant.

Sammy accepted by saying, "Why don't you meet us in the parking lot at 0530."

. . . .

Because of the noise in the jail cellblock, Hugh hadn't slept much that night. After sleeping only a few hours, he was awakened by the on duty guard bringing his breakfast. He was grateful that he did not have to wait for another diabetic attack before receiving his meal. He said grace and asked the Lord to be with him for this upcoming day.

Back at home in Canada, Martha had contacted a lawyer to handle things. She also called the government authorities and told them the story. They told her they would be contacting the Pennsylvania State Police to get to the bottom of the charges against her husband. With a hopeful heart, she sat down to drink her morning tea.

Hugh finished his breakfast and was still hungry. He asked for more food, but they would not give him any. Hugh sarcastically asked, "How about a doughnut then?" The policeman on duty did not appreciate the comment and threatened that if there were any more smart remarks

Hugh would go without any food for the rest of the day. Hugh decided it was a good idea to keep quiet.

The television in the jail had the morning news on. When it showed pictures of the accident, Hugh heard some of the other prisoners talk about killing the dude, if he was in their jail. Hugh kept his mouth shut and prayed that the prison guards would do the same. He worried about what the rest of the day would bring his way.

• • • • • • • • • • •

Sammy was finished with his shower and Frank was just starting his when their mother woke up. She asked Sammy if he slept okay. He replied, "Of course I did, Mom. Frank, TJ, and I went out for a run this morning. Then we came back to take showers. Should we wake the others?"

Hope told him she would call the others and tell them that they would meet in thirty minutes for breakfast.

While they were eating, TJ commented, "I was just thinking, today is Thursday and you all still have those cabins for another week and a half. I think that sometime today or tomorrow someone should go back and cancel the remaining days and get all your stuff out of them. I think that you all are going to need the money and there's no reason to let the cabins go to waste."

The women said it would be a good idea to do something, but to wait to see what the day brings. Kelly said, "Everyone can leave their things at my house. Once things get settled down here, everyone can stay at our home on the farm, if you don't mind a little country living."

Jeb good-naturedly replied, "We're pretty used to country living."

• • • • • • • • • • •

The families headed back to the hospital where Paula got great news. Mark said, "Paula, they said I might be able to head home tomorrow! I can follow up with our family doctor. I told him the doctor we use is at Lebanon VAMC, so he said he would transfer everything just down the road to them. Isn't that great news?"

Paula, with tears streaming down her cheeks, responded, "Yes, Dear, it is. I just hope the others get the same great news."

"They said I can go see the others, if I use a wheelchair. Let's go track them down," said Mark, eager to get going.

Jeb, Sarah, and Rebecca were in the waiting room when the doctor came out. She said, "Hello, Mr. and Mrs. Peachey. My name is Dr. Sullenberg. I just finished the surgery on Jacob's ankle and everything went well. I had to put a couple screws in to hold things in place. He has a cast, which will need to remain on for eight weeks. It's a walking cast, so in a couple of days he will be able to walk on it with the aid of a cane. After a couple of weeks, he won't need the cane any longer. He can follow up with your family doctor in Lewistown. Jacob will be back in his room in about an hour and a half."

They all hugged each other in relief and Jeb said, "God bless you, Doctor."

Heidi and TJ were in the room with Terry when the doctor came in to talk to them. He said, "We did another MRI earlier this morning. We found that Terry has a torn ligament in his neck, but near his spinal cord. This is causing the loss of feeling in his legs. We'll keep a watchful eye on it. He'll be fine, but will have to stay here and start physical therapy. After that, if everything goes well, he'll be able to go home."

Heidi started to cry and the doctor consoled her, "Don't worry, Mrs. Miller. He's going to be just fine."

Terry assured her, "Honey, come on now. You know nothing can keep a good man down. I'm ready to go for a ride right now. I just have to get better so we can take that ride on the Alaskan Highway. Maybe TJ can come with us, if the Navy lets him off."

TJ replied, "Oh, I think I can get a few weeks leave, Dad. I've got 72 days leave on the books now. Look on the bright side, maybe we'll be able to see Sarah and Todd Palin!"

Terry laughed, "Yeah, maybe Todd will take us fishing!"

Kelly was in the waiting room when Todd and Tracy came in. Todd said, "Did you hear anything yet, Mom?"

Kelly told him miserably, "Nothing at all. The only thing I've heard is that Jacob will be fine, Mark is fine, and Terry has a compressed fracture in his neck—nothing on your father."

Todd looked over and asked Hope the same question. She gave him the same answer. They sat waiting—each praying that the wait would not be very long.

. . . .

Detective Karl Shipley came to question Hugh. Hugh insisted, "You can question me all you want. I have told you nothing but the truth."

Det. Shipley said, "Hugh, I have done some online research and found out a lot about you. I found out that you were kicked out of St. Michael's Catholic School in Fitzroy Harbour for assaulting a nun and a priest."

"WHAT? I never went to St. Michael's Catholic School. In fact, I wasn't even raised in Fitzroy Harbour. I moved there less than twenty years ago! I grew up in the city of Montreal and went to public school. I don't know where you're getting your information from, but it's wrong!" argued Hugh.

Officer Shipley replied, "I checked it out by calling the school. They looked on their computer and have your transcripts. You were a below average student and were in trouble many times, until you got kicked out. We have a printout showing that before you were allowed to serve in the Canadian Army you had to get your GED. It was then you went to serve with the British Army in Pakistan."

Hugh shook his head in disbelief and said, "I graduated from public high school in Montreal and then I joined the Army and became a heavy equipment operator. I never left the country. I worked in western Canada in the army before becoming a truck driver hauling materials from Canada to the United States! However, I did have a contract with the U.S. Government hauling for the U.S. Army."

The detective shook his head no and replied, "Hugh, take a look here on my laptop. I pulled up your Facebook page. I have it right here.

It says you went to St. Michael's Catholic School, Class of 1977. It also said that you switched your religion to Islam when you were in Pakistan. We looked up some of your contacts in Pakistan and see that some of your friends have ties with Hamas and the Taliban. Now as you can tell, we have proof on you. Just come clean with us and we'll go easy on you on the terrorism charges."

Hugh angrily screamed at him, "How stupid are you? You first say that I was kicked out of school and had to get a GED to get into the Army. Then you show me a Facebook page that has me graduating high school in 1977. You must really think I'm stupid! Look at my CDL license and you will see my birth date shows that I am 62 years old. 1977 is years after my high school graduation date. Plus, how could I have a high school diploma after I had supposedly been kicked out of high school and yet still have a GED? Doesn't any of this sound ridiculous to you? Obviously, this Facebook page is false! There probably aren't any family pictures on it, are there? That would be, because it isn't my Facebook page!"

Hugh paused to catch his breath, "The only Facebook page I have is under Hugh and Martha Lamadeleine—not Hugh Lamadeleine! I read the newspapers and watch TV news and even I've heard of people hacking into Facebook accounts and changing things around. I will lay money that's what happened here. Now please, take a good look at my birth date!"

The detective looked at the CDL license and the birth date. He saw that it did not match what would have been the birth date of someone graduating high school in 1977. He pulled up Hugh and Martha Lamadeleine on Facebook. He saw his public high school and graduation date was far different than on the Hugh Lamadeleine Facebook page. He began to wonder what other facts they had gotten wrong. He did have Hugh on traffic charges, but now had second thoughts about the other accidents in York County.

· · · · · · · · · · · ·

He turned to Hugh and said, "Hugh, I'm sorry. I'm beginning to wonder what's going on here. I realize the Facebook account could have been hacked into and now I'm beginning to wonder just what else has been tampered with. I'll be contacting your lawyer as soon as I leave here. I will still have to investigate more, but I'll be talking to my boss about this case. I'm sorry, but it might take a little bit longer. As of right now, you are only charged with traffic violations. I'm not promising anything; I still have to check into things further."

· · · · · · · · · · ·

Paula wheeled Mark in to see Terry. As they came into the room, Mark said, "Hey Shipmate, look I'm on four wheels now! How are you feeling?"

Terry answered, "Good enough to go for a ride, but they won't let me."

Mark jokingly replied, "What do doctors know? Let's blow this joint."

After they finished laughing, they exchanged injury information with each other. "Mark, how are you going to get by, if you don't mind my asking? Since I work for the Agency, I'm well taken care of," asked Terry.

"I have short and long term disability at Grove, so they'll take care of me. With Grove's disability, our Navy retirement, and Paula working as a paramedic, we'll get by."

"Well, my friend, you know if you need anything, just let us know. Don't be too proud to ask. We'll say the same to Kelly and Hope. I'm sure they're really going to need some help. We might even need to have a charity ride to help out with things," Terry said. "Just like in the Navy, we sailors and motorcyclists take care of our own."

Paula interjected, "Isn't that the truth! I think I'm going to wheel him over to see how Sam and Joey D are coming along. We'll drop by a little later."

Heidi hugged Paula and said, "TJ stepped out to get me some coffee. I'll tell him you both stopped by and that Mark's doing well."

Sarah asked her son if he was hungry and he nodded. So Sarah, Rebecca, Jeb, and Jacob went to the Café inside the hospital. Jeb pushed Jacob in his wheelchair. He was very happy to get out of his room.

They sat down to eat. After Jeb said the blessing, he mentioned to his wife, "Sarah, the English must be used to seeing us plain people here. Have you noticed that no one is staring at us?"

Sarah answered her husband by saying, "I didn't take notice, but it's nice that they leave us alone."

Rebecca said, "I hate to change the subject, but this sandwich is great! They call it a Philly cheese steak."

Jacob mumbled through his broken jaw, "This tomato soup is good, too. I'm worried about the farm and my wood working business. I know our family and friends will take care of the farm, but what about all my wood working orders that I have lined up?"

"Don't you worry, my son. The Lord will provide; He always has. You must keep faith. Besides you can still work in your workshop with your ankle in a cast. You just won't be able to climb ladders and such," replied Jeb.

Rebecca commented, "After we eat, we should go check on the others and see how they are."

. . . .

The detective came back to talk to Hugh again. "I have some questions for you. Did you go on a three week cruise four years ago?"

"Yes, Martha and I went through the Panama Canal."

The detective then asked him, "Did you loan out your truck while you were gone?"

"Yes, to Carlos Cruz from Lehigh Acres, Florida."

The detective asked, "Can you tell us anything more about Carlos Cruz?"

Hugh replied, "At different times over the next four years, he drove for me for anywhere from two to five weeks when we took a vacation or cruise during our time in Florida."

The detective filled Hugh in on information he had gathered, "Thank you, sir. You've been very helpful. All I can tell you right now is Carlos Cruz is not his real name. We believe he's an Islamic terrorist operating within the United States. He came into the United States through Mexico in some terrorist plot."

The detective looked through some papers and continued, "We don't know why he wanted your truck, but we have a few theories. One theory is that he and others broke into New Cumberland Army Depot and/or Letterkenny Army Depot and used your truck to deliver the load somewhere."

Hugh quickly replied, "That can't be correct! He only drove around the state of Florida. I know this for a fact, because when I came back he only had a little over 4,500 miles on the truck."

The detective remarked, "That's more than enough to travel up to Pennsylvania and back, isn't it? Hugh, I want to advise you that you're not in any trouble for loaning out your truck to this guy. He showed you the paper work with his CDL license, picture, and work history. Do you know how to get in contact with him?"

"My wife has his number. I can call her and get it for you," said Hugh.

The detective said, "If you don't mind, you can call her right now on my cell phone."

Hugh called Martha and she found the number for him. The detective told Hugh that they were working things out and the other charges would be dropped. Then he asked Hugh, "Would you be willing to help out the United States Government by setting up a sting to get this Carlos Cruz?"

Hugh said he would have to hear how it would work and what it would do for him. The detective told him he would work things out with the State Department and the Pennsylvania State Police to see what they would do for him. He said that, at least, they would get him out of jail, back on the road earning money, and on the way home to his wife. Hugh figured he had some things to think about.

• • • • • • • • • • •

The children of Joey D arrived at the hospital. Tracy was carrying a cake, because it was Joey D's birthday. Kelly started to cry. "God bless you, Child! I can't believe I forgot."

Tracy replied, "I thought it would cheer everyone up. Plus, I've heard many times people in a coma can hear and remember what's going on around them. So I just knew that we had to do this for Dad." Kelly called everyone to gather in Joey D's room to celebrate his birthday, hoping he could hear them and feel the love they had for him.

Kelly was at Joey D's bedside with their children. Everyone else filtered in, talking to each other. As the Peacheys came into the room, Kelly realized that they were all together again. Even though the circumstances were tragic and Joey D and Sam were being kept alive by medical machines, Kelly knew they were all blessed to be in each other's lives. She leaned over Joey D and softly said, "Honey, we're all here for your birthday today. I wanted to give you a special gift. I'm going to talk to Jacob and when you wake up, you'll get that present. I couldn't ask for a better husband and father to our children." Tears dropped onto Joey D's blanket and Kelly's son-in-law put his arm around her to comfort her. She smiled at the group around her and said, "Hey, isn't this supposed to be a celebration? How about we start singing?"

After singing a very off-key round of Happy Birthday, Tracy cut the cake and passed it all around. Even the nurses came in for a piece of delicious homemade cake.

Rebecca whispered something to Jeb and Jacob, and then Jeb asked Sammy if he could step outside for a moment. Once outside, Jeb said, "Kelly was going to buy a rocking chair from Jacob for Joey D for his birthday. For all the help your family and friends have given us, I want to repay you. See if you can borrow Kelly's pick-up truck and drive me back to the workshop. Jacob has some rocking chairs back there. It will be our way of repaying you all."

Sammy asked if he could borrow the pick-up and Kelly said, "Of course, but why?"

He grinned and answered, "Don't you worry about it. I'll be back soon."

When they arrived at Jacob's workshop, Jeb loaded two rocking chairs into the back of the truck. Sammy looked at him with a puzzled look on his face. "Well, I figure that Hope is going to be sitting at that hospital for quite a while, too," stated Jeb.

When they arrived back at the hospital and carried the rocking chairs into the room, both Kelly and Hope cried and said over and over how beautiful they were. They thanked both Jacob and Jeb for their thoughtful gift.

Since it was suppertime, the families went to Pizza Hut to eat together. After eating, they headed back to the hospital to sit with their respective family members. Tracy and Rich left from Pizza Hut to go to their home.

When they got back to the hospital, Kelly's minister was standing at the front desk of the hospital. Kelly received permission for him to go up to pray for Joey D and Sam. In the room, he opened his Bible and read James 5:14-15: *Is any sick among you? Let him call for the elders of the church; and let them pray over him, anointing him with oil in the name of the Lord; And the prayer of faith shall save the sick, and the Lord shall raise him up; and if he have committed sins, they shall be forgiven him.*

The minister then prayed for Joey D and Sam. "Father, I offer Joseph Daniels and Sam Adams up to You in prayer for special healing. You know their needs, Father. You have the healing powers, if it be Thy will. Father, we humbly ask for a blessing this evening. Please come into this hospital room and comfort everyone here. Give comfort to Kelly as she deals with the injuries of her husband; and please be with Hope as she grieves with the injuries of her husband. Hope and Sam are so far away from home; help us know how to be helpful to Hope, Sammy, and Frank in their time of need. In Jesus name we pray, Amen!"

Kelly gave the minister a hug and said, "Thank you, Pastor. That was beautiful." Hope came over and gave him a hug too. Both Sammy and Frank shook his hand. At that moment, a couple of loud alarms started to go off! Nurses came running in and said, "Excuse us! You have to leave now!"

Kelly and Hope held tight to each other and started to cry. No one knew what was happening. Was it a code blue? The call went out over the loud speaker for the doctors to report to the ICU. Terry, Heidi, Mark, and Paula all heard the page on the loud speaker and their hearts sank, fearful that it was bad news. Jacob turned to Rebecca with a look of despair as she said, "Oh no! I know that's the room that Sam and Joey D are in. We need to go check on the girls."

Jeb immediately knelt in prayer and said, "Lord, You know what's going on and You know the needs of the Daniels' and Adams' families. Please be with them at this time. Comfort them and, if it be Thy will, please take care of Joey D and Sam." Then rising from his knees, Jeb said, "Let's head up and see what's going on."

. . . .

When Hugh was told he would be going in front of the judge on his traffic charges the next morning, he asked what all of the charges would be. "Operating a vehicle while talking on a cellphone, failure to maintain control of vehicle, crossing the middle line, as well as another possible charge," answered the officer.

"What other charge?"

The officer informed him, "Well, if any of the victims from the accident dies, you'll be charged with vehicular manslaughter."

"But the sergeant told me if I were to cooperate, there wouldn't be any charges."

"I believe he was talking about the hit and run charges," the officer told him. Hugh could feel his anxiety begin to rise again.

When they brought Hugh his evening meal, the guard told him, "Since you're diabetic, we are giving you some extra food. We don't want your levels to bottom out on us again, right?" Hugh thanked him for the extra attention.

. . . .

Mark and Paula were happily surprised when their minister came in for a visit. He asked about the accident and how Mark was feeling. Mark responded, "I wouldn't be any better if I were twins! They said there's a good chance I can go home tomorrow. People think we wear the safety gear to look cool on our bikes; but I'll tell you for sure, the leather jacket, helmet, and boots really saved my hide. Because of them, my injuries were nothing compared to what they could have been. By the way, Pastor, would you mind visiting our friends with us? Some of them are far from home and may need your prayers and comfort, too."

The pastor pushed Mark's wheelchair into Terry's room and Mark introduced Terry, Heidi, and TJ to him. He talked to them for a bit and then offered up a prayer for the Lord to be with them every step of the way. Mark said they were going to Jacob's room next and then up to the ICU. Terry said they would meet them up there.

Rebecca invited Mark and Paula in when she answered their knock on Jacob's door. Mark said, "Our minister is here visiting us and would like to know if he could come in and pray for Jacob."

"I would surely welcome his prayers," responded Rebecca. This was very unusual for an Amish person, but nothing had been normal the last two days.

At the end of the prayer, Jeb came over to shake the hand of the English minister and acknowledged, "Thank you, Sir. I can see you're a man of God and you don't judge us."

"In God's eyes, we are all His children. It doesn't matter which church you go to, as long as it teaches the Word of God," assured the minister, smiling warmly.

At that moment, a call came over the intercom calling doctors to the ICU. Mark, Paula, and their minister said their goodbyes to Jacob and Rebecca and headed directly to the ICU unit. As they rounded the corner, they immediately saw that Kelly, Hope, and Heidi were crying. Sammy explained to the Browns what happened and introduced their pastor. The small group bowed their heads and handed their burdens over to God.

A doctor came out to talk to Kelly and Hope. The two women clung together, praying for good news. Before the young doctor started to speak to them, a nurse called him back into the room saying there was something he needed to see.

Everyone looked around bewildered, hoping it was not bad news. Sammy tried to reassure everyone, "Maybe it's good news that he was called back. We should all calm down. We've prayed; God knows our needs. We have to have faith in Him."

The television in the corner was showing the news of the day; the talk was about Libya. Heidi reminisced, "Remember when the guys were on the USS America back in 1981? They were supposed to be gone for six months and ended up being gone for seven and a half months. They had a three day liberty stop in Palma, Spain. I was able to come from my duty station in Rota, Spain and join them. They really loved that liberty stop. After that, their ship was sent to operate in the Gulf of Sidra off the coast of Libya. Qadhafi claimed over 100 miles off shore and launched some Migs at the ship. The America launched all its F-14s and F-18s to turn back the Migs. After that, they headed down the Suez Canal and into the Red Sea to Gonzo Station. After two months, they had another five day liberty call in Singapore, the City of Lions. They really loved it there! After two more months of Gonzo Station, they headed to Perth, Australia."

TJ interrupted and said, "Yeah, that's where Dad, Joey D, Sam, and Mark all became Shellbacks by crossing the Equator." When sailors cross the equator for the first time, there is an initiation; after that, they are called Shellbacks. Before crossing for the first time, they're called Pollywogs.

Terry laughed as he remembered, "You wouldn't believe how nasty that was, but how much fun it was, too. It was even more fun when we picked up the new crew members in Perth; when we crossed the second time, we got to dish it out to them!"

Mark joined in, "You bet! That was a fun time! I always enjoy being a Shellback. Those Aussies really treated us well down under. They were so friendly! When we'd go out to eat, they would come up to us and want to pay for our meal or buy us a drink. They really went out of their way to welcome you to their city and country. Someday, I want us all to go back there to explore by motorcycle, but also to go sailing there. Sailing is pretty close to a national sport there. One of these days I'm going to buy that cruising sailboat I want. It's just the adventurist in me, I guess."

Kelly added, "My Joey said that he had a wonderful time there. He also told me about receiving the message while on duty that President Sadat was killed. At that point, everything changed and you all were extended another two weeks on station."

Terry agreed, "I do remember that! Tensions were tight. President Reagan was in his first year in office and the Soviets said that no war ship would be allowed to transit the Suez Canal. The Soviet Union had a large Naval Base in Yemen at the time. So President Reagan had our ship and another carrier battle group escort a frigate up the Red Sea and the Suez. We didn't transmit any radio traffic for an entire day. Once we got there, we surprised them. They had their fire control radar locked on us and us on them. It was a stand down. It took both leaders working with each other to work things out. Man, was it tense! A few weeks later, we were heading home! The world didn't even know that there was almost a nuclear war started that day. We knew what was going on and we were worried!"

"Yeah, I remember that feeling. Though nothing compared to the feeling of happiness when we learned we were less than two weeks away from going home. Then we had a fire on board. I remember hearing the shouts—fire, fire, fire! I thought we were goners, but the men were able to put it out. Thank God!" added Mark.

"From what I was told, it took at least two days to fully put out that fire," said Kelly.

"Then we saw the small plane flying with a sign saying, *Welcome Home USS America Battle Group*! The local radio stations were giving updates where the ship was. Looking down at that crowd and trying to find our loved ones was something else. Mothers, wives, and girlfriends were holding signs for their loved ones and all the sailors wanted to jump off the ship to get to them. It was the longest wait in the world waiting for Liberty Call. Everyone was allowed to go in order of rank—Officers, Chiefs, First Class Petty Officers, and each rank after that. All the kisses and hugs that were waiting for everyone was something else."

Mark shook his head and said, "What I remember once we got off base and went to Burger King, was seeing signs in people's yard saying, *Dogs and Sailors, Stay off the grass*! I was so angry about that! We had been protecting vital shipping lanes and after being treated so well in Australia, then we come home to these signs."

Hope added, "Sam's parents got hotel rooms for all of us on Virginia Beach. We went there and Sam was in his dress blue uniform with his ribbons and medals. We were so proud of him. We walked by the front desk and they yelled at Sam to stop. They said he wasn't allowed there because their policy was NO SAILORS ALLOWED! The rest of us could continue to stay there, but Sam couldn't stay with us! We checked out and got another hotel. Almost every hotel on the ocean side of Virginia Beach had the same policy. Sam told us not to worry about it, because he had seen enough water in the last eight months!"

Hope then added, "I do remember going to the two shopping malls in the area; if you showed your military ID and ship's ID card, the stores gave the men a twenty to thirty percent discount. So it wasn't all bad for the men."

The reminiscing came to an abrupt halt when two doctors came into the room. "Hello, I'm Doctor Andrews and this is Doctor Cool. Can I speak to Kelly Daniels, please?"

"And I would like to speak to Hope Adams, in private, if you don't mind."

Kelly and Hope both nervously stood up to go with the doctors. Everyone else said words of encouragement to the girls as they walked to the door, then they prayed for the best.

Doctor Cool spoke, "Hope, the alarms went off because there were some abnormal readings. These readings said that Sam's heart rate and blood pressure increased a little bit. This was a good thing. We know that the minister had been praying at that time and we know that Sam is a religious man. This tells me he was possibly responding to the prayer. However, after that we had a small setback. I remain hopeful for Sam though. It's going to be a long road, but we may be seeing the light at the end of the tunnel. We're still keeping round the clock monitoring on him. Keep talking to him about anything that comes to mind that he would be interested in. I've seen people come out of comas in the past."

Hope thanked him for the information and asked when she could see Sam. The doctor told her they were doing some testing right now, but someone would come out and get her soon. Hope went back to her friends to share the optimistic news.

In the other room, Doctor Andrews was giving Kelly the same information about Joey D. He told her that both Sam and Joey D had a rise in heart rate and blood pressure, but that it had fallen off again. However, Joey D's levels had gone much lower than Sam's had. "I'm thinking that it was a false reading on the machines. I think that Joey D is getting worse. Personally, I'm not sure that either Sam or Joey D has any brain activity at this point. That's something that we are testing. Doctor Cool disagrees with me on this point though. We are, of course, going to continue monitoring your husband and will keep you informed. I just wanted to let you know what is going on at this time."

Kelly felt like the wind had been knocked out of her, but thanked the doctor for everything he was doing for her husband. "Isn't there any hope at all?" she asked him.

"There's always hope. You're obviously a woman who has faith in a higher power. Keep hanging on to that faith. I've seen miracles in this profession." Then he added, "I'll come out and let you know soon when you can come back in to see him."

Kelly joined the others in the waiting room, tearfully telling them what the doctor had told her. It was a very somber group of people, holding hands, each praying silently for the people they loved. TJ quietly started to sing,

O Trinity of love and power!

Our Family Shield in danger's hour;

From rock and tempest, fire, and foe,

Protect us where so ev'r we go;

Thus evermore shall rise to Thee

Glad hymns of praise from land and sea.

CHARLIE RESPONSE
CHAPTER FIVE

The motorcycle escort arrived at the graveyard ahead of the hearse. Because of recent trouble with protesters, motorcyclists and the Patriot Guard Riders formed a wall surrounding the funeral procedures. Blocking both the sight and sound of any protestors, this wall protected the family and friends, who had already suffered an unthinkable loss, from having to deal with hate-mongers.

Sailors, in their perfect dress white uniforms and shiny Bates black shoes, carried the flag draped casket to the waiting vault under the tent. Off in the distance was a small group of sailors with rifles and in the other direction was a lone sailor with a bugle. TJ and his girlfriend, Sally, as well as Sammy and Frank stood at attention and sadly looked on.

The pastor opened his King James Bible to Psalm 23 and looked over the small crowd, "*The Lord is my shepherd; I shall not want.*" He read the passage to the end.

Then as he shuffled the pages of his Bible he continued, "Most sailors travel the world, so let's read Psalm 121:1-8, which is recognized as the traveler's Psalm. *I will lift up mine eyes unto the hills, from whence cometh my help? My help cometh from the Lord, who made heaven and earth. He will not suffer thy foot to be moved; he who keepeth thee will not slumber. Behold, he who keepeth Israel shall neither slumber nor sleep. The Lord is thy keeper; the Lord is thy shade upon thy right hand. The sun shall not smite thee by day, nor the moon by night. The Lord shall preserve thee from all evil; He shall preserve thy soul. The Lord shall preserve thy going out and thy coming in from this time forth, and even for evermore.*"

"The family has requested that we all sing together *Eternal Father, Strong to Save*, otherwise known as the Navy Hymn. This song was President Franklin D. Roosevelt's favorite hymn and to all Navy personnel, it's a beloved song," stated the pastor.

With the help of an electric piano, the small group of mourners began.

Eternal Father, strong to save,

Whose arm hath bound the restless wave,

Who bid'st the mighty ocean deep

Its own appointed limits keep;

Oh hear us when we cry to Thee,

For those in peril on the sea!

O Christ! Whose voice the waters heard

And hushed their raging at Thy Word,

Walked'st on the foaming deep,

And calm amidst its rage didst sleep,

Oh hear us when we cry to Thee,

For those in peril on the sea!

The pastor thanked the crowd for their fine singing. At this moment, the honor guard took a step forward. As the riflemen fired each shot, the women flinched. Tears flowed openly down their cheeks. As the sound of the shots died away, the lone sailor raised his bugle and blew Taps. Very reverently, the honor guard perfectly folded the American flag taken from the casket and handed it to the head of the honor guard. He presented it to the grieving widow and said, "On behalf of a grateful nation." She held the flag lovingly in her hands as she bowed her head in sorrow.

People quietly and respectfully walked through the cemetery to the cars waiting to take them to the fellowship hall for the repast meal.

At the fellowship hall, the pastor blessed the meal. Everyone was soon eating and talking. Some people came over to Kelly, hugged her, and said, "Kelly, I'm so sorry about Joey D." She was exhausted and getting tired of the attention that was being given to her. A few people also talked to Hope, Sammy, Frank, or the other people in their group. People were still talking about the accident and the whispers going on around them made some of them very uncomfortable.

Suddenly, Kelly just could not take all the attention anymore. There were too many questions and too many people looking at her. She missed Joey D! Who could blame her for her feelings? She had thought she could get through this day—but she was wrong. She felt so alone, even with family and friends there. She did not know what her future would be and she did not like the feeling of having no control over things in her life. She told Hope that she was going to the restroom and left the fellowship hall. When she went into the hallway, instead of heading towards the ladies room, she bolted for the exit doors. She hurried toward her Chrysler 200S, fumbling with the door lock button on her key fob.

There is something about weddings and funerals; sometimes, it is the only time that family and old friends get together. Even though we all care for the people we have known our whole lives, so often, we lose touch with them as we grow older and life gets in the way. People were busy catching up with loved ones that they had not seen in a while; no one noticed when Kelly did not return.

Kelly turned her car toward the rural roads of Pennsylvania. She knew there would be no cell phone service out there, so she could be alone with her thoughts. Kelly is gone—unlike Elvis, no one knows she has left the building!

· · · · · · · · · · ·

Back on the Peachey farm, Jacob was working in his workshop making small gifts for his family's new friends from the accident. Because they were all so kind and friendly, he felt that a Welcome sign for their front doors would be appreciated. He lined up the hand carved signs on his workbench, preparing them for staining. Small thank you plaques for the doctors at the hospital were sitting in a neat row on the workbench, also waiting for the staining process. Because of his dislocated shoulder, Jacob was limited to working with only one hand and it was hampering him from finishing these projects in a timely manner. Jacob was beginning to feel just a little useless on his own farm.

It felt good to be back on the farm—Jacob loved being home. He didn't like the restrictions that came with his injuries though. He was on a liquid diet for at least a month, because of his broken jaw. He was getting around on his broken foot alright; but the broken ribs did cause him some pain, whenever he would twist one way or the other. His brother, Mathew, would tease him about not pulling his weight with the farm work. Jacob felt the sting of these jokes sharply. He had always been a hard worker and took pride in his farm. Pushing himself to do more, Jacob tried to hide the pain the work was causing him.

Jeb leaned against the wooden door frame and looked at his son, "Are you going to the sale tomorrow morning?"

"I am."

"I know you don't like to ask for help; but if you get tired tomorrow, please don't hesitate to come to me," Jeb said.

Jeb and Mathew helped Jacob load their goods onto the new trailer the people of their Amish community had built for him.

The drive to the sale brought the accident fresh to Jacob's memory. He would flinch every time a car would pass. When a truck came into view, his heart would stop and he would hold his breath until it went by. Neither he nor Rebecca had told anyone about the nightmares that were keeping him awake at night; he thought it would make him appear weak. He had heard of post-traumatic stress disorder, but thought that only happened to battlefield veterans. It never occurred to him that even an accident could bring it about.

Jacob and Rebecca made the trip to the sale safely. They had a very good day and all their goods were sold. As they were packing up, they heard the fire alarms calling out their distress signal. Their hearts stopped and they looked at each other with worry in their eyes. It would be a long time before they would hear that sound and not go back in their minds to the day of the accident, if ever.

• • • • • • • • • • •

Hugh pulled up outside his comfortable home in Fitzroy Harbour. He had to deadhead home, because the company he worked for had another driver take the load he had been hauling to its destination. He was so glad to be home; he was ready to wrap his arms around his wife in a loving hug. Martha came running out of the house and climbed up onto Hugh's truck to greet her husband. They had not seen each other for two weeks, but to her it had felt like two years. It was certainly a joyful reunion.

As Hugh climbed out of the cab of his truck, Martha exclaimed, "You look like you've lost some weight! Didn't they feed you at all? You know you have to eat with the way your blood sugar is!" They went into the house and straight into the kitchen. As Martha fixed Hugh something to eat, she listened to him as he told her some ideas he had on the long drive home.

"You know the way I've been talking about retiring soon? Well, I've thought about it long and hard and I've decided I want to go out with a bang. I want the two of us to take a vacation and then I want to make as much money as I can quickly. I thought about not going to Florida this year. Instead, I'm thinking about staying up north and running the ice roads. I can make a lot of money in a short amount of time. Then next summer, I'll run lumber again and after that, sell the truck."

"What?!?" exclaimed Martha.

"If everything goes well with the case down in the States, this is a good plan. You said a while ago that you'd like to live in Pine Island down in Florida year round. I could go fishing year round and we could still visit our friends in Canada in the summertime, if we wanted to. If we decided to do this, we could sell this place and invest in 35 foot motorhome. However, if things don't go well down in Pennsylvania, I never want to go back. I'll just retire and we'll spend the rest of our lives here," explained Hugh to his surprised wife.

She tried to soothe him, "Honey, things will be fine. The law will prevail and the good Lord will take care of us. Just do what you know to be right; listen to the FBI and your lawyers. And pray for wisdom and faith. Do that and things will work out just right."

Hugh then told her, "I trust in the Lord, but God helps him who helps himself. I'm worried that everything we've worked so hard for will be taken away in lawsuits. That's why I put most of our retirement money in an offshore account in the Grand Cayman Islands. No one will be able to reach it there. If we sell the house, I'll add the money to that account. With our regular accounts here in Canada and our bank in Florida, they won't think to look elsewhere. They'll think I'm just a poor truck driver, not a truck driver with over half a million dollars stashed somewhere! No one, and I mean no one, is going to take my hard earned money!"

With a look of disapproval on her face, Martha quickly lectured, "Hugh! I think you should read

1 Timothy 6:10: *For the love of money is the root of all evil; which while some coveted after, they have erred from the faith, and pierced themselves through with many sorrows.*"

Hugh looked shamefaced, but turned his back on his wife and walked down the hall.

. . . .

CTN Seaman Frank Adams was nervous about standing in front of all these people, giving them important information. Most were Army Officers and high ranking enlisted—some were even Colonels. He remembered how nervous he used to be standing in front of his speech class at the community college in Mississippi. This was much more intimidating; he was putting so much pressure on himself to perform in an outstanding manner.

His brother, Sammy—Navy Seal and hero—was there with him, but he was the first speaker and he did not know what to expect from this crowd. As Sammy jotted down a quick note that was to be sent to his mother, he advised Frank, "This is different from good old college classes, no one there cared what you said. In fact, I dare say no one even listened to what you were saying then. These people will be listening intently. They want to learn this stuff, because their lives, along with other's lives, depend on them really knowing it." Sammy laughed as he slapped his brother on the back, "Think of it this way, no one here is grading your public speaking performance today." Sammy turned to hand the note to the assistant they had been given for the day.

Frank thought to himself, *Great, people's lives are at stake based on my performance. Mess Cranking was so much easier.* He walked to the front of the room and took a deep breath.

"Officers, Ladies, and Gentlemen, my name is Seaman Frank Adams. I want to welcome you to Fort Indiantown Gap's first ever Introduction to Combat Cryptologic Support in the Battlefield. We will also be adding our Islamic Orientation class. Some of this introductory part is classified For Your Eyes Only, and other parts are classified up to and including Top Secret Code Word. My brother and fellow instructor, Petty Officer Sam Adams has been notified that this is a secure room and everyone here has a Top Secret Clearance. So I'll get started."

Frank told them of the different types of communications equipment they would be using in the field, at base communication sites, in aircraft, and on naval ships. He told them of the cryptologic equipment they would be exposed to while on deployments around the world. He explained who made the equipment, where the equipment came from, and where the codes for the cryptologic equipment came from. Frank instructed, "No matter how high the ranking of the battlefield commander is, the Director of the National Security Agency always has control of everything Cryptologic—SIGINT, COMINT, ELINT, and SATINT."

A Colonel stood up and said, "Your equipment seems fine, but what can it do for me that other kinds can't? And will it work on land, air, or sea?"

Frank, who was getting into the swing of things now, smiled and replied, "An outstanding question; the answer happens to be the reason for this class. I'll break it down for you with four different types of messages and two types of communication centers." Frank looked around the room and saw several people taking notes. Everyone was paying very focused attention to what he was telling him. The fact that he knew this information inside and out, helped him to relax and settle into the role of teacher, for the time being.

Two and a half hours later, Frank dismissed everyone for lunch, saying, "We'll take an hour long lunch break now. When we reconvene this afternoon, my brother Sammy will be taking over."

While her sons were giving lectures ten miles away at Fort Indiantown Gap, Hope was still sitting with Sam at the hospital. His condition was the same, but Hope was still praying for God's will to be done. A nurse walked in and handed Hope a folded piece of paper. She read it with a small smile on her face. As she refolded it, Hope thanked God for giving her amazing boys and she asked Him to guide them safely through the rest of their day.

Back at Fort Indiantown Gap, everyone settled back into their seats after the lunch break. Sammy stood at the front of the room and waited for everyone to get situated. "Welcome back. I'm Petty Officer First Class Sam Adams Jr. Just call me Sammy. I'm a Cryptologic Technician Interpretive. I learned Spanish throughout high school and college. I was also trained as an Arabic and Farsi interpreter in the Navy. I have been in the Navy for ten years, seven of those as a US Navy Seal."

Sammy, confident in his abilities as a speaker, continued, "In this portion of our day together, I'll tell you how Navy Seals can help you in the field." Sammy explained how they could jump from five miles up in the sky with special pressurized suits and oxygen without being seen. Jumping from these heights allows the combatant to get closer to the enemy without being seen on the radars. Doing so allows them to complete their missions, such as gathering information which would be passed on to cryptologic support operators. They then relay it to those who need the information.

Sammy went on to explain how Special Forces can blend into the local indigenous population. In doing so, they can accomplish many different tasks, such as: gathering information, training the people to take care of themselves, giving medical attention, and protecting them in the midst of a skirmish. Special Forces do not just go out to kill the enemy; their primary job is saving lives.

He continued to talk about the invaluable skills of the Seals and the ways they could be used in combat to help other branches of the military. "What sets a Seal Team apart from the other Special Forces is that we specialize on sea, land, and air. However, out on the sea is our forte. For instance, you can have information that resupply goods are traveling down a body of water at night. We can be there to intercept this vessel and take the cargo, so it will not be used against our forces.

We accomplish this at night, without anyone even knowing we are there. We can also train the locals to do this on smaller boats. That way the teams would be able to be used in other areas."

Sammy wrapped up his portion of the lecture for the day telling the audience that they would be loading up in the parking lot to go to the artillery range. He would show them how to paint targets with lasers and then watch an artillery strike. He mentioned that tomorrow's lecture would be in the auditorium and would be information concerning Islam, the Quran, and what it means to a terrorist.

At the hospital, Hope was continually talking to Sam, hoping something she said would get through, and maybe he would respond in some way. She talked about everything she could think of. She told her husband about the lectures the boys were giving. She talked about motorcycle riding trips they had been on. She talked about baseball and the upcoming football season. She asked him if he thought the New Orleans Saints would win another Super Bowl this season.

"Come on, honey! I asked you a question! Are the Saints going to win another Super Bowl?"

"How would I know?"

Hope jumped out of her seat! When she turned around, Mark was standing in the doorway, grinning.

"Oh, my goodness! Don't ever scare me like that again!" exclaimed Hope.

Mark chuckled as he apologized, "I'm so sorry, Hope. I just stopped in to see how things are going. Paula and I are heading home soon, but I wanted to check on things here first."

"No change. Always—no change. It's getting so frustrating!" Hope's face crumpled as she tried not to cry in front of Mark. He immediately walked over to her and enveloped her in a big bear hug.

. . . .

"Good morning, class. I'm Petty Officer Samuel Adams, Navy Seal. I served multiple tours in both Iraq and Afghanistan. I speak Arabic and

Farsi. I'm here today to give a lecture about Islam. We'll be starting from the very beginning to build a strong foundation of knowledge. Without understanding the beginning, you will not understand what the terrorist believes and why he believes it. I want to be clear about this, not all Muslims are practicing terrorism.

"You remember my brother from yesterday's lecture, Seaman Frank Adams. He'll be my assistant today and will pass out some handouts at times throughout the lecture. Today's talk is classified as For Your Eyes Only. Most of it is taught in colleges throughout the country, but I may occasionally refer to missions or other things that are classified. Let's begin.

"Islamophobia is an attempt by the critics of the left to make people who view Islam as a militant threat as xenophobic or just plain psycho. These leftist critics say the Islamophobia is an irrational phobia. I'll tell you that this is a justifiable fear. Here are my reasons:

1. Most conflicts in the world today involve Islam. From Chechnya to Somalia, from Indonesia to Iraq, from Afghanistan to Argentina, from the Balkans to the Philippines, from Kenya to Lebanon, from Tanzania to Yemen, from Syria to Libya. These are all Islamic conflicts.

2. Islam has a history of violence and brutal suppression. I will address more on this later.

3. Al Arian, a professor at the University of South Florida, created the World Islam Studies Enterprise. (WISE) This became a breeding ground for jihadists. The Blind Sheikh, Omar Abel Rahman and his followers studied at WISE. Al Arian has been arrested many times on terrorist charges.

4. FBI Agent Hafiz refused to record conversations with other Muslims even though it was his job. He was supposed to record them planning the first attack on the World Trade Center and other attacks in the future.

5. Al-Farouq Mosque at 554 Atlantic Ave. New York City, NY has been accused of sending hundreds of their people to al Qaeda training camps. There are over 1,200 such mosques inside the USA at this time."

Sammy looked around the room, "So how many of you think that we should learn about Islam and who we are up against?" He slowly looked at each person in the room. Many hands rose to show they also thought this was a very important topic.

"Okay, then—let's get started," agreed Sammy. With that, he launched into the history of the battles of Muhammad.

After breaking for lunch, people started to filter back into the lecture hall, talking about what they had learned earlier and what they might learn during the second half of the lecture.

Sammy stood and began, "Welcome back, everyone. I trust you all enjoyed your lunch. We still have a lot of ground to cover, so I suggest we dive right in. This morning we discussed the battles of Muhammad. The Quran tells about these battles. In fact, the Quran is divided into three parts: worship, love, and battle. Feel free to study more on this individually. In fact, I would encourage this, as it will help you understand the terrorist's beliefs. Through better understanding, we will learn how to deal with them in a more efficient manner.

"Now about some of Muhammad's love interests. Muhammad loved his wife Khadija. Khadija was forty when she married 25 year old Muhammad. Today, Khadija would be called a cougar. She later died and, after that, Muhammad took many wives. These wives were for political and social motives. He did, however, marry Abu Bakr's daughter, Aisha. Abu Bakr was Muhammad's best friend. Muhammad was fifty years old when he and Aisha got married, but Aisha was only five years old!" There was a ripple of noise throughout the room.

At that moment, Sammy heard a knock on the door. A Major opened the door and asked to speak to Petty Officer Sam Adams. Sammy stepped out the door for a few moments, then returned and addressed the class. "Class, today's lesson will have to be continued at a later date. There has been a wildfire reported near the training grounds. My brother and I have firefighting training from the Navy, so we're being sent to head up a couple of the teams going to help. Does anyone else here have firefighting experience?"

The Major told the troops this is a Charlie Response because the fire was threatening, not just wooded area, but houses as well.

A few people stood up to indicate they had experience and were willing to help. Some of them were chopper pilots who could drop water on the fire from the helicopters. In a short amount of time, people were scrambling to get equipment ready.

Sammy went to the Major with an idea. "Sir, why don't we use the Black Hawks to drop us in near the fire with chain saws and fire rakes. We can then repel down and start attacking it."

The Major agreed that it was a great idea. They went to the on-scene leader to share their idea; he also agreed that it was a good plan.

With everyone loaded up, the Black Hawks took off. The forest was so dense that no one could repel into it, so they touched down in a nearby field. Sammy suggested that they climb up and use some chain saws to clear an opening, so people could repel in. Everyone agreed, but it would take some time to get this accomplished.

Sammy's crew charged up the hill and started sawing down trees. It was hard work in the humid, 95 degree weather. The local weather man was calling for severe thunderstorms by late evening. This could help put out some of the fires, but with drought conditions the undergrowth was very dry and burning fast.

A half mile from where Sammy went into the forest, a farmer drove his pick-up into the hay field to see if his property would be in danger. He could smell smoke all around him, but did not think the fire was close to him. Unfortunately, the heat of the engine from his truck touched the dry hay and started his truck and the hay on fire. The farmer ran down the field, but the fire seemed to be chasing him A Black Hawk swooped down to rescue him.

The chopper pilot reported the new fire. Soon, a bulldozer was plowing a thirty foot fire break around the farmer's yard, while fire trucks from the neighboring town were wetting down his house and barn. His buildings were safe for the moment, at least.

A mile up the road, a teenager rode his ATV into a field to get a better look at the fire. He was riding hard and fast, because he did not want to get caught by the authorities. Sparks from his exhaust set off another brush fire, but he did not notice until the flames were quite large. He immediately called 911 on his cell phone. He gave the location of the fire and took off for what he thought was a safe exit, but a fire was directly in his path. He looked around—fire in back, fire to his left, fire in front. He noticed in the distance the bulldozers had plowed a fire break; he quickly headed for it.

Now there were two brush fires on the downhill side of the forest fire, near farms and houses. This was bad. To make matters worse, wind from the approaching storm started blowing between ten to twenty miles per hour. It was whipping up all the fires. Fire companies from Lebanon and Dauphin counties were called in to help. Fire companies from Lancaster were put on standby.

The Major went to the Fire Chief and said that he could call 28th Division Headquarters and get some more man power from Harrisburg and Carlisle, if he needed. The fire chief yelled, "DO IT! We need it before this really gets out of hand!"

The news media trucks and vans were everywhere. They were clogging the roads. At times, rescue vehicles had a difficult time getting to where they were needed the most. The news station helicopters were flying over the fire getting footage of the area, sometimes flying too close to the helicopters watering down the fire. The Fire Chief turned to the Major and complained, "Don't they realize they're endangering people lives!" He picked up his radio and called for police reinforcement to set up a perimeter around the devastated area.

· · · · · · · · · · ·

Kelly walked into the room in the ICU unit in the hospital and hugged Hope. She asked, "How's Sam today, Honey?"

"No change yet, but I'm still praying, and more importantly, still believing!" answered Hope, trying to maintain a good spirit. "Sammy sent me this note this morning; I wanted you to read it. Mark and Paula went home yesterday, so I guess it's just the two of us today." She handed the note to Kelly and then straightened the blankets on Sam's bed.

As Hope picked up the note and handed it to Kelly, Mark popped his head in the door and whispered, "Surprise!" Kelly tucked the note into her pocket and joyfully went to greet her friends.

Paula and Mark hugged the girls while Paula explained, "Mark had a checkup at Lebanon VAMC, but on the way home we had to take an alternate route. Fire trucks were everywhere and smoke has closed down I-81. They said there's a huge forest fire out near Ft. Indiantown Gap, along with some smaller brush fires near some farms on the outskirts of town. This drought has made everything so dry. Anyway, since we had to reroute, we decided to surprise you."

As Paula was talking, Hope turned on the television to WGAL Lancaster channel eight to see if they would be running an update on the news.

The female reporter was giving a rundown on where the fires were, as the camera showed the flames leaping up into the sky. She explained there was a home and horse ranch that were in imminent danger from the fire. The firemen were working tirelessly to save both places. Over 2000 acres had gone up in flames so far. As she was sending the reporting back to the news anchors, she yelled, "Wait! We can see a helicopter rescue going on from where we are. Swing the camera over that way, Scott. They are lowering a basket down in that opening that was cut in the trees. We were told earlier in the day this is where the boys from Ft. Indiantown Gap were sent to fight this fire. Scott, try to zoom in to get a closer look."

"Oh, no! Sammy and Frank are out at Ft. Indiantown Gap giving a lecture today. I just know Sammy would want to be in the middle of things. I'm sure the boys are out there somewhere! I'm not sure how much more I can take!" Hope sunk into the nearest chair.

Mark patted her on the shoulder. "We don't know for sure that they're there at all. *Don't borrow trouble*, that's what my mother always told me. Having said that though, I think we should pray for everyone fighting this fire and all the people who will be affected by it."

They gathered in a small circle and held hands, as Mark poured out their concerns to the Lord. "Father, in the name of Jesus we bring our worries to You. You know the needs of every single person dealing with the fire today, whether they are rescuers, firefighters, or victims. Please give Hope peace of mind that You will take care of her sons. We leave it all in Your loving hands, Amen."

Mark picked up Hope's Bible from the table by Sam's bed and opened it to Isaiah 43:2. He told Hope that he knew of a verse that might be of help to her at this time. *"When thou passest through the waters, I will be with thee; and through the rivers, they shall not overflow thee: when thou walkest through the fire, thou shalt not be burned; neither shall the flame kindle upon thee."*

Mark continued, "I'm sure you remember the story of Shadrach, Meshach, and Abednego from the third chapter of Daniel. When they refused to bow down and worship the images of King Nebuchadnezzar, he had them thrown into a fiery furnace. But these men believed in the one true God and He protected them. When the King called them out of the fiery furnace, verse 27 tells us, *And the princes, governors, and captains, and the king's counselors, being gathered together, saw these men, upon whose bodies the fire had no power, nor was a hair of their head singed, neither were their coats changed, nor the smell of fire had passed on them.* The God who can protect these men while they were standing directly in the flames, can protect your boys, too."

Hope wiped away the tears on her face, while she said, "Mark, you've been a huge blessing to me. Thank you for everything."

"Thank you," said a weak voice in the background. Unfortunately, no one heard it because they had turned their attention back to the reporter on the television.

They saw a person in the basket being raised up into the helicopter. The reporter asked the cameraman, "What kind of uniform is that? It's not Army; it's a blue camouflage. Does anyone know which branch wears the blue camouflage?"

Hope grasped Kelly's hand tightly; she knew that was a Navy uniform. As far as she knew, Sammy and Frank were the only sailors at Ft. Indiantown Gap. Mark tried to assure her, "Don't worry, Hope. God will protect them. Have faith."

No one noticed the tears that slipped from Sam's eyes. They were still paying attention to the television, trying to see who was in the basket.

The reporter received information through her headset and said, "I've just gotten word that the blue uniform is the new Navy working uniform. Military personnel from Ft. Indiantown, New Cumberland

Depot, and Mechanicsburg Navy Depot have all been sent to battle the fires. We have been informed that the local firefighters will concentrate on structure fires while the military will direct their efforts towards the main forest fire."

"See, Hope, other sailors are there too. It might not be Sammy or Frank."

A special weather report broke in on the television: "A severe thunderstorm warning for Dauphin, Lancaster, and Lebanon counties for the next five hours. Severe lightning, high winds, and heavy downpours can be expected. If you're in the towns of Dauphin, Harrisburg, or Harrisburg, prepare yourself and get indoors. This is a huge storm which will converge with two more storms rolling in from the west. Stay tuned for more updates."

Hope cried, "What more can those men go through out there?"

"Don't worry. This will actually help them. It will help put out the fires and keep the danger down." Mark did not mention, however, that the lightning could start more fires or that the wind would play havoc with the efforts of the firefighters. He left the room to go check the emergency room, because he knew they would bring the injured firefighter to Penn State Hershey Medical Center.

In a little bit, Mark came back into the room and told Hope that it was another sailor that they had brought into the emergency room. He had twisted his ankle between rocks on the mountain.

They could hear the wind picking up outside and saw flashes of lightning. All of a sudden, the rain hit the hospital room's windows so hard, they thought it might break. As they moved away from the window, the lights flickered and went out. Seconds later, the generators kicked in and the lights came back on. One of the nurses came in to turn off the alarms, which had started beeping when the power came back on.

The nurse turned to them and asked if anyone had noticed the tears on Sam's cheeks.

"What? What are you talking about?" asked Hope as she rushed to Sam's side. She stroked his wet cheeks and looked around at their friends gathering around Sam's bed.

"I'm going to get a doctor. I'll be right back," the nurse announced as she hustled out of the room.

Sammy, Frank, and the fire were forgotten for the moment.

. . . .

Sammy was lecturing his crew as they were all raking leaves and undergrowth up on the ridge. He reminded them of the basics of firefighting, "For a fire to live, it must have three things: oxygen, heat, and fuel. This is called the fire triangle. If you take out just one of those things, the fire cannot burn. First, however, you need to know what types of fire there are. Number one is alpha fires; these are combustibles. Next, bravo fires; these are oil fires. Charlie fires are electrical fires, and delta fires are uncommon fires, such as magnesium.

"In general, alpha fires are put out in one of two ways: with water, which takes away the heat, or you can take away the fuel. The best way to fight a bravo fire is with foam, which takes away the oxygen. Charlie fires require the use of CO_2, which also takes away the oxygen—never use water on this type of fire. You can, however, take away the fuel by shutting down the electricity. For a delta fire, it's best to just let it burn out, but you can cool it down by spraying water on it."

He looked around at his men, some of whom were not familiar with fires, but who had volunteered anyway. They were working tirelessly alongside the men with years of experience. Sammy continued, "What we are going to be doing here is cutting down trees that are on fire, so the fire can't jump from tree to tree. Once the trees are down, we should be able to control the fire better. This debris that we are raking up acts as fuel for the fire, so we're taking it out of the equation. Our job, right now, is to contain this area; then the big boys can come in with bulldozers, if needed. By taking away the fuel, the fire triangle will collapse. The helicopters are dumping chemicals and water down on the fire. This will cool the fire, also taking heat away from the fire triangle."

An hour later, Sammy's crew met up with Frank's crew. They had cut down trees that were burning and built a firebreak fifteen feet wide. They were all tired, but Sammy shouted; "Now we can go and attack that fire! Move in!"

The winds from the fast approaching storm blew in and whipped up the fire. Up on the mountain, it was worse. Embers had blown about and landed on other trees, catching them on fire. The two crews were working hard putting out brush fires when the downpour came. Sammy looked up at the sky and shouted to all the men, "This storm is going to get really bad in a hurry. Head for the rocks by the power lines and we'll make a quick shelter there."

One of the men joked, "Scared of a little water, Sammy?"

As he was quickly cutting some branches for the shelter, Sammy answered, "Look up there in the sky. That's a tornado sky; I prefer to be prepared. We should be getting hail soon!"

He glanced up and shouted, "Forget making the shelter. Get over by the rocks or where ever you can to get out of the hail!" Thirty seconds later, the hail rained down.

Ten minutes later, the hail had passed them by. They looked below them and saw a path of destruction from a small tornado. Many trees came down and were on fire. 4x4 brush trucks were working their way up to combat these new blazes at the foot of the ridge.

Sammy looked towards Harrisburg and saw the fire was still heading their way. He looked behind him and saw the fire in that direction was still burning, as well. He called everyone together and announced, "We have some time before these two fires meet. We're going to be trapped between the two if we stay here. Now, we can either head down off the mountain or we could go up to the top and build a bigger firebreak, so it doesn't go down the other side. What do you all think we should do?"

They decided to go up and do the best they could. When they were finished with the firebreak, Frank tried to radio down the mountain, but the radio had been dropped and was broken.

Two hour later, the brush units were finally able to reach the area where Frank and Sammy's crews should have been. They saw where they waited out the worst of the storm, but no one was around. They radioed down the mountain to let people know they could not find them. A news reporter overheard this and ran to get her cameraman. She was going to get the exclusive on the missing navy firefighters from Ft. Indiantown Gap.

• • • • • • • • • • • •

Hope, Kelly, Mark, and Paula were watching the report from Channel 8. Hope cried, "I can't believe my boys survived a war, just to come home to this disaster!"

"Have faith. Remember the report. All it said was they weren't where they were supposed to be," said Kelly trying to calm her.

The news reporter was interviewing the fire chief, who was explaining that they were not worried at that point. He was sure that everything was fine.

With everything happening on the television, they did not notice the whispered prayer behind them.

A few minutes later, a news bulletin came on the television. The female reporter smiled into the camera, saying, "I'm standing here with Seaman Adams who was trapped up on the mountain. He's one of the missing firefighters." She turned to Frank and asked, "Can you tell me what happened up there?"

"We took cover from the storm by cutting some branches and throwing together a shelter. Afterward, we decided to make a firebreak at the top, but two fires were coming at us and it looked like we would be trapped. So we went down the other side and circled around the back of the fire to come down," answered Frank.

"Can you tell us where the rest of the guys are?"

Frank looked around as he answered, "Everyone in my crew, except for two, are here. Two of my guys were injured; one has a possible broken ankle and the other twisted his knee. My brother's crew is still on the way down. He has one man with a head injury. We made stretchers to carry the injured guys down. Our radio broke so we couldn't call anyone. I told some firemen where my brother and his guys are and they're heading up there to pick them up."

Everyone in the ICU, watching the television rejoiced, "Thank you, Lord Jesus!"

In the commotion, again no one heard the whispered, "Thank you, Lord."

As Hope turned to tell Sam everything was fine with their boys, the phone rang. It was Sammy calling. Hope began to tell him how worried she was and that she was proud of both her boys when she heard a weak voice, "Tell him I'm proud of him, too."

Hope looked at Sam, fell to her knees, and started screaming! Kelly, Paula, and Mark rushed over to Hope. The nurses heard the screaming out in the hall and came running. Sammy was still on the phone and yelled, "What's going on?"

Frank asked him what he was yelling about and Sammy looked puzzled when he answered, "Mom screamed and dropped the phone. I don't know what's going on though."

Paula picked up the phone and said, "Sammy? Are you still there? Hang on, someone wants to talk to you."

"Son, I'm proud of you. I hope you always know that." Sammy started to cry and dropped his cell phone.

Frank picked up the phone and spoke into it, "Hello, this is Frank. Can someone please tell me what is going on?"

Sam whispered, "Oh Frankie, I'm so proud of you, too."

The nurses came into the ICU room, followed by the doctors. Everyone was asked to clear out of the room. As they were leaving, there was a moan and another small voice was heard, "I love you so much, Kelly."

Kelly looked at Joey D, who was staring right at her and she fainted dead away.

Minutes later, Kelly was on her feet again and being led to a chair in the waiting room. She was having trouble believing that both Sammy and Joey D had come out of their comas at almost the same time. She fell to her knees to thank God for answering her prayers. She had almost lost faith, but through the prayers of her friends she had not.

As Kelly got up to sit in her chair, she felt something in her pocket and pulled it out. It was the note from Sammy that Hope had given her this morning. Unfolding it, she read:

Mom, I want to thank you all for attending the funeral of Private Shawn Sheldon. I know that none of us knew him, but I really believe that's one of the greatest things about military people. We're all here for each other. I realize that attending was especially hard on both you and Kelly; but because you did, the base has organized extra prayer meetings just for Dad and Joey D. There will be several hundred people praying for them. We all know the power of prayer, both in our daily lives and in times of emergency. Thank you for being the kind of parents who taught me these important lessons in life and for having friends who live the same way. Love, Sammy

Kelly refolded the note, knowing she had learned an important lesson about God's love and faithfulness. She would never doubt Him again.

CHARLIE RESPONSE
CHAPTER SIX

Kelly and Hope gathered their families together in the family room of the hospital for visits with Joey D and Sam. They were all so happy to have their loved ones alive and on the road to better health. Joey D and Todd were talking about how the farm was getting along; Sam was talking to Hope about how she had been managing while he was in the hospital.

"Oh, Kelly and I are getting along like a couple of sisters living together at the farm. I do have to admit though, since you and Joey D are on the mend, it's become more relaxed. We were even giving each other pedicures last night," giggled Hope.

Kelly hung up the phone and said that Mark and Paula were on their way and were bringing lunch for everyone with them. She commented that it was turning into a regular party, because Terry had called last night and said they would be coming today as well.

Fifteen minutes later, Mark and Paula walked in carrying several large pizza boxes and boxes of drinks. Mark yelled out, "I've got three cases of Ma's beer. Ma's beer for everyone, including all the kiddies!"

A passing nurse stopped and stuck her head in the door with a stern look on her face. Mark laughed and asked, "Would you like a Ma's beer, too? I mean a Ma's root beer."

The kids laughed and the nurse chuckled as she walked away. Mark looked around and announced, "We have all different kinds of pizzas—cheese, pepperoni, ham and pineapple, and of course, supreme. We also have chicken wings, both honey barbeque and regular. I hope it's enough for this crowd. But first, how about we say grace?" They all bowed their heads as Mark prayed.

They all turned towards the door, as another voice was heard saying, "Amen." Jeb, Sarah, Rebecca, and Jacob, along with Belleville's Fire Chief were all standing in the doorway.

There were hugs all around, as Kelly introduced Jacob to Joey D and Sam. They had heard all about Jacob and his family before. Jacob shook Joey D's hand and said, "Hello."

Everyone was shocked. Jacob said the Fire Chief had brought them to town, so he could have the wires removed from his jaw. He was so glad he would be able to eat solid food now. Sammy spoke up and invited them all to join them for pizza. As they were lining up at the pizza boxes to get their food, Joey D said, "Chief, I just want to thank you for helping to save our lives. I know there were others beside yourself, but since you're here, I really want to show my appreciation."

The Fire Chief looked very pleased and said with a smile, "You're welcome. It's just what we do."

While everyone was eating and talking together, the Fire Chief asked if this had been the first time they had gotten together as a group for a ride. Hope answered, "The boys have been riding together since their Navy days. They rode while stationed at different places all over the world, but since leaving the Navy, we all get together at least once a year for a vacation. Sometimes, we go on cruises; sometimes, we go on rides through different areas of the country."

"Since Joey D and I live so close to Mark and Paula, we get together at least once a month to go for a ride. Terry and Heidi live near D.C., so they try to come as often as they can, as well. Sam and Hope live in Mississippi though, so it's too far for them to come more than once or twice a year," added Kelly.

"So, where did you all go the first time you went on a trip?" asked the chief.

Terry explained, "That would have been our trip through Mobile, Pensacola, and all through the state of Florida." The others nodded their heads, obviously reliving the trip in their minds.

"Oh, yeah! What a ride that was! We went to Daytona Bike Week, too," added Sam.

"Mark and I loaded our bikes into a U-Haul, picked up Terry's bike, and headed down to New Orleans. It took us two days to get there. Terry, Heidi, Paula, and Kelly all flew down. Sam and Hope rode their bikes from Mississippi. We spent two days sightseeing, then packed up our bikes and headed down to Daytona Bike Week.

"We wanted to stop in Mobile on the way to see the Battleship Alabama, so we took the southern route around Lake Pontchartrain. It was so cold that morning, remember? It was 35 degrees at 6:30 in the morning. We definitely wore our leathers," continued Joey D.

Hope cut in, "How could we forget? At least we women rode behind and you guys blocked the wind for us."

"We didn't have the fancy rides like we have today. We were riding Softail Heritages then. We had to stop a lot more frequently too, because the seats were so small and definitely not as comfortable as we have now," added Sam.

Terry boasted, "Yeah, but we were bikers back then and we knew our machines. We thought those EVO engines were great. They were way better than the Panheads and Shovelheads of the past."

Mark agreed, "Isn't that the truth? You couldn't ride 200 miles without needing to fix something, but those EVOs were getting old at that time, too."

"After spending a couple of hours reliving our Navy days seeing the battleship, we were back on our iron horses and onto the super slab we went," said Sam.

"What's a super slab?" queried Jacob.

Sam answered, "I'm sorry. A super slab is what we call the interstate. We hate riding it and avoid it whenever possible. But on this ride, we were on Interstate 10 going from Mobile to Pensacola. By the way, it did warm up to around 60 degrees that day. It seemed like the further east we rode, the warmer it got. I remember riding into Gulf Breeze and then into Pensacola Beach. I've heard claims that Pensacola Beach has the world's whitest sand. The Hispanics in the area call it Playa Blanca, which means white beach. In the summer heat, the sugar white sand is cool on your feet and because it's really fine, it feels so soft to walk on."

Everyone was listening intently to the story as Sam continued, "It was in Pensacola that we all met for the first time. We were all at Corry Station for Naval Communications Technician School. Man, did everything look different! What had been a little town had grown into a big city. Like everything else in life, everything must change."

Heidi took over, "Because we were staying there for a couple days, we found a hotel and unpacked. We walked down the beach and found a decent place to eat. Mmmmmm, we had all-you-can-eat shrimp. Yum! I remember that because I kept thinking people would think we were pigs because of how much we were eating!"

Chuckles were heard from various directions in the small circle of people. The Fire Chief agreed, "I like to eat at all-you-can-eat places, too. Whenever I go to a fancy restaurant, I never get enough food and I always get overcharged. We country folk know where to eat. We go to restaurants that give men's sized portions or we go to buffets."

"Isn't that the truth?"

Heidi continued, "After dinner, we walked back and sat on our balconies to watch the waves roll in. The next day was a day of sightseeing for us."

Paula said, "Would you believe the first place we rode to was the Naval Aviation Museum?"

"But dear, it had changed since we were there last. This time they had F-14s," joked Mark.

"Like you didn't see enough of them on the aircraft carrier," laughed Paula. "After the museum, we rode to Corry Station to see if it had changed, too. Basically, it didn't. We even went to the Enlisted Club and the Petty Officer's Club to check it out."

"That's where I noticed big changes. I couldn't get over how young the kids were that were allowed in the EM Club. I even asked where their parents were," said Joey D.

Kelly responded, "Dear, I told you then and I'll tell you again— those weren't kids. They're young sailors, like we were a long, long time ago."

"And like I told you then— they might have uniforms on and might be marching down the street, but they must have been some Junior ROTC cadets from some high school. The nerve of some of those sailors, they called me SIR!" said Joey D.

"Well, what about me?" exclaimed Heidi. "They called me Ma'am!" Everyone chuckled at Heidi's obvious insult.

"The next day, we were speeding along on Route 98, which we nicknamed the beach road. It goes all around the beaches of the Florida panhandle and down the west coast. It had been a dream of ours to take this ride. We had our Harleys for quite a few years by that point and it was our first extended trip together. As we rode, we saw beautiful sunsets and sunrises, smelled the fresh ocean air, and heard the waves breaking all around us. We took rest stops in Apalachicola and Manatee State Parks. It was amazing!" remembered Sam. He looked around at his friends and silently thanked God for every one of them.

Continuing on Sam said, "We stopped to visit Hope's grandmother and she turned us on to Route 41, the Tamiami Trail. It travels from Tampa to Miami, which I thought was another great ride."

"Speak for yourself!" Heidi interjected, "There was a bridge—so, so high—going from St. Petersburg to Clearwater. Scared me to death! Do you guys remember that? It was so windy; it was blowing our bikes around. I was terrified and I'll never forget it. Another thing I'll never forget is seeing the statue called the Kiss in Sarasota. It was one of my highlights on that trip."

Bobbie Jo, Kelly's daughter-in-law, asked, "Kiss? I've never heard of that one. What was it a statue of?"

"You know the photo taken right after World War II ended, when the sailor grabbed a pretty girl and bent her over backwards for a kiss? Well, they have a statue just like that. We stopped and took pictures in front of it. I really wish that I had known about it when I was in the Navy. I would have liked to have mine and Terry's picture in front of it in the same pose in our dress uniforms. Now I just have to be happy with the picture of us in our biker clothes," said Heidi wistfully.

Hope picked up the trip down memory lane, "Remember that nice hotel on Ft. Myers Beach that we stayed at? Some local people told us to get up really early and go to Sanibel to collect shells."

"We collected so many that we had to get a box to ship them home," laughed Kelly.

Terry added, "While the girls were out doing their thing for the day, we men hired a guide and went fishing for grouper, snapper, and redfish. The hotel's chef cooked up what we caught and we had a fantastic dinner that night. We spent about three days there. It was great! Everything about that trip was great. I still wear all the Harley-Davidson t-shirts we picked up along the way."

Sam continued the reminiscing, "I liked going to see the Thomas Edison and Henry Ford Winter Estates. I think we all enjoyed seeing their houses and that huge banyan tree. The road leading up to the estates are lined on both sides with royal palms on both sides for about six to eight miles. It really is beautiful!"

"Sounds like you all enjoy traveling a lot." Jacob looked down at his hands and asked, "I don't want to sound out of place, but do you take the time to thank God for the good times you've had? Do you think to praise Him for the wondrous things you see?"

"Jacob!" exclaimed Rebecca.

"No, it's okay. It's a good question. We do. Every morning, we have Scripture study and prayer. We give thanks before every meal we eat and before every ride we pray for our safety. At the end of every day we thank Him for the day's blessing and most of all, for keeping us safe. On Sundays, we ask around for a good church to attend. We try to share the love of Jesus Christ where ever we go. I want to thank you though, for being concerned about our eternal salvation. Keep up the good work," said Joey D as he patted Jacob on the back.

Jacob looked at Rebecca and smiled.

"Pappy, these places sound fun. You took me to the ocean a few times, but we never collected sea shells before. Can you take me there someday?"

Joey D pulled Peggy Sue onto his lap and snuggled her as he answered, "I promise, I really will do most anything you ask me to. As soon as we all feel much better, we'll rent a place for a week or two down there and see how much things have changed. We'll have tons of fun!"

"Anyway, when we left Miami Beach we rode up to Daytona Beach. We found our place that we were staying and took it easy for a while."

Terry said, "There was a big sign across the road that read, *Welcome to Daytona Beach*. You should have seen all the bikes lined up on both sides of the street; they were even parked in a row down the middle of the street. Tens of thousands of motorcycles were everywhere; it was crazy! When anyone would ride by on a Japanese motorcycle, some of the Harley riders would throw rice at them, yelling 'Rice burners!'"

"Why would anyone do such a thing?" asked Rebecca.

Terry answered, "Because Harley-Davidsons are made in America and most riders back then were into riding American made products. I agree with your line of thinking though, it's not a nice thing to do. However, having said that, I do think it's wise to always buy American, whenever possible. At that point in time though, Japanese motorcycles were more reliable, cheaper, and had a better ride than American bikes. Eventually, Harley-Davidson designed a better bike and ever since then they have kept up with the market of Japanese products."

Heidi added, "Of course, we didn't throw any rice. We actually started out riding on small Japanese motorcycles. I've always believed that it doesn't really matter what you ride; what matters is that you ride."

"Why does it matter where you buy your goods from?" asked Rebecca.

"I know your family eats the food you grow and you buy from your Amish community as much as you can, because that supports your way of life. The reason I believe we should buy American is simple; it supports our way of life. It's that easy. When we buy from other countries, we're taking jobs away from Americans. If the jobs go away, it obviously makes us a poorer nation in more ways than one. Our citizens won't be earning money. We won't have the ability to make our own goods eventually, which in the case of another world war would be disastrous for our country. The more we give away, the more we become a weaker nation. Our food is grown somewhere else; our goods are produced somewhere else; our fuels are bought from somewhere else. We're slowly becoming dependent on other countries. When a country isn't self-sufficient, it opens the door for other governments to walk on in. At that point, we start losing our rights and history dictates that the first right to go is usually the freedom of religion. I don't want that to happen, but it seems that most people just don't care anymore," answered Heidi.

Terry interrupted, "Maybe this isn't the right time or place for a lecture, Honey." He took Heidi's hand and squeezed it lovingly. "My wife is passionate about certain subjects and that happens to be one of them."

"Here's one thing it's always the right time for—witnessing. We witnessed to many bikers that week during Bike Week. So many didn't know that the only things you had to do to be a Christian is to believe that Christ is the risen Savior, ask Jesus to forgive you of your sins, and try to sin no more. I remember one man asking me how much it was going to cost him. I told him that it would cost him his eternal life, if he didn't. We prayed together and he accepted Christ that same day," said Sam.

Joey D started talking about one of his favorite things they did on the trip, "We saw on the news there was a snow storm brewing on up the east coast, which was going to bring a lot of rain down to Florida, so we decided to stay for a while longer than we had planned. We all agreed that it might be fun to test drive some new Harleys. So we went and did that. They were so great, so much improved that we all decided to buy touring bikes. I bought a sweet Twin Cam 88 Electra Glide. We had to order them and have them shipped to our homes, though. We all traded in our bikes to buy the new ones, so after that we were pedestrians for the rest of the trip."

Rich, who had been as quiet as a mouse, asked, "What did you guys do? Did you go home right away?"

Sam answered, "We left two days after we sold the bikes. We walked everywhere; we hung out on the beach and saw different motorcycle events going on. Back then, it was a lot rougher than it is now. There were drunks everywhere, but there were places that the average person could go. It was there that we first got involved with the CMA."

"What's the CMA?" asked Jacob.

"The CMA is the Christian Motorcycle Association. It's a group of motorcyclists who go to various functions and witness for Christ. They hand out Bibles at all the gatherings. Even though they're a solid group of believers and some people think that Christians are no fun at all, they do have a good time at these functions. It's not all work and no play for them. I think it shows non-believers that you can be a Christian and still party and play. We are members of both Harley Owners Group and the CMA. Along with large biker functions like Daytona Bike Week, they also have monthly meetings; they raise money to reduce the cost of the Bibles they hand out; and they also do charity work in their local areas. Their local events are family friendly. You can take your children to them without fear of inappropriate conduct. It's a great organization!" explained Sam.

At that point, a nurse walked in to say that she needed to take Sam and Joey D back to their room to be seen by the doctor. Everyone else could wait here, if they wanted to, the doctor would come in to talk to them shortly.

They continued talking among themselves while they waited. Heidi started to clean up the pizza boxes and empty cups from the room. Soon enough, the doctor walked in to talk to them.

"I got a call from the Navy and they wanted an update on Sam. I told them what I could. I need to do a thorough check up on both Sam and Joey D tomorrow. Right now, everything seems to be looking pretty good. Joey D and Sam are pretty tired after the long visit you've just had though. I'm going to let you all go in to say good bye, then I want them to rest for the remainder of the day." After making this announcement, the doctor looked at Sammy and told him that his CO wanted him to call ASAP.

Everyone left the family room to say their good-byes, while Sammy was left in silence to make his call. "Eagle One, this is Blue Tango One reporting as ordered."

"Blue Tango One, this is Eagle One. I received the update on your father. It certainly is great news for your family. Bravo Zulu for your outstanding work on both the forest fire and the class you're teaching. I've heard that your brother and you are doing a great job on the lectures. People are learning a lot from the two of you. I know you need to finish up the last part of your lecture, which you'll do tomorrow. After that, there's a situation that needs to be addressed. A Blackhawk will bring your gear and special equipment for you. We'll talk more tomorrow at 1600. Eagle One out."

As Sammy walked to his father's room to say good-bye, he saw the television in the waiting room was on Fox News and something caught his eye. He walked over to take a closer look. He shook his head as he noticed the USS Ronald Reagan pulling out of port. Frank was assigned to the USS Ronald Reagan and now it was leaving without him. Sammy wondered if its leaving had anything to do with his new assignment. He sighed as he walked out of the room, knowing he would have to wait until 1600 tomorrow to find out. Sammy walked into his dad's room and told him so long for now.

As everyone was gathering their things to leave, Kelly said, "Let's all meet somewhere for supper and then everyone come to my farm for the evening. We can watch a movie or play some games. I'll make some snacks. We'll have a good time."

Everyone agreed that it sounded like fun and off they went.

· · · · · · · · · · ·

Sammy and Frank stood in front of the class and called it to order. Frank started the video recorder and turned on the Smart Board, while Sammy addressed the class, "Thank you all for coming out on a Sunday morning. Since most of you are here for weekend drills, it probably wasn't a real problem for anyone. Our class was cut short last time because of the forest fire, but that is, after all, why we're here—to protect and serve, not just overseas, but here as well. Let's review what we covered last time."

When Sammy had given the review and was sure that everyone had a good understanding of the material, he said, "Now I will address the meat of this course. This is very important information in combatting radical Islam.

"In the Quran, a society is based on the unity and equality of believers. It is a society in which moral and social justice will counterbalance oppression of the weak and also economic exploitation. Muhammad brought a revelation that challenged the established order of things. The Quran includes rules that concern a person's modesty, marriage, divorce, feuding, intoxication, gambling, diet, stealing, murder, fornication, and adultery. It also talks about false contracts, bribery, and the abuse of women.

"When Muslims came into a town or city the people are given three choices: 1. Convert to Islam. 2. Accept Muslim rule and pay a poll tax as protected people. 3. Battle by the sword.

"Abu Afak was 100 years old when he converted from Islam to Judaism and wrote something about Muhammad's teaching of all creation and what is forbidden or permitted. So Muhammad sent a servant to silence Abu Afak. Then a poet wrote something against Muhammad and he had him killed, as well. He told his followers to 'kill any Jew that falls into your power.'

"A small tribe of Jews remained in Medina. They surrendered, but Muhammad had them all beheaded, with the exception of one woman with whom he had relations; but when he was done with her, he also had her beheaded. It is written in Quran 5:51, *Take not Jews or Christians as friends.* I find this disturbing, because our own government always wants to make friends with Islamic Nations."

Sammy and Frank spent the entire morning lecturing the class about Islam. They believed that to defeat your enemy, you must thoroughly know your enemy—and Sammy had extensively studied this subject matter.

"I think it's probably time for a bit of a break. When we return, it will be a couple more hours before we wrap it all up," Frank announced to the class.

Sammy stepped outside and called his CO again. Eagle One informed him that his brother, Frank, would be going with him for the beginning of this assignment. After that, Frank would rejoin his crew onboard the USS Ronald Reagan. When they reported to base, they would be supplied with desert battle dress uniforms and other necessary clothing. Sammy was told that they would have time to go back to say good-bye to everyone after the lecture, but to be back at the Gap by 1800 hours. Sammy asked what to do about the rental car and was told to leave it; the Commanding Officer of Ft. Indiantown Gap would take care of it.

"Hey, Frank, come over here." Sammy gave the information to his brother.

"What's going on? I thought we would be with Dad for a while," responded Frank.

Sammy answered, "I don't really know. Obviously, it's classified. We'll find out once we get in the air on the plane, after the Blackhawk drops us off."

They went inside to get ready for the remainder of the day. Sammy printed up some hand-outs for the class, while everyone was making their way back to their seats. When he was finished, he stood at the podium and called for everyone's attention.

"This afternoon, we'll be covering some high profile Islamic leaders—both past and present. We need to understand how these militants think, really get into their brains. Let's start with Ibn Taymiyyah…"

Sammy taught the class about important Islamic leaders and how they relate to today's situation in the world. He explained that the Islamic militant founders were consumed with hate for the western world, focusing on the United States. Sammy showed how inconsistent and hypocritical some of these beliefs are. He then tied them together with today's current events to show how dangerous the Islamic militants can be.

Frank put an outline on the white board of different ways to undermine Al-Qaeda and other militant Islamic organizations. Sammy went over these points one by one with the group. Then he talked about how they are now using money as a new terrorist weapon, "I want you to remember this—Sharia Finance is the new weapon. The financing and investments of United Arab Emirates is in America and funding the central banks of Iran and Syria. Sharia Finance could be a new major threat! Could Muslims get into American political power and use Sharia Finance against us? I believe so—by giving financial aid to Islamic countries, devaluing our dollar, over-taxing our businesses and people, thus making us a poorer nation. Maybe some are already in our government, slowly chipping away at us. We must be vigilant on both sides of this coin. The terrorists of today are much more sophisticated than ever."

Sammy shuffled his papers into an orderly pile, while he made his closing remarks. "Seaman Adams and I would like to thank you all for your attention throughout the lecture. I know it's a lot of information to absorb, but it's important information nowadays. Remain safe, people, whether you go abroad or remain stateside. My prayers go out for your families, as well."

On the way out of the building, Frank called Kelly's home and asked if someone could bring his sea bag to the hospital. Sammy said it would be nice to pick up some Chinese food to take with them to the hospital and Frank agreed.

When Sammy and Frank arrived in their father's room, they explained to Hope they only had time to eat supper and then had to leave quickly. Everyone in that room understood leaving in a flash is something that just happens in the military. Sam and Hope kissed their sons good-bye. Sam held them each just a little longer than normal in big bear hugs. They understood it was hard for him to let them go this time.

Everyone bowed their heads as Joey D prayed for a safe journey and a speedy return for the boys. He asked God to be with Hope and Sam, as they would be worrying about their sons. He also thanked and praised God for the continued recovery of Sam and himself.

Once more, hugs were given all around; even some of the nurses came in to say good-bye and give a hug. On the way out the door, each boy turned, saluted his father, and then they were gone.

CHARLET RESPONSE
CHAPTER SEVEN

"Have either of you considered what you'll do when you're released tomorrow?" asked the doctor of Sam and Joey D.

Joey D answered, "I'm going to Westminster Woods Nursing Home in Huntingdon for my recovery and therapy."

Sam looked at Hope and responded, "Hope and I talked about it a long time and I've decided that I'll go to Westminster Woods as well. I think Joey and I would push each other in therapy and that might help us progress faster. I don't want Hope to be living on her own down in Mississippi. This way, she and Kelly would be there for each other, the same way Joey D and I will be here helping each other."

The next morning when the medical transport arrived, the orderlies wheeled Sam and Joey D out in wheelchairs. Kelly and Hope loaded the rocking chairs, flowers, and all their other things into the back of Kelly's pick-up.

It was a nice trip for the girls down Route 322, then over on Route 22 West. Some motorcyclists passed Kelly's truck and Hope commented, "I wonder what the guys are doing?"

"If I know them at all, they're wishing they were the ones riding those motorcycles right now," chuckled Kelly.

Kelly went on to talk about the new bypass around Lewistown, saying, "There used to be a lot of bad accidents here, but this new bypass made things much safer. It was so bad here that there used to be more than fifty crosses along the side of the road, one for each person that died there. It earned the nickname Death Valley. The locals used to have a saying, 'In order to get to Happy Valley, you have to go through Death Valley.'"

"Oh, my goodness! That's terrible!" gasped Hope.

As they drove through Huntingdon, Kelly pointed out Juniata College and told her, "This is a small private college—super expensive.

Most of the locals can't afford to go here even with the Huntingdon County discount."

They drove into Westminster Woods, past some upscale houses, "Wow! Are these the houses the boys will be staying in?"

"Unfortunately, no, Hope. These are retirement homes. If you live in these and need medical attention, you would just go to the nursing care facility, where the boys are going. You only get a single room there, but it's pretty nice. It's nicer that some of the hotels we've stayed in."

After going through the registration process, Sammy and Joey D checked out their rooms, which were, indeed, pretty nice. In the lounge outside their rooms, the television was tuned into the lunch time news. A Special Report came on about a military helicopter in Afghanistan going down with both Navy Seals and Army Rangers on it. The reporter said that there had been a number of deaths, but that it was unconfirmed at that time. Everyone held their breath and looked at Hope, not knowing how much more she could handle. "I have to know if they're alright," she said, as she lowered herself into a nearby chair.

Kelly hugged her tightly as she comforted her, "Just breathe. The only thing you know is they're on a special mission. You don't even know where they are; they could be anywhere in the world. Now pray, Hope."

Nodding her head, Hope immediately sank to her knees and pleaded before the Lord to protect her sons. She prayed for all the men that were in the helicopter and their loved ones. She finished her prayer with the request for strength no matter what the circumstances ended up being.

The other people in the lounge watched Hope, whispering among themselves. An older couple asked Sam if Hope was alright.

A nurse came over to tell them it was meal time and asked if they wanted to eat in the dining room or in their private rooms. She added that Kelly and Hope could join them for a fee, if they chose to. They decided to join the other people in the dining room.

The dining room was a pleasant place with plenty of sunshine streaming in the windows. A volunteer was playing soft tunes on the piano in the corner. A local minister blessed the food before they ate and then he said a few words about God when they were finished.

Sam's room was just two doors down the hall from Joey D's. There was a little place for families to sit and talk or watch TV, if they did not want to be in the big lounge. A while after they returned to their rooms, a nurse came to tell them it was time to start their physical therapy. She added that if they wanted to get out of there quickly, they would need to push themselves. Kelly laughed as she said, "That won't motivate them too much. You should say if you ever want to ride your Harley again, you have to push yourself."

Nurse Debbie commented, "Oh, you ride motorcycles?"

"No, we ride Harleys! There's a difference!" joked Joey D.

"I ride a Honda 750 Aero and love it," added Nurse Debbie.

When Sam asked why she bought an Aero, she answered, "Because it was small and I wanted something to learn to ride on. I didn't want to spend a fortune on a Harley, so I bought the Aero used."

"Did you know that for just about a thousand dollars more, you could have bought a brand new 883 Sportster—more power, better fuel economy, and a higher resale value," lectured Joey D.

Sam added, "Another advantage to owning a Harley-Davidson would be the Harley Owners Group. It's a great group to belong to. We go on group rides with our local chapter all the time. We also raise money for various charities. There are different incentives for riding, such as: mileage pins, points for riding to different states and countries. With these points added up at the end of the year, you qualify for free gifts.

"Most states have a H.O.G. Rally each year. Plus, they have a program with your membership that if your bike breaks down, they will pay to have it towed to the nearest Harley Dealership. There is also a plan that will cover your tow vehicle too. Another benefit about being a H.O.G. member is that you get H.O.G. discounts at Best Western Hotels. I know Honda and other manufacturers don't offer what Harley-Davidson does. In your case, I would recommend a 1200 Sportster or if you plan to travel a bit, maybe a Softail Classic. We know a girl that rides a 2003 883 Sportster that has over 180,000 miles on it. She bungees a duffle bag on the back and goes on extended trips with her husband, who rides a Softail Heritage. You'll find that Harley's prices are competitive to metric motorcycles."

Sam looked sheepish as he apologized, "I'm sorry. Once we start talking about motorcycles, it's hard for us to stop. Please don't feel like we're lecturing you. As long as you have your knees in the breeze, it truly doesn't matter what you ride."

· · · · · · · · · · ·

Hugh sat in the office with his attorney, waiting for the video conference call to be set up. This was to be a meeting between his side and the attorneys from the Commonwealth of Pennsylvania. He made a comment about the wonders of modern technology to his lawyer, Mr. O'Malley.

On the video screen the attorney representing Pennsylvania, Mr. Dewy, opened the call explaining, "We have an attorney, Mrs. Lewis, here as a mediator. Her job is to get us to come together on this law suit so we don't have to go to court, thus saving everyone both time and money."

Mr. O'Malley told everyone the facts of the accident and the treatment his client had received from the Pennsylvania State Police. He then presented their side of the case, "The treatment my client endured was most unsatisfactory. He was accused of causing not only this accident, but three others as well. My client gave the police the information that he was in southwest Florida at the alleged times of the other accidents. After that, he was denied basic essentials, such as food and water. This caused Mr. Lamadeleine to go into a hypoglycemic attack and as a result of that, lose his job. Even though he has been diabetic for some time, he always controlled it by eating properly at regular intervals. We are seeking $1,000,000 in damages, plus coverage of legal fees."

Mr. Dewy commented, "That's ridiculous! Mr. Lamadeleine would never have made that amount of money. Give us proof of pain and suffering amounting to that much."

The attorneys began to argue among themselves and Mrs. Lewis sarcastically commented that she was so glad she had gotten this assignment. She settled the lawyers down and they all got down to business.

After four hours of video conferencing, a deal was finally reached. The Commonwealth of Pennsylvania would pay off the loan on Hugh's truck, pay Hugh $250,000, and pay for his legal fees. Both parties were satisfied with this deal. Mr. Dewy told Hugh that he would receive a check within the next two weeks.

Once Hugh was home and told Martha all that had happened in the case, he called his realtor to put the house up for sale.

"Martha, Honey, we can finally enjoy life. I'll be able to take you to all the places I've seen driving around the country in my truck. We can finally retire to Florida and only come back up north in the summertime to see our friends. All I have to do is call Carlos to drive the truck and let the terrorist task force take care of things. Once things settle down from that, I'll either sell the truck or hire a driver for it."

Being a Christian, Martha had never liked the idea of a lawsuit, but she was happy that Hugh was finally able to retire—being an over the road truck driver's wife had been very lonely.

· · · · · · · · · · ·

TJ pulled his Heritage Softail up to the front of the barracks where Ensign Sally Morgan lived on Norfolk Naval Base. They were headed to Bayside Harley-Davidson in Portsmouth, because Sally was thinking about buying her own bike. When they walked into the dealership, a salesgirl recognized Sally from her previous visits and called out, "Sally, welcome back. How can I help you today?"

"Hi there, Maryann, it's nice to see you again. Well, I just recently finished the Harley Riders Edge class for beginners and I wanted to test drive a Sportster 883 Low," answered Sally.

They chatted as they walked over to a shiny two tone colored motorcycle. Maryann showed Sally different features of the bike as Sally sat on the seat, testing the feel of the motorcycle. Maryann commented,

"I think this is the perfect bike for you. I can have one of the service guys come get the bike and get it ready for a demo ride if you'd like. Of course, we require the proper safety gear to be worn. Will that be a problem?"

"Not a problem at all. We rode here on TJ's bike, so I have all my gear here," answered Sally.

A little while later, when she returned from her demo ride, Sally was all smiles. TJ asked what she thought of the bike. Sally flashed her mega-watt smile at him and excitedly replied, "It's just so awesome! It's the most perfect bike! I love the Birch White and Sunburst Red two-tone paint; it's my favorite. I don't think I could ask for a better bike right now. What do you think?"

"Well, I'm the one who told you to look at the Low, so obviously I think it's a pretty good fit for you," bragged TJ.

Sally asked Maryann to work up some numbers for her while she picked up some things in the store's clothing department. She added that she would need a luggage rack and back rest installed on the motorcycle. Sally chose a couple of jackets and some chaps, as well as a rain suit.

When Maryann came to give her the figures, she was considering buying a helmet that matched the paint color of the motorcycle. Sally asked Maryann to run a loan application through Harley-Davidson for her and told her the amount she would put down on the bike. After a short amount of time, Sally was told that her financing was all arranged and was asked to go into the finance office to sign her paperwork.

After the paperwork was taken care of, Sally and TJ had to wait a couple hours for the service department to get the bike ready to go, with the new back rest and luggage rack. Sally asked TJ if he thought she should also purchase some saddle bags.

"I think you should," he said. Then he added, "But they're on me. Consider them a gift."

Sally gave TJ a quick hug of gratitude. "Oh TJ, you're just too good to me."

TJ took Sally's hand as they went in search of Maryann to get Sally signed up for both Ladies of H.O.G. and her membership in H.O.G.

Sally was telling everyone that she came across that she just bought her first motorcycle and was so excited. Maryann took Sally's picture to put on the wall of new Harley owners. When they finally brought Sally the keys to her new bike, they had several salesmen revving up the motors of bikes in the showroom to celebrate the new Harley owner. Sally was beaming as the attention was centered on her.

Before they left, Sally made an appointment for her 500 mile warranty check the following week. It was finally time to take her bike home. TJ told her she should take the lead on the way home, so they would be traveling at a speed she was comfortable with. As always, before climbing on his bike TJ asked the Lord to give them safety on the road.

Sally smiled on the entire ride back to the base. They stopped at the front gate to get her base stickers for the motorcycle. When they got back to her barracks, TJ told Sally they would get together the following day for another ride.

TJ checked his cell phone and saw that his mother had called. She hadn't left a voice-mail, so TJ called her number right away in case something was wrong. She answered and told him his father had some good news to tell him.

"Son, I had a doctor's appointment today and got nothing but great news. I've been doing physical therapy at the Lebanon Valley VA Medical Center and they told me my shoulder is outstanding. I have almost full range of motion. My ribs are doing much better, even though they are still sore. My neck is okay. I can turn it now, though there is slight stiffness."

"Dad, that's great news!"

They talked for a while and TJ told them Sally had just bought a motorcycle. Terry said to tell her congratulations.

For the next couple of days, TJ and Sally rode around the Tidewater area. Sally liked riding to Virginia Beach, but not during rush hour. It was just too much traffic for her at this stage of her riding experience. TJ let her take the lead most of the time, so that she gained some confidence in her riding skills. They had fun together and grew closer over time.

• • • • • • • • • • •

At an undisclosed forward operating base (FOB) in Afghanistan, the message came that Seaman Adams was to be promoted to Petty Officer. The CO was to have the short ceremony in the field. All the Petty Officers stood in line for the initiation into the brotherhood of Petty Officers. The emblem of the Petty Officer is the head of an eagle, but sailors have always called it the Petty Officer's CROW. Before the promotion ceremony, the soon-to-be new Petty Officer must have his new patch sewn onto the left arm of his uniform. Immediately after the ceremony comes the initiation.

Every Petty Officer will *tack on* the crow so it does not fall off. This is done by punching the new Petty Officer in the arm where the crow is. Most of the guys do not hit very hard, but there are some that will hit with all their might. Most of the time this results in a black and blue arm; sometimes, the men cannot move their arm for a few days. It is a rite of passage and no one complains about it.

Sammy walked up to his brother to tack on his crow and acted like he was going to decimate him, but instead he stopped about an inch from his bicep. He announced so everyone could hear, "When you fully tack on a crow, you have to follow through with your punch. You hit with your fist and follow through hitting with your elbow. Since this is my little brother, I'm just sighting my punch. You all can hit him first and I'll get my time with him later."

Frank smiled at his brother, as he pretended to be frightened. Sammy continued, "Now, little brother, you have to hold your sleeve real tight when you get hit to take the wrinkles out of your sleeve. Otherwise, the wrinkles can cut your arm and out here in the boonies that could mean an infection."

Frank started to get worried since he was he was with a bunch of Navy Seals. He knew he was going to get hit hard and it was going to hurt; but he wanted to be part of the brotherhood, so he welcomed the initiation.

By the time the thirtieth sailor tacked on Frank's crow, his arm was really starting to hurt and he had a hard time moving it. Sammy was called away for a few minutes. When he returned he said, "Little brother, come here."

By this time, everyone on the team was calling Frank *little brother*.

Frank walked over to where his brother was standing and Sammy continued, "I have to leave, so it's time for me to tack on your crow. Now brace yourself! Remember, I hit really hard, so pull your sleeve tight and get ready."

Frank gritted his teeth to prepare for the hit. Sammy pulled back his arm and then just lightly tapped Frank with his fist and then his elbow. Everyone laughed at Frank, even though they all had thought that Sammy would hit really hard, too. Sammy pulled Frank into a brotherly embrace and slapped him on his back as he said, "Congratulations, little brother. I'm so proud of you."

The two brothers said their farewells and Sammy went to pack his gear for the mission. He and his fellow Seals, along with the Army Task Force 160, otherwise known as Night Stalkers, were heading out to rescue some Army personnel from an intensely dangerous situation.

Sammy was in charge of this mission and laid out his plans to the men on the helicopter ride to the drop-off point. The helicopters would be utilized later upon the evacuation of the injured Army men. Because of the thorough planning by Sammy and his superiors and the unfailing cooperation of the men in his charge, the rescue mission went off without a hitch. Even though many of the enemy lost their lives that day, there were no Navy or Army losses.

As the wounded Army soldiers were being loaded into the helicopters, Sammy and his shipmates were unloading the dirt bikes that they would use to get out of the hot zone, while drawing the enemy away from the other soldiers.

The evacuation was going well when they received a radio transmission that two divisions of the enemy were advancing on them. They had to get out of the area quickly because they were such a small force, so Sammy called in for an air strike to help cover their retreat.

The small band of sailors took off down the mountain on their dirt bikes, taking care at each hairpin turn to stop and lay in explosives. Each explosion resulted in rocks and trees raining down, covering the pass. They did this the entire way down the mountain. Finally, they reached the flat land and thought they were home free.

You know the old saying, *when you drop your guard is when you are headed for disaster?* Truer words were never spoken.

Newly promoted Petty Officer Frank Adams was busy setting up computer networks between different Forward Operating Bases when he received word that his brother Sammy had been injured.

"Is he all right?"

"He'll be fine soon enough. They were down off the mountain and thought they were in the clear, when a roadside IED went off, throwing Sammy from his dirt bike. He injured his knee and ankle. They treated it the best they could in the situation they were in, but he's going to be out of action for at least two weeks," answered the radio operator.

"Was anyone else hurt in the blast?"

"No, everyone else was alright. Sammy was just in the wrong place at the wrong time, I guess. Bad luck for him. His bike was damaged and unfixable, so they destroyed it. He had to ride in on the back of another guy's bike. I just thought you'd want to know about Sammy and I was thinking you should tell your folks he's okay. There was a different helicopter that went down today and they might be freaking out. I know my mother would be," said the radio operator.

Frank thought about that and decided it was pretty good advice, so he asked the CO to place the call to his parents. He received orders that he would be heading back to his ship, the USS Ronald Reagan. His orders included special instructions not to change his appearance by cutting his hair or shaving, as he would be needed for special assignments.

• • • • • • • • • • •

Kelly asked, "Do the boys know that Sam was transferred here?"

"I haven't talked to them for about four days now, so no, they don't," answered Hope.

Kelly assured her that if they called the hospital looking for their dad, the hospital would let them know where they were.

At that moment, Hope's cell phone rang. When she answered it, the voice on the other end said it was Captain Robert Casey, Sammy's

Commanding Officer. Hope started to cry, anticipating bad news. She handed the phone to Sam. "It's Captain Casey, Sammy's CO."

Sam took the phone, "Good afternoon, Sir. This is retired CT Chief Sam Adams. My wife can't talk right now. What can we do for you?"

"Sammy sent me a message to please contact you and ease your mind about some things. Neither Frank nor Sammy were on the helicopter that recently went down."

Sam grabbed Hope's hand and told her, "Our boys are alive. They weren't on that helicopter!"

The Captain continued, "Petty Officer Sammy Adams was on a different mission. While coming back on a Special Ops dirt bike, he crashed when an IED went off ahead of him. He twisted his knee, but other than that is fine. Petty Officer Frank Adams is on a classified mission, but will be returning to his ship, the USS Ronald Reagan, soon."

"Petty Officer *Frank* Adams? You must be mistaken, Sir; Frank is a Seaman."

"No mistake. He was promoted to Petty Officer Third Class. You have two very remarkable sons. I'm honored to be their Commanding Officer at this time. One of them should be calling you soon. Good-bye and God bless."

The call was over, but Sam could not talk for a moment. When he collected his thoughts, he looked up to see Hope looking at him, obviously worried about what he had heard. He told her everything the Captain had told him. Kelly hugged Hope and Joey D slapped Sam on the back at hearing the good news. The other people in the lounge were congratulating them, as well.

Hope's cell phone rang again. It was Heidi calling. "Hope, have you heard anything about Sammy or Frank?"

Hope repeated everything Captain Casey said. Heidi said, "Oh, that's good! I got the information at work just a bit ago and decided to call, in case you hadn't heard. I have to make this a quick call; we're having all kinds of trouble happening that we have to take care of. I'll talk to you later. Bye."

• • • • • • • • • • •

When Frank arrived back onto the aircraft carrier that was his second home, he checked in at his work space, still carrying all his gear. His other uniforms and belongings were still onboard the ship, at his same rack and locker down in berthing. It was suppertime, so he joined his shipmates for a walk to the chow hall.

On this ship, there was more than one option of where you could eat. There are mess decks back aft for regular meals and forward mess decks for fast food. Frank chose to eat in the aft mess deck; tonight they were serving steak and lobster, vegetables, and rice, with strawberry shortcake for dessert.

Frank looked around at the bustling mess hall and smiled to himself. The smell of the delicious food was making his mouth water; he had not eaten in nearly 24 hours. He attacked his plate with gusto, as he talked with his shipmates, telling them all that had happened since he left. It was good to be back. The life of a sailor was one that Frank dearly loved.

The sailor next to Frank leaned over and whispered, "Better watch out, here comes Hargrove."

Frank looked over his shoulder and saw the Mess Deck Master of Arms, Petty Officer First Class Hargrove angrily striding in the direction of Frank's table. Frank took a deep breath and focused on his food. He had problems in the past with this man, who for some unknown reason had taken a deep dislike to Frank. Hargrove always gave him a hard time. It was the one thing about this ship that made Frank uncomfortable.

"Petty Officer, that is not a standard U.S. Navy uniform you are wearing on my mess deck! Your hair is also unsatisfactory! Navy regulations state that you must shave and it looks like you haven't shaved in weeks," yelled Hargrove forcefully.

Frank calmly answered, "You're right, I haven't shaved for weeks. I need time to explain that."

The Mess Deck Master of Arms, however, was in no mood to listen to Frank's explanations. He put Frank on report for his appearance and for talking back to him. He then ordered Frank to get into the proper uniform and get a haircut. Frank tried to explain that he had other orders, but again was cut off.

Frank was sent to the Executive Officer (XO), Captain Derek P. Hargrove. The Mess Deck Master of Arms was also there to present his charges against Petty Officer Frank Adams. Frank brought with him his Temporary Assignment of Duty orders. The XO looked over them and then threw them onto his desk. He told Frank that he expected him to immediately get into the uniform of the day and present himself to the barbers for a Navy regulation haircut and shave.

The XO continued, "Boy, you're in the real Navy now and you need to look like it. I know you are just getting back onboard, but this is MY ship. You will obey MY laws on MY ship."

"Aye, aye, Sir. May I say something about these charges and what I've been doing?"

The XO answered, "I don't care what you've been doing. I'm the boss here and you better not forget it. Now get out of my sight. You have five minutes to be in the uniform of the day. Then go straight do to the Barber Shop to get your hair cut. I want a high and tight haircut. I don't care what the Navy Regulations say about haircuts, you will follow my regulations."

Frank saluted and left.

The division chain of command on this ship was a great group of people, Frank thought; but this particular XO was power hungry. Frank went back to his bunk and changed into his naval working uniform of the day. He walked down to the Barber Shop, where he had head of the line privileges, to find the barber already waiting for him.

Back at the Ships Signals Exploitation Space, Frank dropped his things off at his desk and went in to speak to the Division Officer. He told him about his orders and what happened with the XO. The Division Officer told him to get to work; he would take care of things.

Later that night while Frank was sleeping, the Chief came down and told him to get up ASAP and get into his dress white uniform. Flag was in the SSES. Flag is the carrier's task force commander and a rank of either Rear or Vice Admiral. The CO and XO were also there when he arrived.

Frank wondered what was going on when a video conference came over the system. It was the Vice Admiral in charge of JSOC Operations in the Middle East. He informed Frank's superiors that Frank would be on call throughout his stay on the USS Ronald Reagan and then commented, "I'm wondering what kind of operation you're running there, that would treat a sailor the way Petty Officer Adams was treated earlier today."

"I'm sure I don't know what you're talking about," responded the XO.

"Of course, you don't. Petty Officer Adams, did you know you made Petty Officer Third Class eight months ago?"

Frank answered, "No, Sir. I did not."

"I didn't think so. Your XO contacted Washington, D.C. and withdrew your recommendation; so even though you were selected, you didn't make it. When we investigated, we found that your record has been spotless," commented the Admiral.

The XO spoke up and said that he had withdrawn the recommendation, because Frank did not finish his Seal training, thus disqualifying him for promotion.

The Admiral argued that the reason Frank did not finish was due to an injury he received when trying to help another injured sailor. Then, "Petty Officer Adams, you are awarded the rank of Petty Officer from eight months ago; you will also receive back sea pay, as well. When you get the work finished, you'll be able to take the next exam for Petty Officer Second Class. Good luck, Sailor."

Frank replied, "Thank you, Sir! I should have no trouble as I already have all the requirements for Second Class finished."

"Great job, Petty Officer. Now, I'll move on to other issues. Captain Hargrove, I'm very upset an officer would do such a thing, as to withdraw a recommendation for promotion for a sailor who has such a pristine record. In addition, I heard about you giving the Petty Officer a difficult time about his hair and uniform today, when he was under my specific orders to NOT cut his hair or facial hair. I know, for a fact, that Petty Officer Adams told your cousin, GM1 Hargrove about these orders and he told him to shut up about them. Could it be that the two of you are working against him?"

The Admiral continued, "What really has me for a loss of words is when you told the Petty Officer this was YOUR ship and he had to obey YOUR regulations."

The Captain of the ship, Captain Washington, turned to the XO and said, "You said this was your ship? It is the United States Navy's ship. From things I've been hearing about you, I don't think your time as XO will be long."

"These are all just lies," mumbled the XO, Captain Hargrove.

The Admiral continued, "What you are unaware of is that Captain Washington's aid, Petty Officer Yolinda Rose sent me copies of over fifty occasions where you misused your authority—from rescinding promotion recommendations to failure to obey your own regulations. We've been told that you would blackmail people to do things for you, saying that then you would not put charges in their personnel files. I can assure you that after today, you will have a few things in your file. We have witnesses of what you told Frank, so charge one is conduct unbecoming of an officer and misuse of authority.

"Charge two is misuse of government funds. We have photographic evidence of you using Navy vehicles and boats for your own personal pleasure. We have photos of 168 different times that you did this."

The Admiral stood up and looked ominously at the XO, "Charge three is even more serious—espionage. We have evidence of you photographing different areas within the ship and e-mailing the photos to a known agent. We have evidence that you took M-16s and .45 caliber handguns from the ship's armory, selling them to an undercover agent. I wonder if your other cousin, the Gunners Mate, has anything to do with that one."

The Admiral sat on the corner of his desk and shook his head, saying, "We've been looking at you for a long time, Captain Hargrove. It's so disappointing when one of our own goes bad. Captain Washington, I order you to take Captain Hargrove and Petty Officer Hargrove into custody at this time. They'll be shipped out on the next flight to Guam.

I will also advise you that JAG is coming onboard to continue the investigation. You are all dismissed."

· · · · · · · · · · · ·

"Honey, I'm home. Great news! The doctor said I can go back to work, as long as it's light duty. I told him that where I work, it's all light duty," said Mark laughingly. He was sure in a good mood.

As he rounded the corner into the living room, he saw Paula crying. "Oh Baby, what's the matter, Honey?"

Paula let Mark put his arms around her as she sobbed. "I had two Charlie Response calls today."

"Tell me about them," Mark said softly.

"The first one was a 21 year old male and his girlfriend on a crotch rocket. He was traveling at a high rate of speed when he lost control in a turn and did a low side fall. Neither of them were wearing helmets."

Mark thought to himself, *I know where this is going.*

"The boy was thrown from the bike and his body hit a parked car. He sustained head trauma with internal injuries; I don't know if he'll make it' or not. He's just a boy and his little girlfriend is only 16! She went down with the bike and was pinned underneath it. She had no protective clothing on, just short shorts, flip flops, and a bikini top! She also had head trauma and quite a lot of road rash to her face. She looked like she would have been beautiful!" cried Paula.

Mark held his wife and let her cry out all her frustrations and fears. They talked about the importance of protective gear and riding lessons.

"What about the other call?"

"It was an Amish buggy going pass the Chrysler dealership on Route 30; a car came from behind and hit it. The two people in the buggy sustained minor injuries and were taken to Chambersburg Hospital. Both accidents just made me think of our accident a few months ago. I went to the Chief and told him I needed some time off. He agreed. I didn't tell him that I've been having nightmares about our accident. I know it's PTSD. I've been put on vacation for seven days."

Mark told her that she should go to the doctor and talk about things before it gets worse. Paula agreed to go. Some injuries are just hidden.

CHARLIE RESPONSE
CHAPTER EIGHT

"So where are these bikes I'm supposed to bless?" asked Commander Ed Ruby, the ship's chaplain.

"They're sitting at the end of the pier, Sir," answered TJ.

Having been given three day passes at the same time, both TJ and Sally decided to really break in her new bike with a road trip down the Skyline Drive.

The Chaplain laid his hands on the Harley-Davidson motorcycles and started the blessing, "Oh, Heavenly Father, we come to You on this beautiful day and give thanks for all of our blessings. We ask that You keep Your watchful eye on the path of these bikes, both at home and in all of their journeys. We ask that You keep Your protective hands around the riders and always bring them home safely. May Your mercy, grace, and love shine upon their every path. Amen."

As they thanked Chaplain Ruby, he said, "This was the first motorcycle blessing I've ever done."

TJ said, "We really appreciate that you took the time to do this for us. The Commanding Officer appointed me Motorcycle Safety Officer of the ship. When I come back, maybe we can get together and give a ship wide blessing of motorcycles. What do you think?"

The Chaplain said he thought it was a great idea. TJ had the Chaplain take a photograph of him and Sally. Then TJ took a photograph of the Chaplain by their bikes. He thought it would make a nice article in the ship's newspaper and newsletter to the families.

Sally and TJ each put on their leather jacket with the required high visibility vest over their leather jacket. Naval Regulations call for all motorcyclists to wear high visibility jackets or vests and helmets.

They started up their Harley-Davidsons and TJ said, "Kick stands up! Remember to tell me if I go too fast for you." Sally said that she would. They pulled away from the pier, down Hampton Blvd. past other ships on different piers. Since the two of them had already topped off their gas tanks the night before, they quickly put Norfolk Naval Base in their rearview mirror.

In no time they had passed the Norfolk Naval Air Station (NAS) and were headed over the Hampton Bay Bridge Tunnel. With the rumble of the Harley exhaust pipes in their ears (music to any Harley lover), they pointed their bikes in the direction of the capital of Virginia. The city of Richmond is deep in American history, being the capital of the Confederate States of America in the Civil War.

With about an hour of riding behind them, they rode into Williamsburg and headed for the local Harley shop to pick up t-shirts as souvenirs. Leaving Williamsburg, TJ turned onto Route 5, a more enjoyable road to ride on than the interstate. They followed Route 5 into the beautiful city of Richmond, found the Harley shop, and picked up a couple more t-shirts.

"Wow, this is a beautiful part of the country for riding. All this fresh air has made me hungry and my behind sure could use a break," announced Sally. "Let's find somewhere for lunch."

Grinning, TJ replied, "Sorry, I forgot you're a newbie on the bike. Your backside must be almost numb by now. You're really doing a great job for your first long ride."

They found a nice little diner and had a good meal, a good conversation, and a good rest for Sally. They talked about the plans for the rest of the trip, their family and friends, and their hopes and dreams—all those things that couples talk about when they are starry eyed about each other.

After they finished eating and resting, they got back on the bikes and headed down the road once more. They rode all around the area, stopping in towns like Scottsdale, Unionville, Orange, and Madison to get pictures for the ABCs of Touring Contest for H.O.G., picking up t-shirts all along the way.

They rode further north on Route 231 when they saw signs for the exit to the Skyline Drive. They were just east of Shenandoah National Park, when they decided that Sperryville looked like a nice place to stop for the night. Surrounded by the Blue Ridge Mountains and just a stone's throw from the entrance to the Skyline Drive, there was beautiful scenery rolling out in every direction from Sperryville. Unfortunately, all the bed and breakfasts in town were completely booked, so Sally and TJ rode out onto Route 231 and headed towards Winchester.

In Winchester, they got a room at the Sleep Inn and Suites. TJ told Sally she could have the bed and he would take the pull out couch in the living room of the suite. They took their things into the suite and then walked next door to the Golden Corral for supper.

When they were finished with their supper, they walked hand in hand back to their room where they changed into their swimsuits and climbed into the Jacuzzi to relax. After being in the Jacuzzi for 15 minutes, Sally commented that a dip in the swimming pool sounded like a good idea to her. "Even though this is very relaxing, I think I just need to move my muscles around more than just sitting in the hot tub".

TJ agreed and they gathered their towels and walked to the hotel's indoor pool. After swimming and playing around for a while, TJ took hold of Sally's hand and asked, "Do you trust me?"

"Of course, with every particle of my being," she said with a questioning look in her eye.

"Then will you dive under water with me with your eyes closed?"

"Okay, but this better not be one of your pranks," Sally said with a warning tone.

"Just trust me."

After taking deep breaths, under the water they both went. While holding Sally's hand, TJ pulled something shiny out of his swim trunk's pocket. He put a diamond ring on her finger and she opened her eyes. Sally quickly went to the surface of the water and looked at her finger with tears in her eyes.

"Ensign Sally Morgan, will you do me the honor of becoming my wife?"

Sally excitedly grabbed TJ, hugging and kissing him.

"Well, what's your answer?"

But she couldn't answer him because she was crying so hard.

"If you don't answer me, I'll think that your answer is no," TJ teased.

"Yes, I'll marry you!" Sally cried out.

TJ felt a huge wave of relief flow over him. They both looked at her ring as if it held a magical promise of future happiness. "I thought since we're both in the Navy, the best place to propose would be in the water."

Sally looked at him with shining eyes, "It was perfect, TJ, just perfect."

Later on, when they were watching television, Sally asked, "When do you want to get married? Have you given it any thought?"

"I've given it a lot of thought, actually. It's up to you, of course, but I was hoping for a military wedding. There's really only two times we could get married—either before the ship leaves for our six month deployment or after I get back. What do you think?"

Sally snuggled under the arm that TJ put around her and thought for a minute, "It will take some time to get everything ready, but given the circumstances I think I would rather get married at least a month before you leave. Maybe I should talk to my parents before I give you any kind of solid answer on that."

They talked long into the night about plans they would like to make for the wedding and plans for their future.

The next morning when Sally woke up, TJ was nowhere to be found; so she picked up the phone and called her parents. She told her mother that she and TJ were engaged and they excitedly talked of the romantic way that he proposed. Mrs. Morgan told Sally that TJ had talked to them weeks ago, asking for their blessing and that they couldn't be any happier about it. They briefly talked about plans for the wedding and Sally told her mother that they wanted a military wedding. They both wanted to walk under an archway of sabers that their fellow shipmates were holding up.

After quite a lengthy time on the phone, Sally said she needed to go find TJ, but that she loved her parents very much and couldn't wait to see them again.

Just as Sally hung up the phone, TJ opened the door of the suite with his arms loaded down with food.

"Awwww, you're awake already. I was hoping to surprise you with breakfast in bed," said TJ with a mock pout on his face. "I got up early. You were still sleeping when I was finished with my shower, so I headed downstairs to check out the breakfast situation. I didn't know what you would want so I brought a little of everything."

They spread the food out on the tiny table in the corner.

"You're so sweet. Aren't you eating?" asked Sally as she spread cream cheese on her bagel.

"I already ate, but I think I could still help you out some with all this food," said TJ, sitting in the chair next to Sally.

After eating, TJ started to load up the motorcycles while Sally was in the shower. When Sally was ready to go she came outside, "Oh, look at this glorious morning!" She held her face up into the sunlight, closed her eyes and took a deep breath of the crisp morning air. *Could life be any more perfect*, she thought to herself.

They quickly looked at some brochures from the area and remarked that they would have to come back to the area sometime to do some kayaking in Front Royal. The two of them got on their bikes and headed south. At the exit for the Skyline Drive, they took pictures of each other by the sign. There was another family there also taking pictures, so Sally took a couple of pictures of them together under the sign and they took pictures of Sally and TJ under the sign.

Sally quickly posted the picture on Facebook with the caption, *my soon to be husband and I on our motorcycle trip down the Skyline Drive*. She wondered how many comments she would get since none of her Facebook friends knew of the engagement yet.

They rode about three miles and then stopped at the Shenandoah Valley Overlook. They took pictures across the valley to Signal Knob. TJ read a sign that said Signal Knob was a Civil War communications post on Massanutten Mountain.

A couple more miles down the road, they stopped at the Dickey Ridge Visitor Center. There they looked at the exhibits and watch an informational video.

Back on the bikes, they rode 12 miles before stopping at the Range View Overlook. With an expansive view of the ridges and the valley below, it was the perfect place for taking more pictures. Sally posted another picture on Facebook and captioned it, *Glad you're not here. I'm enjoying my time alone with TJ.*

"Did you know this road is 105 miles long and has 75 different overlooks on it?" TJ asked.

"Sounds like we're going to be on and off our bikes a lot today," remarked Sally.

"How about we head over to the Luray Caverns and do some time off the bike exploring? They're the largest caverns in the eastern United States. There's a pipe organ there called The Great Stalacpipe Organ. I think it would be interesting and would let us stretch our legs a bit today."

"Sounds good to me."

After exploring the caverns and visiting Shenandoah National park, they decided to stop for lunch. As she kneaded her thigh muscles, Sally remarked that it was amazing to her how sore one could get just sitting on a bike. When they were finished eating and resting, they decided to fill up on gas. They figured out what they were getting for fuel mileage, TJ was getting 50 mpg and Sally was averaging 66 mpg. They made jokes about this being the way to travel, especially if you were trying to save your pennies.

TJ and Sally spent the rest of the afternoon seeing the sights along the Skyline Drive, as well as the National and Historical parks along the way.

They decided to stop for the night at the Massanutten Resort. They got a room with two queen sized beds and then went to supper at the Blue Ridge Restaurant. While they were eating, TJ told Sally they were near Whiteoak Canyon. He explained that there were six beautiful waterfalls, perfect for taking photos and, if she wanted to, they would ride there first thing in the morning. However, for tonight the resort had an indoor water park, so as soon as they were finished with their meal, they changed into their swimsuits.

They had fun taking their inner tubes down the various slides. Then they rented boogie boards and went to FlowRider, which is an indoor wave pool. Sally said, "I love it here; we should come back here for our honeymoon."

TJ hugged her and said, "That sounds perfect to me. We don't have time to try everything this time and I don't want to miss anything. I would love to come back here."

After they played around in the wave pool for a while longer, TJ took Sally aside and announced, "As a surprise, I booked a Massamutten Signature Massage for you. It's Swedish and deep tissue massage combined with aromatherapy, heated towels, and different oils and balms. You have enough time to go get ready for it, if you leave now."

"Oh TJ, I can see already that you're going to be the type to spoil me. And I'm going to be the type that lets you," Sally teased. She reached up and kissed him. "Thank you so much."

"Go have a relaxing time. I'm going to boogie board a bit longer and I'll see you up in the room later," said TJ, smiling, very pleased with himself.

Sally was feeling very relaxed later when she walked into the room. She smiled to herself as she noticed that TJ had worn himself out and was sound asleep, still in his clothes, with Sports Center playing on the television.

She changed into her pajamas and climbed into the other bed, appreciating the fact that this bed felt like sleeping on a cloud. In a matter of about two heartbeats, Sally was also sound asleep.

They woke up refreshed at 6:30 the next morning. When TJ remarked that the restaurant did not open until 9:00, they decided to find a fast food joint.

After a quick breakfast at McDonald's, they headed for the waterfalls and spent an hour taking pictures there. Then they headed down the Skyline Drive once again, visiting and taking photos of all the many wondrous sights that God had created.

At the end of the Skyline Drive, they rode towards Staunton to find the Harley dealership for another souvenir t-shirt for each of them.

Over lunch they decided to head east on I-64 to go to Thomas Jefferson's home, Monticello.

Once they got there, before the tour started, TJ mentioned that he should call his mother.

· · · · · · · · · · ·

Kelly called Heidi to see if she and Terry could come up for a visit on the weekend. As they were talking, they devised a plan to get the entire gang together for a surprise visit to Sam and Joey D at Westminster Woods. Everyone would meet on Saturday morning at the Daniels' home and ride over together.

Heidi was excited to tell everyone that TJ was going to get married, but decided to wait until everyone was together with Sam and Joey D. It was hard not saying anything with everyone talking about the things that had been going on in their lives. They stopped on the way to the nursing home for lunch at Original Italian Pizza. After they ordered, Kelly reminded everyone that this was a surprise visit. She was sure Sam and Joey D were going to be so excited, as it had been a while since they were all together.

At the nursing home, they all signed in at the welcome desk and went to the lounge. Kelly and Hope went in to see Sam and Joey D, then wheeled them down to the lounge on the pretense of taking a walk. The boys were very excited to see all of their friends.

When the commotion of the greetings settled down, Heidi stood up and said she had some good news to share with everyone. "Let's hear it, girl," said Sam.

"TJ talked Sally into getting her motorcycle license. Earlier this week she joined the Harley family, when she bought a new 883 Low."

"That's great!"

"Always room for one more on the road!"

Heidi smiled and continued, "She joined more than one family this week. She and TJ went on a trip to ride the Skyline Drive. While they were gone, TJ slipped a diamond ring on her finger! We're going to have a new daughter-in-law!"

"Congratulations!"

"When's the big day?"

"Did they set a date yet?"

Heidi told them that they wanted to get married about a month before TJ leaves on deployment, so they would have the date set in a few days. Everyone thought that was a good idea.

"It's such a short time to get ready, is there anything that we could do to help out?" offered Paula. Heidi explained that they wanted a simple military wedding, but if she came across anything helpful, she would let her know. She added that they should probably check to make sure that Sam and Joey D would be able to get a pass to go to the wedding in Norfolk.

So Heidi and Paula went over to the nurse's station, explained the situation, and asked if the policy allowed patients to leave the area. Debbie, the nurse, said that it would be up to their doctors. Usually doctors considered all the facts; such as how they are recovering, how their therapy is progressing, and if they had a trained medical professional going along with them. All these things would factor into the decision.

Paul spoke up and told the nurse she was a trained paramedic and asked if that would count as a trained medical professional. Debbie answered that it was completely up to the doctor. She said she would speak to Sam and Joey D about it; then speak to their doctors.

Back in the lounge, Heidi's cellphone rang. She answered and her face lit up when she heard TJ's voice on the other end.

"Hi, Mom. I'm sorry to bother you. Are you in Pennsylvania this weekend?"

"Yes, we are."

Heidi put TJ on speakerphone so that everyone could congratulate him on his engagement. It was then they all heard him sniffling.

"Mom, I know you already told everyone about the wedding, but I have something to tell you. When I was turning the keys in at the hotel this morning, Sally met up with an old boyfriend in the parking lot. I came out and found a note on my bike. She loaded up her bike into the back of his truck and ran off to Mexico with him. Sally's gone AWOL, Mom! She called off the wedding!" cried TJ.

You could have heard a pin drop in the lounge. Heidi, with tears in her eyes, asked her son if he was alright.

Terry consoled TJ, saying, "Son, you know I've always liked Sally—this is just so hard to believe. She's always been such a wonderful person. Are you sure she isn't just playing a joke on you?"

TJ answered, "I'm sure she's not playing a joke on me, because I'm playing one on you all!" TJ was laughing so hard he was almost hard to understand.

Heidi rolled her eyes and shook her head. "TJ, someday your pranks are going to get you into some very big trouble."

"I'm sorry, Mom. Everything is fine between us. I'll call you later tonight to tell you about our trip and if we've come up with a date. I love you guys. Good-bye."

After a good afternoon with Joey D and Sam, everyone decided it was time to leave and let the boys get some much needed rest. They all headed to Hoss's Steak and Seafood across town, which made Joey D very jealous, because he loved Surf and Turf dinners.

With everyone gone, Joey D and Sam settled in to watch the Pirates and the Phillies play while they ate their dinner.

. . . .

Frank logged on to his laptop and opened his e-mail account. Before looking at any of his e-mail, he wrote one to his mother. He was hoping to get in contact with her before the Navy did.

As soon as his brother, Sammy, was released from medical leave from injuring his knee, he had volunteered for another mission. In the course of this mission, Sammy had once again played the hero, saving several sailors by sacrificing himself, thus getting hurt again. Since this injury required surgery to remove shrapnel from Sammy's abdomen and leg, TJ was pretty sure Sammy would be forced to take some real time off from the excitement that he seemed to crave.

Always the hero, Frank thought as he finished writing his mother about Sammy, begging her not to worry; it was not as bad as it sounded. Sammy would be just fine. In truth, Frank was enormously proud of his brother. He just wished he would not take so many chances—no one was invincible.

Since it was the weekend, the message traffic was not very heavy. Frank turned on one of the spare receivers to listen to Armed Forces Radio. They were broadcasting the Pittsburgh Pirates vs. Philadelphia Phillies baseball game. Frank opened the study manual for Petty Officer Second Class for CTN to study for the promotion. Near the end of his twelve hour watch, a call came into the workspace. It was the doctor asking if Frank wanted to come down to see his brother. He left immediately.

Frank looked at his brother and cringed; he looked pretty beat up. Sammy opened one eye and said, "Little bro, we have to quit meeting like this." He gave Frank a crooked smile and continued, "I'm tired and sore, but you should have seen the other guy."

Frank lectured, "You have to quit trying to be everyone's hero. I was sent a message about what you did. Do you have to stay behind every time? Isn't it about time you let one of the others earn some accolades? Remember the first rule of being a Petty Officer—learn how to delegate."

"Yeah, but I do it so well," said Sammy cockily. "Aww, I'm just teasing you. Actually, I'm really tired and sore right now. Could you come back down a little later? I need some sleep."

Frank said he would be back and left the room. He turned at the doorway and looked at his already sleeping brother. "I'm proud of you, Sammy," he whispered.

· · · · · · · · · · · ·

Hope and Kelly were leaving for church soon; but Kelly always took longer to get ready, so Hope thought she would have time to check her e-mail. She saw that she had a note from Frank and opened it. Kelly came running to check on her, when she heard Hope gasp.

Kelly held Hope's hand while she finished reading what Frank had written. Hope took a deep breath and put her son in God's hands, knowing it would do no good to fall apart.

Hope always thought most religions were the same. However, she found there were differences between her Baptist church back home and the Methodist church that Kelly went to. They talked about the differences; such as, baptism, use of the different versions of the Bible, and women preachers. They decided that as long as they prayed to the same God, then to each his own.

After church, they went to a buffet lunch at the Sunny Ridge Restaurant. Several people came up to them to ask how Joey D and Sam were doing. Many people offered to pray for them, so Hope asked if they would also pray for her son, Sammy, and explained why. Hope began to realize how much she really liked being in this small town country atmosphere. The food was great and the people were very friendly. It was a relaxing and welcoming feeling.

After eating, the women went back to Kelly's home to pick up their things for the trip to see Sam and Joey D. Hope quickly answered Frank's e-mail, now that she was in a better frame of mind. She told him that she loved him and to take good care of his generally reckless brother.

Sam took one look at his wife and knew something was wrong. "Honey, what's wrong? Have you heard from the boys?"

"You always could read me better than anyone." She proceeded to tell Sam what Frank had written.

"Wheel me down to Joey D's room. I have to tell him this; we need to pray as a group about it," Sam said, looking very upset.

When Sam told Joey D the news about Sammy, it was obvious the small group was in some distress. A nurse's aide was outside the room and heard everything, so she told her co-workers what happened. Nurse Debbie immediately came to the room and asked if they needed to talk to someone, maybe a social worker.

Sam answered, "Yes, I do need to talk to someone—God." The small group of close friends grasped each other's hands and bowed their heads.

Later that evening, Kelly and Hope ate supper with Joey D and Sam. They wanted to maintain some kind of family togetherness, especially on Sundays. After supper, Hope said they better head back to the farm in case there was any more word on Sammy.

• • • • • • • • • • •

Later in the day, Frank went down to the medical unit to check on Sammy. The doctor said Sammy was recovering well and was okay to fly to Guam and then back to the States. Sammy was heading home the next morning.

Frank sat with Sammy for a while. They talked, teasing each other and lightly rough-housing. Then the doctor came in and said that he should go soon—Sammy needed his rest.

Frank would not be able to come back in the morning in time to see Sammy before he left the ship. So they said their good-byes. Sammy said, "You keep doing a good job. If at all possible, I'll come to San Diego when you come home."

Frank nodded his head. As he was heading out the door, he turned and said, "You tell Mom *hello* from me when you get home; give her a kiss for me, too. See you later, Brother."

• • • • • • • • • • •

TJ and Sally took the super slab of I-64 home to Norfolk. She was anxious to show her friends her diamond ring. After eating supper, Sally went to her barracks and TJ went to his ship. They were both very tired from their busy weekend. TJ called Sally's cell. "Remember, you're coming to chapel with me tomorrow on the ship. We're scheduled to talk to the Chaplain afterwards."

"Yes, I know." They said good night and hung up.

Sally was alone in her barracks. She started uploading all of the pictures from the weekend onto her computer. She picked out a special few and posted them on Facebook. Her friends started commenting on Facebook, asking if she was home now. They wanted to come right away to see her ring and talk about wedding plans.

The first to show up were Ensign Sara Jane Dell and Ensign Victoria Hertz, Sally's two best friends. The three girls met at and graduated together from the U.S. Naval Academy. Now all three officers were stationed together at the world's largest naval base in Norfolk, Virginia.

Sara Jane grabbed Sally up in a big hug, while Victoria inspected the ring. They were very excited for their friend. The other girls on their floor filtered in when they heard all the excitement. Sara Jane pulled her silky, dark hair over her shoulder as she bent down over the ring. She said, "Oh Sally, this is a beautiful engagement ring. How did he propose?"

Sally told them the story and one of the girls asked her if they had set a date yet. "Not yet," she said, "but we know we want to do it before TJ is deployed."

"What's the reason for the big rush? You're not...ummm...?" asked one of the girls, with raised eyebrows.

"Obviously, you don't know Sally very well if you have to ask that. Sally is a good Christian girl; she's got morals," answered Victoria.

Sally explained that they wanted to get married at least a month before he left. They wanted to have time to adjust to married life before one of them had to leave for a lengthy time. "We're supposed to talk to TJ's chaplain tomorrow before we can set a date," she added.

The next morning, Sally was very cheerful as she dressed in her dress white uniform. She could not wait to see her husband-to-be. She drove her car to Pier 12, where the USS George Bush CVN-77 was docked. As she locked her car, she noticed what a sunny, beautiful day it was.

Sally showed her military ID card to the brow watch and was waved through. Half way up the brow, she stopped, turned toward the ship's stern, and saluted the flag. By the time she had requested permission to come aboard the ship from the Officer of the Deck, TJ was waiting for her. He signed her in as a guest and they headed to the Chapel.

TJ introduced Sally to Commander Ed Ruby, the Chaplain of the USS George Bush. TJ explained they had just gotten engaged and were interested in having the wedding performed by him at the base chapel. Commander Ruby talked with them briefly and told them he would make up a list of available dates for both himself and the chapel.

TJ showed Sally to a seat before the chapel service began. The Chaplain opened the service with prayer and then led them in the singing of a few songs. TJ pointed out his Commanding Officer, Captain Trent Baker and his wife, Kandi. Captain Baker had a deep bass singing voice that carried throughout the room. He would raise his arms in the air to give praise to God, when they sang the words of the chorus *when we all get to heaven*. Most of the crew on the ship and those in his chain of command knew that the Captain was a man of God.

After the song, Chaplain Ruby exclaimed, "When we all get to Heaven, we will be shouting Victory! I want to welcome everyone to our Protestant Service here on the USS George Bush. As always, welcome to our Commanding Officer and his wife. And today, we have a guest of Lt. TJ Miller. Welcome to our service, Miss Morgan."

He looked around at the people in their seats and said, "Let's sing another song, lifting our voices up to God."

The congregation started singing,

There's within my heart a melody
Jesus whispers sweet and low
Fear not, I am with thee,
Peace be still
In all of life's ebb and flow.

Jesus, Jesus, Jesus
Sweetest name I know
Fills my every longing
Keeps me singing as I go.

After the singing was finished, TJ surprised Sally by getting up and moving to the front as the Chaplain said, "We will now have a solo by Lt.TJ Miller. he will be accompanied by Petty Officer Locke on the piano."

TJ talked a little about the song he was going to sing. "Some people think that the famous big band leader Tommy Dorsey wrote this song, but he didn't. It was written by Thomas Andrew Dorsey, who was the son of an African American revivalist preacher. It is called, *Precious Lord, Take My Hand.*"

TJ's baritone tones filled the room. When the final strains of music died out, the congregation clapped their hands, shouting, "AMEN!"

"What a treat that was, Lt. Miller. God has certainly given you a great voice," exclaimed the Chaplain.

When TJ sat down, Sally leaned over and whispered, "I've never heard that song sung any better in my life. You did such a great job!" Smiling, TJ settled into his seat.

Chaplain Ruby spoke, "We have some good news this week. Our own TJ Miller has proposed marriage to his girlfriend, Sally Morgan. Our congregation will soon be growing by one. Praise the Lord! This fits right in with the message this week on Proverbs 31."

He started reading verse 10, *Who can find a virtuous woman? For her price is far above rubies. The heart of her husband doth safely trust in her, so that he shall have no need of spoil...*

After the preaching the Chaplain said, "Now we will sing the Navy Hymn, also known as *Eternal Father, Strong to Save.*"

After the service, the people lingered, talking in the chapel. Several people congratulated both TJ and Sally. The Commanding Officer and his wife walked over to speak to them, as well. "Congratulations to the both of you. Miss Morgan, I'm Captain Trent Baker and this is my wife, Kandi," said the CO.

"Thank you, Sir. I'm pleased to meet you."

Kandi asked if they had set the date yet—a question they seemed to hear a lot lately. Sally explained they wanted to get married before the ship deployed.

"Well, dear, I'll have to invite both of you for supper one evening. Also, when the ship deploys, you might find it easier to cope if you're part of the Navy Wives Club. We would welcome you with open arms. The Chaplain's wife is normally here for church, but Grace isn't feeling well, from what I hear. She's also part of the Navy Wives Club."

Captain Baker said, "TJ, you and your fiancé are invited to join me for lunch in the Wardroom. Chaplain Ruby, you're invited also."

TJ said, "Thank you, sir. What time do you want us there?"

"Right now. My wife and I always eat lunch together after Chapel."

When they arrived in the Wardroom, other officers were already there. When the Captain and his wife entered the room "Attention on Deck" was called out. The Captain told everyone to take a seat and relax.

The Culinary Specialist brought everyone non-alcoholic drinks. Soon, bread and salad was served to everyone; followed by a delicious main course of baked grouper with rice and mixed vegetables; and for dessert, fruit cocktail.

Most of the conversation at the dinner table was by the Captain or his wife. Kandi mentioned that she was happy that she was not the only woman in the Wardroom today. She thanked the four female officers of the ship and Sally for coming.

The conversation in the room quickly turned to whether the Naval Academy football team would be as good as in years past. Captain Baker had played on the football team at the Academy. TJ had been on the team as a backup punter and backup field goal kicker during his time there.

Eventually, the Captain said, "I'm sorry to have to break up this get-together, but I do have a meeting I must get to. Miss Morgan, I wish to express my happiness in meeting you. You seem to be a fine young lady for Mr. Miller. I hope the two of you will have a long and happy life together."

"Thank you, Sir. And thank you for inviting me today," responded Sally, shaking the Captain's extended hand.

Chaplain Ruby handed TJ a folder containing the coordinated dates that both he and the Base Chapel had open. TJ thanked him and said he would be in touch with him about it.

TJ escorted Sally off the ship and they went to the Vista Point Center to get information about available dates and menu options for the reception.

CHARLIE RESPONSE
CHAPTER NINE

Hope was more upset than she had let on about Sammy's injuries. She tried to play it off as pretty normal, because she did not want to upset the others. They had all had so much upheaval the past few months. She was not sure, however, that she could maintain this facade for long without talking to Sam. She picked up the phone and dialed the number to his bedside telephone.

Sam answered the phone, "Well, well, a special phone call from my special lady. How are you doing, Babe?"

Hope told Sam about the insecurities and doubts that she was feeling. Her boy was far away and injured and the mother in her just wanted to be with him, taking care of him. She told Sam that she had gotten word that Sammy would be transferred to Bethesda Naval Hospital, outside of Washington, D.C. He would be all alone there with no family and she was having trouble dealing with it.

Sam, who knew Hope better than anyone, let her cry it out for a bit. He knew she was not wallowing in self-pity, but that she needed time to get all of her feelings out. When she had poured out all her concerns, Sam quietly began talking to her, calming her. He reminded her that their sons were both not only adults, but also military men. And they both had a functional, personal relationship with God. They were never alone; God was always with them. He continued, "As soon as we get off the phone, I want you to do something for me. Get your Bible and look up Hebrews 13:5. Read the last half of that verse, highlight it, cling to it, and remember it every time you have doubts."

They talked for a few more minutes and then said *good-night*. Hope retrieved her Bible from where it sat on her nightstand and opened it to the verse Sam had given her. She smiled to herself as she read aloud, "*for he hath said, I will never leave thee, nor forsake thee.*" It was a promise—a promise from God. Sam was right; her boys were never alone.

Hope fell to her knees and lifted her voice up to God, "Lord, thank You for Your promises. Forgive me for being a child of doubt; teach me to rely solely upon Your word. Be with my family, Lord, for You know their needs better than I do. From this moment on, I will place all my worries at Your feet. Remind me often of Your promise to never leave me. In my Lord Jesus' name I pray, Amen."

. . . .

In Chambersburg, Paula was just coming in from grocery shopping when the phone rang. Mark answered it. The woman calling was an attorney from Dewy and Stewart Attorneys of Law in Harrisburg, PA. She told Mark that she was representing Hugh Lamadeleine's trucking company and would like to set up a meeting between herself and all the motorcycle riders. At the meeting she planned to offer compensation on behalf of the trucking company—indicating that it was a sizeable offer.

Mark told her that she was welcome to come to his home and he would inform the others, if the offer seemed acceptable. He told her he would prefer to do it this way, as his friends Sam and Hope were going through a rough time right now; their son had been hit by a mortar shell recently in Afghanistan.

The attorney agreed and said she would be there within the next two hours.

Mark told Paula the attorney was coming and the reason for the visit. She commented, "Just remember, you should never take the first offer."

"I know, on the one hand we don't want to seem greedy; but on the other, both you and I have been off work for a while now. So with that in mind, we can at least listen to their offer."

The attorney found her way to Mark and Paula's home with the help of the GPS navigation system in her red Dodge Charger. Mark welcomed her in saying, "That's a nice car you have there. I thought all lawyers drove BMWs."

She smiled. "That's what my father drives, but he's a partner in the firm. My name is Jamie Stewart. You have a lovely home, Mrs. Brown.

Is there somewhere we could sit and spread out some papers?" She held out her hand in greeting to both Paula and Mark.

Paula showed her into the dining room and asked if she would like coffee. Miss Stewart replied, "Just a glass of water, if you don't mind. Thank you." She took a sheath of paperwork out of her briefcase and sat down. Paula handed her a glass of ice water and sat down across from the lawyer.

"I've already spoken to the Millers, Adams, and the Daniels. They all said for you to hear the first offer; then you can meet with them to discuss whether the offer will be accepted. We can all get together later at Westminster Woods to discuss things further, if needed," Miss Stewart informed them.

Mark told her that his wife, Paula, had been having symptoms of Post-Traumatic Stress Disorder. She was having nightmares about the accident and was on medical leave right now from her job as a paramedic. She was also taking Paxil for her anxieties. Miss Stewart said, "I wasn't aware of this, so it's good that we met. Do you have any proof of her treatments?"

Paula handed her some papers, "Here's the bill that was sent in to the insurance company."

Miss Stewart said she had to make a phone call and went outside. She came back in and said, "I have great news for you. I have an even better offer. Here is what we propose. These papers are for you to take to your attorney, Abraham David; but let me explain everything to you now."

She shuffled through some papers and settled in to talk, "First and foremost, all your doctor bills for the injuries you received will be paid, both now and down the road. Your legal fees will be covered. Terry Miller will be compensated $250,000 for his pain and suffering. Mark, you will receive $100,000 for your pain and suffering. Your amount is less than Terry's, because your injuries were not as great. Paula will receive $50,000 for your PTSD and all your behavioral health appointments are covered, as well. For both Sam Adams and Joseph Daniels, we're offering $500,000 each, plus an additional $50,000 each for their wives for the stress they have gone through."

Mark sat in thought for a minute and said, "Let me make a phone call. I'll be right back." After a few moments, Mark came back and asked Jamie if she could meet tomorrow with their lawyer at Westminster Woods. They made the appointment for 1 p.m.

After Miss Stewart left, Mark said, "Wow, I didn't expect to get this much on any offer, let alone on the first offer." Paula agreed it was a nice offer.

· · · · · · · · · · ·

TJ and Sally compared the notes for the Norfolk Base Chapel and Vista Point Convention Center, looking for a mutually available Saturday. There were no openings for seven months. Sally started to cry, but the Religious Program Specialist mentioned there was a Friday opening in three weeks at both the chapel and Vista Point. Sally wiped the tears from her face and thanked the RP Petty Officer Ben Long for his vigilance in finding her an open date for her wedding.

Ben asked his assistant, Dawn, to loan Sally the computer program that made announcements and thank you cards. Sally thanked them and said she would get it back to them in the next couple of days. Ben had been such a help to her in every way so far, so Sally thanked him for his help. "Ma'am, you can come here anytime and I will help you with anything. That's what I'm here for."

Sally went back to her room in Spruance Hall to work on creating the perfect wedding announcements. Victoria and Sara Jane gave their opinions on which design to use and the wording of the card. Sally added all the important information to the inside of the card, such as directions and phone numbers. On a separate sheet, she included a dinner choice of grilled chicken or grilled salmon.

When she was finished, she called TJ to make sure that he remembered to book the honeymoon hotel room at the Hilton Hotel at Virginia Beach. They talked for a bit and made a dinner date for that evening.

After working on addressing the envelopes for the announcements, TJ and Sally went to Pizza Hut for supper. TJ had been unusually quiet all evening and Sally could not take it any longer. "So, when are you going to tell me what's wrong? You know, you're not entitled to keep secrets from me anymore."

TJ told her the ship was leaving this coming Monday. He had to leave in the midst of all the wedding preparations and was worried that she was going to be angry with him.

"Are you kidding me? Is that all it is? Are you going to be back before the wedding?"

"Of course, I will."

"You know, TJ, it hasn't been a secret to me that I'm marrying a Navy man. I know that to some degree, your life is not your own. Don't worry about it, I've got this handled," assured Sally.

Knowing that Sally was capable of taking care of things and understood TJ would not always be around took a heavy load off his shoulders. Finally, TJ relaxed and they had a great evening together.

The next Monday, TJ was up on the flight deck of the ship waving to Sally down on the dock. The enormous aircraft carrier was ready to leave dock side.

Once all the dock lines of the ship were removed from the pier, the Quarter deck announced, "Shift colors." (The American flag is called the *colors*. When a ship is moored to the dock, they run the colors up a flag pole on the stern of the ship. However, when the ship is underway, the flag is run up the mast of the ship. So the order *shift colors* means taking down the flag at the stern and putting it up at the mast.)

One long blast of the ship's horn sounded telling everyone that the ship was leaving the dock. Toby Keith's song Courtesy of the Red, White, and Blue started playing on the ship's loudspeakers. Every year, the crew of the ship votes for a song to be the breakaway song. It will be played every time the ship comes into or leaves port.

Sally continued waving at TJ until he left the deck to make his underway reports. "Every time I hear that song, I'm going to think of TJ leaving," she said to the lady next to her.

"Look at the other side of it. Whenever you hear that song, remember he's that much closer to being back in your arms again," the lady said.

Sally turned to thank her and suddenly realized it was Captain Baker's wife. "I'm sorry, Mrs. Baker. I didn't realize it was you."

"That's okay. Don't worry; the ship will be back into port before you know it. My husband says these shakedown cruises are good for making sure the ship's operating fine. It's also kind of a trial run for the sailors and their families to prepare them for the longer deployments."

"By the way, we received your wedding invitation in the mail. Thank you so much for inviting us. The Captain said he was honored to be asked and that we will be coming. I'm really looking forward to it. I just love weddings. Who made your announcements? They're really pretty; I loved them."

Sally told her that she had made them from a computer program the Base Chapel loaned her. They talked for a few more minutes about the wedding plans. Then Kandi asked, "Would you like to meet me for lunch later?" Sally said that would be lovely and they made plans to meet at the Breezy Point Officer's Club.

TJ finished his reports and turned them into the bridge. He checked with various personnel that all the circuits and receivers were in good working order. Before long, they would pass the Chesapeake Bay Bridge Tunnel and sail out into the Atlantic Ocean.

The USS George H.W. Bush CVN-77 was the Navy's newest aircraft carrier. She was 1092 feet long and completely redesigned from top to bottom. Her motto was *Freedom at Work*.

The sailors that are assigned to a new ship when it is commissioned are called Plank Owners. They get a certificate and when the ship is decommissioned, they have a ceremony. TJ was a Plank Owner of this ship.

While the USS George Bush was at dockside, TJ made sure the men in his crew received all the training they needed and then some. As well as going to Cryptologic Technician School and Advance Shipboard Communications-Crypto School, they also trained in firefighting, damage control, security, and weapons training. TJ wanted his men prepared for anything. They had worked hard getting this ship ready for launch and now came the real test, the shakedown cruise.

TJ went out through the hatch on the O-3 level by their workspace, which was one level below the flight deck. He looked out, seeing nothing but endless water. When he scanned the horizon, he noticed some very black clouds moving in. He knew they were near Cape Hatteras, where the waters are always rough.

TJ figured he better go find out if anyone was likely to be seasick if there was a storm. He sent a few men down to sick bay to get the patch. He told the newbies, "If it gets really rough when you're off duty, I'd suggest tying yourself in your rack, so you don't get tossed out of bed and get hurt."

The Bridge made an announcement over the 1MC, "Cover all guns, close all hatches, and clear the weather decks. Make all preparations for heavy seas." TJ thought, "Sounds like I was right about the storm."

In the midst of the storm, TJ turned on his laptop to check his e-mail. There were a couple from Sally—one saying good-bye and she loved him; the other wanting to know how the cruise was going so far. As he was reading, he heard the beep from Skype telling him he had a caller. It was Sally.

After they talked for a few minutes, Sally asked how the weather was; she had heard there was a storm off the coast. "Oh, everything is going great so far. The storm isn't too bad; there's just a really relaxing slow roll. I swear it's going to put me to sleep soon."

Just as he said that, the loud boatswain pipe sounded and the loudspeaker announced, "Man overboard, man overboard port side. All hands, man your man overboard stations."

"Honey, I have to go!" TJ exclaimed. In the blink of an eye, he was gone, running up to the work station.

Back in Spruance Hall, Sally was worried. Sara Jane and Victoria asked what was bothering her. She told them and they started to pray together for the safety of the man who had gone overboard, as well as the men who would be in on the rescue mission. This situation was dangerous.

TJ asked the Division Chief if the message was sent out for the man overboard. The Senior Chief told him the message was sent out along with the ship's position.

An hour later, the Captain announced, "Secure from man overboard drill."

The Captain has a dummy that the Navy calls Oscar. The Captain or Executive Officer throws the dummy overboard to test the crew. No one ever knows that it is a test beforehand. Each division must send an *all present and accountable for* report to the bridge.

TJ went back on line to tell Sally what happened. Victoria and Sara Jane spoke to him, telling him how worried Sally was.

"Why were you so worried? You knew it wasn't me; I was on Skype with you."

"I know. I guess it was just an over-reaction. I knew in my head it wasn't you, but I still worried."

They talked for a while before TJ said, "I should go. It was a long day and who know what lies ahead in the night."

As he was talking another announcement was heard, "Fire, fire, fire. Fire in the Aft Galley Port side. Away the response team from the aft repair lockers."

TJ said, "See, what did I tell you? It's going to be a long night."

"Oh, my! Aren't you scared about the fire?"

"Why? We have a professional crew onboard. They can handle it. It was in the galley, so my guess is a deep fryer caught on fire, or something like that. Don't worry about it; I'm not."

They talked for five more minutes when the Captain came on and announced, "Secure from fire detail. Fire put out by Culinary Specialists. Good work, men!"

"See, I told you not to worry. Everything is fine. OH, MY!!! I think we just hit something!" TJ exclaimed.

Sally screamed, "What did you hit? Are you alright?"

TJ held his sides as he laughed heartily. "We're okay. We just hit a big wave."

"Don't scare me like that! You're not funny, you big tease!"

The announcement came over the loudspeaker that it was time for evening prayer. Chaplain Ruby came on and said, "Father, we ask You to watch over us as we sleep. Please watch over the crew that is working the night shift; keep their attention on the tasks at hand. Keep your watchful eyes on our families ashore, giving our sailors one less thing to worry about. Father, give us a restful, peaceful night. In Jesus name, Amen."

TJ added, "And Lord, please be with Sally. Keep her calm and take away her fears and worries. Let her know she can count on You to be with her through every situation. Thank you for giving me a woman who cares so much about me. Amen."

"Amen. I feel better after that. Thank you, Honey," said Sally, already calmer.

TJ and Sally said their good-nights and logged off of their computers.

• • • • • • • • • • •

Jamie Stewart had an appointment at Westminster Woods with Sam, Joey D, Terry, Mark, and their wives. Lunch had already been served, so the dining hall was free for them to use for the meeting. It provided more privacy than the lounge.

She shook hands with each one. Sam introduced her to their attorney, Abraham David, who said, "It's a pleasure to meet you, Miss Stewart. Let's get this meeting started."

They all sat around a long wooden table. Miss Stewart started, "We all know why we're here. On our end, the offer is the same as before. Hugh's insurance company will cover all medical bills and we have made offers individually. We believe they were fair offers."

Attorney David cut in, "I told you on the telephone we want $4,000,000 each for Mr. Adams and Mr. Daniels, and $1,000,000 each for Mr. Miller and Mr. Brown. We also want Jacob Peachey taken care of too. We believe that Canadian Lumber never had a policy about driving while texting, driving while talking on the phone, and also operating a computer while driving. Because of this, they are just as much at fault as Mr. Lamadeleine.

"We're ready to go to court on this. The American public is not so happy with Mr. Lamadeleine or Canadian Lumber Inc. I also want a training plan put in effect by Canadian Lumber, so this never happens again. Trust me, the negative media coverage isn't something Canadian Lumber needs right now. Also, something else that has been brought to my attention; Mr. Lamadeleine sued the Commonwealth of Pennsylvania and he has every right to do that. But we are asking that he donate $25,000 out of his court winnings to every fire department that he put at risk with his irresponsible actions."

With that, Mr. David told his clients it was time to leave. Miss Stewart asked for some time to make a few phone calls.

"I'm alright with that. We'll wait outside."

Miss Stewart called them back into the room and waited for everyone to take their place at the table. She stood up and said, "My job as the mediator was to make a deal that all parties would be happy with. I have spoken to my clients and we have a new offer. We would offer $100,000 to be divided equally between all the fire departments that worked this accident scene. Jacob Peachey will receive $50,000. He has already agreed to this. Paula Brown will receive a total of $75,000 for her work with the fire department and her PTSD. Mr. Brown will receive $375,000 for his injuries. Mr. Miller will receive $500,000. Mr. Adams and Mr. Daniels will each receive $1,500,000. Mrs. Adams, Mrs. Daniels, and Mrs. Miller will each receive $50,000 for their anxieties and travel expense to see and take care of their husbands.

"I will step out now and let you discuss this with your clients, Mr. David. However, this is the final offer. If you don't accept today, it will be taken off the table and we will see you in court."

Mr. David said to his clients, "I believe this is a more than fair deal, but if we hold out for a while longer we might get more."

Hope said, "I don't know if everyone here would agree with me; but I feel like, as Christians, we shouldn't get greedy and wait for more. If it's a fair offer, then it's a fair offer."

They all agreed. Mr. David called Miss Stewart back into the room to tell her they accepted the deal. Miss Stewart stepped back outside and printed out documents from her laptop onto a printer in her car. She handed checks out to everyone. They were all surprised they received their checks so swiftly. Canadian Lumber Inc. paid Mr. David's attorney fees and the case was closed.

All parties were satisfied and happy. Joey D said, "I wish we could go celebrate somewhere, but Sam and I can't leave the nursing home."

"I know—I'll call over to Hoss's Steak and Seafood and order it for take-out. Then after we eat, I'll make a Dairy Queen run to get all of us some treats," offered Kelly.

After a delicious meal of rib eye steaks and tilapia, they wrote their Dairy Queen order on a list to make it easier for Kelly to remember. Good news, good food, and good friends—God had surely given them much to celebrate on this day.

• • • • • • • • • • •

The ship docked at Pier 12. The Sea and Anchor detail was secured and after the brow was put up to the Quarter Deck, the Captain announced Liberty Call. TJ picked up some classified paperwork that needed to be taken to CincLantFlt. He figured it gave him an excuse to see Sally, so he offered to hand deliver them. After an excited greeting, he and Sally made plans to go to Bayside Harley-Davidson where they were having a H.O.G. Chapter ride that evening.

When Sally got off duty, she went to her barracks room to change out of her uniform and into riding clothes. TJ went back to the ship to change out of his uniform and then they met for their ride. They arrived at the dealership where other H.O.G. members were gathering. About thirty or more already were there. The destination of the ride was for their evening meal at the Hampton Golden Corral on Mercury Blvd.

The employees at the dealership already knew that TJ and Sally got engaged on their ride, but the H.O.G. members did not. The Chapter Director went over to congratulate the couple. TJ had been a member of the chapter for a couple of years and was one of the chapter's Road Captains. A Road Captain would plan out the ride and then lead the riders in safety. One Road Captain would ride ahead of the group and then another would ride behind. On most chapter rides, such as this, the riders would split up in smaller groups of 5-8 in a group. This way it was safer going through intersections; it would also keep other vehicles from cutting into a long line, possibly causing an accident. A rider had to go through a Harley-Davidson training course and get certified before he could become a Road Captain.

There were ten people in TJ's group, including him and Sally. Everyone arrived there safely. After TJ said the blessing for the meal, they had a great time eating and talking. TJ then led the group of sailor H.O.G. members back to the base.

CHARLIE RESPONSE
CHAPTER TEN

Frank sat down and took a deep breath. He had just worked his twelve hour mid watch. Now, two hours later, he was sitting down to take his Petty Officer Second Class exam. He had used every available minute he had studying for this test. He felt prepared, but still nervous in the pit of his stomach.

The test was 175 questions. You were graded on how you scored against the rest of the sailors taking the test. However, you were not promoted by the test scores alone. You received points for your time in service, time in grade, and points from awards such as, medals or letters of commendation. These points were then added to the points from your test and points from your evaluations, or performance appraisals. When all the points were added together, you needed to exceed a previously determined number of points to be promoted.

A truly bad sailor would likely get a 2.8 evaluation score, but Frank had received a 4.0 on his Evals, the highest score possible. He knew that he also had three points from medals he had received, but he would lose points for time in service and time in grade. He would have to make this test count by getting as high a score as possible.

This test was a multiple choice test. Frank kept a tally of the answers he knew he had correct, answers he had guessed, and answers he had narrowed it down to two.

He believed he had 164 correct answers, leaving eleven that he either had narrowed down to two possibilities or had guessed outright. He figured that he had done pretty well on the test, so the only things that would hurt his chances now were his time in service and time in grade. Instead of worrying about things that were out of his control, he decided to get some sleep.

The USS Ronald Reagan was operating in the Arabian Sea. At any given moment, its jets could hit targets in Iraq, Afghanistan, Syria, Oman or Yemen. Both Russian and Iranian intelligence aircrafts attempt to fly near enough several times a week to check out the ship's defensive capabilities. When this happens, the USS Ronald Reagan would launch its fighter jets to intercept them, not only protecting its own ship, but the entire battle group.

Frank fell asleep as soon as he lay down. He slept through the launching of the F-18s alert. The Super Hornets were going to intercept a Russian intelligence aircraft.

Frank was awakened to the familiar sound of the buzzer from the bridge. Then the bridge announced, "General Quarters, General Quarters. All hands man your Battle Stations. Set Condition Zebra throughout the ship. All hands move up and forward on the starboard side and down and aft on the port side. All Battle Stations must be manned in five minutes. This is not a drill, this is not a drill. General Quarters, General Quarters. All hands man your Battle Stations."

The order *up and forward on the starboard side* means on the starboard side of the ship the crew will go up ladders and move forward to the front of the ship. The order to *move down and aft on the port side* means all ladders on the port side are to go down to the next deck, no one is allowed to go up. It is done this way so the crew would not be running into each other when trying to go up a ladder when everyone is coming down and vise a versa. There is a passageway that goes side to side through the ship so people can go from the starboard side to the port side.

Frank jumped out of his rack and put on his pants and boots. He did not bother lacing up his boots; he wrapped the shoe string around the boot and tied it. He grabbed his t-shirt and shirt, putting them on as he ran up the ladder to his work place, also his battle station.

When Frank came in through the doorway, he asked what was going on. The Leading Petty Officer CTN1 Dan Coates answered, "An IL-38 May took off from Yemen, heading our way. Then a second May took off. It's been years since two Mays have taken off and both headed our way. Captain Washington launched the alert F-18s. Now we have been told to send up half of our Fighters to intercept them. Hopefully, this is just one of those stupid stand downs, but our intercept people are getting all kinds of stuff. We're sending the messages on whatever they get. That's what's going on."

In the end, everything turned out okay. The recon planes were just gathering information that could be useful at a later date. Now they knew how the Navy ships would respond. However, the Navy learned how they react to things, as well. Captain Washington announced orders to secure from General Quarter once the aircraft left the area. The men raced out of their battle stations to the mess decks since they had been at their stations for five and a half hours. Frank hurried to the forward mess decks so he could get his food faster, he had to relieve the day shift soon.

· · · · · · · · · · · ·

The medical helicopter landed on the landing strip at Bethesda Naval Hospital. Captain Robert Casey was there waiting for his Navy Seal. Sammy was taken to his room and his Commanding Officer said, "I'm proud of you, Son. You take care and get better. I'll be around to see you. Your mother is outside waiting to see you. Bravo Zulu, Sailor!"

Hope came into the room, trying not to cry. She went over to hold his hand. Sammy said, "Don't cry, Mom, I'll be okay. Think of it as God's way of making me slow down. They brought me here to take out some shrapnel that the Army Hospital in Germany couldn't get out. Coming in, I went through the metal detectors and set them off. I guess I have that to look forward to the rest of my life."

Hope told him not to joke around, but she still laughed anyway.

Sammy asked about his dad and Hope said that he as well as expected. He was doing his physical therapy. Both legs were still in casts and would be for a while yet. Sammy asked about Joey D and the rest of their friends. Hope told him they are doing well too. She stroked Sammy's hand and said, "I know you must be tired after such a long flight. I'll let you get some rest and I'll be back in later."

"Thanks, Mom. I'll see you soon."

Sammy's doctor came into the waiting room to speak with Hope. He said, "It's been three days since Sammy's surgery. We know that you haven't been back to your husband for four days now. We believe that he needs you up there."

Shaking her head, Hope quickly rejected the idea of leaving Sammy, "My son needs me here, so here I stay."

"Let me finish. We're transferring him to the Altoona VA Medical Center. You'll be able to see both your son and your husband in the same day." Hope told him that was great news. The doctor continued, "We're flying him up by medical helicopter; he'll be checking in up there four hours from now. He already knows, so why don't you just pop in and tell him that you'll see him in Altoona."

Hope drove from Bethesda, Maryland to Altoona in the new car she bought just before going to Bethesda. When she arrived at the Altoona VA Medical Center, she saw that Sammy was already there and settled in a room. She fussed with his bedding and everything in his room, making everything just so.

When she finally settled down enough to sit and talk with him, she told him all about her new car. She had taken a photo of it with her iPhone and showed it to him. She told him all about the features it had, such as keyless entry and touch start, rain sensitive windshield wipers, back up camera, and blind side monitoring.

"It has heated and cooled leather seats, a dual-pane panoramic sunroof, and a media center with a voice activated GPS. You can also answer your phone through the media center. It really is a great car and bonus, I'm getting about 30mpg on the highway," gushed Hope, still going on about her new car.

"Yeah, I know the car. Some of the officers on the teams have bought that car for their wives. What happened? Did you win the lottery or something?" Sammy asked.

"In a way we did win the lottery."

Sammy exclaimed, "What?"

Hope told him about getting the settlement from the lawyers. He said, "Wow! That's great, Mom! I'm happy for you and Dad."

Hope told him, "Bad news though, a couple weeks ago our home was destroyed by a tornado. It's the second time the house has been in the path of destruction. First, Hurricane Katrina and this time, it was a tornado. Your dad and I have discussed things and we've decided to move away from hurricanes and tornadoes. We're giving you the land to do with as you please. You can sell it or build on it or even rent it out. Whatever you want, you can do it—no questions asked."

"Number one, I don't want to take your hard earned money. Number two, I don't think it's fair to Frank," argued Sammy.

"Don't worry about Frank. We're taking care of him. I talked to him on video chat and made him an offer. He's taking the money I offered and we're giving you the property. We got the insurance money from the house already; we got $150,000 for that. We gave your brother half of it and you get the property."

Sammy started to tell her again that he could not take their money, but Hope just cut him off. She told him the amount they received from the settlement. She told him they were giving him and Frank each a certain amount of the money and part of it would be going to their new church.

"We rode a lot of the roads around here and really love this area. We love the people around here; they don't get hurricanes very often; they don't have tornadoes. Winter can be bad, but most often, it's not too bad. We're happy here, so we've decided to find a place to buy in this area."

Sammy agreed with his mother that it was a good idea, "I'm so happy for you both. Have you thought about where to live?"

"Down in Shade Gap, there's a builder who's building a beautiful log home on 44 acres of grassland and timber. It has three bedrooms, three and a half bathrooms, a huge kitchen with a dining room, and a huge family room with a fireplace. We were told the deer and turkey hunting is great. It isn't quite finished, but that means we can have it finished to our taste. The builder also said he can make it completely wheelchair accessible for Dad while he recovers," explained Hope. "So, what do you think?"

"Did you go back home for your things in Mississippi?" asked Sammy.

"Kelly's son and son-in-law went down for me and salvaged what they could. They put everything in a storage locker in Shirleysburg; when we buy a place I'll go get the stuff out."

"Is this what you both want to do?"

Hope thought for a moment, and then answered, "Every couple talks about their dream home, and this would check off a lot of our boxes. We like being near Joey D and Kelly, and we like the other people in the Shade Gap area. I found a church that I like there, too."

"Then I'm happy for you! I love you both and want whatever makes you happiest," Sammy said.

"I'm going to do it. I'll call the builder tomorrow and tell him we're taking it and to make it ready for a wheelchair," decided Hope.

• • • • • • • • • • • •

Frank woke up to his LPO Dan Coates screaming, "Wake up, you slimy Pollywogs. Today, you become Shellbacks."

Sailors are called Pollywogs before they cross the equator. Once they cross the line, they become Shellbacks, if they go through the initiation. The Shellback initiation goes back for centuries. The Pollywogs are awakened around 4 a.m. They are led down to the mess decks and given green scrambled eggs for breakfast. (Food coloring at its best.) The Shellbacks pour hot sauce on the eggs while they are being eaten. During this time, the Shellbacks fly the Jolly Roger flag on the ship.

Later on in the day, when the ship crosses the equator is when the real initiation begins. Pollywogs have to wear their uniforms inside out and backwards. They have a large, red P painted on the front and back of their shirts. They have to crawl everywhere on their hands and knees. The ceremony takes place on the flight deck. The Shellbacks are dressed as pirates. They have homemade paddles with which to spank the Pollywogs, who have an obstacle type course they have to go through. The sailors crawl through a chute filled with garbage from the mess decks. Once out of the garbage chute, they are led over to the person playing King Neptune. He has lard all over his belly and a cherry in his belly button. The Pollywog is told to eat the cherry, but as he tries King Neptune grabs his face and rubs it over his lard filled belly. Everyone laughs at this. Then King Neptune shouts, "Get this Pollywog scum out of my presence."

At the end, the Pollywog climbs up a ladder and jumps into a large metal container filled with water. They have to swim underwater and come up at the other end. They are then asked what they are and they reply, "A Shellback, Sir!"

After going through the Shellback initiation, Frank went back to his bunk to get some sleep. When he finally got up, he went to supper and was happily surprised to find out they were serving T-bone steaks.

Later at work, Frank skyped his parents and told them about becoming a Shellback. His father, Sam, said, "Welcome into the brotherhood of King Neptune, Son. I remember how much fun it was for me when I went through it; but let me tell you, it's a lot more fun when you get to dish out the initiation."

· · · · · · · · · · · ·

On an impulse, Mark drove to M&S Harley-Davidson in Chambersburg. This used to be a favorite haunt of his—he was always dropping in for a part for his bike or a new t-shirt for his wife. Today, he just missed the feel of the place and wanted to walk around a bit.

As soon as he walked in the door, he saw it—frosted ivory and vintage gold paint with quartzite graphics, 110 cubic inch motor—the most beautiful CVO Screaming Eagle Road Glide he had ever seen.

The salesman walked over to Mark ready to make his sales pitch, but never had the chance.

"Work me up an out-the-door price. If you want to make a sale today, I'm ready to write a check today," he said, as he settled onto the seat. The salesman hurried off to get to work.

After Mark signed the papers, he decided to get new gear to go with the new ride. So he bought a new leather jacket, boots, gloves, and a couple of t-shirts.

He pulled his cell phone out of his pocket and dialed Terry's number. He could not wait to tell him about it; he also had a bit of information he wanted to pass on.

"Hey, Dude! I just bought a new Screaming Eagle Road Glide. It's so beautiful! I can't wait 'til you see it. I'm here at M&S in Chambersburg and you should see the bikes they have in stock here. I think you'll love the Screaming Eagle Ultras they have. One is Black Ember and Rio Red, but the other one is all you. It's Twilight Blue and Candy Cobalt with flame graphics," explained Mark, grinning like a kid in a candy store.

"They had one of those down here too, but it already sold. I want the blue one! Do you know what it costs?" Terry asked excitedly.

Mark put the salesman on the phone with Terry and the deal was worked out. Both men would be picking up their new motorcycles the following day.

The next day was Friday. Heidi and Terry took a half a day off from the NSA to drive to Chambersburg. They planned on spending the weekend with Mark and Paula. They would go pick up the bikes that day and on the next day they would ride to see Joey D and Sam and show them the new bikes.

When they went to pick up the bikes, they were surprised when the dealership gave them each new helmets with intercom systems. Papers were signed, license plates were transferred, and photos were taken to put on the wall of fame in the Harley-Davidson dealership.

As they were ready to leave, Mark shouted, "Man, it feels so good to get back in the saddle!"

"Yes, it does, Brother! Yes, it does! And I've got the appropriate song for this moment," said Terry as he slipped a CD into the stereo. *Back in the Saddle* by Aerosmith played loud enough for everyone in the shop to hear. Most of the people in the shop knew of the accident and gave them thumbs up. Only a true biker would know what it is like to be back in the saddle again.

Mark said to Terry and Heidi, "The H.O.G. Chapter is riding this evening to a little restaurant for supper. Do you want to go?"

"We do, if you do."

"We can ride over to our place, ditch the car, and then ride back to the dealership to show off our new bikes—I mean meet up with the Chapter and ride to eat."

When they got back to the dealership, everyone welcomed them back and congratulated them on their new bikes. The Chapter Director had the riders gather around for a prayer for safety. He said that after what happened to our brother Mark, he knew the safety prayers were very important. "Lord God, please be with us while we ride. Please grant us safety tonight. We give Thee thanks for the fellowship this evening and for the food we will receive. Thank you Lord, Amen."

The ride went well, the food was good, and the fellowship was nice. The ride back to Mark and Paula's was uneventful. The four of them got out cards and played Phase 10 long into the night. Life seemed to be getting back to normal.

The next morning, the women were the first to get up. They were planning to ride through the hills of the countryside before going to see their friends. When Heidi stepped out of the shower, the smell of homemade cinnamon rolls greeted her. Paula wanted to make even breakfast seem special.

When all had eaten their fill of delicious rolls, they readied themselves for the ride. Mark led the way, followed by Paula, and then Terry brought up the rear with Heidi on the back of his new bike.

They headed out of town and were soon enjoying the sweeping turns in the rolling hills of the countryside. They headed toward Allen's Valley Road, a motorcyclist's dream. Allen's Valley Road is a smoothly paved two lane highway with a labyrinth of over one hundred turns. The frequent sightings of whitetail deer are both a delight and a reason for caution. As they rode, Mark's voice would periodically come over the intercom, giving them the historical high points of the various places they went through.

"I was reading a book about this area the other day and it has some unique history. During the French and Indian War, the British officer, General Forbes, along with other officers, was building roads in this area. Can anyone guess who one of his aides was? Anyone have a guess? It was none other than our first president, George Washington.

"I also read something pertaining to Cowan Gap State Park, which we will be going through soon. In 1775, a Loyalist named John Cowan was in Boston and met Mary Mueller, who was a Patriot. Her parents forbade their marriage; so after the Revolutionary War ended, they eloped. A few years later, they were heading south to Kentucky when their wagon broke while crossing the Conococheaque Creek, which we just went by.

"John made a deal with the Tuscarora Chief, trading his horses and wagon for land, which is now called Cowan Gap. John and Mary Cowan received a peace pipe and tomahawk rites to the land. Three slashes were made in a tree to sow peace with the Tuscarora Indians. Now, the surrounding mountains are called the Tuscarora Mountains. I'll bet you'll never guess who they were named for."

Terry complimented Mark on his impressive command of history and made a mental note to send a few historical books to him for Christmas.

They rode to a Cowans Gap State Park in the Tuscarora Mountains and pulled into the parking lot. Terry exclaimed, "Wow! I never get tired of this ride and to think, there's more to come. I can't believe that on the weekend after Labor Day, hardly anyone is here. It's supposed to be really nice today too, up around 84 degrees."

"I grew up around here and I never will get tired of it. I guess we should get going though; I thought we could get something to eat here, but I see the stand is closed down already," said Mark.

They continued riding on Allen's Valley Road. The trees provided a beautiful canopy over the road and, on a hot day like this, nature's cool shade was much appreciated. At the end of Allen's Valley Road, they turned left onto Fannettsburg Pike to head toward the town of Burnt Cabins. They stopped at the Burnt Cabins Gristmill so Paula could get some buckwheat cake mix, which she loved.

Mark, being the historian of the group, explained the strange name of the town, "Native Americans once owned this land, but by 1750, eleven squatter cabins were on the Indian's land. The homes of these squatters were burnt by the provincial government to maintain peace with the Indians. In 1998, the entire village of Burnt Cabins, all 44 homes, was put on the National Register of Historical Places. Burnt Cabins Gristmill is also on the National Register of Historical Places. Paula loves their buckwheat cake mix, so that makes it famous enough for me."

They got back on their bikes and turned them toward Shade Gap and Huntingdon. When they passed the Shade Gap welcome sign, Mark gave another history lesson over the intercom.

"Now look ahead of us. Do you see the way the two ridges come toward each other? Don't you think that would be a great place for an ambush? It was—Native Americans would get the high ground on each side and ambush settlers as they passed through the valley. It became known as the Shadow of Death. Matthew 4:16 says, *The people living in darkness have seen a great light, on those living in the land of the shadow of death a light has dawned.* I'm pretty sure the Lord wasn't talking about Shade Gap, but it reminded me of it. Now it's known as Shade Valley for the shade it gives."

They rode on through small towns on their way toward Huntingdon. Heidi asked if they were planning to eat soon. Paula said that she was getting hungry too. Mark answered that there was a great place in Mill Creek called Topp's Diner and they could stop there, if everyone agreed.

They pulled their iron horses into the parking lot and walked inside the diner. The girls ordered grilled chicken salads for their lunch. Mark and Terry ordered Philly cheese steaks with sweet potato fries.

As they waited for their orders to come Terry commented how much he had enjoyed the ride so far. It had been too long for his peace of mind since he had been on a bike.

"I know what you mean, it's nice riding behind my hubby again," Paula said, as she smiled at the love of her life.

Heidi added, "This ride is nice. For some reason this new bike seems more comfortable than the old one. Also, those mini history lessons along the way have been interesting."

"Hey, you know how excited I get when I read new things. I just have to fit them into my everyday life somehow," protested Mark, knowing that he was being teased.

Everyone enjoyed their lunch and the company that came with good friends spending the day together. After leaving a generous tip for the waitress and paying their bill, they walked out into the sunlight and climbed back onto their motorcycles for the ride to Huntingdon to see Sam and Joey D.

They walked into the nursing home and were directed to the lounge where Sam, Hope, Joey D, and Kelly were watching the Penn State football game. After a warm greeting, Mark asked if they would all like to go outside with them. Mark wheeled Joey D out in his wheelchair and Terry wheeled out Sam. The girls followed behind.

"Wow! What beautiful bikes!" exclaimed Sam. This was definitely one of those moments when he wished he could get out of his wheelchair. He missed the free feeling of the wind in his face, the sun on his back, and even the ache in his shoulders from an all-day ride.

They stayed outside in the parking lot talking about the new bikes, the old bikes, and the mutual love for motorcycles they all shared.

"We wanted you both to see the bikes. We were hoping it would provide a little incentive in the physical therapy room," Terry said.

Mark added, "And we wanted to give you something to look forward to when you get out of this place."

Both Sam and Joey D expressed their gratitude for the men bringing the bikes for them to see. Then they went inside and had a very pleasant visit.

One of the nurses told them that if they took Cold Springs Road outside of Westminster Woods, it would lead them to Route 26. She said that Route 26 was a really nice road for a ride; her boyfriend took her for rides down that road. Since Penn State was playing an away game, the traffic would be non-existent, so today would be the perfect day to ride it.

When it was time to leave, they made a group decision to follow the nurse's advice and take Route 26. They had not been to #1 Cycle Center in State College in a long while, so they decided to ride with that destination in mind.

When they had been on Route 26 for just a few minutes, Terry said over the intercom, "Friends, I think we're in for a treat here." The road was smooth with great scenery; it had sweeping turns and twisty curves. It was the kind of road that bikers live for.

At one point, as they were riding past a dairy farm, they stopped to help the farmer get his cows off the road and back into the pasture. The farmer offered them money for helping him, but Mark told him to add a little extra to the offering plate at church and to say a prayer for them.

They had ridden through several state parks when Terry's voice came over the intercom and asked, "Is the entire state of Pennsylvania filled with state parks or is it just in this particular area?"

Mark told him that the Pennsylvania State Park system was the largest in America. Terry responded, "Wow, I believe that!"

At the top of a mountain, they pulled into an overlook to view the Jo Hays Vista Valley. It was a nice place to take some pictures of rolling hills and beautiful farm land. The pine trees left the air smelling of Christmastime. Heidi and Paula both agreed that it was a beautiful place. Heidi was thoughtful for a moment, and then said, "People who have never been to Pennsylvania would probably think of major cities, like Pittsburg or Philadelphia, but Pennsylvania has an awful lot of rural land too. I think we're looking at some of the best right here!"

Mark lectured, "Pennsylvania got its name from two parts. Sylvania means woods and Penn comes from William Penn. So, it means Penn's woods or, as we now know it, Pennsylvania."

"Time to get on the road before we get another history lesson," Terry laughed as he clapped Mark on the shoulder. "I'm just kidding, my friend. We really do need to get on the road, though, so we can get to the dealership before it closes."

Down the mountain they went with Mark leading the way. For safety, they all dropped into a lower gear because it was a steep road filled with sharp turns. At the bottom of the mountain was the intersection of Route 26 and Route 45, a featured ride in the Harley-Davidson Touring Handbook.

They followed the route that would take them to the #1 Cycle Center. They found the roads at this point to be smooth and mostly straight, bordering many farms. In what seemed like no time at all, they saw the Harley-Davidson Bar and Shield sign. Moments later, they turned into the parking lot and saw some buildings and a huge silver horse statue. They had arrived at their destination. As they put their jackets into their saddle bags, they all talked over each other remarking what a nice ride it had been. Then they went inside the dealership together.

Once inside, they noticed the building was divided into separate areas for the different departments: motorcycles, apparel, service, and parts. Upstairs on the second floor were areas for the local H.O.G. Chapter meetings, discount items, used motorcycles, and a refreshment area. As they walked around looking at everything, they saw a motorcycle on display that Evil Knievel used in one of his jumps. Talking among themselves, they decided that was pretty cool to see.

They walked around and bought some casual clothing. Mark saw a brown leather jacket and chaps set. He called Paula over and said, "Honey, I think this would go great with my new bike."

She agreed, but said, "Just two days ago you bought a new jacket."

Mark saw a guy going to purchase one just like his and asked what size he wore. They found they wore the same size and made a deal with him to buy the jacket from Mark for $75 less. Mark grinned at Paula and said, "See—problem solved." He picked up the brown leathers and headed for the cashier.

They walked around outside while a local customer and his wife showed them all the out buildings and other things. There was a pavilion with a fire pit and a building where they had nightly rentals and apartments. There was even a small race track at the bottom of the hill. They wandered over to the horse statue to get their pictures taken; first, a group photo and then a separate photo of each family together.

• • • • • • • • • • • •

Sara Jane and Victoria took Sally to the dress shop for the final fitting. Everything went well and the dresses were beautiful. Sara Jane said, "Let's do some celebrating this evening; let's go to Breezy Point Officers Club."

Sally did not really want to go there because she wanted to wait for a call from TJ. They reminded her that he was on OOD Watch (Officer of the Deck) until midnight and there would be no way he could call her until then. So they drove to the officer's club.

When they had arrived and were waiting for a table, Sara Jane complained impatiently, "Where's our table? There's nothing but a bunch of men in here."

The hostess arrived and escorted them to the banquet hall. Sally was busy taking off her jacket when they walked through the door, "Surprise!"

The room was full with over fifty women yelling and throwing confetti. It was Sally's bridal shower. So many women were there and Sally was so surprised, it took a few moments for her to realize that her mother, Cindy, and her sister, Soledad, were in the crowd.

The two sisters hugged each other. Sally asked how long she was home for. Soledad, a Navy nurse stationed in Georgia, answered, "I've got four weeks leave. I've got plenty of time to spend with you and the folks. I can come to this and your wedding, too. I'll even still be here after your honeymoon. I have time for all of it in one vacation. So, how have you been?"

"You don't even need to ask. I've never been happier in my life. I have a good Christian man that I'm going to marry soon. And apparently I have wonderful friends who have gotten much better at keeping secrets—I had no clue about today. There's nothing more I could want in my life; it's like I live in a fairytale," answered Sally, her face glowing.

Sally went around greeting and hugging everyone. She saw her Aunt Grace had come from South Carolina and her Aunt Polly had come from Ohio. She was grateful that she came from a family with such close bonds. Then she noticed her Grandma, Mary Morgan, who had flown in from Florida. The two of them lingered over their hug, "Grandma, it just wouldn't have been the same without you here. I'm so glad you came; you've always been there for me. I love you."

"I wouldn't have missed this for the world, Sweetie," replied her grandmother.

Cindy came to Sally and said, "Honey, I'm glad you're having such a great time. Grandma O'Malley couldn't come, because she isn't feeling well. She plans on being here for your wedding. She'll fly up from Sarasota."

After all the games and eating, it was time for Sally to open her presents and there were lots of them. Some were from people who could not make it for different reasons, so they mailed their gifts to Cindy, Sally's mother. There were some very nice gifts. Grandma Morgan gave her a nice sundress. She said that she could wear it anytime since, being in the Navy, she would always be around a beach somewhere.

While Sara Jane and Victoria cleared away the gifts and put them in the cars, Sally thanked everyone for coming and making this a special day for her. Grandma Morgan said, "The special day is coming soon—this was just a fun day!"

• • • • • • • • • • • •

The four friends left #1 Cycle Center with their saddle bags full of goodies. They decided to take a different route back. The day was sunny, crisp, and lightly breezy; just the kind of day motorcyclists love.

They had been riding for a while when Mark's voice came over the intercom, saying, "Do you see the stream on our left?"

They all replied in the affirmative. Mark then asked if they thought there was good fishing down there. Terry replied that maybe some small trout would be in the stream.

"You're right. This is a famous trout stream. A lot of brook, brown, and rainbow trout are caught here. President Jimmy Carter would fish here when he was the president. He stayed in a nearby farm house and wrote about the experience in a fishing book he wrote. I guess you all got another history lesson from me again," Mark said while laughing. They turned onto Route 22 and the road sign said it was William Penn Highway, which prompted Mark to ask if anyone knew who this was named after.

Teasingly, Heidi said, "Was it named after George Washington?" They all laughed at Heidi's joke.

The group decided to stop and get some supper and a room in a hotel. They were leaving early in the morning and it was already getting late. After they got a couple of rooms, they changed into some of the clothes they had bought at the Harley dealer earlier that day. They had a wonderful dinner at Woody's Bar-B-Q and headed back to their rooms, so full they even turned down dessert.

The next morning, they woke up, got ready, and checked out. They rode to Hoss's Steak and Seafood for their weekend breakfast buffet. After eating, they rode out to Westminster Woods to see Joey D and Sam.

They told Sam and Joey D about their ride and how nice the weather was. Mark said, "I thought about taking them to see the campus of Penn State, but with it being a football weekend I thought against it. I figured we could all ride up there sometime and show it to them, as well as going to the museum in Boalsburg."

"That sounds great!" agreed Joey D. "Hey, would you guys like to stick around and attend the Sunday service with us?"

They all agreed and headed into the chapel, pushing the wheelchairs ahead of them. After the service they said good-bye to the guys, saying they were going to Altoona to visit with Sammy in the VA hospital. Sam asked them to tell Sammy that he loves him and he's proud of him.

"Nothing would make me happier than delivering that message for you," said Terry.

At the VA hospital, the nurses allowed them to wheel Sammy out to the parking lot to see the new bikes. He said, "What beautiful bikes! I'm certainly not ready for one of these though; I think I'll stick to my Heritage."

After visiting for a while, Sammy said he was feeling a bit tired out, so the visitors decided to leave. Sammy told them of a restaurant not too far from there that they should try out. They headed to the Prime Sirloin Buffet and noticed that Apple Harley-Davidson was close by. They pulled into the parking lot and saw that the dealership was closed on Sundays, so they went to the restaurant.

After a really good meal, they headed back out on their motorcycles. They spent the day riding from one little town to the next on interesting roads that crisscrossed their way through the countryside. Much later in the afternoon, Mark said, "You all know we started our ride on Route 30, but now we are further west than where we started, even though we're now back on Route 30 again. Pretty soon we'll be heading over the tallest mountain yet. It's going to be fun!"

They passed by McConnellsburg as they glided through the wind toward some really nice twisty roads near Tuscarora Summit and Buchanan Summit. At the peak of one summit sat a restaurant that was used as the local hang out for riders. As they passed it, Mark told them, "I was going to pull in there for supper, but there are just too many people today. We'll continue on for now. Do you all want to stop at the Milky Way Restaurant in Ft. Loudon or ride the extra hour until we get to Chambersburg before we stop?"

All of them at once said, "Milky Way."

They made a left hand turn onto Route 75 and pulled into the Milky Way Restaurant parking lot. There were other motorcyclists there. Everyone was out enjoying the nice September day.

The waitress asked them what they wanted to drink. All four of them ordered water. When she brought four tall glasses of ice water and set the straws down for them, she asked if they were ready to order. They all ordered hamburgers and French fries.

While waiting for their food they talked to the other motorcyclists. They talked about all the rides they had done and those still on their wish list. The others were jealous of all the travels the four of them had done in the Navy. Mark invited them to join Chambersburg's H.O.G. Chapter and come to the next meeting.

They finished their meal and each had some soft serve ice cream. Heidi said, "I really like this place. The food is great, the service is great, and the atmosphere is outstanding. We can eat here anytime."

Everyone else agreed. They got on their bikes and rode the rest of the way to Chambersburg. Mark showed Terry how to get to I-81. Terry said, "I guess we kept Sheetz gas stations in business this weekend."

Everyone laughed and said they would see each other the next time. The next stop for the four of them would be their own homes and beds.

CHARLIE RESPONSE
CHAPTER ELEVEN

It was winter, but spring was in the air in Western Australia. The temperature during the day was in the mid-70s and the sun was shining. The USS Ronald Reagan was coming into port for much needed liberty for its crew in Fremantle and Perth.

When the ship anchored out in the harbor, the men left the ship by either the ship's launches or the two passenger ferry boats provided by the city of Perth. Not everyone went ashore right away however. One third of the crew would stay onboard to run the daily operations of the ship.

As the ship approached Fremantle, the crew manned the rails in their dress blue uniforms. The entire length of the ship was lined with sailors. It was an awesome sight to behold! A helicopter flew overhead and took a photograph of the ship with its crew on deck.

The Captain called out, "Set the special sea and anchor detail!" and the anchor dropped. The crew knew Liberty Call was near. For the past week, the crew thought this moment could not get there quick enough, but now the seconds seemed to drag even more slowly. Finally, the Captain said, "Secure from manning the rails."

The crew was so excited; they knew their time to go ashore was near. They went to their berthing to pack for liberty.

CTN1 Dan Coates came into the berthing and said, "Commander Brown wants to talk to us ASAP."

Dan Coates was not onboard when Frank went home on emergency leave, nor was he assigned to the ship when Frank returned. He had only been onboard for two months, but he already did not have a good opinion about Frank. He felt that Frank received too much attention and he wanted the attention all to himself; after all, he was the leading Petty Officer. He also did not like Frank because he was a handsome young man, tall and in good shape. Dan was short, overweight, and balding.

Up in the work space, the Commander said, "Everyone has been working hard for the past three months without any time off, and since we only stand comms watches, I came up with our own duty section watch relief. The ship says duty section relief is at 0700 each morning. I say relief is 0930. That way everyone will get an extra three hours of sleep when ashore. Petty Officer Coates, do you have the duty section made out?"

"Yes, Sir," responded Petty Officer Coates. He read out who was on which duty sections. Frank was on section one and Petty Officer Coates was on section six. He gave the import duty section list to the Lt. Commander, who turned it over to the Captain.

The Commanding Officer decides which section stands watch on any given day. Petty Officer Coates assumed that he would choose duty sections 1 and 2 the first day, 3 and 4 the second day, and 5 and 6 the third day.

Petty Officer Coates turned to Frank and sneered, "Boy, I really messed you over in this port!"

"So, what? Everyone has to stand the duty one day; who cares which day it is?" replied Frank, shrugging his shoulders.

Just then the Captain came over the ship's intercom and said, "I'm switching the in port duty section roster for this port. Duty sections 3 and 6 will have the duty today, duty sections 4 and 5 will have the duty tomorrow, and 1 and 2 will have the third day; then we will repeat."

Five minutes later, the ferry boats pulled alongside the USS Ronald Reagan and the Captain called out, "Liberty call for Officers and Chief Petty Officers will commence at this time." These are some of the sweetest and most anticipated words a sailor will hear onboard a ship.

Petty Officer Coates went to the Commander and said, "Wait, Sir, I have to change the duty roster. I need to put myself on section 1 and Frank on section 6. I'm meeting a girl on shore today."

"Sorry, no way. And if I hear you say one more word about it, I'll cancel your liberty for this port," said the Captain as he turned to walk away.

Frank grabbed his overnight bag, which was sitting on his berth already packed. The entire division had agreed to get rooms at the Kings Perth Hotel in the Perth city center. Finally, it was Frank's turn to go ashore. He made it to the Quarter Deck and said, "Request permission to go ashore, Sir."

The Officer of the Day looked over his uniform to make sure he was presentable to go ashore and then checked his military ID card and liberty card to make sure they matched. The OOD said, "Permission granted, Petty Officer. Stay safe and have fun."

On the ferry, the first mate offered free drinks, either soda or something harder. There were a few sailors that liked the free beer offer, so they stayed onboard drinking until they were drunk. However, the Captain would get angry and take away your liberty card for the day if you were caught. To Frank's way of thinking, it was certainly not worth the risk.

Frank ended up on a different ferry than his friends did, so he was by himself. Just in case something like this happened, they had all planned on meeting at the hotel at 6 p.m. Frank did not mind because he liked walking around by himself; it was a good way to explore and see Fremantle and Perth.

The ferry docked at Fleet Landing. People lined both sides of the red carpet walkway, waving both Australian and American flags, and shouting, "Welcome to our country!" The men would shake the hands of the sailors and the women would hug and kiss them. Frank thought to himself, *Now this is the way to be greeted when coming into a port!*

One of the Australian sailors ran up to Frank as he was walking through the crowd. "Are you Petty Officer Frank Adams? I've been watching for you, which was pretty hard in this crowd."

"Yes, I'm Frank Adams."

"My name is Petty Officer Mick Poxon; I'm from the HMAS Arunta," said the sailor.

Frank stopped walking and looked him, "Oh my goodness, it's so nice to finally meet you! We talk on the circuits all the time when we're sending messages back and forth."

Mick slapped Frank on the back and yelled, "Good to finally see you, Mate. Did you get your hotel room at the Kings Perth Hotel like I told you? This crowd's crazy! Let's get out of here."

Frank answered, "I got my room ordered through the ship's special services. It's so great to be here! Well, well, well—who are these pretty ladies?"

Two very pretty young women had walked up to them and were standing off to the side when Frank saw them. He instantly noticed the girl with the long, golden blonde hair and the large green eyes. Apparently not shy at all, she extended her hand to Frank and said, "So, you know Mick? My name's Sue Poxon. Mick is my big brother. This is my friend, Rose Wallace."

Mick, Frank, and the girls had been talking for a while when Seaman Dugan O'Reilly joined the small group. Dugan introduced himself to Mick, Sue, and Rose.

Sue asked Frank if he had any plans or if he'd like to grab some lunch. So it was decided that she would take the guys to the bank to exchange their money and they would grab lunch at the Sandrino Café before they headed to the hotel in Perth.

They had a great lunch of wood fired ham and pineapple pizza and Bianca sandwiches. The conversation was great and they learned a lot about each other. Frank liked the things he learned about Sue. She was close to her family, was a Christian, and was going for her BS in nursing. Frank had never felt as comfortable with any other girl as he already felt with Sue.

After lunch, Sue offered to drive them to the hotel in Perth. Along the way they discussed the sights Frank wanted to see while he was there. He wanted to pack in as much as he could in the time he had.

Sue said, "With my brother being in the Australian Navy, I know what it's like for a sailor to visit a foreign port and not know where to go or what to see. If you want, I could take you to a few places, if you would like to go with me?"

"I think I would love that. Not only seeing the sights, but also seeing more of you," smiled Frank as he entwined her fingers in his.

"So, where would you like to go first?"

"The hotel."

"Hey, I'm not that type of girl!" snapped Sue.

"Wait a minute! I want to go there so I can get my room and drop off my clothes!" laughed Frank, defending himself. "We can do whatever you want after that." Frank was pretty glad that Sue was not that kind of girl, but instead was the type of girl who valued herself.

Sue and Rose waited in the lobby of the hotel, as the boys checked in and went up to the rooms. They came back down and were happy the girls seemed eager to spend time with them. They headed for the car. Rose got in to drive and Frank said, "For once in your life Dugan, be smart, sit up front with her, so Sue and I can sit together."

They decided to go to Kings Park. On the drive Sue and Rose told them about the park and the things you could do there.

"It's a great place for long walks, picnics, and ceremonial events. Some people even choose to have their weddings there. This park is big, over six million people visit every year," Sue told them.

"Sometimes, I like to just go there to sit by myself and read a good book," said Rose.

"Me, too," agreed Sue. "It's nice to just be peaceful and watch the people seeing the sights. The sunsets can be great, too."

"I can't wait until we get there. It's on my list of things I wanted to do," said Frank.

Sue reached over to hold Frank's hand. Frank squeezed her hand and smiled.

"One of the things you'll want to see is the Memorial Project. This place has the most memorials in Australia. There are the State War Memorial Precinct, the 10th Light Horse Memorial, the 2/16 Battalion Memorial, and the list just goes on and on," explained Sue.

"I think you should be my tour guide. I do want to pay my respects to your memorials, but when we go I want to be wearing my uniform," said Frank.

They parked the car and went through the entrance to the park. Frank and Sue walked around holding each other's hand. Rose and Dugan went in another direction to be alone. Sue and Frank found a park bench and sat down. After a while, Sue noticed the pensive look on Frank's face.

"What's wrong?"

"Over 25 years ago, my dad's ship pulled in here. My mother flew over to meet him. Mom and Dad's best friends were here too. They loved it so much here. Dad told me the best thing about that particular cruise was Australia and the Australian people. Boy, was he right. I've only just met you today and I think you're the nicest person I've ever met."

Sue smiled as she asked, "Why would that make you sad?"

"It doesn't really. I was just thinking about my family." Frank told her about his dad's accident and recovery in the nursing home and about Sammy's accident and that he was in the VA hospital.

"So you see? I'm just feeling guilty about being so happy that I'm here with such a wonderful person, having such a great time and not being there to help take care of them," explained Frank.

"I see why you feel the way you do; you're very devoted to your family. It's one of the first things I picked up about you. You talk about them all the time and with such pride in your voice. Do you want me to take you back to your hotel? Wait, better yet—call them on my phone." Sue immediately reached into her bag to retrieve her mobile phone.

"No way! The charges for calling out of the country would be astronomical!"

"You just let me worry about that," reassured Sue.

Frank dialed and his mom answered. "Hello, Mom. I'm calling on my friend Sue's phone. I have you on speaker phone."

Sue yelled, "Hello, Frank's mom!"

"Frank, aren't you supposed to be in Australia?"

Frank told his mom he had landed in Australia that day and had met Sue, who was the sister of a friend. They talked about Sam's condition and Hope told Frank he was doing great and had come a long way toward recovery. After a few minutes, they expressed their love and said they would talk again soon. Frank hung up and handed the phone back to Sue.

"Thanks, Sue. That was a really nice thing you did."

"I know from Mick how hard it can be to be away from family."

Frank leaned forward and kissed her on the cheek. "That just won't do," said Sue, as she leaned forward and kissed Frank.

There was a smile on Frank's face as he looked into Sue's eyes. He took a deep breath and whispered, "I don't want to say this too fast and ruin things, but I already feel a very real connection between us that I think is worth exploring. I really would like to get to know you better. Do you feel the same or is it just me?"

"I never wanted to get involved with a sailor, but this little bit of time today was enough to convince me that I want more time to get to know you too," admitted Sue.

"I guess first things first. I'm a Christian. I know Jesus Christ as my Savior. I need to know what your beliefs are," questioned Frank, holding his breath.

With shining eyes, Sue assured him that she, too, had a deep personal relationship with Jesus. She told him that a missionary from Ft. Myers, Florida, had come knocking on their door one day and invited them to the Baptist Church on James Street. They went as a family and one by one, they had all come to know Christ.

They sat for so long, just talking, that they did not even get to see the park. Finally Sue asked Frank if he would like to go to Cottesloe Beach to watch the sunset with her.

"Whatever you want, you're the tour guide. Let's add another dimension though and grab some food to take with us. A picnic in the moonlight sounds pretty perfect," suggested Frank.

Sue called Rose on her phone and told her to meet them at the car in ten minutes. They dropped them off, picked up cheeseburgers, fries, and milkshakes, and headed for the beach.

There is something wonderful about wrapping your arms around someone special in the silvery moonlight and talking late into the night. It is the stuff that magic moments are made of. When Frank noticed that it was after 2 a.m. he suggested they needed to get going. Sue agreed and said that she should have been studying for a test she had coming up; but, oh, she was so glad that she had spent the evening this way instead.

Sue drove Frank back to the hotel. They kissed good night and she said she would be back at the hotel around 10 a.m. Frank said he would be waiting for her.

Frank tossed and turned all night; he just could not get his mind to shut down. Every time he tried to sleep, Sue would pop into his mind. When he finally was able to doze off, he was awakened by Dugan coming in very late and not very quietly. About 5:30, Frank finally gave up and got up. He answered some e-mails, posted some pictures, and wrote on his blog about his short time so far in Australia.

Sue found her mind wandering as she took her test. She told herself she must concentrate on the task at hand, but she could not stop thinking about Frank. She really liked this one; the only problem was that he was from another country. She wondered if she could leave her home for any man. Finally, she decided she was putting the cart before the horse. It would be best if she just put everything in God's hands. She knew He would always lead her where she was supposed to go. With a short prayer, she left it with God.

She finished her test before anyone else and turned in her paper. She drove to the Kings Perth Hotel. The front desk buzzed Frank's room, but no one was there. It was 9:30. Where could he be?

Frank finished eating breakfast, then went and bought a dozen roses for Sue. He saw her waiting in the lobby. He snuck up behind her and said, "Have you been waiting long?"

"Only my whole life," she said, hugging him.

They spent a wonderful day visiting the sights at Kings Park, where they took a guided tour. They went on the Bushland Nature Trail and to the State War Memorial. Frank was so moved by the memorials that he felt he needed to pray, "Father, we give thanks for such brave men.

We know that You welcomed them with open arms and that they heard, Well done, they faithful servant. We ask that You bless these grounds and everyone in them, together with their families. In Jesus name, we pray. Amen."

An employee of Kings Park said, "Thank you, sailor. That was beautiful."

After they walked on the Lotterywest Federation Walkway, they went to Stickybeaks Café to eat lunch. They were walking around Botanic Garden when Frank admitted, "I'm really enjoying my time with you. I like it, just the two of us alone. Just think—we have the whole day to ourselves."

"It's great, isn't it?"

"It sure is," said Frank, as he linked his fingers with her.

Later in the afternoon, they went to the Aquarium of Western Australia, reported to be the best aquarium in the world. On the way there, Sue explained to Frank that in the 1970s, Morris Kahn was diving with his son and his son ascended too quickly. Morris tried to stop him, but it still damaged his son's eardrums. While sitting on the beach, he thought what it would be like to never dive again. So in his mind he started to build Coral World, so people would never have to suffer from diving. They would be able to go underwater in a building or tube and look at the marine life. He built several Coral Worlds around the world. In 1991, Underwater World in Perth was purchased. On January 1, 2001, the aquarium was launched as The Aquarium of Western Australia (AQWA) to showcase marine life and the unique regions of Western Australia.

Frank really liked looking at all the sea creatures in AQWA. They had a good time. Sue said, "Do you see what time it is?"

Frank said, "I guess we better eat supper and then figure out what we're going to do for the rest of the evening."

Sue asked Frank if he would like to go on the Perth City of Lights Dinner Cruise on the Swan River. Frank said it sounded great. It was a beautiful evening; perfect for a dinner cruise. The twinkling stars intertwined with the city lights from Perth creating a breathtaking skyline. Frank took pictures of Sue, captivated by the sparkle in her eyes.

"I love the lights of Perth in the evening. This is the most romantic thing I've ever done in my life! The scenery is perfect, but it doesn't compare to the company," Frank said.

"Then why don't you do something about it?"

"Well, what do you want me to do?"

"This!" Sue leaned close to Frank and tenderly kissed him.

Wednesday morning finally rolled around, and with it came the time when Frank had to head back to the ship to do his duty. Sue drove him to the fleet landing. As he was heading out on the ferry, she called loudly, "Remember to keep it stiff and come knock me up tomorrow."

Frank's jaw dropped and some people on the ferry teased him. "Mr. Goody Two Shoes has got himself a wild woman."

An Australian deck hand on the ferry said, "Hold it, Mates. It's not what you think. The Sheila is old school British and Australian. Keep it stiff means to keep a stiff upper lip. Come knock me up means to come knock on my door."

Frank checked into work. He wondered what this duty day would bring. As it turned out, it was an uneventful day. Everyone was able to sleep in their racks in shifts. Some slept in their work chairs. Frank thought that 9:30 a.m. could not get there quick enough. He was not allowed to bring his laptop inside the workspace, but he was still able to send a couple of e-mails to Sue telling her that he was thinking about her.

Frank was upset. Everyone was relieved by the next shift except him. He sent the oncoming shift to look for Petty Officer Dan Coates. Frank walked out of the office to his berthing and retrieved his cell phone. He decided not to mind the overseas calling charges and he called Sue. He told her that his relief never showed up and he had to stay there until he was properly relieved by another CTN.

The noon meal was being served so Frank went down to eat. He heard rumors about Coates being drunk and staying at the Kings Perth Hotel. Frank called the hotel, but no one could find him. At this point in time, Frank had not reported Petty Officer Dan Coates for unauthorized absence. In fact, Frank was becoming worried. Notwithstanding the friction between him and Petty Officer Coates, it was unlike Coates to be UA. Frank started to wonder if something had happened to his shipmate. Finally, Frank called the ship's Master of Arms and told him that CTN1 Dan Coates was missing.

A message came in that there was a typhoon in the Indian Ocean. As of that time, the USS Ronald Reagan was on alert status. That meant they had to be ready to sail at a moment's notice. However, if the typhoon stayed in the north, then the ship would have to stay in port for six extra days. Frank mentally crossed all his fingers that the typhoon would just stay put.

Two days later, Lt. Commander Tom Brown came onboard. The Master of Arms had Coates in custody; the Shore Patrol had found him in a drunken state. Frank had never been relieved and was tired and angry. One of his fellow shipmates said, "You know, God is testing you. You need to forgive him. If you can, I'll bet the Lord will have something great in store for you."

"That's easier said than done, but you're right. I'll let it go," said Frank.

Frank called Sue on his cell phone, "Hello, gorgeous. I'm finally off and I get an extra day, too."

They arranged to meet in thirty minutes. They kept talking while Frank packed his bag. Sue said, "I can't wait to see you!"

"I know. Me too! I don't understand it. I've only known you for two days, but I think about you all the time," Frank told her.

"Well, hurry up, Sailor! I'll meet you at the Fleet Landing lickety split; then you won't be missing me anymore," joked Sue.

· · · · · · · · · · ·

Terry called Lt. Junior Grade John Beam, one of TJ's best friends. Terry said, "I've got the thirty football tickets for Saturday's game."

They had invited TJ's close friends from the ship, including Captain Baker, Commander Ruby, John Beam, and Tim Slaughter. Mark Brown would also be there—he loved all kinds of football.

The game was Navy against Georgia Southern. Captain Baker had the ship's bus take them all up to Maryland. This would not be your typical bachelor party. TJ's stance on alcohol was common knowledge. It would be a dry party, but a memorable one never the less.

As the bus wound its way through the eastern countryside, most of the sailors were singing Anchors Aweigh and other Navy songs. They pulled into the parking lot a couple of hours early and set up grills and picnic tables for tailgating.

During the game, the announcer came over the loudspeaker, "We would like to announce the upcoming nuptials of Lt. TJ Miller, former team member of the Naval Academy team and currently stationed on the USS George Bush. TJ is here with all of his bachelor party buddies. Stand up, gentlemen!"

The pro Navy crowd cheered.

The game ended with Navy winning 13–7. It was a very close game that could have gone either way.

When TJ made it back to the ship, he called Sally to let her know he had made it back safely. He told her about the day and said he would send pictures to her phone. They hung up after making plans to attend church together the next day.

CHARLIE RESPONSE
CHAPTER TWELVE

Frank greeted Sue with a big hug and kiss. He said, "I'm sorry about what happened yesterday; I was upset about the circumstances, but I'm over it now. I've got today and the next two days to play; then I have duty on Tuesday."

"Well, we can do whatever you want to do today, but I thought we could stay in Fremantle and go to the Fremantle Market. After that, we can go to the beach. Tomorrow is my graduation and my family is having a picnic get together at our place. Sunday morning is church, of course, but after that we could go to Adventure World or out on my dad's sailboat. It's all up to you, even though it doesn't sound like I'm giving you any choice here," said Sue, laughing as she realized she sounded like a dictator.

Frank agreed with the plans that Sue had put suggested. She added, "Dad said that if you agreed to come to my graduation, my party, and church that HE invited you to stay at our place. We have a guest room that you can stay in. I think this is going to be my best weekend ever!"

"I know this is the best time in my life and I see it only getting better," agreed Frank.

Sue pulled the car into the parking lot at the Fremantle Market. "This has more of a historical feel to it than Perth. What do you think about eating an early lunch?"

They eased their way over to Cicerello's Restaurant for some fish and chips. When they had filled themselves good food, they slowly walked around the market. Being partial to bookstores, Frank found himself browsing a bit in Elizabeth's Secondhand Bookshop and Magpie Books. He bought travel books about the various places in Australia and picked up a couple of books on sailing.

Sue spent a lot of time picking out fresh fruit. Frank liked watching her smelling this and thumping on that; it felt very domesticated to him. He could easily imagine, in the not too distant future, the two of them doing the grocery shopping together for their own home. It gave Frank a very pleasant feeling and he decided it was something he should think about further. He had never had these kinds of feeling about any girl before.

They spent a lovely afternoon wandering around the market and then they decided to visit the Maritime Museum. When they left there, Sue said that she had a surprise for Frank. He asked where they were going, but Sue was very secretive about it.

Frank was pretty surprised when they ended up at Hillary's Yacht Club in Perth. Sue took Frank's hand and they began walking down the pier. She told him all about the yacht club and then said, "Did you know that today is National Talk like a Pirate Day?"

"Really? How fun is that?"

They had come upon a beautiful sailboat named Flying Dutchman, when Sue surprised Frank by calling out, "Captain, oh captain! Request permission to come aboard."

A man came onto the deck of the boat from the cabin. He was barefoot, wearing a t-shirt and shorts. He had red hair and a red beard and was wearing a pirate bandanna.

"Arrrgh! Why do ye landlubbers want to come aboard me vessel? Are ye mates after me rum?"

Sue answered him saying, "Oh, fairest of Captains, we be mates and we have no need of yer rum, because we don't drink rum."

Sue was laughing pretty hard by this time. The Captain pulled out his saber and exclaimed, "Arrrgh, mates! Ye may come aboard me vessel of the seven seas, but if any funny stuff goes on I'll make ye walk the plank!"

"Oh fairest of Captains, this is the American sailor I've been telling you about. This is Petty Officer Frank Adams of the U.S. Navy. Frank, this scurvy pirate is Captain Henry Poxon, who is also me dad."

The two men shook hands and Frank said, "Captain, glad to meet you."

Henry replied, "Aye lad, glad to meet you; you may call me yer lordship. I'm only kidding, you can call me Henry. Would you like to see my vessel?"

"Of course. She looks like a fine boat from what I can see."

"That she is, mate. She has taken every nasty blow I've ever put her through. She sails well and is fast for her size. Would you like to take a look around?"

Henry and Frank wandered away talking about the boat and Sue realized she had been abandoned for the time being.

A lady came onboard and asked for help carrying the food. Sue introduced Frank to her mother, Emily Poxon. Emily said, "We've heard a lot about you, Frank. I'm so glad to meet you."

"I'm pleased to meet you too, Mrs. Poxon."

"Please, call me Emily," Sue's mom told Frank. Everyone went down to the car and grabbed a bag of food.

When they had put all the food into the galley, Emily told Sue and Frank that they, along with some friends, were going for an evening sail and would have supper when they dropped the anchor. She asked if they would be interested in joining them. They quickly agreed.

With Henry's instruction, Frank adjusted the genoa as they sailed down the Swan River. They talked along the way and got to know each other pretty well. Once they anchored, Frank was introduced to the other sailors joining in on this supper cruise. It was a beautiful evening, with a wonderful sunset. The sail back was just as beautiful—Frank loved seeing the city skyline. He took night time pictures of the city lights by balancing his camera on the boat and using a high ASA setting of 1600.

When they came in for the night, Sue showed Frank to his room and everyone went to bed early. It was going to be a big day for everyone the next day.

The graduation and the party went well. Frank felt as if he had known these people his whole life because they made him feel comfortable and welcome. The graduation party was at Cottesloe Beach. Everyone had a great time. Henry also taught Frank how to paddleboard. So it was another wonderful day for Sue and Frank.

The next day they went to church. Frank recognized some of the songs they sang. He told Mr. and Mrs. Poxon that his Baptist church in Mississippi used the same song book. There was a guest speaker, who was a missionary that his church in Mississippi also supported. Somehow these small facts made the United States feel not so far away.

They spent the rest of the day sailing on the Indian Ocean and enjoying the Lord's Day. Frank said how much he enjoyed the time on boat and just being with everyone. Henry gave him some lessons while they were on the boat. He went over the points of sail: Close Haul, Close Reach, Beam Reach, Broad Reach and Running. He taught him navigation, chart plotting and gave him lessons at the helm. Henry asked him if he had ever learned how to *heave to* and Frank said, "No." He told him that *heave to* would be used to stop the boat to eat, pick up a man overboard, or any other reason you might stop. He taught him how to set the asymmetrical spinnaker sail when they were running down wind. Henry said, "You'll probably forget all this, but I'm going to teach you anyway; you might remember some of it."

They made it back to the dock safe and sound. Back at the house, they saw that Mick was waiting for them. It was the first time they had seen him since the day Frank had docked. They talked for a while and then everyone headed to bed early to prepare for another big day. The whole family would be going to Adventure World together.

In the morning, they ate a hearty breakfast after saying grace. As they all loaded into the car, Emily checked to make sure they remembered to bring their yearly passes. After a pleasant ride, they finally arrived and walked across the parking lot to the entrance gate. They decided to ride the water rides later in the day when it was warmer, so their clothing would dry more quickly.

Henry challenged, "Let's see if the American can drive a race car."

They went to the Grand Prix Race Track and waited in line for their turn.

"In America, they don't make us wear helmets," Frank told them.

"Maybe that's why the insurance rates are so high, because of the law suits from all the injuries."

Frank thought about that for a moment and agreed, "You might have a good point there."

At the end of the race, Mick said, "You drive too much like a NASCAR driver. You bumped into everyone on the track."

Sue added, "I liked it; it helped me to win."

They raced three times and three times Sue won. Frank said he had the slowest car and that was the reason he had to bump his way through the field. Henry laughed at that and argued, "If you had the slowest car, you wouldn't have been able to bump people."

"Well, it wasn't fast enough to pass anyone," insisted Frank.

They rode a few thrill rides; ones that shot them up in the air and others that spun them in dizzying circles. They all agreed that they should ride the Rampage next, before finding some lunch to eat. The Rampage was the scariest ride there.

After riding it Frank confessed, "I'm sure glad we didn't eat before riding that!"

They chose to eat lunch at the pizza stand. After eating, they rode the Rail Rider, which is a ride where you peddle a two person car four meters above the ground all around the park. It is a peaceful and relaxing ride. Both Sue and Frank thought it was very romantic. Frank held Sue's hand the whole way.

"I really love this ride, because we have a chance to be together," he said to Sue. She leaned forward and kissed him, just at the place where the park's camera took a picture.

"Hey, Mate! I saw that!" yelled Mick.

"Me, too!" echoed Henry.

Emily consoled Frank, who was turning quite red in the face, "Frank, don't let those two get to you. It's not like they've never had a girl kiss them before."

Sue and Frank took the next ride on the Sky Lift; the rest of the family said they would meet them at the Power Surge. They settled into the seats for the ride. Frank wrapped his arms around Sue and whispered into her ear, "I'm going to remember this day forever." She turned to look in his eyes as he continued, "I know this sounds crazy; we've only known each other a few days, but I'm falling in love with you. I already can't imagine my life without you in it."

Sue hugged him and said quietly, "I've waited my whole life to hear that from someone who meant it. I know what you mean though, it is fast. I guess when you find the right one, it's obvious right away. I love you too, Frank."

They kissed and felt like they were floating over the park. They settled back to enjoy the view in each other's arms. Sue confided, "I already told my family that I thought you were the one for me. They said they had already noticed in the way I talked about you and the way we acted together. That's why Dad started teaching you about sailing already. He thinks you may be joining the family soon."

Her face became serious as she drew her brows together. "I have to talk to you about something. There are things about my family that I haven't told you yet. Dad was a businessman in Great Britain before we moved here. He's what you Americans call a day trader. He deals in the stock market and he's pretty good at it. We aren't super rich, but we can afford things."

She continued, "Dad bought into different internet companies when they were small and now they're not so small anymore. I've been fairly selective with whom I associate, because I didn't want anyone to take advantage of me for my parents' money."

"I can see your point there; but it's your parent's money, not yours. I recently came into some money myself and didn't tell anyone about it for the same reason. So, we each have access to sizable money and didn't tell each other, but have fallen in love anyway. I'm pretty secure in the knowledge that you don't love me for my money. How about you?" said Frank.

"I'm in complete agreement with you. You know, maybe Dad could help you invest your money in some low risk accounts, but enough talk about money for now. Today, let's just have some fun," answered Sue.

When they exited the ride, they linked hands and walked toward the Power Surge ride to meet Sue's family. The rest of the day was a blur of rides, food, and family fun. Frank had to admit he already felt like part of the family.

The next morning, Mick and Sue drove Frank back to Fleet Landing so he could work his duty day. As they all got out of the car, they heard gun fire. Frank yelled for them to take cover and they all hit the ground behind the car. When Frank peeked around the car to assess the situation, he saw a Fremantle Police officer lying on the ground.

He went running toward the officer and saw the gunshot wound in his chest. The officer was having trouble breathing. Frank rolled him over, knowing he would have to treat him for a sucking chest wound. "Mick, give me your ID card and call for an ambulance. Sue, do you have any tape?"

"There's some in my car."

"Run and get it!"

Frank put the ID card over the hole in the officer's back and taped it down securely. He took off his t-shirt and used it as a pressure dressing on the officer's chest.

He asked Sue to come over to him, "Honey, the gunman appears to have fled. I think Mick's chasing after him, so I think it's safe. I need you to take my driver's license down to the Shore Patrol and tell them what's going on. Otherwise, I may not be allowed back on shore; I'm obviously not going to make it back on the ship on time."

While Frank was still keeping direct pressure on the wound, the police arrived and took his statement. He would keep pressing on the wound until emergency personnel arrived. At some point, after the ambulance had taken away the downed officer, Frank's Commanding Officer, Captain Washington, arrived on the scene and saw Frank covered in blood.

Captain Washington told him he could go back to the ship and get cleaned up. He also told Frank that since he had taken over during Petty Officer Coates' missed duty, and since Coates was now confined to the ship, Frank could have the remainder of the time in port off. He would just need him to provide a phone number where he could be reached. Captain Washington looked at Frank sternly, "Be back on the ship at 0900 Monday. Don't make me come looking for you." Only the twinkle in the captain's eye gave Frank a clue that he was being teased.

Sue was happy for the extra time with Frank, so she waited for her hero boyfriend to return from the ship. When he finally stepped onto dry land again, the news media mobbed him for interviews. Frank gracefully deflected any praise for his actions, "I didn't do anything special. Any military man would have been qualified to do the same. I just happened to be in the right place at the right time. The real hero is the cop who was chasing the bad guy in the first place."

Because Frank was an American sailor and had been heroic in a foreign country, the news story made it back to the United States. Sam and Hope were bursting with pride when they saw it. The nurses at Westminster Woods said they must be special parents to raise two heroic sons.

Back at Sue's family home, they made a big deal out of it and had a special family dinner in honor of Frank's actions. When he offered to help with the dishes, Emily said that a hero should not have to scrub pots; but Frank told her his mother had raised him right, as he ran the hot water into the sink. She looked at him and thought to herself, *Yep, this one's a keeper. I'm so happy for Sue.*

The next morning, the family went sailing to Rottnest Island. Frank had his camera in his hand the whole day, taking pictures of the wildlife and Sue's family on the beaches; but his favorite subject to photograph was Sue—Sue on the beach, Sue with the flaming sunset behind her, Sue looking at the old shipwreck on the island, and Sue on the boat.

He was flipping through the pictures he had taken that day while they were all eating dinner. He saw a picture of an animal he did not recognize and asked Henry about it. "Oh, that's a quokka. It's a marsupial and pretty friendly. There was a Dutch explorer that came to the island and saw these animals that he thought were really large rats. So he named the island Rottnest, meaning rat's nest. What he really saw though was the quokka. Just a little history lesson for you."

When everyone was finished eating, Frank again filled the sink with hot water to wash the dishes. Emily told him to sit back down; she did not expect guests to do dishes. But Frank said, "My mother had a rule for us kids; if you didn't help prepare dinner, then you helped clean up." He leaned down and loudly whispered, "Besides, I'm trying to impress your daughter."

"There's no need for that. I'm pretty much already impressed," laughed Sue.

The next day they had a great sail back. Henry had Frank take the helm to teach him how to fall off the wind and get back on course. Then he had Emily take the helm.

"I want you to stand up here in the middle of the boat. Do you feel the wind?"

Frank lifted his face to the wind and said, "Yes, I feel it."

Henry said, "Good. Now hold onto the shroud and walk between the headsail and main. Tell me if you feel any difference in the wind."

Frank grabbed a hold of the shroud, walked around, and exclaimed, "WOW! I can hardly hang on!"

Henry lectured, "We call that area the Slot. Now, I want you to take the helm again. We are in 12 to 14 knots wind. Do you notice where we are heading now—how the bow wants to head towards the wind?"

"Yes Sir."

Henry looked pleased, "Good, you're learning."

The sailing lesson continued all the way back to Hillary's Yacht Club. Frank jumped onto the dock and handled the lines with ease.

"Good work, mate! I'll make a sailor out of you yet. Come back onboard and get dressed. We're going to eat in the clubhouse tonight."

Later that evening, Frank sat on Sue's porch swing alone. Henry walked over and asked if anything was wrong. Frank told him that he felt the Lord was leading him in an unexpected direction and he was just having a conversation with God about his anxieties. Henry sat down and asked Frank if he needed any advice.

"My whole life I've planned things out well in advance. That's just the way I've always handled my life. And then I met Sue. I feel like my heart has spun upside down and sideways in just a few days. I know that I love her and I can't imagine my life without her in it anymore. It just feels so fast and unexpected. I'm already at the place that I want to plan our future together. I know this is going to sound too fast for you, but I want to ask Sue to be my wife. I've been praying for guidance and I believe this is the path that God has set for the two of us," explained Frank, holding his breath at the end, expecting Henry to object.

Henry sat quietly for a few minutes just looking at the birds in the trees. Finally, he spoke, "Frank, I really like you and I know that you have a special relationship with God. Emily and I have spoken about this and we realized this was coming soon, not this soon, but soon enough. Emily and I would be honored to have you as our son-in-law, but we would like it if you took your time getting married."

"That actually works out perfectly. I can't get married right away due to being on the ship. I'll be transferred to a shore site in a year— that's when I'd like to get married," Frank informed him.

"Unfortunately, right now you're talking to the wrong person," teased Henry. "Maybe you should talk to Sue."

"Would you mind taking me into town tomorrow? I have a few things I need to organize and a ring to buy."

The next day, the family went to the beach for a fun afternoon, followed up with a bonfire on the beach. Frank pulled out some chocolate covered strawberries that he had gotten for Sue. "I have something for you," he said, handing her the box.

"Oh, I love these!" As she spoke, Sue looked up in the sky as she heard the drone of a small plane. The plane was pulling a long, yellow banner and she squinted to read the words. "Will...you...marry...me... Sue?" She gasped as she looked back at Frank, now down on one knee.

Holding the emerald cut diamond ring nestled in the velvet box out to Sue, Frank felt his heart pounding as he waited for an answer. He didn't have long to wait though.

"YES!" she cried and hugged him. Crying tears of happiness, she showed her mother the ring and they jumped for joy.

Later that evening, Sue called her friend, Rose, on her cell phone to tell her of the engagement. Rose told her that she and Dugan had run off and gotten married the second day they were together.

"Dugan is going AWOL. He went to the ship, got his clothes, and isn't going back. He's already got a job and everything," said Rose.

"Rose, that's stupid! Don't you know if he's caught he will go to jail for years?"

"That's a chance we're willing to take," snapped Rose.

On Saturday, Sue, Frank, and Henry went sightseeing on the motorcycles. They had a great time showing Frank around the countryside. Henry asked Frank how he liked the ride so far. He answered, "It's just so awesome. I have so many pictures. No one will believe I did all this until I show them all the pictures. I can never repay you for everything you've done for me. You've shown me so much, given me the time of my life, and most of all, given me your daughter's hand in marriage."

Emily had dinner ready by the time they returned. Over the hot, homey meal, they all discussed what to do the next day—Frank's last day in Australia. "First and foremost, we all need to go to church, of course. After that, though, I just really want to spend time with Sue. We can do whatever she wants to do," remarked Frank.

"Oh, my! We forgot to take Frank to the Perth Zoo! We could do that after Sunday dinner tomorrow," exclaimed Sue.

"Sounds fine to me. Maybe I can visit my relatives in the monkey cages," joked Frank.

After supper Sue and Frank took a walk around the city, holding hands. Sue asked if Frank was going to tell his parents or would they tell them together. Frank said, "I have a good idea! Let's go on Skype and tell them together. We can introduce our parents, too."

They got online and managed to get a connection with Sam and Hope at the nursing home. Frank introduced Sue and everyone. He told his parents how nice the Poxons had been to him. He told them all about the different adventures he had enjoyed since he had been there. Finally, he told them all about Sue and how much he loved her. Sue interrupted Frank and held up her left hand, "Frank, you sure do go about things the long way around, don't you? Mr. and Mrs. Adams, Frank asked me to marry him. I'm very excited about joining your family and I can't wait to meet you some day."

Congratulations were freely given and Sam and Hope seemed very excited. They briefly discussed the plans that two young adults had for their wedding so far. Frank told them it would not be for at least a year.

"That gives me extra incentive to get better. Frank, TJ's getting married next weekend. They're getting married on base and having a full military wedding in the Norfolk Base Chapel," said Sam.

They talked for a while longer and then said their good-byes.

The next morning at church, Sue showed everyone her diamond engagement ring. The pastor announced the engagement from the pulpit and said, "Our little Sue has grown up." He said a special prayer for the young couple and wished them a long, happy life together.

They spent the afternoon at the Perth Zoo and had a good time, but that evening everyone seemed to be down. They knew it would be the last time they were together for quite a while. Frank and Sue spent their time sitting on the porch swing or walking outside. Sue cried a lot.

The next morning, they ate breakfast together. They debated who should take Frank back to the docks. Frank settled it himself, "Please, everyone come. I don't want Sue to have to drive herself home. She'll be too upset and I'll worry."

They loaded up the car with Frank's belongings. Sue cried all the way to Fleet Landing. Henry felt bad that his daughter was hurting. He wished he could take the hurt away for her, but he also knew she needed to learn to lean on God in tough times.

They pulled into the parking lot at 8 a.m. Sue walked with Frank to the docks. They held each other tightly until the ferry came to take Frank away. Frank held Sue's hand and prayed, "Dear God, I'm leaving this woman that I love completely in Your hands. I trust You to keep her safe and sound for me. Be with her in the near future; she's going to need You to calm her fears when she worries and when she's lonely. I'll be a great distance away from her, but You will always be right there with her. Help her to remember that. Thank You for bringing her into my life. In Jesus name, Amen."

As the boat pulled away, Frank felt the tears coursing down his cheeks and was glad that Sue could not see him cry. It would only upset her more. He thought to himself this was harder than leaving for boot camp or deployment. It was the hardest thing he had experienced yet.

When Sue and her parents arrived home, they saw that Frank had left roses and cards for them. Emily opened their card and saw that it was a thank you card. Inside was a gift certificate for the yacht club. Frank had written, *Think of me when you have this meal.*

Sue opened her card and a handful of pictures of herself and Frank fell out. On her card Frank had written, *Think of me whenever you look at these. LOVE YOU FOREVER!*

Sue fell to her knees and wept.

CHARLIE RESPONSE
CHAPTER THIRTEEN

Hope and Kelly drove to Altoona to pick up the recently released Sammy from the VA hospital. The next morning they would drive over to Chambersburg to meet Paula and Mark, who were going to ride their motorcycles to meet up with Terry and Heidi. Mark loaded their luggage into Kelly's car and away they all went.

Heidi had lunch ready for everyone so they would not have to make a stop on the way to Virginia. Everyone was excited; it was not often they had such a happy occasion to celebrate. Heidi and Terry's son was getting married and it was the topic of conversation at lunch. What would the chapel look like? Had Heidi seen the bride's dress? Was TJ nervous?

After lunch, it was time to get on the road. Terry was going to ride his Screaming Eagle Ultra Glide with Paula and Mark. Heidi decided to drive her Lincoln MKZ though, because she was concerned about their clothing getting ruined in the saddle bags of the bikes. TJ was their only son, in fact their only child, and she wanted to look her best for his wedding.

The small convoy pulled onto Route 29 and Terry took the lead. They were happy to be ahead of the rush hour traffic. Traffic around them was speeding along at around 75 mph, but they held steady at 65 mph. "No need to get a ticket or get into an accident before we get there. Slow and steady wins the race," said Terry. Everyone agreed with him.

It seemed like no time at all before they were on the bypass around Richmond, Virginia. Just a short time later, they went through the Hampton Bay Bridge Tunnel and could see the Norfolk Naval Base. They all followed Terry to the hotel where TJ had reserved their rooms. They planned to unload all the luggage and freshen up before they went to meet TJ.

The girls were impressed with the rooms, which had been recently updated and were quite comfortable. Hope gently bounced on her bed, testing the firmness. The rooms that TJ had reserved were all near one another, so it was easy to visit from room to room. TJ had told them to come over to the ship and he would give them a tour before they went to the wedding rehearsal and rehearsal dinner.

When they arrived at Pier 12, they called TJ who went to the ship's Brow Watch to let him know to let them up to the Quarter Deck. They all stopped midway up the brow, faced aft, and put their hand over their heart. Sammy rendered a hand salute. At the Quarter Deck they all said, "Request permission to come aboard, Sir."

"Come aboard," he answered and gave them each a visitor's pass.

TJ met them and showed them around the massive aircraft carrier. The first place he took them was the hangar deck and from there to his stateroom that he shared with his roommate. When he took them to his workspace, the Ship's Signal Exploitation Space, they were very impressed. This is where all the Cryptologic Technicians work. Since they had all held the same position in the Navy, they were very interested in seeing this part of the ship.

"I know Joey D and Sam would have really enjoyed seeing this part of the ship; but like us, they would have been lost with all this new equipment," said Hope, in awe of the recent technology.

Sammy commented, "Maybe when Frank comes back from his cruise, he could give them a tour of the Reagan."

TJ called from the SSES over the 1MC to ask if the Captain was on the Bridge and ready for them. He was given an affirmative answer and they went to the Bridge to meet the Captain, where he personally gave them a tour of his Bridge.

The Captain told Hope how much he thought of her son, adding that he was a great Division Officer whose men respected him. "Thank you, Sir. That means a lot coming from his Commanding Officer," said Hope, very pleased.

They chatted for a few more minutes, then Hope thanked the Captain for the great honor of giving them his time. She said they needed to think about getting ready for the wedding rehearsal. Hope shook the Captain's hand and smiled warmly at him, saying that she looked forward to seeing him at the wedding.

They drove to the Norfolk Naval Base Chapel for the wedding rehearsal. RP1 Ben Long and RPSN Dawn Fetters greeted them and told them they were the first to arrive. They went inside and sat down in the chapel to wait for everyone else.

Sally's parents came in with Sally and her sister, Soledad. They were closely followed by Sally's friends, Victoria, Cassie, and Yu.

People filtered in and started milling about, talking to one another. Some were TJ's friends and some were Sally's. There were a great many introductions going on. Relatives and friends mingled and talked, teased and got to know each other. Snippets of conversations could be heard over the general din from time to time.

"Hey, Half Witt finally made it somewhere on time. Thanks for coming, Buddy," TJ joked with his friend, Lt. Doug Witt.

"Thanks for asking me to be in your wedding. This is going to be so fun!"

Sally's cousin, Fiona, walked in. Sally rushed over and gave her a big hug. "Fiona, thank you for coming." After catching up for a few minutes, Sally said, "Fiona, remember when we would sit on your bed and plan our weddings together? Not one of those plans looked anything like this, did it?"

"Nope, but none of those plans had you marrying a handsome officer in the Navy either. TJ sounds like a good man. I'm so happy for you," Fiona answered, squeezing Sally in a tight hug.

Sally asked Fiona how she liked her duty station. She said, "You wouldn't believe what it's like being a female officer onboard a ship. I thought I wouldn't get any respect, but I do. Both the enlisted and the officers aboard respect me and I'm grateful for that."

"You're stationed out of Mayport, Florida, right?"

"Yes, I am."

"Did you know my sister, Soledad, is stationed near you at Kings Bay Naval Sub Base in Kingsland, Georgia? She's a Navy nurse there."

"No way! I didn't know that she was that close. We'll have to get together while we're down there," Fiona exclaimed.

Kelly's daughter, Tracy and her husband, Rich, arrived in the midst of the general chaos. Tracy had their new son, Richard Daniels, in her arms and Rich had five year old, Peggy Sue, by the hand. TJ introduced Sally to Peggy Sue, their flower girl, and her parents. He told her that he and Tracy had grown up with each other as Navy brats. Sally said, "I'm pleased to meet you. You have such a sweet baby. Can I hold him?"

"Oh, sure. Go right ahead. Anyone that can put up with TJ has to be a good person. You must be a really special girl to land him, because the other ten girls he asked to marry him didn't work out. He always backed out in the end."

"What!?!"

Tracy doubled over laughing, "I'm only kidding! TJ played the same joke on Rich and I told him I would get him back someday. So make sure you talk to him about paybacks."

Sally laughed along with Tracy. "Okay, I will." She decided this was a girl she could really get along with.

As if Tracy read her mind, she said, "I really would like to get to know you better. You and TJ have a permanent invitation to come to the farm anytime you want to."

"You better be careful, because we just might take you up on your offer."

The last people to arrive were Todd Daniels and his wife Bobbie Jo. Their son, Joseph, was going to be the ring bearer. TJ introduced them to Sally, and Todd also invited them to come for a visit.

"We were such close friends when we were growing up and we've kept in touch throughout the years. I hope and pray that we never lose track of each other," said Todd.

"We just won't let that happen. I grew up in a Navy family, too. I know how important friends and family are. I'll give you my Facebook information and my e-mail address and we can all stay in touch," Sally reassured him.

It was then that Dawn came to them and said, "Chaplains Ruby and Henderson are ready to begin. We need to go inside."

Chaplain Henderson handed out programs to everyone who was involved in the ceremony. They all went through the different portions of the wedding, practicing until each one was confident in their task at hand.

At the end of the rehearsal, they were directed to the Vista Point Center where the Millers were holding the rehearsal dinner. TJ had set the whole thing up when he made the reception plans. For dinner they were serving barbecue wings, hamburgers, and hotdogs with all the fixings. Potato salad, cole slaw, and macaroni salad, followed by cake and fruit salad rounded out the meal.

Chaplain Ruby gave the blessing and then said that Terry Miller wanted to say a few words. Terry stood up, "I want to thank everyone for coming this evening. Normally, rehearsal dinners are for the family and those who are part of the wedding party. However, we chose to do things a little differently. We invited the friends and co-workers of TJ and Sally, so you could all get to know us and we get to know you too. It's nice to put faces to some of the names I hear all the time. You're all a big part of our children's lives; I wanted to get to meet you tonight, because tomorrow will be hectic and we might not get the chance then.

"Some of you may not know this, but TJ comes from a Navy family. We were from the enlisted ranks as Cryptologic Technicians. All of his friends growing up were the sons and daughters of CTs. He studied hard and worked hard to get to where he is and we're very proud of him. We're very happy that he is marrying such a wonderful girl as Sally. She comes from a good family. I hope and pray that we will become one seamlessly blended family. We come from humble beginnings and we used the Navy as a stepping-stone to get ahead in life. We like adventure, so we ride motorcycles and we also like to go sailing. The Navy has always been a very big part of our lives and always will be. With that being said, the biggest part of our lives has always been our only son, TJ—we're not losing a son, we're gaining a daughter. Welcome to the family, Sally."

Sally's father, Captain James Morgan shook Terry's hand and said, "Thank you for throwing the perfect rehearsal dinner. I like that it's casual and comfortable, making it easy to mingle and get to know everyone better. Leave the formal stuff for tomorrow, I say."

"Thank you, Sir."

"Please, don't call me *sir*. We're going to be family now, just call me James. I agree with you in the hopes that our families will be close. Who knows? We may be sharing grandchildren in the near future.

"You know, I like sailing, too. Someday, we should rent a boat and go sailing together with our wives. The Norfolk Naval Base Special Services rents sailboats just a few blocks from here."

"I'd like that. I'm going to the Annapolis Boat Show in a few weeks with the intention of buying a sailboat. You could come with me, if you'd like. I'm thinking of buying a 32 to 36 foot Catalina," replied Terry.

"You know, that actually sounds like fun. Let me know the details. I'll drive up and we can make a day of it. Thanks for the invite. By the way, the sailboats that the Navy has for rentals are Catalinas. I've heard they're pretty good."

Everyone was enjoying the get together and the food. TJ walked over to Sally's father and asked, "Sir, are you getting enough to eat? Can I get you anything?"

Sally's father answered, "I'm fine TJ, just fine. I'm enjoying a nice conversation with your father. We're making plans to get together in a few weeks."

Sally and TJ were trying to make sure they spent some time with each of their guests. Sally walked over to her Grandma Mary Morgan and hugged her. "I'm so glad you were able to come, Grandma. Are you enjoying yourself?"

"Of course, I am, Dear. I'm so happy for you. Just look at all the family members and friends that came for you; you're so lucky to have so many people that love you. You have a wonderful, caring man in TJ and I hope the two of you have many years of happiness," Grandma Morgan answered, holding Sally close.

"Oh, thank you, Grandma," Sally said, with tears in her eyes. Her emotions were getting the best of her. "I better go fix my mascara. I love you so much, Grandma."

Sally excused herself and made her way to the ladies room. She fixed her make-up and spent a few moments getting herself under control.

On her way out of the ladies room, Sally ran into her other grandmother, who gave her a lot of advice on how to keep her man happy and her marriage running smoothly. After a few moments, Soledad and Fiona joined them.

Soledad and Fiona talked about how close the bases they worked at were to each other. They exchanged cell phone numbers and e-mail addresses so they could stay in closer contact. Lt. Doug Witt overheard them talking and said that he, too, was stationed at Kings Bay Sub Base. He was on the submarine USS Florida SSGN-728. He asked if they would exchange e-mail addresses and Facebook information with him, too. Both girls agreed and included their cell phone numbers. They talked for a while and got to know each other. Doug told them he liked to ride his Harley, go sailing, fishing, camping, hiking, and paddle boarding.

Soledad told him about the dangers of motorcycling. Doug said, "You should talk to TJ's dad about that. His two best friends aren't able to be here, because a truck driver hit them. Terry was injured, as well, and so was his friend, Mark, over there. I'm aware that people get injured and even killed on bikes all the time, but so do people in cars and trucks. If you respect the bike and follow the rules of the roads, the odds are in your favor. Your sister loves it; she took the Harley Riders Edge Beginners Class before she started riding. TJ could take you for a ride or even I could take you. Fiona, that goes for you too; I'll take you for a ride if you want."

"I would like that. When we get back home, I'll call you and we can set something up."

Eventually, people started drifting out, heading for wherever they were calling home for the night. TJ and Sally stood at the exit, thanking everyone for coming. TJ went back to his ship and Sally went to stay with her family at home, instead of going back to the barracks.

Around 3 a.m. Soledad noticed that Sally was not in bed, so she got up to look for her. She found her on Facebook, playing games. Sally said she was so anxious she could not sleep. Soledad fixed them hot chocolate and they dipped chocolate chip cookies in it and talked until Sally finally felt like she could sleep.

Sally was not the only one having a difficult night. At four in the morning, TJ was still wide awake, worrying. Would he hear the alarm in the morning or would he sleep through it? Sally had teased him earlier that if he was late for the wedding, she would not wait for him and he would not get a second chance. What if she meant it?

TJ was so anxious that he tried to calm his nerves by taking a walk on the flight deck. He walked up to the bow and sat down with his feet dangling over the side. He promptly fell asleep there.

At 0655, Captain Baker yelled on the ship's intercom, "Will the drunk asleep on the bow of my ship wake up and report to me ASAP!"

TJ woke up and ran down to his Division for morning muster and told them he had to go to the CO's and would explain later. He knocked on the Captain's door and heard, "Enter."

TJ entered and the CO said, "State your business, Lieutenant."

"I'm here because you called for me."

"I didn't call for you. Someone is playing a wedding day prank on you. I'm waiting for a drunken sailor who was sitting on the bow of my ship. You're relieved, Lt. Miller."

TJ looked down at his shoes, unable to believe that on his wedding day, he had gotten himself into trouble. "I'm sorry, Sir. That sailor was neither drinking nor was he drunk."

Captain Baker stared at TJ for a moment and said, "And you know this how?"

TJ took a deep breath and replied, "Because he is me. I couldn't sleep and went out for a walk around 0400. I sat down to watch the tide roll in and fell asleep."

For a split second there was absolute silence and then the Captain started laughing and said, "I think I've heard it all now. It's a wonder you didn't fall overboard. That would have been some wake up call." The Captain shook his head, still laughing and added, "You better start getting ready for your wedding, Mr. Miller. I'll see you there. Don't worry about anything; you're not in any trouble for this morning. You're excused."

"Thank you, Sir."

TJ mustered his men and then went down for breakfast in the crew's chow hall. He ate a few doughnuts and drank some coffee. Since nothing was really going on, he went to his stateroom to shower and shave. He got dressed and went to pick up his leave papers. TJ went back to his Division and reminded them to be at the chapel before 1300.

Sally woke up feeling a little groggy after her sleepless night. She ate a light breakfast and went into work. She asked again if everyone was coming to her wedding. The Department Head told her the office was shutting down at 1100 so everyone could go home and get ready. They would all meet at the base chapel at 1245 to see Sally tie the knot. Sally picked up her leave papers and drove back to her parent's home to start getting ready for her big day. Time was drawing near.

In her old room at her parent's house, Sally had plenty of help getting ready. Aunt Grace, Aunt Polly, and her mother were all helping with her hair, makeup, and dress. It was a very special time for Sally; she knew she would never forget the advice given to her from these very special women in her life.

All morning long, Sally's father spent his time polishing his sword and shining his shoes. He made sure that Grandma Morgan and Grandma O'Malley were both ready and then went to get Sally. "T-minus now! It's time to go!" he yelled through the door.

Sally's mother, Cindy, opened the door and Sally's father suddenly could not breathe. He saw his daughter standing in front of a tri-fold mirror in her wedding gown. At that instant, the man who commanded an entire ship full of men could not stop the tears trailing down his cheeks.

"Oh, Honey! I've never seen anyone more beautiful than you are today," he said softly to Sally.

Cindy cleared her throat, "Ah-ahem."

"Oh, right. Of course, except for your mother," he corrected sheepishly.

"Now you've got it right, Dad. Good save," said Sally and they all laughed.

TJ opened his locker to get his formal dress uniform and it was not there! He asked his roommate, Jim, if he had seen it and he said, "No, I haven't. Just put on your dinner dress whites instead."

TJ tried to put on his other uniform and it did not fit! *What on earth is going on?*

"It must have shrunk," he said to Jim.

"Are you sure you're not just getting fat?" asked Jim. "Try your other one."

TJ pulled out his extra uniform and saw that it had grease all over the front of it. He tossed it on his bunk in frustration. He could not believe that today, of all days, things were going this horribly wrong.

"What am I going to do?"

Jim offered a solution, "Why don't you ask around the ship and see if you can borrow a set?"

"Good idea."

TJ was very anxious and felt like he was not thinking straight at all. He was positive he had just had his uniforms cleaned and had put them in his locker. He started asking around and went to the Quarter Deck, where he was informed that all Department Heads and Division Officers had already left the ship, with the exception of himself and his roommate, Jim. They said they only officer left on the ship was the Commanding Officer, who was on his way down now.

The Commanding Officer walked in, looked at TJ, and shook his head. TJ knew he had really messed up this time.

"Okay men, bring them out!" said the CO, with that fun loving sparkle in his eyes. A sailor walked into the room carrying TJ's formal dress uniform and his dinner dress whites. They had taken them and swapped them out with different ones as a joke. TJ couldn't believe that the Captain would take the time to pull a prank on him.

TJ breathed a sigh of great relief. "Good one, guys! Very funny. Just be ready for some payback!"

Everyone laughed and slapped TJ on the back. "Let's all get ready now and see if we can get to the church on time," TJ said as he rushed out of the room.

Sally's friend, Dawn, played the piano as people were ushered into the chapel. She had a list of songs requested by Sally and TJ. When the chapel was half filled, RP1 Ben Long sang a solo, *Joyful, Joyful, We Adore Thee*. People continued to file in; the chapel was filling up.

Attention on Deck was called as the Commander in Chief of the Atlantic Fleet came through the doors. The Admiral and his wife sat behind the Morgan family. Chaplain Henderson had some members of his congregation help out and when the chapel had no more seats, people were directed to the overflow room where the wedding was transmitted via a video camera and shown on a large screen by a LCD projector.

It was finally time for everyone to take their places. Dawn played Richard Wagner's *Bridal Chorus* and the processional began. Terry and Soledad, as the best man and maid of honor, came down the aisle in slow measured steps, followed by four other sets of attendants. Terry had worried that he would stand out, being the only one besides the bride not in a uniform. However, his tuxedo was white and blended in fairly well.

Two attendants pulled the white runners up the aisle. Peggy Sue was precious as she carefully dropped exactly one petal at each pew. Joseph, the ring bearer, kept his eye on the pillow trying not to drop the rings, but stood at perfect attention the whole time he was with the men up front.

Everyone stood up and turned to see the coming of the bride. TJ watched Sally walk confidently down the aisle and had to quickly wipe the tears from his eyes. She was lovely, and he could not believe that she was his!

Chaplain Henderson asked, "Who gives this woman to be wed?"

Holding back tears, Capt. James Morgan responded with a crack in his voice, "Her mother and I do." He did an about face and went back to sit next to his wife. No longer would Sally be his baby girl; she would be Mrs. Terry James Miller III.

Sally and TJ had planned a very traditional wedding and it went off without a hitch. Neither one forgot the others name during the exchange of vows; but when they were exchanging rings, Sally's hand was shaking so hard TJ wondered if he would ever get the ring on her finger. It was a moment they would never forget, because it was captured forever on video.

TJ and Sally walked to the front and lit the Unity Candle. When they returned to their positions in front of the Chaplain, he said, "As a surprise to Sally, we will be hearing another solo. The soloist will be singing the A.H. Malotte rendition of *The Lord's Prayer*."

TJ treated everyone to the smooth, baritone melody raised to the rafters. Sally closed her eyes, listened to his voice, and beamed with pride. She gave TJ's hand a gentle squeeze as he finished.

Chaplain Ruby said, "TJ and Sally have decided to have their first meal together as the Lord's Communion." He gave them their Communion and then had them face their families and friends as he announced, "It gives me great pleasure to be the first to present to you Mr. and Mrs. Terry James Miller the third."

People started to clap and some of the sailors whistled loudly. As TJ and Sally walked down the aisle to the back of the chapel, a small band played *Anchors Aweigh*.

The Chaplain then said, "Since this is a military wedding, the Arch of the Swords ceremony will take place outside."

Everyone started filing outside to watch the Arch of the Swords ceremony. At the door, each person was given a tiny bottle of bubbles to blow at the newlyweds as they walked by.

As a surprise for the special day, the Admiral would be taking part. Normally, Admirals and Captains do not do this, but TJ and Sally were very much respected even by their superiors.

Detail, attention.
Detail, dress right, dress.
Detail, forward march!

They marched about ten feet when the Admiral called,
Detail, march!
Detail, halt.
Detail, center face.

The Arch Detail turned and faced each other.
Detail, dress right, dress.
Ready, cover.
Detail, draw swords.

They all drew their swords from their holsters.
Detail, attention.

They brought their swords to their chests.
Detail, parade rest.

They moved their left foot to the side and put the tip of the sword to the ground.

When Chaplain Ruby came outside, the Admiral called,
Detail, attention.

They came to attention and brought their swords to their chests.

The Chaplain said, "Now presenting Mr. and Mrs. Terry Miller."

People cheered and millions of tiny, iridescent bubbles floated through the air.
Detail, present swords.

They raised their swords up into the air.
Detail, blades to the wind.

The swords were turned with the sharp end facing up into the sky.

As TJ and Sally walked up to the arch, Captains Parks and Baker put down their swords in front of Sally and said, "Rite of passage is one kiss." TJ kissed his bride and they proceeded under the Arch of Swords. Once they reached the end, Sammy and Cassie lowered their swords and the Admiral yelled, "Rite of passage, Sailors!"

TJ bent Sally over backwards and gave her a proper Navy kiss. As they passed from beneath the arch, Cassie gave Sally a spank on her behind with her sword, which is the traditional Navy love tap.

TJ and Sally walked down to the horse drawn carriage that was waiting to take them to Vista Point Center. TJ asked the driver if he could take the scenic route, so they would have a few minutes of private time.

When Hope arrived at Vista Point Center she pulled out her cell phone to call Sam. She told him how beautiful the wedding had been and said that the Navy had videotaped it—she was sure they could get their hands on a copy. Sam asked how Sammy had made out with all the standing around with his injuries. Hope answered, "Sammy did very well. He was even in the Arch of the Swords with the other officers. He and I are having a really good time. Oh Honey, I have to go now. I see TJ and Sally's carriage coming up the drive. I'll talk to you later tonight."

Hope sent a quick e-mail to Frank telling him that the wedding was over and she was thinking of him and Sue getting married. She told how cool the Arch of the Swords was and that she was at the reception hall waiting for the celebration to start. Hope thought this modern technology was really something. Just a few years ago, no one had the internet on their cell phones and now it was commonplace to surf the web through smart phones.

The horse drawn carriage drew up to the doorway and people lined up to take pictures of the beautiful couple arriving. As they walked under the archway of red, white, and blue balloons, the emcee introduced them. They made their way to the head table, stopping a few times to chat with friends or hug and kiss family members.

Appetizers of chicken skewers were brought out for everyone while they waited for the meal to begin. Once the newlyweds were seated, Chaplain Ruby blessed the meal and the salads were served.

Terry was nervous about giving the speech as the best man. He grabbed a microphone as people were still being served their salad. "Can I have everyone's attention please? I'm wearing two hats today—first, I'm TJ's dad and second, I'm the best man. I'd like to give the toast now. To TJ, the best son a father could ever hope to have. He's a good, young, Christian man who has worked and studied hard his whole life. I'm so proud of you. Sally, I'm so glad my son was smart enough to choose you as his wife and partner in life. I couldn't have asked for a better daughter-in-law. May both of you trust God to guide and direct you throughout your lives. I wish you both a long and happy life together." Everyone raised their glasses.

Everyone seemed to enjoy their dinners of either grilled chicken breast or grilled salmon. TJ had not eaten since he had the doughnuts early in the morning and was starving. He ate both a chicken dinner and a salmon dinner. Sally teased him about eating both.

While they were eating, people would tap their silverware on their glassware. This was a signal for the newlyweds to kiss. TJ said, "I'm starting to like all this kissing, but I'd really like it if they would give me a chance to eat something."

"Well, I'm pretty sure they'd rather watch us kiss than watch you eat. In fact, I'd rather see that too," she teased him.

As people were finishing their meals, Soledad, as maid of honor, took charge and said, "Everyone can continue to eat, but right now we're going to have the happy couple cut the cake."

Heidi whispered in TJ's ear, "Please do not smear cake all over her face. It's just tacky and there are a lot of high ranking officers in attendance."

TJ and Sally stood by the nautical themed wedding cake and smiled for the people who were taking photographs. A delightful guitar rendition of *Sailing* played in the background. TJ presented his sword to his bride to cut the cake. He put his right hand over hers as they cut the cake with his ceremonial sword. They each took a piece and fed it to the other. Then the top of the cake was taken away to be frozen and kept for their first anniversary.

After everyone had eaten their fill of cake and mint candy and nut mixes, and the food had been cleared from the tables, TJ, Doug, and Ski grabbed microphones and started singing all the old Navy songs. People all over the large hall joined in as they sang,

M' father often told me when I was just a lad,

A sailor's life was very hard, and the food was very bad,

But now I joined the Navy, I'm on a man-o-war,

And now I find a sailor ain't a sailor anymore!

Don't haul on the rope; don't climb up the mast,

If you see a sailing-ship it might be your last,

Get your civvies ready for another run ashore,

A sailor ain't a sailor, ain't a sailor anymore!

The "Killick" of our mess, says we're had it soft,

It wasn't like this in his day, when he was up aloft,

We like our bunks and sleeping bags but what's a hammock for?

Swinging from the deck head or lying on the floor?

There is one hard and true fact about a large room full of sailors—they can sing. They sing long, they sing loud, and they sing with passion. When the men were finished with the song, someone yelled out the name of another song, *Don't Forget Your Shipmates*, and the singing started up again.

When they finished this song, people were clapping and cheering and the Admiral was shouting, "Oooo rah!"

Lt. Doug Witt said into his microphone, "On the tables in front of you are papers with the lyrics to the next song. We would respectfully request if you are able to, stand up and sing the newest version of Anchors Aweigh with us. Over the years different verses have been added. This first verse is the official verse that everyone has learned in Navy Boot Camp ever since 2004. The second verse will be more familiar to you."

Everyone in the room stood and sang,

Stand, Navy, out to sea,

Fight our Battle cry;

We'll never change our course,

So vicious foe steer shy-y-y-y

Roll out the TNT,

Anchors Aweigh,

Sail on to Victory

And sink their bones to Davy Jones, Hooray!

Anchors Aweigh, my boys,

Anchors Aweigh!

Farewell to foreign shores,

We sail at break of day, of day,

Through our last night on shore,

Drink to the foam,

Until we meet once more,

Here's wishing you a Happy Voyage Home!

Everyone cheered, raised their glasses, and shouted, "Ooooh Rah!" Terry said, "Emcee, I think it's time to start the music. It's time for the first dance."

TJ pulled Sally close and they slow danced to *Just the Two of Us* by Grover Washington Jr. Gliding across the dance floor, surrounded by the people they loved the most, Sally found perfect contentment in the arms of the man she loved. They danced together, the center of attention, until her father tapped TJ on the shoulder and asked, "May I cut in?"

When the song was over, the emcee shouted, "It's time to liven things up people!" *Celebration* played out loud and clear over the speakers and people started to dance. Sally and her mother disappeared for a while and when they returned, Sally was in her dress white uniform. She wanted to have fun and dance, but could not do that very well in her wedding dress. Now, she was ready for a party.

The emcee was good; he kept the music lively and the people dancing. He took into consideration that most of these people were connected to the Navy and mixed in with the other songs he played, songs like *In the Navy*, *Where the Boat Leaves From*, and *Son of a Son of a Sailor*. They line danced to *Boot Scootin' Boogie* and the emcee brought the house down when he played Toby Keith's *Courtesy of the Red, White, and Blue*.

This was a lively group of people and they all had fun. Sally was out of breath as she was swung around the dance floor by one person after another. Several hours later, Terry and Heidi asked TJ and Sally to step outside with them to catch a breath of fresh air.

Heidi pressed a tissue to her forehead and said, "Wow, it sure is warm in there!"

Sally agreed and said, "Obviously, I should take up dancing for exercise. Who knew it would wear me out like this? But I'm having such a good time. These memories will last my whole life!"

Terry said, "I know you're not opening your wedding gifts until you get back from your honeymoon, but we wanted to give you ours tonight." He pointed out a brand new Jeep Grand Cherokee with a large white bow across the windshield. He dropped the keys into TJ's hand and continued, "It's the new Grand Cherokee Overland Summit and it's loaded. It has a backup camera, rain sensing wipers, forward collision warning system, and a command view sunroof with dual panels. Trust me; this baby has plenty of goodies for you to play with."

"I love that light blue color," said Sally.

Heidi told her, "It's called Winter Chill Pearl."

TJ just stood there—speechless. Finally, he turned and grabbed both of his parents up into a big bear hug. "I can't believe you did this. It's too much; it's way, way too much!"

Heidi hugged TJ back and said, "Nothing is too much for our only son."

"Actually Son, that's not even all," said Terry, nodding at Heidi. She turned and handed Sally an envelope.

Sally tore the envelope opened and her jaw dropped as she saw what was inside. Shaking, she handed it to TJ. He slowly slid the $20,000 check out of the envelope and stared at it as if it might magically disappear. He looked at his mother and she laughed at his amazement, "Like I said, there's nothing that's too much for our only son. We wanted to help you buy new furniture for your new home. Don't worry, we can afford it."

TJ and Sally both cried as they hugged Terry and Heidi, thanking them over and over. "Let's go look at your new car," said Terry as he secretly wiped at his eyes.

When they later walked back into the reception hall, TJ went over and talked to the emcee. "Could I make a request? Would you play *Good Ole Boys Like Me* and dedicate it to my father? It's his favorite song."

TJ got their suitcases and Terry helped him carry them out to the new Jeep. When they returned inside, TJ and Sally said their good-byes and hugged their parents, then they slipped out into the darkness to begin their new life together.

As they drove out of the parking lot, TJ looked at Sally's fingers interlaced with his and lifted her hand and kissed it. "Well, Mrs. Miller, we're linked together for life. Do you feel any different yet?"

"We've been together for two years and only been married for five hours, I can't wait to see what the next fifty years brings us. If I know you at all, I think it's going to be quite an adventure," Sally said as she squeezed TJ's hand in hers.

They stopped at the base on the way out of town to pick up their new base sticker to make things easier when they returned. TJ then whisked his new bride off to Virginia Beach where they would spend the weekend enjoying the King Neptune Festival.

CHARLIE RESPONSE
CHAPTER FOURTEEN

Nurse Debbie had the nursing assistants wheel the patients out of their rooms down to the day room, like she did every morning. Everyone was waiting for Joey D and Sam to tell their sea stories. Many of the patients looked forward to hearing these stories, because they never had the opportunity to travel much. Many of them were now in their late 80s and 90s and would never get to travel again.

Finally, they brought Sam and Joey D into the day room and Ms. Grace said, "Glad you two could join us. What are you going to share with us today?" Ms. Grace was 93 years old and enjoyed listening to the stories very much.

Joey D answered, "We're going to share one of our motorcycling adventures from the days when we were stationed in Honolulu, Hawaii. I was onboard the USS Chosin CG-65 and my family lived in the base housing."

Sam said, "And I was on the USS Port Royal CG-73 out of Honolulu at the same time. My ship won the Battle E, which is an award given by the Navy to ships in different classes in each fleet for battle efficiency. I like to bring that part up, because that meant we were the best!" He laughed as he nudged Joey D.

Joey D rolled his eyes and shook his head, but continued on anyway. "Most of the time, my ship was out when Sam's ship was in and vice versa. We didn't get to see each other that much, but our families still spent a lot of time together and our kids played together. Mark and Terry were both stationed in San Diego at that time. One time when we were both in port at the same time, our parents came and took the kids back to the mainland for a couple of weeks. We decided it would be a good time to explore the island from the seat of our bikes. Kelly was on the back of mine and Hope rode with Sam. What a beautiful ride it was going around that island!"

Sam said, "I had been on a charity ride previously for the Honolulu Children's Hospital and we were riding the same roads. We took off north with the ocean on our left and the Waianae Mountain Range on our right. Man, it was so beautiful. It really made me appreciate the wonders that God created in those first seven days. We rode up to Kaena Park and what a pretty place that was, too. All around the island we rode—if there was a pretty sight to be seen, we rode to see it. I didn't want to miss a minute of it. We saw Sacred Falls Park. This was before it closed down due to tragic circumstances, but we were lucky enough to see the park firsthand. We rode many miles that day, for sure. We finally ended up in Waikiki where we spent two nights at the Outrigger Waikiki."

Joey D went on with the story. "We ate a traditional Hawaiian meal of poi and lomi salmon with pineapple and then went to the beach where we saw the most amazing sunset. The sky was a riot of colors, one blending into another. I'd never seen anything like it before. The next morning we went for another ride on the motorcycles, but then we came back for an afternoon of fun and sun on the beach. We also did some surfing while we were there. We had to rent surfboards, because we couldn't carry them on our bikes. That night we went to a pig roast and watched some fire dancers. We had a blast! The next morning, we checked out and rode back to the base."

"That reminds me of the guy we saw that had a rack built onto his bike to carry his surfboard on top. We should have done something like that to our bikes," laughed Sam.

Joey D laughed along with Sam, "Yeah, we could have, but it would have looked pretty stupid on our touring bikes."

One patient who was listening to their story asked if either Mark or Terry and their wives ever came over to see them. Joey D answered, "Oh sure, they came over a few times. We would show them around the island and around the other islands, too. They really loved going to the Hawaiian Polynesian Culture Center. And since everyone was affiliated with the Navy, they wanted to see Pearl Harbor and the Arizona Memorial. One year when they came over, we got tickets for everyone to go to the Pro Bowl game. We even got to meet some of the pro football players. They came to the different military bases to visit. We even played them in a game of slow pitch softball for charity."

Sam added, "We all played Captain's Cup sports on base. We played a lot of softball, volleyball, and 8-man flag football. In Hawaii, softball was played year round in different leagues. We played in all the leagues we could. Joey D played third and I played shortstop. Joey D was a wide out on the football team and I was the quarterback. In volleyball, I was a setter and he was an outside hitter. But if you want to talk about two man beach volleyball, we ruled!"

"We also played church league softball. I remember when we got transferred to Norfolk, Mark, Terry, Joey D, and I were all there together with our families. We played in a church league. In that league, Joey D played third base and I played shortstop. TJ was 17 years old at the time and played second, while Terry played first. Mark played right centerfield and Hope was in left centerfield. Kelly was our catcher and Heidi was our pitcher. We won the league two out of three years in Norfolk."

While Sam talked, Joey D looked around at all the people listening. He silently thanked God for putting them in a place with people who were not only willing, but eager, to listen to them talk about the good times in their lives. At least, this rough patch they were going through made it possible for them to reach out and meet all kinds of people.

Hopefully, they were brightening someone's day by talking about their adventures; some of these people really needed a bright spot in their day.

· · · · · · · · · · · ·

Frank was awakened by the sound of the bridge announcing the mail plane had just landed. He was excited and hoped that within a few hours he would finally get mail for the first time in almost two weeks. Normally they received mail every day, but since leaving Perth the mail had been rerouted to Diego Garcia and then flown to them.

Frank tried to fall back to sleep, but was too excited. He was hoping to hear from Sue, his future wife. The thought of those two words, *future wife*, made Frank smile.

An hour later, Frank got up and got ready for work. He showered and shaved. His uniform was already pressed and ready. His boots were polished, but he buffed them anyway, just to kill time. Finally, he wandered to the mess decks. He saw that they were serving Chili Mac. Usually, when they served this there was a storm coming.

He asked the mess crank where everyone else was, as the mess decks seemed relatively empty. "They're still up on the flight deck fastening down the aircraft for the upcoming storm. They say it's supposed to be nasty for a couple of days."

Frank screwed up his face and said, "That's just swell. Our communications will be down most of the time then."

Frank ate Chili Mac and then went to the forward mess decks and got a hamburger, fries, and ice cream. His dad had told him that in order not to get seasick, you must have a full stomach. He knew the ship would be rocking and rolling, so he was working on filling up now.

Since he was still about half an hour early, he went to the ship's store and bought some instant oatmeal. Just like any good Eagle Scout, Frank believed in being prepared at all times.

Suddenly, Frank heard one of the sweetest sounds onboard a ship, "Mail call!"

He knew it would take a while for the Division's Mail Clerk to go get the mail, so Frank continued to take his time at the ship's store.

Before he left, he ordered flowers to be sent to Sue—he was sure she would be surprised.

When he arrived at his Division, Frank was still twenty minutes early. They were passing out the mail when he walked in. In the pile of mail he received, Frank had four letters and five post cards from Sue and several letters from his family, as well.

Frank read through the post cards first and then put them aside to pin to his bulletin board. He stacked the letters from Sue in order from oldest to newest. He had read through two of the letters and then it was time for him to relieve the watch.

Frank went through the usual routine that he went through every time he started a shift. He was hoping if he got everything finished quickly, he would have time to read another letter. However, a major satellite channel went down due to the upcoming storm. That meant he had to spend his time finding a better channel that would work and also bring up the backup HF circuits.

Frank's mind was not wholeheartedly on his work, it was on a stack of mail sitting on his desk unopened. He did his work mechanically; because it was so familiar to him, he could almost go on auto pilot.

"Attention on deck!" The Admiral of the Battle Group came into the work center. He handed Lt. Commander Tom Brown some written messages and said, "These messages must be sent ASAP because we're heading into a typhoon."

Frank typed up the message to the HMAS Arunta, the helicopter ship that Sue's brother Mick was on. The message told them to alter course and head away from the typhoon. When Mick acknowledged the message, he said, "Godspeed, Mate."

Frank told him, "We're staying our course."

Mick typed back, "I'll be praying for you, my friend!"

In the middle of sending messages, it was time to do the daily crypto change over. They all went about their assigned duties and after four hours everything calmed down.

Frank was finally able to get back to Sue's letters when they went for mid rats, midnight chow for the mid watch. She wrote about Dugan

O'Reilly getting caught by the Shore Patrol. She said Rose was planning to go to the States as soon as Dugan could send her some money.

Sue told him that she had memories of him wherever she went in town. Those memories were all good ones, but sometimes they made her cry. Frank had never felt so far away from someone he loved as he did now. Silently, he prayed that God would keep Sue close to His heart.

Frank read through his other letters and was grateful that he came from a family that liked to keep in touch often. He said another quick prayer for Sammy, who was having doubts about his ability to remain a SEAL team member. Frank hoped that once he went back to his team, his confidence would return.

As Frank was returning to his rack the next morning, he heard a lot of noise and asked what was going on. He was told that the Captain said everyone in Deck Department and Air Department had to prepare for heavy seas. Everything that was loose must be securely fastened down. The guys on the flight deck had to triple tie down the aircrafts to make sure they would not be swept overboard by high waves. The ship's Gunners Mates had to cover all the guns so they would not be damaged or destroyed. Anything that was left loose could be lost overboard or do possible damage to the ship.

Frank put his earphones in and turned on his iPod—maybe some nice easy listening music would help him sleep through the storm.

For the next two days, they were confined to the inside of the ship. The ship rocked and rolled violently at times, but made it through the storm in one piece. There were a few injuries from people being thrown out of their racks; it reminded Frank that his father had told him sea stories of being tied down in his rack during storms. That night, Frank got some rope and tied himself in. It got so bad at one point that the ship's anchor was torn away from the ship!

· · · · · · · · · · ·

TJ and Sally were finally asleep. It had been a long day and it had taken several hours for them to relax enough to fall asleep.

At 0100, both Sally's and TJ's cell phones started ringing and they woke up. Groggily, they hit their talk buttons and listened to the pre-recorded messages. Sally sat straight up in bed, "WHAT!?!"

She looked at her new husband in alarm, "Are they serious? ALL military are to return to their bases? All leaves and passes are canceled due to the attack? What attack?"

TJ jumped out of bed and turned on the television. "It's got to be a joke," he said. "Don't panic yet."

On the television was a special news report. The reporter was saying, "The President and his Cabinet are in an undisclosed location at this time." Behind her, on the street, was mass panic. People were running in all directions and smoke filled the area. The television cut away to footage of a burning White House, then switched footage to show the Pentagon also in flames. The reporter's voice continued to give information, "At this time, we must ask everyone to remain indoors. We know that Washington, DC, New York, and areas in Virginia have been targeted. The USS George Washington, also, is in danger of sinking. We just don't know enough information right now. The terrorists could be anywhere. Hold on…I've just received word that Norfolk Naval Base is also in flames."

The reporter's voice droned on as the screen flashed image after image of devastation. TJ looked at Sally and shook his head in amazement. Just at that moment, they heard some F-18s fly overhead. "I think it's the start of World War Three. We have to get out of here. Grab everything." TJ swung into action stuffing all their things into the duffle bags.

Tears were streaming down Sally's face as she quickly got dressed, "But we just got married today," she wailed.

TJ stopped and hugged her, kissing her upturned face, "I'm so glad you married me, Honey. I love you. But it's time to go earn our paychecks, Baby." He grabbed the bags in one hand and Sally's hand in the other and ran out the door and down the hallway.

As they ran down the stairs, they heard gunfire. It was closer than he thought. They ducked and ran to their car and were hit…….by water balloons. TJ's so-called friends, Doug, Ski, John, and Sammy had just pulled off the master of all pranks on him.

"Cut it out, guys! Haven't you heard? World War Three has started. We've got to get back to base quickly!"

"Oh, we got you good! He still believes it! We are the masters!" cried John.

Sammy explained the television footage was put together by the Mass Communication Specialists on the USS George Bush. They had spliced a lot of movie footage together and added the reporter over it. They had then bribed workers in the hotel to help them pull the prank of the year on TJ and Sally.

"But we heard gunfire!" argued Sally. Sammy sheepishly held up a handful of firecrackers.

At first, Sally and TJ were mad—they thought the prank had gone too far. However, after about two minutes, Sally just busted out with a huge belly laugh over the whole thing. Relief spread through her that war had not just broken out. In fact, she felt pretty special that so many people had gone to so much trouble to pull this joke on them.

"Oh, trust me, paybacks will be forthcoming," threatened TJ, but he too laughed.

When Sally and TJ woke up the next morning, they were still tired and upset for their lack of sleep. "What a way to start a honeymoon," yawned Sally.

They showered and went to find some breakfast. Sally said, "It's our first breakfast as man and wife."

"There's going to be a whole lifetime of first coming up for us," agreed TJ.

After breakfast, they grabbed their cameras and went for a walk down the beach. They had walked for just a short time when they looked out into the water and saw a school of dolphins swimming by. TJ teased, "Look, even the dolphins have come to congratulate us!"

They walked a long way down the beach with no particular destination in mind. When they had been walking for a while, they came upon a sand sculpture competition going on. The sculptors had started very early in the morning and their creations were beginning to take shape. Sally took some pictures as TJ talked to some of the competitors. They found out the Blue Angels were performing that day and would be flying over that same beach.

"I've seen them perform many times before, but I've never seen them fly over the beach before," said Sally.

"We'll hang around so you can get some pictures," offered TJ.

Boats and people were everywhere for the King Neptune Festival. TJ noticed there some people surfing out in the ocean. He looked longingly at the waves building up. "I wish I hadn't broken my board," he said.

"Hey, let's go to the Freedom Surf Shop and see if there's a board you like. It'll be my wedding present to you," said Sally.

At the surf shop, TJ had a hard time picking out just one board. There were so many. Finally, he settled on the Channel Islands K-whip, about six and a half feet long. It was white and yellow with yellow spiral designs on it. TJ preferred a single skep over multiple ones.

The sales person helped him carry it out to the Jeep and asked if they had any rope to tie it down. When they said they did not, he suggested going back inside to buy tie down straps because they were safer than rope anyway.

It took so long at the surf shop they missed the Blue Angels flying over the beach. TJ apologized, but Sally did not really care. The Blue Angels would be around for a long time to come. She would see them another time.

Sally and TJ spent the rest of the afternoon at the beach. TJ surfed and met other surfer dudes and had a totally bodacious time. He caught a few good waves and in very short time he was commanding his board.

TJ looked around and saw a nice set of waves coming. He paddled hard and got on a nice wave. He was throwing buckets as he cut back and then gained speed. He cut back again and did a floater. Sally took pictures of him with the telephoto lens; she could not believe the moves he was making with his new board. TJ had taught Sally how to surf a while back, but she could not do the cut backs as well as TJ. Sally was a real Gidget at heart; but on the other hand, she loved motorcycling, too. She guessed she was just an adventurist like her husband.

When TJ got back out in the ocean, one surfer said, "Dude, you really iced that wave! Totally rad! What's your name, Dude?" TJ told him and the dude said his name was Sky.

TJ saw a large wave forming and started paddling really fast and yelled, "Banzai!" He was charging as he caught about the seven foot wave. Everyone on the beach stopped and yelled about the huge wave. Sally was taking pictures of TJ with the telephoto lens.

TJ did a monster of a cut back to the top of the wave. He caught some air as he did a 360 and came back down into the wave. He came back up and did a floater. Everyone cheered and some called TJ the Big Kahuna. He was really rippin'! He rode the wave the whole way to shore and Sally ran over and hugged and kissed him.

"Honey, that was da bomb! You were really rippin' out there. I couldn't believe it!" exclaimed Sally.

Sky came ashore and yelled, "Dude, you're a mega ripper! Brah, that was totally rad!"

TJ said, "Sky, I want you to meet my Sheila. We just got married yesterday; her name is Sally. We're both officers in the Navy, though I've been in longer than she has, so I outrank her."

"Aloha, Sally."

"Aloha, Sky."

"It's been great to meet you, Sky," said TJ. "Right now I think me and my lady are going to get some grindage. If I don't see you later tonight, I'll be dawn surfing tomorrow and Monday. You can meet me here."

"Okay, Dude," said Sky. "Sally, nice to meet you and if you know any other bangin' Sheilas like yourself, feel free to introduce them to the adventures of Sky."

As they walked to dinner, TJ said, "Honey, thank you for the board and most of all thank you for giving me some time out there on the waves. You can't believe the way it felt out there. I love surfing, sailing, and riding my Harley. They give me the feeling of freedom I enjoy, but surfing has much more danger to it, No matter how good you are, you always wipe out."

"I have to admit, it was pretty cool watching you. All these girls were talking about the hot dude on the white and yellow board. I wanted to tell them that you were mine and to eat their hearts out. Then even the dudes were commenting about your style out there. I was so proud!" said Sally.

After dinner they went back to their hotel room. Sally was downloading all the pictures she had taken into her MacBook Pro. TJ was reading the local paper, waiting for her to finish. "Hey, Honey, there's a local singer named Robbin Thompson playing at the Jewish Mother tonight. My parents used to play songs by him all the time. Do you want to go hear a set or two?" TJ asked.

"Sure, sounds fun."

They walked hand in hand to the Jewish Mother in the bright moonlight. When they got there, they ordered a sandwich and iced tea and sat down to enjoy the music. After the first set of songs, Robbin took a break. TJ walked over and talked to him for a bit. He told him that they were both sailors from Norfolk on their honeymoon. TJ let him know that his parents played his music all the time and he loved it.

When Robbin returned to the stage he said, "I want to welcome a couple of fans of mine, here on their honeymoon. Congratulations TJ and Sally!" Everyone cheered and clapped for them. Robbin then said, "TJ, I know you know this song. I want to dedicate it to you and your bride."

As the notes of *Candy Apple Red* swelled and filled the room, TJ stood on his chair and sang right along with Robbin. The music played until late into the night. TJ knew most of the songs by heart and was not shy about belting them out.

When it was time for the last song, Robbin announced, "This next song of mine was loved so much in Richmond that it became the State Song of Virginia. So please stand up for *Sweet Virginia Breeze*."

This was one song even Sally knew. They both stood up and sang along.

He must have been thinking about me
When he planted the very first dogwood tree…

When that breeze starts blowing through those trees
You know everything will be all right.
Sweet Virginia Breeze.

Sally shouted over the noise, "Man, this guy's great! I love this music."

"I heard him all the time growing up. He's proof positive that some people never make it big that are loaded with talent. It sure is a shame!" TJ yelled back.

They left Jewish Mothers and strolled back towards the hotel. TJ had his arm around Sally when traffic stopped at the red light on Pacific Avenue. Some beach music was playing on someone's car stereo. TJ swung Sally around and started dancing with her. Unfortunately, seconds later the moment was ruined by the THUMP, THUMP, THUMP of the bass coming from a young kid's car with a hip hop station playing excessively loud.

TJ shouted, "Yeah, I remember when my daddy used to let me borrow his car, too."

Other people on the street laughed, until the kid jumped out of his car and ran at TJ with a switchblade. Someone screamed, but TJ easily took the switchblade away from the young punk and restrained him, twisting his arm behind his back.

"You better watch who you pull a weapon on, little boy. One of these days, you're going to get hurt by someone a little less polite than I am," said TJ as he handed the kid off to the police officer who had come running instantly.

TJ said he did not want to press charges, but the officer told him that the kid had just been bailed out for assault with a deadly weapon when he pulled a knife on a girl. "He won't make bail this time. I don't care who his daddy is, I'll make sure he won't be bonded out," promised the officer.

The next morning, after TJ spent some time in the water with his new surfboard, they put on their dress whites and drove to the base chapel for church. They walked into the chapel and saw their families already there, standing in the aisle talking amongst each other. Sally's mom, Cindy, saw them first and commented, "Wow, we sure didn't expect to see you two today."

Heidi hugged her son and new daughter-in-law and asked how they were enjoying their honeymoon. Sally told her they had a wonderful time at the beach the day before and how impressive TJ had been surfing.

"That's funny that you should mention surfing. We were at the beach yesterday and saw some dude down the beach on a really big wave that actually got air and did a 360," commented Terry.

"That was TJ!" exclaimed Sally.

"No way! TJ, that was you? I thought you broke your board," said his dad.

With a smug smile on his face, Terry answered, "That was me. Sally bought me a new board for a wedding present." He looked toward the front of the chapel, "We better get to our seats. Church is getting ready to start."

Chaplain Henderson welcomed everyone and made a special welcome to the new Mr. and Mrs. Terry Miller III.

After the service, they all agreed to spend some time at the King Neptune Festival and then get some lunch together. As they walked around the festival, Sally's grandmother said, "In my day, the family didn't go with you on your honeymoon."

"Well, you know what they say, Grandma—the family that prays together, stays together. I didn't know they meant ALL the time, but…" with that Sally shrugged her shoulders. Everyone laughed, glad that Sally was happy to share her honeymoon time with them.

After they ate lunch, they walked down on the beach together. TJ said to Mark and his dad that they should rent a couple of surfboards and catch a couple waves with him. Cindy commented to her husband that he should join them.

"What? Dad knows how to surf? Unbelievable," exclaimed Sally.

Cindy explained, "When your dad and I were first married, we were stationed in San Diego and he learned to surf and sail there. Then, we went to Hawaii and he surfed all the time. After that, he was so busy working and raising our family that he just didn't go anymore."

They all had good times that day, the kind of fun that you tuck into the back of your mind so that later, you can draw it out and savor it. The men all surfed together and later in the day, even the girls went out on the boards. Sky showed up and so did Cassie and Victoria. Sky thanked Sally for bringing some bodacious babes for him this time.

In the evening, they all sat around a roaring bonfire and told sea stories. Sally's father, James, sat there looking at his precious daughter laughing with her new husband, obviously happier than she had ever been. And it made him feel good inside.

"There it is! You found it," exclaimed Cindy, leaning in to whisper in his ear.

"What?" he looked puzzled.

"You finally found your smile. I thought you had lost it," she told him.

"I haven't had this much fun or felt this relaxed in a long, long time," he admitted.

"That's what you get for acting like a captain all the time. Like I've told you before, you have to have fun sometimes."

"You were right, my love. I think our son-in-law and my new friend, Terry, are going to teach me how to live again," said the Captain as he leaned in to kiss his wife slowly.

Early the next morning, TJ took Sally to Brenneman Farm Apartments. He pulled out the key that the rental lady had given him and opened the door for Sally. "It's a two bedroom, two bathroom corner apartment. It comes with all the appliances, including a washer and dryer. There's a fitness center, swimming pool, a club house, and let me show you the walk in closets," TJ said.

"Oh, look! There's a fireplace! I only have two questions—can we afford it and when can we move in?" exclaimed Sally.

An enormous smile broke out on TJ's face, "I already paid the deposit and first and last month's rent! We're going to buy furniture today and move in right away. Dad and Mark are going to help us."

"Are you serious? Oh, TJ, our first home! We're going to be so happy here," Sally said as she hugged him.

They went to Haynes Furniture Store and picked out furniture for the bedroom, living room, and dining room. Sally said, "We shouldn't buy anything else until we open our wedding presents. We don't even know what we have."

TJ arranged for the furniture to be delivered. They stopped for lunch at Taco Bell and decided it would be fun to open their wedding gifts now. They stopped at Sally's parent's home and loaded up all the presents.

Sally and TJ sat in the middle of their brand new empty apartment, surrounded by a massive pile of presents. They opened them one by one, very carefully recording in a notebook who gave them each one.

When they had finished, TJ remarked about the insane amount of things they had received. Sally said, only half seriously, "I can just feel the love radiating from this pile of presents. Can't you?"

"Radiating love, huh? You're going to feel the love radiating from somewhere, but it won't be these presents," taunted TJ, as he grabbed for Sally and chased her around amidst the wrappings. When he finally caught her, he kissed her and looked at the mess they had made. "Gee, I just love how you've decorated the place, Mrs. Miller."

"Why thank you, Sir. It's just a little talent I have," Sally said. She looked around and said, "You know, TJ, I can't wait to have family gatherings and friends over for visits. It's going to be so much fun having our own place."

"So why do we have to wait?" asked TJ. "I say we call everyone up and have them come over for dinner tonight. We can have a house blessing."

"But we don't have anything here! No furniture, no kitchen things; we don't even have toilet paper!"

"So we'll order pizza and my mother will bring some toilet paper. We'll have the important things—God, family, and love. Those are the only things we'll ever truly need," said TJ.

Sally smiled and hugged her husband, "Sounds good to me."

CHARLIE RESPONSE
CHAPTER FIFTEEN

TJ entered Captain Baker's office as bidden. "Sorry to bother you, Sir, but I need to request seven to ten days leave," TJ held his breath and grimaced.

"For what reason?"

"Both Sally and her father received promotions, as you already know. Admiral Morgan wants the entire family to take a trip with him to celebrate," answered TJ, nervously waiting for the answer. It was a long leave to request, but it would be hard to let down the Admiral, too.

"Is the Chief away during any of this time?"

"No, Sir. Neither is anyone else. I would need from Monday after work through the following week's Thursday evening."

After shuffling some papers around and looking closely at the memo he found, the Captain asked, "Did you know I just got a message for a change of ship's orders?"

"No, I didn't, Sir." Now TJ was really nervous. The orders could say anything. They could be shipping out earlier than he thought or maybe, if he was lucky, they would be sitting tight for now.

Captain Baker looked at TJ for a few moments and then said, "We're having a special meeting this afternoon; but I'll tell you now, if you can keep it to yourself." TJ nodded his head in agreement. "Due to some unforeseen problems, we will not be deployed next month. We'll be going back into the yard to have some improvements and repairs done. Our deployment has been delayed until May of next year. Since you didn't really take a honeymoon and I'm also in a pretty good mood, I believe that I will sign your leave papers now. But keep what I've told you in confidence, please."

"Aye, aye, Sir. That I can do," said TJ, with a smile on his face. He couldn't believe his luck; that meant that he would be home for Thanksgiving, Christmas, and Easter! Also, leaving in May meant they should be home for Christmas next year, too.

The celebration of both Sally's and her father's promotions was a ten day ride down the Blue Ridge Parkway to see the autumn colors and sightsee. Mark, Paula, Terry, Heidi, Sally, and TJ were going to ride their motorcycles, while the Admiral, his wife, Cindy, and their daughter, Soledad, followed in their car.

They all met just north of Richmond, Virginia and rode across the state to Waynesboro, where they stopped for lunch. They were all excited and talked a lot about the sights they would see. Before they left the restaurant, they all joined hands as Terry asked the Lord not only for safety and guidance, but also that the trip fill them with memories that would last a lifetime, as they bonded together as a family.

The motorcycles led the way onto the Blue Ridge Parkway. Four miles down the road they stopped at America's oldest continuously operating show cave, Grand Caverns, where they took the tour.

All along the way down the road, they stopped at various viewpoints and pull offs. The fall foliage was brilliant, the forest dressing itself in showy colors. They pulled out their cameras several times to take pictures of the magnificence of God's paintbrush over the mountains. When they hiked up to the summit of Sharp Top and saw the view from there, Sally said, "Oh, I do love the changing of the seasons."

They made it safely to Nelson County, Virginia, where they spent the night at the Natural Bridge Hotel and Conference Center. Terry told the others they should spend the following day exploring the sites in the area. Soledad asked what was in this area to see and do. Terry said, "There's the Natural Bridge, of course. But there's also the Natural Bridge Caverns, the Monacan Indian village, and the Virginia Safari Park. We could also hike up to Crabtree Falls, which is the highest cascading waterfall east of the Mississippi River. What does everyone think?"

They all agreed it sounded pretty good. They would not want to miss these sights, so they reserved their rooms for an extra night.

They enjoyed visiting the sights the next day. TJ stood in front of a sign at the Natural Bridge and read aloud, "The Natural Bridge was once called the Bridge of God by the Monacan Tribe. None other than the father of our country George Washington surveyed it, but King George III deeded it to Washington's friend, Thomas Jefferson."

That evening they ate at the Colonial Dining Room. As they waited for their meals to arrive, Sally said, "I really had fun today. The best part was going to the largest indoor butterfly exhibit in Virginia at the Natural Bridge. I loved seeing the swarms of butterflies, all those Monarchs and the Blue Morpho, but my favorite was the Yellow Tiger Swallowtails." Soledad's head bobbed up and down as she agreed with her sister.

Once again the next morning, they started the day with a prayer of gratitude for the blessings they had received thus far and a plea for God's hand in safety over the little group.

Day in and day out, the group wound their way through the mountainous sights along the Blue Ridge Parkway. They saw many wonderful things and were educated in historical facts along the way. They went to Appomattox, where the Civil War officially ended, and to the National D Day Memorial. They hiked up many trails to see the view from the summit or to visit a waterfall. They even went to the Andy Griffith Museum and saw Wally's service station and Floyd's Barbershop.

Cindy joked, "I wish I would've seen Aunt Bee during our stop here. I would have asked for her recipe for apple pie." Everyone laughed.

There were many charming little places that Paula and Mark decided they were going to come back to at a later date. Paula wrote the name of each place in a little notebook: Little Switzerland, NC; Station's Inn Motorcycle Resort; Fancy Gap, VA.

On the fifth morning, when they arrived at the Linn Cove Viaduct, one of the most photographed sections of the Parkway, the Admiral drove in the front and Cindy took pictures of the bikers coming towards her. Then they let the bikers pass them and she took pictures from behind them.

They went to the mile high swinging bridge on Grandfather Mountain. Heidi struggled a bit with the height of the bridge, but she managed to inch her way across it. While they were on the bridge, Mark told them all, "Did you know that the Cherokee called this river *Eeseeoh*, meaning the River of Cliffs? It later became known as Linville Falls. The river starts on Grandfather Mountain and goes down over 2,000 feet through a beautiful gorge."

After lunch, the Admiral told them he had a surprise for everyone. They needed to follow him as he led the way, but not to worry when they left the Parkway. They rode along wondering where they were going. Just outside of Ashville, North Carolina, they turned onto a long, winding road that cut through the forest like a jagged scar of stone. It was not long before Sally gasped. "Oh my goodness, we're at Biltmore Estate! I love this place. It's always been a dream of mine to stay here someday," said Sally, looking around her in wonder. "Why do you think we're here?"

They pulled into a parking lot down the road from the Inn on Biltmore Estate.

"Surprise!" yelled the Admiral as soon as he stepped from the car. "What do you think? We're staying here tonight. Don't worry about the cost, it's on me. My little girl has always dreamed of staying in this place, so I figured, why not?"

They had perfectly appointed balcony rooms with king sized beds and impressive views of the estate. They took a tour of Biltmore House, the largest home in America. The women were teased about the possibility of breaking their necks as they tried to see everything at once, but they had never seen anything so opulent and breathtaking as they saw in that home. After the tour, they ate at the Stable Café, which had been the estate's stables in the 19th century, and then they went out to explore downtown Ashville.

Sally walked hand in hand with her father, when she leaned in and kissed his cheek. "Thank you, Daddy. You've made another one of my dreams come true."

Jim blushed and ducked his head down so no one would notice. "Nothing's too good for my baby girl."

The next morning, they headed out onto the road again. They saw beautiful scenery and had a great time being together. On Tuesday, they were going to ride the famous length of road known as the Tail of the Dragon on Route 129. The Tail of the Dragon is an eleven mile stretch of road that has 318 turns at the southern tip of the Great Smoky Mountain National Park. People come from all over the world to ride or drive on this challenging road. At the Deals Gap Motorcycle Resort was the Tree of Shame, where they hung pieces of motorcycles that had wrecked on the Dragon. It was shameful for a motorcyclist to have a bit of his bike hanging there.

Terry, Heidi, Mark, Paul, and TJ were excited to ride the Tail of the Dragon, but Sally was nervous. She confided to TJ, "Honey, I'm a little scared about this. Are you sure I can handle this?"

TJ grabbed Sally around her waist and said, "Trust me; if I didn't think you could handle it, we wouldn't be going. You've ridden this entire trip without a single problem. You're going to love it."

They decided to take the ride in stages. First, they would go through it slowly, so they could all get used to the sharp turns. Then they would ride it again, but this time they would stop at various points to take pictures. The final time, they would ride it faster for those who wanted a thrill.

TJ had a small video camera attached to his handlebars. Mark had one attached to his helmet. Cindy was going to record them from behind with her video camera. They would have plenty of footage of this ride.

By the end of the third pass, Sally was smiling from ear to ear, "Yeaaaah! That was way more fun that I thought it would be. There were time my pegs were scraping on the road, I was leaning so far! That was completely exhilarating!"

Everyone complimented Sally on her riding, which was really good for a beginner. She said she could never have done that ride if she had not taken the safety courses. Before they left, they bought t-shirts and pins and patches to commemorate riding the dragon's tail.

They decided it was a good idea to compliment such an exciting ride with one a bit tamer. They were going to ride the Cherohala Skyway. Nicknamed *a Drive among the Clouds*, the Cherohala Skyway travels through the Cherokee National Forest and Nantahala National Forest. It is a smooth, wide road and has many places to pull off for photographs.

When they stopped for lunch, Cindy told the others, "I've traveled all over the world with James and I don't think I've ever seen sights as beautiful as we've seen on this trip. I think the Cherohala Skyway has the most magnificent sights I've ever seen. Sure, the Tail of the Dragon was exciting, but for beauty nothing beats this road. I just can't get over it; it's been this close to us for years and we never came before."

As they ate lunch, the men hovered over the open map spread out on the table, sometimes over their food even. They went over the different routes to get home and finally decided to forego the back roads and hop onto the interstate to get home as quickly as possible.

When they had finished eating, they pointed their bikes and the Admiral's car in a northerly direction and got onto the interstate. They were making good time, traveling about 70 miles per hour, when TJ and Mark noticed some dark clouds ahead of them. TJ switched the stereo on his bike to the weather band radio. They heard that a severe thunderstorm was heading up the coast. There were warnings for severe lightening, heavy downpours, high winds, and the possibility of hail and tornado warnings for the next three hours. They pulled off the road and told everyone what was heading their way.

Heidi said, "Terry told me that on his GPS the next exit is Orangeburg, South Carolina. I looked on my iPhone and found a place. I called and they have rooms for us at the Fairfield Inn. They have a swimming pool and a Jacuzzi. There's also a fireplace to cozy up to. They said with the pending storm, we could park our bikes underneath the store frontage to keep them safe from the hail. They said there's even a large screen television by the fireplace so the guys can watch the World Series."

They all agreed they should put up for the night for safety's sake. They pulled back onto the highway and made a beeline for the hotel.

They checked in the hotel and put all the bags in their rooms. With the storm coming, nobody wanted to go out to eat, so they called Papa John's to deliver pizza along with soft drinks.

The pizza came and they gave the delivery girl a nice tip for coming out with inclement weather coming. They ate and watched the news for the weather report. Pretty soon, it started to get windy and very dark outside. They jumped when they heard the first clap of thunder and when the lightening slashed through the sky, Heidi and Sally went to the windows to see the storm approaching.

The weather person on the television announced, "I'm seeing rotation on the Doppler radar right here in this area." He drew a circle on the screen where there was a cluster of bright yellows and reds on the radar. "If you're in Orangeburg, you need to seek shelter at this time. Go to the most secure place in your home," he urged.

"We're not home; where do we go?" cried Heidi, looking for a place to hide.

"I think our best bet is to stand in the middle of the hallway. That would give us support on both sides. I think that's what we should do," the Admiral yelled, while he herded the women to the hallway.

At that moment, the warning sirens started their shrill wailing. Just a few minutes after the sirens sounded, it sounded like the roar of a freight train going by. TJ held tightly to Sally, as he wiped away the tears streaming down her cheeks. After the roaring noise passed by, there was utter and complete silence. Those who were huddled in the hallway looked at each other in amazement. Heidi had her hand over her mouth and her eyes were wide open with terror. "Was that a tornado?" asked one of the women.

Mark answered, "I don't know, but that silence is eerie. I think we should go check it out and see what happened and if there are any damages or injuries."

The men went out to the lobby and saw that the hotel had not suffered any damage, neither had any of their vehicles. Just as they were telling the women that everything seemed okay, there was the loud screeching of tires and then the horrible grinding of metal on metal and glass shattering. The following screams were heart stopping, but they spurred Paula into action.

She quickly grabbed the small medical bag that she brought and went running in the direction of the screaming. Mark dashed after her and the sight that greeted him was sickening.

Two cars had run off the road and hit a bus stop shelter, where people had taken refuge from the storm. The shelter was smashed almost beyond recognition and people were still screaming inside. As they were running toward the scene, one of the cars back up and drove away.

"Memorize that license plate number, Mark!" shouted Paula, as she assessed the scene.

Paula called 911 and reported the accident. She informed the dispatcher that she was a trained paramedic and could do what needed done until the ambulances arrived. She put Mark on the phone and he gave them the license plate number and description of the car that fled the scene.

The call went out to the first responders, "Charlie response. Multi-vehicle accident, two cars crashed into a bus stop shelter. Five people injured. A paramedic from Pennsylvania is on the scene giving us information about the injuries. Standby for updates on the victims."

Mark, Terry, and TJ set up road flares from the hotel. They directed traffic around the accident until the police and fire responders arrived. As the first ambulances arrived, Paula directed them to the four people who were inside the shelter. When the next group arrived, she directed them to the person in the car. The rescue crew was quickly overwhelmed and asked for more help over the radio. Paula offered to help and they directed her to the least injured of the victims.

With the rain pouring down around them and the lightning flashes blinding them, the guys continued to direct the traffic away from the accident. The rain caused the road to become slippery and one car slammed on its brakes and flipped over off the road. TJ ran to the car and yelled to the paramedics. He pulled the man out of the car, just as it caught on fire; then helped him away from the car before the man collapsed. TJ ran to alert the paramedics about the man's condition.

The police finally showed up and took over the job of taking care of the traffic. They thanked Terry, Mark, and TJ. Other first responders showed up and Paula was sent back into the hotel. The police would be talking to all of them later. The Admiral had been watching everything that happened and was very impressed by what he saw. He made a mental note to put TJ up for a Navy lifesaving medal. He would also make sure that Paula was rewarded in some way too.

"Ugh, I hate cold pizza," grunted TJ.

The front desk clerk heated it up for him and then said, "It's the least I can do for you all. You guys are heroes."

TJ laughed and said it must just come from having been trained by the Navy. He explained that they were all either in the Navy now or had been in the Navy before. The clerk commented that maybe he should join the Navy too; right now, he was working while going to college. The Admiral took his name and said he would see about getting him into a NROTC scholarship program.

They went up to their rooms and changed clothes. The hotel clerk said he would put the wet clothes in the dryer for them. Everyone huddled around the fireplace to get warm and finish eating the pizza. No one really cared who won the World Series, but since the Rangers were the underdogs, they pulled for them.

The next morning was cooler, but otherwise was a perfectly sunny day. There was no trace of the stormy weather. After loading their things into the bikes and the car, they went to eat breakfast. After they had filled up on eggs, bacon, and pancakes, they gathered around in a circle and held hands.

The Admiral lifted his voice up to the heavens in prayer. "Heavenly Father, we come unto You this morning to give praise. Praise for bringing each of us safely through the storm uninjured. We are grateful for the knowledge that Paula has that helped ease some of the suffering of the victims of the horrible accident. We are so thankful for the wonderful fellowship we have enjoyed on this trip. I stand here amazed at the glorious world You have created for us. We were surrounded by its beauty and majesty this past week and I'm grateful for those memories. Please be with us as we journey home; help us and others on the road to remain attentive. Take us home safely, Lord. In Jesus Christ's name I pray, Amen."

They headed out onto the road and in no time they were hugging the Atlantic seaboard on the Coastal Highway. The ride that day was pleasant, but uneventful. They stopped for the night in Morehead City and stayed at the Peppertree Atlantic Beach.

From the beach, they lingered over the sunset before they walked over to the restaurant to get something for supper. After they ate, Jim, Cindy, Mark, and Terry went back to the hotel. Everyone else went for a walk along the beach. Soledad said, "Maybe we should go and give these two love birds some alone time."

"I think it's nice that we're walking together. Just think, I'm the only guy among all you beautiful women. I'm the luckiest man on the beach!" TJ exclaimed.

"TJ, you offered to take me for a ride on your bike before. I wasn't really thrilled about it then; but now I'm thinking maybe, it wouldn't be so bad after all," Soledad commented.

"Sure, I'll take you for a ride. I even have an extra helmet with me."

After visiting the North Carolina Maritime Museum the next morning, they got onto the ferryboats to take them to Route 12. Soledad got on the back of TJ's Harley for her first ride ever on a motorcycle. TJ had given her some pointers, telling her to never take her feet off the foot pegs, even when they were stopped. He also told her not to try to lean or not lean through the turns, instead she should just look over his shoulder in the same direction they were turning.

Riding along the seashore, they saw people riding horses on the beach next to the water. Over the intercom, Mark said, "I wonder how many beach bums will step in horsey poo poo on the beach today."

"Oh my goodness, only you would think of that," said Paula.

Mark said, "I'll just stick to my Steel Horse that I ride."

"Are you wanted?" asked Terry.

"Yes, dead or alive," finished Mark, singing the lyrics.

Soledad got back into the car after the ride and said, "Okay, I get it now; riding is awesome!"

They stopped to have supper together before they went back to Norfolk Naval Base to check back from leave. At supper, Soledad asked TJ if he would call his friend, Lt. Witt. TJ asked her why she wanted him to. She said, "He wanted to take me and Fiona for a ride on his motorcycle and I said no way. Well, maybe you could call him and have him ask me again." TJ said he would e-mail him that night.

The Admiral, TJ, and Sally went to the base and turned in their leave papers before heading home. Mark and Paula, and Terry and Heidi stayed at Sally and TJ's apartment for the night. The next morning, Sally cooked breakfast and told them to feel at home while she and Terry were at work. Paula said, "Thanks, Dear, but we really should be going."

"C'mon, we just spent ten days on the road!" Sally exclaimed. "I think you need a break from the road and a chance to relax. Just chill out today and make yourself at home."

TJ inspected the men for morning muster. He was pleased with the way the men kept everything in tip top shape. He handed out three day passes as a reward for a job well done.

CHARLIE RESPONSE
CHAPTER SIXTEEN

The doctors at Westminster Woods told both Joey D and Sam they would be able to go home for the holidays, as long as their home met with certain handicapped guidelines. Since both families were almost finished building new homes close to each other in Shade Gap that would not be a problem. Their new houses were equipped with extra wide passageways, easy access tubs and showers, and higher commodes with handrails, along with other special features.

Both families were excited with the impending visits. The doctors said that based on how well these visits home went, they may release them to go home, as long as they had home care available to them. Both men still had casts on both legs, so it would be difficult for their wives to care for them alone. Both Hope and Kelly went out and bought used vans with wheelchair ramps, so they could transport their husbands more easily.

Joey D told Kelly that he could not wait to see their new home. It was hard having only seen it in pictures. One thing he was sure of, no matter where they lived, he missed being home with Kelly. Sam agreed, but since he and Hope had relocated to the area from Mississippi, everything would be totally different for him. Even though he had always moved from base to base and ship to ship, his home base had always been in Mississippi. Hope told him they could still visit back home from time to time.

Before the holidays arrived, Frank would be coming home from his deployment. Sam wanted to go meet him in the worst way, but when the doctor gave him the reasons it would be a bad idea, he agreed. He told Hope that he would hold down the home fort, while she and Sammy went to meet Frank. Anyway, Frank had said he would be home for Christmas this year, so he would have both his boys home for the holidays—he could wait for that.

Sammy and Hope flew out to San Diego. They picked up their rental, a Town and Country minivan, and drove to the Navy Lodge San Diego. They rented adjoining rooms and were unpacking their bags when Hope got a phone call. Hope talked for a few moments, hung up, and turned to Sammy. "They've arrived! I'm so excited!" she said.

Twenty minutes later, Sammy and Hope were waiting outside as a taxicab pulled up. The door opened and out stepped Sue and her family. "You must be Frank's mother. I'm Sue! I'm so excited to finally meet you!" Sue immediately hugged Hope tightly. Hope hugged her back, relieved that she was so friendly.

"And you must be the hero that Frank always talks about. You know you are his inspiration. He's always trying to live up to you. I'm so happy to meet you, too!" said Sue, as she grabbed Sammy up in a hug, too.

"Welcome to our family," said Sammy, feeling instantly at ease with her.

Henry shook hands with both Hope and Sammy, saying, "G'day, Mates! I'm Henry, Sue's dad and this lovely Shelia is my wife, Emily. So glad to know you both."

As Sammy helped them inside with their bags, he said, "The Navy Lodge is really close to the base, so we won't be fighting the traffic the whole time we're here. There's a lot of nice hotels in San Diego; but we figured this is nice and inexpensive, which is a plus since we didn't know how long we would be here."

"This is fine, it's just fine," reassured Henry.

They made small talk about the flight and their layover in Hawaii. Then Henry said to Hope, "Can I say one thing to you?"

"Uh oh, should I be worried?"

Henry laughed and said, "Of course not. I just wanted to tell you that I think you and Frank's father raised a really fine young man."

"I'll second that!" agreed Emily. "Do you know when he was in our home, he did the dishes every night, even though I told him not to. He said that his mama raised him right and he would never want her disappointed in him."

"Thank you. I'm proud of both of my sons."

Sue went over and hugged Hope again as she said, "You should be, Hope, umm, I mean Mrs. Adams."

"Honey, you can call me Mom or Hope, whatever you are more comfortable with. My preference would be Mom though," said Hope, as she smiled warmly at Sue.

"Are there any updates on your husband, Hope?" asked Henry.

Hope nodded her head and told him, "The day after we return home, he'll be transported home to spend the holidays with us. He's looking forward to meeting you."

After getting to know one another better, they decided to go to Applebee's for supper. Hope told them it was one of Frank's favorite places. At the restaurant, their waitress said her name was Sheila. Henry, Emily, and Sue laughed. "I'm sorry; we don't mean to be rude. In Australia where we're from, all the girls are called Sheilas," said Sue. Hope explained to the waitress that her friends had just gotten off the plane from Australia; they were all here to see her son who was in the Navy.

As they were eating their supper, the manager came over and introduced himself. He asked if everything was satisfactory. When they replied that everything was delicious, he said that since they had all come such a long way to see one of the Navy boys, he would give them dessert for free. They thanked him and said they would look over the menu. Henry commented, "That was very nice of him."

Meanwhile, things on the USS Ronald Reagan were anything but calm. Everyone on board was getting edgy waiting for the next day. They all enjoyed the liberty ports they visited and they had accomplished a lot during their time away, but they were especially excited about seeing their families again. It sure was hard for the sailors to sleep that night.

The CT communication shack was shut down. Frank had sent out the 120 page end of cruise report, called the Situation Report, and the message they were shutting down. Now there was nothing to do but wait until they heard *Liberty call, liberty call.*

It was hard to wait those last few hours. The crew filled their time in any way they could. Some of them watched TV in the lounge and some played cards long into the night. Frank looked through the pictures of his family and of Sue on his computer. It seemed to him that the ship was going much slower than usual. This was definitely the worst part of the cruise. He felt a little homesick knowing that he was so close to everyone, but still so far away.

Frank finally went to sleep around 0300, but was awake again by 0600. He went to see how far away from the pier they were. He was told it would be a few hours still. He was also informed there would be a uniform inspection. Finally, he had something that would fill up a little of his time. He prepared his dress blues and got them ready for inspection. He also made sure he could see his reflection in his shoes. Frank showered and shaved, and put on his uniform and new hat. He kept some masking tape with him to take the lint off his uniform right before the inspection.

During the inspection, Frank was picked as one of top five most impeccably groomed and won the right to leave the ship early. Wow, listening to Sammy and his dad about keeping dress uniforms and dress shoes just for inspections had really paid off! Maybe he should listen to them more often!

Frank went to the lounge and saw on the TV that the local media was really playing up their arrival. It was not just the aircraft carrier USS Ronald Reagan coming into port; it was the entire battle group that served with it. The destroyers, cruisers, submarines, refueling ships, and supply ships were also coming home. It was worthy of some time on the local news.

Sometimes, it was a thankless job being in the military. Most of the time the media would not report the good things they had done, like rendering aid to a cruise ship in trouble, or delivering food and medical supplies to areas around the world hit by disasters. Most often, the world only heard when they were bombing someone; unfortunately, there was very little balance.

Frank saw an airplane fly out to the Battle Group pulling a banner that read, *Welcome Home USS Ronald Reagan Battle Group*. There were so many crew members with their cameras pointing to the sky that TJ thought it was pretty funny looking, so he snapped a photo of it. He was getting more excited; the time was getting closer and closer. Frank could not wait to see the faces he loved on that pier.

At the hotel, there was a scramble as they all needed the bathrooms to get ready. Sammy put on his dress blue uniform and made sure that his medals and shoes were shiny, as they ought to be. Sue wanted to rush right over to the pier to wait for Frank; but Sammy assured her that it could take hours, before they had the ship docked and everyone disembarked. They decided to go eat some breakfast at the Richard Pancake House. No one really felt like eating much, but they gave it their best effort.

Finally, it was time to go to the base and wait on the docks with all the other families. They were all very excited. Even Sammy, who had been through this many times, caught the fever of excitement. Once they arrived at the base, they listened to the radio hoping to find out how soon the ship would be there.

They stood on the pier with thousands of other people waiting for those they loved and missed. The Navy band proudly played patriotic and naval songs, and sometimes the crowd sang along. People held onto large signs and banners they had made for the returning patriots.

Sue was grateful that this day was perfect in so many ways—the sun was shining; she was surrounded by loved ones; and she would finally get to hug and kiss the man she would soon marry. She stopped cheering and privately thanked God for her wonderful life.

Finally, the escort sail and motorboats came into view with the huge carrier. The crowd grew even more excited, waving their signs, jumping up and down, and cheering loudly. The tugboats went out and greeted the ships by firing water from the fire cannons. The men on the ships were manning the rails in their dress blue uniforms. It was certainly a sight to behold!

The people on the ships could see the pier now, but the ship slowly crept along. Even the sailboats were sailing past them! Frank yelled out, "Hey, we better raise some sails on this ship so we can get there faster!"

A shipmate shouted back, "What do you want to raise, the John B sail?"

Frank scanned the faces of the thousands of people waiting on the pier. How would he ever find his family? Amazingly, he suddenly zoned in on a waving sign with the word Australia on it. When he was able to fully focus on it, he realized he had found them. Henry and Emily had a sign that said, *We came from Australia to see you.* Hope's sign said, *Welcome home, Son!* Sammy waved a sign that read, *Frank, you're still my little brother.* But the one that made him crack a smile was Sue's, *Frank, how about lunch?*

Other ships helped tie the ship to the pier; then they helped bring the Officer's brow and then the Enlisted brow up next to the ship. A voice from the intercom system said, "Attention on the USS Ronald Reagan, secure from manning the rails." A loud cheer went up from the crew. They knew it would not be long now until they were on dry land.

Frank had a meeting to attend, so he headed to his workspace. Lt. Commander Brown said, "We're going to stand down to a six section duty section while we're in homeport. It will be easy to figure out your duty day. Today is Wednesday; duty section five has the watch."

"That's not fair! That means I have duty tomorrow. I've got a wife and kids at home. I only get to spend one night at home and then have to come back to work in the morning!" complained CTN1 Dan Coates.

"You made up the Watch, Quarter, and Station bill. Would you rather have duty today? Because I would be happy to arrange that for you," said the Lt. Commander, glaring at him. "You don't hear Petty Officer Adams complaining about things, do you? His mother and brother came from the east coast, along with his girlfriend, and her parents from Australia. His duty is Friday. Not only that, after he stands his own 24 hour duty on Friday, he's taking Petty Officer Baer's duty on Sunday, so Baer can spend some time with his kids. Baer is going to take Frank's duty on December 23rd, so Frank can go see his father. Everyone in this Division is working things out among themselves, except for you." Coates shifted uncomfortably in his seat as the Lt. Commander continued to scowl at him.

Finally, the Lt. Commander shifted his attention to the rest of the group. Since these people had been out to sea for the last eight months, he wanted to give them some advice about safety and readjusting to family life. Then he reminded them of the days when everyone needed to be back to the ship.

"Men, in closing, I want to tell you that everyone up the Chain of Command has been talking about how great our ship has done on this deployment. Also, everyone up **our** Chain of Command on this ship has been very complimentary of the great job we did in our Division. So, congratulations men for a job well done! Now, go out and have some fun, but please be careful out there. Use your heads!" On the way out the door, the men let out a loud Navy OOOOH RAH!

Frank carried his travel bag with him, along with his computer and camera. He was ready to storm off the ship, but he knew he still had a while to wait.

"Now on the USS Reagan, shift colors." The flag came down from the mast of the ship, while simultaneously a flag was raised on the stern of the ship. The ship was officially docked at this time. They were no longer at sea! The men started to bid each other good-bye, shaking hands, and slapping one another on their backs.

Over the intercom came, "This is your Captain speaking. Now on the USS Ronald Reagan, Liberty Call will commence for Cryptologic Technician Petty Officer 2nd Class Raymond Kosack, who is the winner of the First Kiss contest." The First Kiss dates back to a photograph of a sailor kissing a girl in New York City at the end of World War II. Whenever a ship hits port, that ship holds a drawing to see who gets to become the person off the ship first who gets that first kiss. Photographers gather around to photograph that kiss.

In no time, it seemed that the call came over the ship's intercom, "Now on the USS Ronald Reagan, Liberty Call for all new dads!" Reporters were swarming trying to get that prize winning shot of a father seeing his child for the very first time. One of the baby's had a sign attached to him that read, *Daddy, I've waited my whole life to see you!*

People were so engrossed by the new fathers and their babies, so not many really noticed when the Captain called, "Liberty call for the five sailors who won this morning's uniform inspection."

Suddenly, Frank's heart was racing and he couldn't breathe. He started taking quick shallow breaths. A ship's Master of Arms was standing beside him and said, "Sailor, stand up straight! Take a deep breath and hold it! Now let it out slowly. Things will be fine. Is this your first cruise?"

Frank answered, "Yes, and my mom is out there. My girlfriend from Australia and her parents are out there, too."

The Master of Arms said, "I know you. You're that sailor that saved the cop's life in Australia, aren't you?"

Frank told him that he was. The talking helped calm him down. Before he knew it, Frank was saluting the brow and making his way ashore!

Hope, Sammy, Sue, Henry and Emily were waving their signs frantically. Sue screamed, "THERE HE IS!"

She wanted to take off running, but Sammy held her back. He told her that no one was allowed to go beyond the rope. Finally, Frank was beyond the rope and she took off with tears running down her cheeks. TV and still cameras were on the two of them. Hope and Emily were taking pictures, too.

When they had all passed Frank around for hugs and kisses and then passed him around again, Frank finally had the opportunity to say, "Henry, Emily, and Sue, welcome to America!"

A passing reporter overheard Frank and asked what he meant by that; so Frank told him the story of how they met, fell in love, and would be married next year. After writing everything down, the reporter wandered off in search of some more interesting stories from the reunited friends and families of the crew on the ship.

Sammy said, "How about we get out of here and grab some lunch?"

Everyone agreed. Frank wanted to grab some fast food instead of going to a fancy restaurant, so they found a McDonald's and ordered their food. Frank ordered a twenty piece McNugget chicken, fries, and a large milk shake. His mother exclaimed, "Wow, Frank, you must be hungry!"

Sue said, "That's my man—he eats like a big horse at times."

The manager asked him what ship he was on and Frank said the USS Ronald Reagan. The manager asked, "Isn't that the one that just came back from deployment?"

"Yes, I'm one of the first off. The officers and chief petty officers are getting off now. The rest of the crew will be off within 2 hours."

The manager said, "In that case, your meal is free today. It's my way of saying, 'Welcome Back Home and thank you for your service.' That is, all your meals are free." They all thanked the manager. They said the blessing at the table and asked a special blessing for the restaurant manager. Afterwards Frank laughed as he said, "If I would have known I was getting a free meal I would have ordered the fifty piece McNugget."

They went back to the lodge and Frank and Sammy put on more comfortable civilian clothing. They sat outside for a while and caught up. Frank only let go of Sue's hand to put his arm around her. Hope told Frank how his dad was doing and showed him some pictures of the new house.

Sammy told him that he put a double wide trailer on the land in Mississippi and rented it to a second cousin. "Do you remember little Jimmy Adams?" Sammy asked.

"That little guy? Of course, I remember him."

"Well, that little guy is now about five foot, ten inches tall and about 180 pounds. He's married and working as a bulldozer operator now. He didn't have enough money for a down payment for a home, so I'm renting to him on a rent-to-own deal."

Frank told them that he had to work a 24-hour duty on Friday and also on Sunday. He said on Sunday they should all come onboard for church service and then they could eat lunch with him on the mess decks afterward.

They talked about the holidays and the various comings and goings of everyone. Frank said, "My leave starts Tuesday, but I couldn't get a flight home until Wednesday afternoon."

"Well, Sammy and I are leaving Tuesday afternoon, so we have time to get the new house ready for everyone coming for the holidays.

I'm so excited—your dad gets to come home for Christmas! They will transport him Christmas Eve and, if everything goes well, he'll be able to stay until January third. Frank, when do you have to be back on the ship?" said Hope.

"I have to be back by midnight, January 3rd, because I have duty on the 4th."

After a few hours of catching up, it was time to get ready for supper. They had reservations at Humphrey's Restaurant. Frank and Sammy put their dress blue uniforms back on because Humphrey's was a classy place. Henry noticed Frank's sleeve and asked, "Frank, is there another stripe on your sleeve?"

"It took long enough for someone to notice! I was promoted to Petty Officer Second Class." Frank received a round of congratulations from his family and felt pretty proud of himself.

"Good for you, Frank, good for you!" approved Henry.

They were shown to their table at the restaurant. Henry commented how classy the place looked. Sue exclaimed, "What a view! Look at all the sailboats on the bay. It is so pretty!"

The waitress came to take their drink orders and Frank asked if they had Cherry Coke. She said they did and when she brought it there were even cherries in the glass. "I haven't had a Cherry Coke for so long," said Frank, after he took a long drink from his glass.

Everyone thought their meals were first rate and the view was second to none. As everyone was talking about how much they loved their meals, Frank said, "I have a surprise for everyone tonight. Attached to this restaurant is a place called Backstage Live and we're going there for a concert. Someone special is singing tonight, but that's all I'm going to say right now." Everyone speculated on who it could be, but Frank kept his secret.

They went to the Backstage Live concert and were surprised that it was none other than Australia's own, Olivia Newton John! They enjoyed the concert and knew most of the songs she sang, so they sang along. They had a really good time and told Frank so; he just smiled smugly, because he knew there were more surprises coming.

Everyone was stunned when Olivia Newton John called Sue up on stage. "This next song is especially for you. Your future husband, Frank, wanted this song dedicated to you, but I wanted to bring you up on stage as I sing it."

Sue cried tears of joy as Olivia sang *Hopelessly Devoted to You*. After the song, Olivia said, "I wish you nothing but happiness in your life together."

When Sue went back to her seat, she hugged and kissed Frank. Hope wiped her tears and asked, "Where did you learn to be so romantic, Son?"

"I learned by watching Dad, that's where."

"I think I'm going to love your dad," smiled Sue through her tears.

The next morning as they ate breakfast, Frank told them he had another surprise for them. They all climbed into the minivan and Frank drove as he talked, "In 1851, Americans took a 139-foot yacht over to England to race for the Challenge Trophy. The Americans raced the famous yacht called America and they won. They brought the trophy back to the New York Yacht Club and the Challenge Trophy was later named the America's Cup. No one was able to beat the Americans for 133 years! In 1983, a team from Australia in a boat named Australia II beat Dennis Conner in a boat named Liberty. Australia II had a secretly designed keel called a winged keel. It is now being used on some yachts today."

Frank turned a corner and continued with his history lesson, "Dennis Conner formed a team from the San Diego Yacht club in 1987 and won the Cup back. Fast-forward a decade. In 1995, Dennis Conner sailed the Stars & Stripes USA 34. It was supposed to go against New Zealand's Black Magic. The Yacht Club told Dennis that the other American boat was faster, so instead of using the Stars & Stripes USA 34 that he had been winning with, he changed boats to the Young America USA 36. Black Magic won and the Cup went to New Zealand. I know you must be asking yourselves why I am telling you all of this. Today, we're going to see a replica of the 1851 America and take a whale watching cruise on it."

"WOW!!!"

Frank further said, with a gleam in his eye, "That's not all. We're also going to see Dennis Conner's Stars & Stripes USA 34!"

Henry and Sue both said, "WOW! How cool is this!"

Sue said, "I would give anything to just step foot on one of those America's Cup racing yachts."

Frank teased, "Will you give me a kiss and marry me?"

"Of course, I'll give you a kiss and marry you."

Frank teased and said, "I'll hold you to that."

They arrived at the pier and there was the Stars & Stripes.

"What a beauty!" breathed Hope.

A man stepped up and asked, "Are you Petty Officer Frank Adams?" Frank told him he was. The man continued, "We have some others coming to help fill in as crew members for you. Dennis will be your skipper today for the match race with Abracadabra USA 55."

Hope was astounded, "Excuse me? Did you say match race?"

The man smiled, "Yes, Frank booked this boat months ago. You're going out in the harbor to race and he paid extra to have Dennis Conner along as Skipper. You may not get to take the helm; that will be up to Dennis. However, you'll be raising and adjusting the sails and grinding on the winches."

Everyone was amazed that Frank had given them this rare opportunity. Sue grabbed him and kissed him, whispering, "I think you made my dad's day; no, wait, his life with this. In fact, I love it too."

Sammy took Frank aside and offered, "Little brother, let me pay my share of this."

"No way! This is my big Christmas gift to everyone."

They were in awe as they stepped onto the sailboat. They had their cameras out and took pictures of each other by the equipment. Then Dennis Conner came onto the boat. They were very excited and paid close attention as he went over was would be expected of them. As they showed Dennis the things they already knew, he was impressed.

In fact, they made such an impression that on the last leg of the race, Dennis allowed Sue to take the helm. The men took over the grinders and the sails were perfect. Stars and Stripes 34 surged ahead of Abracadabra USA 55 and won. You would have thought they had won the America's Cup from the way they cheered and screamed.

Dennis looked at them with approval and commented, "You all worked well together. Sue, you really know how to stay on course; you hardly ever had to adjust the helm. You would make a great sailor."

Sue blushed as she thanked him.

Henry and Dennis had formed a little bit of a friendship that afternoon and Henry asked him to go sailing on his boat in Perth. Dennis said it would be nice to go sailing there without having to worry about the Fremantle Doctor, which is the name used for the strong afternoon breeze on the water down in Perth and Fremantle. Henry and Dennis exchanged e-mail addresses and Dennis asked Henry not to give his address out to anyone. "I won't even give it to my family members," assured Henry.

Before heading to the sailboat America, they had time to buy some souvenirs. They bought t-shirts and jackets to commemorate their time on the Stars and Stripes. Henry also bought a Stars and Stripes model for his desk at home.

They hurried to the pier to catch the America whale watching cruise. They saw three large pods of whales and took many pictures of them. The whales were in fine form, blowing air from their blowholes and flicking their tales. There were even several baby whales swimming along. The sunset as they sailed back in was gorgeous. Sue laid her head on Frank's shoulder and said, "This has been the best day ever. I'm so glad we could spend it together."

After a delicious dinner of seafood, they went back to the hotel. It had been such a busy day that everyone was soon sound asleep. The next day would be more relaxing, as they planned to spend it at the San Diego Zoo.

Sunday morning, Frank was back on the ship for morning muster. Soon, the whole family would arrive for church. When they arrived, Frank met them at the Quarter Deck. With both Frank and Sammy in their dress blue uniforms, Hope was proud, not just of how good looking they were, but also that they had both grown into responsible, respected, and God-fearing young men. She took Sammy's arm as they walked to the chapel and Frank introduced them to the chaplain, Commander David Dubbs.

After they enjoyed the ship's church service, Frank showed them all around the ship. They bought a few more souvenirs in the ship's store and then Frank took them up to the ship's bow. He told them that he liked to sit up there whenever there weren't any flight ops going on. Sue commented that it was extremely high and told him to be very careful when he was up there. Frank was touched that Sue cared enough about him to worry, even about the small things.

Eventually, Frank had to get back to work. When the family was leaving, he told them they should go to the beach. "You can't visit San Diego and not spend at least one day at the beach." They decided it was a good idea and went to the hotel to pick up their swimsuits.

The next morning, Frank took his mom and Sammy to the airport; then he spent the rest of the day with Sue and her parents exploring San Diego. After eating dinner at Kansas BBQ, Frank went to the ship's Quarter Deck to sign out for leave; then they all went back to the hotel.

The next morning, Sue waited impatiently for the rest to finish getting ready for the flight to Pennsylvania. She paced from the window to the door, from the door to the bed, and from the bed back to the window again. They ate fast food on the way to the airport to save time. They turned in the rental car and carried their luggage to the check in counter.

They had a short layover in Chicago, just long enough to eat lunch in the airport. Sue was amazed at the moving sidewalks. Frank challenged her to a race to the end of it. Sue felt like she was flying when she ran from one end to the other. She was glad that this area was pretty close to empty, since she and Frank were behaving like children. However, she laughed pretty hard when Frank missed the end of the walk and tumbled head over heels.

They made their connecting flight to Harrisburg, Pennsylvania, and relaxed the rest of the way there. Once they landed and picked up their baggage, they went to the car rental to get the Jeep Grand

Cherokee Frank had arranged for them. He explained to Henry that he wanted a four wheel drive, just in case it was snowy.

They loaded up the Jeep and got on the highway. Frank had not yet been to his parent's new house, so he set up the navigation system to show him the way. When they pulled into the driveway, he was delighted there was at least two inches of snow on the ground.

This would be the first time the Poxons had ever seen snow! Sue reached down and touched it with her fingers, "Frank, it feels so soft, but it's so cold after you hold it for a while."

Frank showed Sue how to make a snowball and said, "This is what we do with it." Frank threw the snowball at Sammy as he came out the door.

The snowball hit Sammy on the shoulder. He quickly made one to throw back at Frank. "Let me help you with your bags," Sammy said to Sue and Mr. and Mrs. Poxon. "Little brother, you can get your own."

Hope followed Sammy out the door and said, "Welcome to our home. Did you enjoy your flight?" When they said they had, she took them in for a tour of the house, leaving Sammy and Frank to carry in the bags.

Sammy put the last of the logs into the fireplace and asked Frank to help him split some more firewood. A short time later, Sue went out to watch them. When she went inside, she said, "Mom, come out here and look. I've got a lumberjack for a future husband." She took a couple of pictures of the boys splitting logs.

When they finally went back in the house, Hope offered them hot chocolate and homemade chocolate chip cookies. Sue shivered and asked how cold it was. Hope told her it was 28 degrees.

"It's a lot colder than 28 degrees! I'm not that dumb."

Hope laughed. "I'm sorry, Sue. I forgot you're from Australia. That's 28 degrees in Fahrenheit, but around minus four degrees in Celsius."

"Wow, that's cold," Sue said while rubbing her frozen fingers.

The next day, Sammy and Frank were outside splitting more wood when the Westminster Woods van pulled up with their dad. Frank went running to help him inside, but hugged him tightly first. Sam was in tears as he went through his new home. He couldn't believe how beautiful and cozy it was. Frank introduced Henry, Emily, and Sue to his dad and they settled in to get to know each other.

Kelly and Joey D lived next door to the Adams; Joey D had come home in the same van. Sometime after lunch, Hope told Frank to take the Poxons over to meet them. Henry asked how far away it was. Hope showed them through the window the Daniels' house in the distance.

They walked over, their boots making crunching sounds in the snow. Sue thought the noise was funny and giggled most of the way. Joey D and Kelly were very happy to meet the love of little Frankie's life. They talked for quite a while before Kelly and Joey D's children started filtering in for the holidays. After introductions, Frank said they should get back home and let the Daniels have some family time. They walked back home in the falling snow, while Frank and Sue held hands.

CHARLIE RESPONSE
CHAPTER SEVENTEEN

"Do you think we decorated enough?" Sally asked TJ for the tenth time.

"Stop worrying. It looks beautiful," reassured TJ.

Sally stopped on the way to the door to straighten one of the stockings hanging above the fireplace. She heard a car door slam and went to open the door for TJ's parents, who had come for Christmas.

After a round of hugs and kisses, Heidi asked what the delicious smell was. Sally told her she had pies in the oven. Meanwhile, TJ carried their bags to the guest bedroom.

"Are you sure this isn't going to be too much trouble for you, Sally?" asked Heidi.

"Are you kidding? I've been waiting to entertain for Christmas in my own home since I was a little girl. My mother always made it look so fun."

Pretty soon, the doorbell rang and TJ opened the door to admit Sally's parents, James and Cindy Morgan. They all warmly greeted the newcomers and Cindy said that Soledad, Sally's sister, would be there in about two hours. TJ asked, "Admiral, did you have a good trip over?"

"Now, now, my boy, I think since we're off base and I'm out of uniform you should probably call me James. We had a nice drive over, not too much traffic this afternoon."

Soledad arrived on time and Sally soon had a tasty supper of baked ham and sweet potatoes on the table. TJ asked the blessing and thanked the Lord for all the good things that had happened to them over the last year. After that, they all filled up on the good food and then Sally brought out the pies, apple and pumpkin.

When they had all eaten their fill, they put on their dress uniforms and went to the Christmas Eve service at the Norfolk Base Chapel. Chaplain Henderson welcomed everyone to the service and they sang a few traditional Christmas hymns. The candlelight from the holiday decorations flickered as the reading of the birth of Jesus Christ was heard by all who attended. A reverent quietness filled the chapel as the Chaplain told of the lowly birth of the King of Kings. When the sermon was finished, they stood as attendants passed out candles and lighted them. Holding the candles, everyone sang *O Holy Night*.

The Morgan family walked out together. Sally reminded them, "Remember we're going to eat around 1 p.m. If you want to come over earlier, you can." They said their good-byes and everyone left for home.

In Shade Gap at St. Luke's United Methodist Church, the Daniels' and the Adam's families went to the service on Christmas Eve. Everyone at the church was excited to finally see Joey D again. They welcomed Sam and his family very warmly too. Kelly introduced everyone who was visiting from out of town.

Kelly and Joey D's grandkids, Joseph and Peggy Sue, sang with the children's choir. Then the pastor read from the second chapter of Matthew and very straightforwardly told the congregation of Herod and the birth of Christ. After the simple service, the church had hot chocolate and cookies in the fellowship hall downstairs. The people spent their time talking and laughing with each other.

Henry was asked how they would have spent Christmas in Perth. He told them, "We go to church on Christmas Eve. Then on Christmas Day, Santa Claus comes in on a sailboat or a surfboard and delivers gifts. We open gifts and then later we get together as a family and eat our meal. Afterwards, we would go to the beach, because it would be in the mid-30s, which is around low to mid 90s here. We spend the day surfing or sailing. It's totally different than here, but so far I like the change."

After the fellowship at the church, the people walked through town singing Christmas carols while a little bit of snow fell. It seemed fitting when they sang *It's beginning to look a lot like Christmas* with the snow falling as they sung. A school bus picked them up at the other end of town to take them to their cars at the church. Everyone wished each other a Merry Christmas and they went on their merry way home.

When they got back to Hope's the phone rang. She answered it, then said, "Emily and Henry, it's for you."

It was Mick calling from Australia. His ship pulled in to port early. He was supposed to come home in February, but came home early due to a bent shaft. He said that he and Becky had gotten engaged. They had been dating for three years. Emily said, "It's about time! We're so happy for you, son. Have you set a date?"

Sue came over to talk to her brother and was happy when he said that he was finally going to marry Becky. "Oh, I'm so glad! I really like her—she just feels like family."

They told everyone the news when they hung up the phone. Everyone congratulated them and Frank said he was sorry to have missed meeting her while he was in Perth.

The phone rang again and this time it was Mark and Paula. They told Sam they had just gotten back from delivering toys with their H.O.G. Chapter. Most of the members had driven their cars, but a few had braved the winter's cold and rode their bikes, like they did. Mark said they were going to try to visit on Christmas or the following day.

Henry said, "It's the same in Australia. H.O.G. does a lot of charity work there also. I say H.O.G. stands for Hearts of Gold!"

"Amen to that, mate!" agreed Sam.

The Daniels' house was filled with grandchildren after the church services. They gave each child one gift to open. They ate pie and pecan rolls, and drank coffee or hot chocolate. After the children had put out the cookies for Santa, Tracy started putting coats on the kids.

"I really hate to see you go, but it's starting to snow harder now. I want you to get home before the roads get too bad," said Joey D.

"I need to get the kids in bed anyway, Dad," said Tracy.

Soon, there was more than six inches of snow on the ground. Todd went home and brought out his Morgan horse and hooked up the sleigh. Joey D said he was too tired that evening to go out for a ride, but he would on Christmas Day. He asked Todd to take the sleigh over to the Adams and see if the Poxons would like a ride. He said they probably had never been on a sleigh ride before. So Todd drove his horse driven sleigh over, with the lanterns glowing softly and the sleigh bells jingling.

Henry and Emily took the first ride and loved it. Hope covered them with a warm blanket, so they were cozy when they rode through the snow in the field. There was little traffic on the road, so there was no sound in the field except for the sound of the horse's hooves. "It's so quiet; I swear I can hear the snow falling," said Henry.

When they pulled back into the yard, Emily thanked Todd for taking them. "That was the most peaceful thing I've ever done in my life," Emily told him.

"I'm so glad you enjoyed it."

Sammy, Frank, and Henry helped Sam into the sleigh, so that he and Hope could take a turn around the field too. Hope asked if he had taken his mom and dad out for a ride earlier this evening. Todd said that his dad had decided he would enjoy a ride better tomorrow, when he had rested up a bit. Hope invited him to come in for a warm drink and a snack when he was done giving rides.

Finally, it was Frank and Sue's turn. They got under the blanket as Todd drove the sleigh away into the night. Sue commented how peaceful the quiet night was and Frank told her how much he was enjoying his first sleigh ride.

"What? You've never done this before either?" Sue was shocked.

"Honey, I grew up on different Navy bases around the world and then in Mississippi, where there isn't really any snow. Then I joined the Navy and was stationed in San Diego and there's no snow there either. So to answer your question—no, I haven't done this before. I'm really glad I'm doing it with you for the first time." The two kissed and held hands under the blanket. "You're so pretty with snowflakes in your hair and on the end of your nose," Frank told Sue as he brushed snowflakes off her face.

At the end of the ride, Todd went into the house with Frank and Sue and announced, "Here I am. I've always been a sucker for homemade cookies, so I guess I can stay for just a little bit."

They were having a good time talking as Todd warmed himself by the fire. Then he heard tones go off on Hope's scanner. "Oh, no!

Too many tones—that could mean a structure fire. I'm the Chief of Company 14 of Shade Gap's volunteer firemen," Todd told them.

Sammy said, "Both Frank and I have fire fighter training from the Navy."

Then the tones and siren for Company 14 went off. Todd said, "That's me. I'll have to drive the horse over to the barn."

"We could help out. I could drive us there in my Jeep," offered Frank.

"Alright, I never turn down good help. Hope, can you call Bobbie Jo to come take the horse over to the barn for me?"

Off they went on a Charlie Response to a structure fire in a place called Black Log. Several other fire companies were also called to help fight the fire. Todd told Frank to follow behind the fire trucks with his four ways on.

Hope bowed her head where she stood at the kitchen counter and prayed for the safety of not only her boys, but everyone connected to the fire. As soon as she finished, Kelly knocked on the back door. She told Hope she was going to the fire hall to make coffee and sandwiches for the men, because when they eventually came back they would be cold and hungry. She asked if someone could go sit with Joey D, because she would probably be gone most of the night. It was decided that Hope and Sue would go with Kelly to the fire hall, while Henry stayed with Joey D and Emily stayed with Sam.

At the fire hall, Sue fought back tears as she worked on making plenty of coffee and hot chocolate. When they had plenty of food and hot drinks made, they loaded them into the back of the pickup truck and went to deliver them to the men. Then they headed back to the fire hall to make another big batch of everything.

"With a cold night like this and being this close to Christmas, I'm almost willing to bet that the cause is one of two things, a wood burning stove or an overloaded electric plug," commented Kelly.

When they were working on more sandwiches, Kelly excused herself and went to talk to someone. When she was finished, she came back and told Hope and Sue that it was a house fire. Two adults and two children, ages five and three lived in the house. Thankfully, no one was hurt; but they had lost everything!

Kelly said, "I'll call the Red Cross to get the ball rolling on getting them a place to stay. I'll also work on getting a clothing drive set up for them. We also need to make sure those little ones have presents from Santa." She stopped a moment to gather her thoughts and then she was off to do her job.

After she called the Red Cross, Kelly called her pastor and told him what was going on. They worked together to get things in order for the family as quickly as possible. In Orbisonia, near Black Log, other people were doing the same thing. The southern end of Huntingdon County was coming together as a community in a time of crisis. They pulled together to help a young family, who had just lost everything on Christmas Eve; and most of the people did not even know who they were helping.

Sue was getting a firsthand look at what true Americans are all about, not the Hollywood version that tears America down. She was seeing hard working people coming to the aid of their fellow citizens in any way they could and she was impressed.

Already Kelly had a load of clothing and presents for the family loaded in the back of her truck. She drove out to the fire scene to deliver her load to the Red Cross volunteers there. The fire was not even out yet and the family was being provided for, due to the giving nature of good Christian families.

Kelly talked to the Red Cross and the small family and told them that a member of her church, Mr. Peterson, had an empty mobile home that he was willing to give them for four months' rent free. After the four months, they could work out further details with him. Kelly gave the Red Cross Representative Mr. Peterson's phone number.

Mr. Peterson was already hard at work getting the small house ready for the devastated family. He even put up a small Christmas tree for them and put some presents under it. He wedged an envelope into the branches of the tree—inside the envelope was a check for $500 from the church to help them in their time of need.

Kelly went back to the fire hall and loaded another round of sandwiches and hot drinks, along with bottled water, into her truck. Sue, Hope, and Kelly dropped them off at the fire scene. When they saw the burned out shell of the house, they prayed and praised God that no one was hurt. Then they turned and went home.

It was 2:30 in the morning and Joey D was sound asleep when Kelly went in the house. Henry was asleep in the rocking chair. She tried to wake him to move him to the couch, but he said he would go ahead and walk back over to the Adams' house.

Sue decided to wait up for Frank. She was worried and trying not to cry. "Mom, those flames were so high! All those men are putting themselves in danger. I'm scared for Frank."

Emily put her arm around Sue and tried to comfort her. She reminded Sue that Frank had extensive training by the Navy in firefighting. Eventually, everyone went to bed, except for Sue.

It was almost 5 a.m. when Sammy and Frank came in, cold and covered in soot. Sammy went to the bathroom to wash up. Frank was creeping quietly to the other bathroom when he saw Sue curled up on the end of the couch asleep. He noticed that her nose was red and her eyes were puffy from crying. He took a quick shower and went back to the couch to sit with her. She shifted and he wrapped her in his arms. Frank immediately fell asleep.

Hope was the first one up and she proceeded to get breakfast ready for everyone. She saw Frank with his arms wrapped protectively around Sue, still sleeping soundly. "Well, look at the love birds," she commented to herself.

Hope was making her boys' favorite breakfast, scrambled eggs and her famous biscuits and gravy. She was just putting the biscuits into the hot oven, when Sue wandered into the kitchen and sat at one of the stools at the island rubbing her eyes. Moments later, Frank also came into the kitchen. He kissed Sue and then kissed his mother. "Merry Christmas to my two favorite ladies!" he said, happily. He looked at Sue's still swollen eyes and kissed them gently, "You worry too much, Sweetie. I'm okay."

Sue smiled and told him she was alright, "I know. I just love you so much, so I worry when I think you're in danger. It was just a lousy night."

Sammy came into the kitchen, sniffing the fragrance in the air, "I assume I'm smelling biscuits, which I hope will be accompanied by some delicious gravy soon. Frank, we should head outside and split some more firewood before breakfast." So they shuffled out into the snowy backyard to work up an appetite.

Hope called them in for breakfast and each of them brought in an armload of wood. Sam bowed his head and thanked the Lord for keeping everyone safe last night. He prayed for the family whose home had been lost and praised God for the community that stepped in to help them. He asked God's blessing on the food and said amen.

Everyone dug in and enjoyed the filling breakfast. Hope already had the turkey in the oven and good smells wafted throughout the house.

Over in the Daniels' house, Kelly made the coffee and mixed up the pancake mix. She then went into the bedroom to help Joey D into his wheelchair. In about four hours, the rest of their family would be coming for the Christmas celebration.

Joey D made it out to the kitchen and kissed his wife, "Merry Christmas, Honey." They sat down to eat and she told him all about fire of the night before. He said, "We should think of something to do for the family."

"How about we invite them to Christmas Dinner?" asked Kelly.

"That's the ticket! Good idea, let's do that!"

Kelly called Todd on the phone. He said as soon as the kids were done opening their gifts, he would drive over to see if the family would like to join them.

• • • • • • • • • • •

In Virginia Beach, TJ and Sally woke up to their first Christmas morning together as husband and wife. It was a chilly Virginia Beach morning. It had rained overnight, causing some dampness in the air. It was only 54 degrees at 8 a.m., quite different than Pennsylvania at 28 degrees, with six inches of snow on the ground. Sally started to get breakfast when Terry and Heidi came out to the kitchen and said Merry Christmas.

After they finished eating, Terry and TJ washed dishes as Sally and Heidi stuffed the turkey and put it in the oven. Heidi said, "TJ, I'm seeing the presents under the tree and am having a hard time believing that you've waited this long to open them. You could never wait when you were younger."

"Sally wanted to wait until her parents arrived, so we could all open gifts together as a family."

The vegetables were fresh and ready to be cooked. Everything was ready. There was nothing left to be done, so they sat down with coffee and cookies in front of the fireplace to talk together. Sally received a flurry of phone calls from her friends, one right after the other, all wishing them a Merry Christmas.

Sally spoke to Fiona for quite a while. They talked about the weather; Fiona told her it was only 72 degrees in Mayport. She also told her she had worked duty the night before on Christmas Eve. Then she teased, "I know something you don't know."

"What do you know that I don't know?" asked Sally.

"Well, I know that Soledad has been spending a lot of time with Doug Witt lately."

"What?!?" exclaimed Sally, wondering why Soledad was keeping this fact from her.

Fiona explained that Doug and his shipmate Lt. Jg. Bruce Bair had taken herself and Soledad on several motorcycle rides lately. Fiona would drive up to the base in Kingsland, Georgia, to meet them whenever she could. They had ridden on a couple of Toys for Tots runs together, as well as rides around the countryside of Georgia. After riding for the day, they would all go out to dinner together. Lately, she noticed that Soledad and Doug were spending a lot more time than just riding together though.

"Soledad didn't tell me anything about any of this! Do you think it's serious?" asked Sally.

"Well, they meet each other for lunch several times a week. I know that Doug was talking about trying to get a flight up there to surprise her. He said that he would fly up there, even if he could only spend four or five hours with her. He's been sitting at the airport on standby. So, what do you think? Does it sound serious to you?"

"Wow!"

"Exactly! Anyway, I thought I would give you a heads up that he may arrive at any time. I thought it would be great if you got her reaction on video. If you do that, you have to send it to me though," confided Fiona.

"I will, I promise. I need to go now, Fiona. Thanks for the info. I can't wait to tell TJ this! I don't even think he knows anything. Bye for now. Have a great Christmas!"

TJ could not believe that his good friend, Half Witt, was dating Soledad and had not told him anything. As they were talking about it, there was a knock on the door. Sally opened the door and there stood Doug!

"How did you get here so fast? Fiona just told me ten minutes ago?" Sally asked, surprised.

He told Sally he was lucky enough to catch a flight quickly. He said he had a three day pass and he hoped it was okay with them that he just showed up like this. TJ slapped him on the back and said he was obviously getting better at keeping secrets these days.

Sally called her parents to find out when they would be leaving to come over and her mother told her they were walking out the door right then. Sally then turned to TJ and Doug, with a gleam in her eye, and said, "I have an idea! You guys come with me."

They all went out to the dumpster and found a box big enough for Doug to fit inside. TJ hauled it up to the apartment and wrapped it with festive Christmas wrapping paper. Sally asked Doug if he thought he could hide inside the box for about half an hour. Doug said that he would do anything for Soledad.

A short while later, Doug was tucked safely inside the box and TJ held the video camera as Sally opened the door for her parents and sister. Sally said that she was so excited this year about the holiday and wanted to open gifts right away.

Everyone settled around the Christmas tree and TJ said, "Soledad, you have the biggest gift this year, so you get to go first."

Soledad pulled the bow and when the box opened, out popped Doug, singing *You're All I Want For Christmas*! She screamed and then stopped breathing for a few seconds. Then she started crying and ran into Doug's arms, while everyone else looked on, happy for the new couple.

After everyone opened their gifts, the men went into the living room to watch football and the women went into the kitchen to finish making the Christmas meal. Sally joked that there were too many cooks in the kitchen, but they all stayed to help anyway.

The men were talking sports amongst themselves, picking who they thought would win the games they were watching. All of them except TJ picked the Dallas Cowboys to prevail over the Arizona Cardinals. TJ thought Arizona would win because the Cowboys had not been playing well for a while and the game was at the Cardinal's home field. Sally's father said, "With me taking over Destroyer Group 20, I have connections. If the Cardinals win, I'll have you transferred to Greenland for a three year unaccompanied tour of duty. You think you could handle three years away from Sally?"

TJ laughed out loud and said, "I stand by my choice."

Eventually, Sally called them in for dinner. TJ sat at the head of the table and gave the blessing. They all dug in to a tasty dinner of turkey, mashed potatoes, noodles, corn, and cranberry sauce. Sally was complimented many times over on her first holiday dinner. After dinner, the men cleared the table and washed the dishes to give the women a break.

TJ went out to the garbage dumpster with Sally to help put the garbage out. As they were walking back in, James yelled, "TJ, get back in here now!" TJ and Sally broke into a run, thinking something was wrong. They burst through the door to hear James say, "TJ, did you tell your wife that you are being transferred to Greenland for three years?"

"What?!?" cried Sally. Her father pointed to the television screen which read Arizona-27, Dallas-26. The men were heartily laughing, but poor Sally was just confused. Her dad explained the joke he had played on TJ.

When the Morgans were getting ready to go home, the Admiral offered Doug a place to stay. "I wouldn't want to put you all out, but thanks anyway."

"Nonsense, we have an extra room and Soledad is staying as well. Get your bags and come on," ordered the Admiral. They said their good-byes and drove home.

. . . .

When Todd's family was finished opening their presents, they all piled into the car for the drive to his parent's home. He stopped by to ask the Scotts if they would like to join them for Christmas dinner later. They accepted and Todd told them he would be back to pick them up around noon.

Little Joseph was happy to see his Mee Maw and Pappy when they finally arrived. He went running to them, shouting, "Merry Christmas, Mee Maw and Pappy! Did Santa Claus come to see you, too?"

"Yes, he sure did! Why don't you go and see what he brought. I'm pretty sure there's something under that tree for you," said Joey D after he gave Joseph a big hug.

Joseph yelled, "Alright!" He went running over to the tree and poked through the presents. Bobbie Jo told him he had to wait until Uncle Rich and Aunt Tracy got there. Joey D told Joseph to come over and tell him what presents he had gotten that morning.

The Myers pulled into the driveway. Peggy Sue jumped out of the car and ran into the house yelling, "Merry Christmas!"

Tracy got little Ritchie out of the car seat and into his carrier. Kelly said, "Here, let me have my little boy. Merry Christmas to all!"

Kelly told her, "Todd invited the fire victims, the Scotts, to eat Christmas dinner with us. He's going to pick them up at noon, so I think we should open our gifts sooner rather than later, but I brought a gift for each of their family members too."

The children were happy opening their gifts. Pappy and Mee Maw were happy being with their grandchildren on Christmas morning.

Todd went to pick up the Scotts. He brought them back to the house and introduced them to everyone. "This is Leroy and his wife Monique. This is their five year old son, Tyrone, and their three year old daughter, Latisha."

The Scotts were genuinely welcomed by all who were there and Joey D gave each of them a gift. Monique said, "You didn't have to do that. Inviting us for dinner was more than we expected. Thank you so much!"

The kids received teddy bears with the Navy symbol on their bellies. Leroy and Monique opened their gift to find Navy hoodies. They were appreciative of the gifts. They said they were unsure how they would have managed Christmas without the kindness of complete strangers. Kelly put her arm around Monique and said, "Well, we're not strangers anymore, are we?"

They went to the dining room table for the Christmas meal and Joey D said the blessing. He thanked the Lord for all the blessings they had received and for their new friends, the Scott family.

After the meal, Todd asked the Scotts if they had ever taken a sleigh ride before. They said they never had, so he went to the barn and hooked up the horse and sleigh. He took them for a nice long ride before he took them back to their new home.

Frank and Sue enjoyed their first holiday together. They went outside to build a snowman. When they realized they did not know how, they went back inside to ask Hope. When she finished giving them instructions on the best way to build one, she also told them how to make snow angels. Frank opened the door and held it for Sue when they went back outside. They believed they built the best snowman ever and took pictures of it and posted it on Facebook. They were making the most of their time together.

When it was time for supper, they gave thanks, not only for the food, but also for the Poxons visiting them. They wished it would happen many more times in the future.

Kelly and Joey D's family had the tradition of making homemade ice cream every year on Christmas. They called the Adams family and invited them to join in the fun.

Kelly showed the women how to cook the ingredients and put it in the container. The men carried it outside and packed ice and snow all around it. When he started cranking the handle, Todd told them, "The key is to keep turning it at a nice even pace. You also have to keep packing it with snow. We put some salt on the snow to make it even colder. Right now, the crank is pretty easy to turn, but after twenty or thirty minutes, you'll think your arm is going to fall right off. That's when it's done and we can take it in and eat it."

When they took it inside, Kelly handed the dasher to Rich and told her guests, "We always take turns getting the dasher. They all keep pretty good track of whose turn it is."

"What's the big deal about getting the dasher?"

Rich licked the dasher, rolled his eyes, and said, "Yummy, that's good! The person that gets the dasher gets the first taste of the ice cream!" Kelly filled everyone's bowls and they all enjoyed the ice cream. Everyone agreed it was the best ice cream they had ever had. Hope said she would have to get the things so she could make some at her house too. Kelly said they not only do this at Christmas, but also whenever there was a big snowstorm.

"We figure once a blizzard hits, we're not going anywhere anyway. We might as well sit tight and make ice cream," Kelly explained.

When they had gone home, Frank said, "Dad, you know what we forgot to do today?"

Sam thought about it for a moment and said, "What?"

"We forgot to watch the football game. I was actually having such a good time that I completely forgot about it," said Frank.

Both Sam and Sammy looked at Frank with their mouths wide open, and then Sam said, "You know what? I don't think I even care. I had a really good time today. This has been a great Christmas."

"Me too," echoed Sam.

Puzzled, Hope looked at her men, "I think the world is going to end or something. These three have never forgotten about sports before!"

Throughout the week, it stayed in the low 30s. Hope took her visitors to visit some state parks and showed them the sights in the area. She was hoping the water would be frozen at Trough Creek State Park so they could ice skate, but unfortunately it was not. The Poxons said they would have to come back sometime during the summer months. It would give them all something to look forward to.

Sam had to go to Westminster Woods to be checked out by the doctor. The Poxons said they would like to go along to see where he had spent so much time after the accident. At the nursing home, Sam introduced everyone to Sue and her family. Sam was a talkative, friendly man and while he was a resident of Westminster Woods he had talked a lot about his sons. Some of the other residents asked Frank if he had any pictures of when he was in Australia. Hope said they really did not have time right now, but they could come back the following day for a presentation. Sam's nursing home friends were very excited about it and the nursing home said they would set a room for the picture show.

On the way home, they all stopped at Original Italian Pizza and filled up on ham and pineapple pizza. As usual, Frank ate twice as much as anyone else and then wiped his mouth and said, "Okay, so much for that. By the way, what's for supper?"

The following day, Hope called Kelly to invite her and Sam to the iPhoto presentation of Frank's leave in Australia. Kelly said she would put Joey D into the van and meet them there.

When they arrived at Westminster Woods, everything had been set up for them. There were about 75 people waiting to see the pictures. As Frank was going through the pictures, people would ask questions. Frank asked Sue to answer them and explain some of the sights they were seeing.

Afterwards, Nurse Debbie talked to Frank about her son. She said that she wanted him to go to college, which they could not easily afford. However, her son wanted to join the Navy and was constantly telling her the good he could do if he were in the Navy. Frank told her about the Navy ROTC Scholarship and the benefits it could have for her son.

He gave her his e-mail address and made arrangements to talk to her and her son about how to land the job you want in the Navy. He told Debbie that he would do all that he could to help them out.

Frank was dreading New Year's Eve, because he knew it meant his time with his family and Sue was coming to an end for a very long time. It was snowing again, so Todd brought the sleigh out. They had a pleasant time going out for rides, but the snow kept coming down harder and harder. By 7 p.m. there was over ten inches of snow on the ground. Most of the people who had plans to go out for New Year's Eve were canceling their plans, because the forecast called for up to twelve more inches. It was going to get nasty outside, not the kind of weather you want to get stuck in.

In the early afternoon, Frank had taken the Jeep out to pick up more bread, milk, and eggs, along with other food basics. While he was out, he also stopped at the hardware store and bought an ice cream maker. While he was there, he saw a nice Winchester Model 94 30-30. He asked the clerk if there was a waiting period to buy the gun. The clerk said he could buy it and carry it out. As Frank paid for it, he was pleased with himself for finding it, because he always liked this style of gun—he thought it looked like a cowboy's rifle.

When Frank returned to the house, Kelly and Joey D came over and she showed them again how to cook the ice cream. As the boys were outside turning the crank of the ice cream maker, Frank told Todd about the rifle.

"Are you going to shoot it at midnight?"

Frank quizzically looked at Todd and asked, "Why would I do that?"

"Well, out here in the country, we take our guns out and shoot them up into the air to shoot in the New Year. It's been going on here for over a hundred years!"

They talked about it a while longer and Frank decided that he would take out his gun at midnight. Sammy said he wanted to get in on the fun too and so did Sue. Todd suggested that the next day they should set up a target in the field and have some target practice. They all agreed that would be fun.

TJ and Sally were spending New Year's Eve alone. Soledad and Doug had gone back to Georgia and their two sets of parents had gone to their own homes. While TJ and Sally were listening to fireworks going off all around them to ring in the New Year, gunshots were echoing off the mountains in Pennsylvania.

In the afternoon on New Year's Day, TJ put on his wetsuit, took his surfboard, and went for one ride on a wave. When he came back in, he said that he had done the first wave of the New Year on Virginia Beach. Sally took pictures of him and sent them to the local paper.

Back in Pennsylvania, Frank loaded up the all the baggage in the Jeep. The Adams and the Poxons bid each other a teary farewell. In the short time they had together, they had become very fond of each other.

While Frank was driving down the highway, Sammy called. Frank answered on his Bluetooth device. Sammy told him that he just got the call to go back to Little Creek and he would have a desk job for now. His medical leave was finally over. Frank said, "Well, big brother, you take care of yourself and don't try to rush things. More than anything though, try to avoid papercuts."

Once Frank's plane landed in San Diego, he picked up a rental vehicle and drove to the Navy Lodge. He stayed the night. In the morning Henry drove him to the ship for his 24 hour duty. He said good-bye to Sue at the hotel, because he would not be able to get off in time to see them off to the airport. It was more difficult than he imagined it would be. He did not even know when he would be able to see her again. He knew he would be deployed again soon and did not really know what would happen after that; but he knew it would be many months before he would be able to put his arms around her again.

Sue called him many times that day; it was harder for her to let him go. Frank's Division Officer Lt. Commander Tom Brown noticed how hard coming back onboard had been for Frank. He told Frank to invite Sue and her parents to come to the ship for supper that evening.

They ate in the USS Ronald Reagan's chow hall. After eating, they went up on the flight deck and spent time just being together. They looked out over the water, watching yachts and sailboats go by the naval base for a little while.

Frank took them down to his berthing, but he was not supposed to have any females there, so they did not stay long. Finally, they could not delay the inevitable any longer. It was time for them to go. Frank walked them to their vehicle. He kissed Sue good-bye and held her close while she cried. After a few minutes, she straightened up and said, "I'm okay now. I'm glad I was given the gift of a few more hours with you. I'm going to hold onto these precious memories until I see you again. Don't worry. I'm a tough girl."

It was a very long walk back to the ship for Frank. It was all he could do to just walk up the brow of the ship.

CHARLIE RESPONSE
CHAPTER EIGHTEEN

Two months later, Frank was on a conference call with his parents in Pennsylvania and Sue in Australia. He told them about all the people on the pier saying good-bye to the sailors leaving for their deployment on the ship. They would be gone for several months.

Frank was telling them all that was going on in his world. "Our new CTN, Seaman Apprentice Martina Gonzales came in to learn how to bring up the circuits last night. This is her first duty assignment after A School. The Chief put her on my watch. She seems to be nice and eager to learn."

The ship's horn sounded one blast, meaning it was leaving the pier. The Captain called, "Shift Colors." They were now underway again. Sam and Hope told their son so long for now. They would talk to him again later and would send him care packages throughout the cruise.

Sue said that if she closed her eyes, she could see San Diego in her mind and that made her feel closer to him. After they talked for a while longer, Frank said that he needed to go to lunch and then get to bed.

After Frank woke up and ate supper, he went back to work. Some people were somber and others were excited. Martina was feeling homesick already. Frank tried to make her feel better. He told her that it was normal and everyone feels homesick from time to time. He said the best way to get past it was to stay busy and keep her mind occupied. Frank assigned her to work the message desk to keep her mind off her troubles.

Martina was so busy that she almost missed midnight rations. Frank had to go tell her and two others that they needed to go eat. He would eat after they came back.

Frank established the backup communications with the Carrier Battle Group ships, USS Chancellorsville CG-62, USS Preble DDG-88, and USS Higgins DDG-76. All three ships were manned by good men and the USS Ronald Reagan was honored to have them as part of the battle group.

The first night shift went well. When communications started to slack off around 0400 Frank held a mini training session. He wanted his watch section to be well trained and prepared for any situation.

They finally fell into a normal routine after the first few weeks. They were sailing to the Sea of Japan for some exercises with the South Korean Navy. On the afternoon of March 11, the ship's alarm for General Quarters went off. "This is not a drill, general quarters, general quarters. All hands man your battle stations."

Once battle stations were manned, the Commanding Officer announced that a 9.1 earthquake hit mainland Japan and there were tsunami warnings for the Sea of Japan, South China Sea, and most parts of the Pacific Ocean.

Reports had wave heights of 133 feet hitting the Miyako and Sendai areas of Japan. After securing from general quarters, some of the women started a clothing drive on the ship. They gathered anything they thought would be helpful to the Japanese people.

Within the first few hours, the crew of the USS Ronald Reagan gathered blankets, pants, shirts, jackets, socks, towels, shoes and stuff toys from sailors throughout the ship.

The Captain received orders to steer the aircraft carrier towards Japan and help out anyway they could. The ship was used as a refueling platform for the Japanese Navy, Japanese Coast Guard, and US Navy helicopters to fly to the mainland with supplies. They would also to bring back injured people to be treated at the ship's Sick Bay. During those first few days, over 500,000 pounds of supplies were flown off the USS Ronald Reagan. Here was a warship being used for good and most of the people of the world would never know it.

A few days later, the ship was forced to move to avoid a radioactive plume from the Fukushima Nuclear Power Plant accident. More than a dozen helicopter crewmembers from the ship had to go through the decontamination process. Days later, the crew conducted a radiation decontamination of the ship to remove any radiation hazards.

Sam and Hope were very worried about Frank. They had not received any letters or e-mails from him for two weeks. In Australia, Sue was also worried. She called Hope to see if they had heard anything from him lately. They knew where he was and what was going on in that part of the world. They were worried about the nuclear reactor that they saw on the news. Sue told Hope she was not sleeping well and could not stop thinking about Frank.

"Sue, hold on, I've got a call coming in. Let me put you on hold. If we get cut off, I'll call you back."

When Hope answered the call, she heard Sammy say, "Mom, I only have a minute to say this, so don't interrupt. Frank and most of the crew are fine. Some of the helicopter crew were treated for radiation and are now okay. The ship will be leaving the area very soon. Please don't worry. I have to go now. Love you. Bye."

Hope went back to the call with Sue and told her everything Sammy had said. She told Sue that sometimes you just have to put all your worries in the hands of God. Sue said she would do that now. They talked a few more minutes and hung up.

A few weeks later, Japan's Minister of Defense praised the United States for giving Japan help in her hour of need. Frank made the comment that it felt good to help a country in trouble and have it recognized.

Frank was talking to Martina about where he would like to be stationed next. "You know what? I wouldn't mind being stationed on the USS George Washington. Her homeport is in Japan, so you could serve on a ship and be stationed in a foreign port. My re-enlistment is coming up and I've been thinking quite a bit on where I'd like to be. I know I could request just about anywhere in the world, but since Sue and I will be getting married, I kind of want her to become familiar with the United States first. With that in mind, I'll probably request Norfolk or Washington D.C. or maybe I'll just stay onboard here for another year, since we're going to the yards in Washington."

Martina looked thoughtfully at Frank and asked, "You really care a lot about Sue, don't you?"

"More than anyone will ever know. I never wanted to be tied down. I wanted to see every part of the world. I wanted to be assigned to both East Coast and West Coast ships. I bought into that whole dream of a girl in every port, you know?"

Martina nodded her head; she was familiar with that dream. Frank said, "Then I met Sue and my whole world changed. It immediately changed the way I thought about my future. She was everything I wanted."

"Frank, that's so sweet!"

"I told Sue and my family that the ship now has a Facebook site. They can go to it anytime and it will keep them informed of everything that's going on here. You should tell your family about it too. I'm sure Jose would like it too."

Martina said she would tell them and she thanked him for the information.

. . . .

TJ and Sally had their last full day together before TJ went out on deployment. They went for a motorcycle ride and stopped for lunch out on the road. When they came back, they loaded up TJ's surfboard and went down to the beach by Terry and Heidi's hotel.

Sally and TJ's parents watched TJ as he caught a few waves before they went out to supper. It figures, thought TJ, just as surfing was starting to get good, his ship was leaving for its first long deployment. TJ was excited to go, but he was also miserable about leaving. He was going to miss so many things—Sally, their anniversary, riding, surfing.

After surfing, they met with Sally's parents for supper. When Terry asked the blessing he included prayers for TJ and his shipmate's safety. After eating, they said their good-byes and said they would try to meet on the pier if possible.

TJ and Sally went back to their apartment and spent a very rough last night together. Sally knew it was going to be hard on her. She had taken the whole next day off, partly because she knew her face would be red and swollen once TJ actually left. Her boss understood and the Navy made allowances for things like that.

Sally thought she would lighten the mood, so before the alarm went off the next morning, she woke up TJ. "Oh, no! The power must have gone out! You're late! Get up now!" she screamed at him. TJ bolted out of bed, still mostly asleep. He tried to gather up his clothes quickly and got his foot caught in the lamp's electric cord. He fell over as he tried to untangle himself and that is when he noticed that Sally was doubled over laughing.

He finally succeeded in freeing his foot and caught Sally up in a bear hug. He kissed her soundly and threatened, "Oh, girl, live in terror of the payback! I'm going to get you so good."

As Sally drove him to the base, there was an unusually large amount of traffic. TJ started to worry that he would indeed be late. He called the Chief to tell him he was stuck in traffic and was relieved when he found out the Chief's arrival was also hampered by the traffic.

When they finally arrived, on time, Terry, Heidi, Jim, and Cindy were waiting to say good-bye by the officer's brow. They laughed as they realized all the ship's company walking down the pier would snap to and quickly render a hand salute, when they unexpectedly saw the Admiral.

An hour after taking away the brow, the shift colors sounded and everyone waved and cheered. TJ yelled, "I'll see you in Italy!" TJ and Sally planned on meeting each other when the ship pulled into Naples, Italy in about six weeks.

It was a beautiful day for sailing down the Elizabeth River. TJ called Sally on his iPhone to tell her one more time that he loved her and would miss her. TJ then took one last look at America, as they sailed away and he went to work.

· · · · · · · · · · ·

While the USS George Bush was leaving Norfolk, Virginia, the USS Ronald Reagan was pulling into Phuket, Thailand for four days of liberty. The night before, the ship's closed circuit TV broadcasted a message from the Commanding Officer. He outlined the rules for leaving the ship in this country. There were things they were not allowed to do and places they could not go; because, unfortunately, Thailand was becoming a dangerous place for visitors from other countries.

When the ship pulled into different ports around the world, many of the sailors chose to do charity work. The Chaplain set up different places for them to help out. This time they helped at the Baan Klong Sai

School and Muang Phuket School, painting and doing construction. The people of Thailand were quick to notice the humanitarian efforts of the Navy lately.

Once the ship left the port, the mail clerk on the ship dropped a box on Frank's desk. He opened it excitedly. His mother had sent him a care package full of goodies. He shared it with his shipmates and they were all grateful. Some of the men did not get mail very often. Frank was lucky that his mom and Sue kept sending him a regular supply of care packages and letters.

· · · · · · · · · · · ·

On Memorial Day Weekend, Mark and Paula, and Terry and Heidi went on a charity ride for Rolling Thunder, a group that raises money for POW/MIA and other veteran's issues. Almost one million riders joined in the ride this year. As they rode near the Lincoln Memorial, they saw the Lone Marine.

Every year, the Lone Marine stands in his dress blues holding a hand salute for everyone passing by, as a thank you to the riders joining the Rolling Thunder ride. This year, the Lone Marine had held his salute for over three hours with a broken wrist. That is gratitude!

When they returned home, Heidi called Sally to tell her that she was missed. Heidi asked if Sally was all packed up and ready to go to Italy to meet TJ.

"My stomach is so upset, because I can't wait to get going. I'm leaving in eight days and I'll be there waiting for him to come ashore. TJ said he has the first two days off in port, so at least we'll be able to have fun for a couple of days."

While Heidi spoke to Sally, Terry was calling Joey D and Sam to tell them how much bigger Rolling Thunder had gotten.

Joey D said, "Next year I'll be riding with you."

Sam told Terry he would be more faithful in his rehab assignments, so they can all ride together again.

To keep herself busy, Sally went for rides with the H.O.G. chapter and joined the USS George Bush's Navy Wives Club. She found that the Navy Wives Club was really helpful in almost any situation, from plumbing problems to late night phone calls of sympathetic crying over loneliness. They got together once a week and planned all the events surrounding the ship's future homecoming.

A few days before Sally was to fly over to Italy, she had Victoria, Cassie, and Yu Yang over for dinner. Sally cooked a pot roast dinner that included mashed potatoes, noodles, peas, and corn. She also baked a cake for dessert. Victoria said, "You didn't have to go through all this trouble for us."

Sally said, "Yes, I did. I'm here alone all the time. I can't cook meals like this just for me. I was hungry for pot roast and thought you might want a home cooked meal, too."

"Well, you can call us over anytime," said Victoria, licking her lips

The girls decided to spend the night at Sally's apartment. They watched movies late into the night, only interrupted by a late night run to Taco Bell. The next morning, they decided to extend their fun by spending some time on the beach. By the end of the day, they were glowing from the sun and feeling very relaxed. They made plans to meet each other at church the next day.

· · · · · · · · · · · ·

It was early Saturday morning as Terry and Heidi pulled into Port Annapolis. Terry carried the ice cooler onto their brand new sailboat. It was a beautiful 35 foot Catalina. The nicely outfitted boat had all the bells and whistles that you would need to spend a lovely few days on the water. With two queen sized beds, a gas powered stove and refrigerator, and solar panels to run all the electronics; it was a completely functional sailboat. The Catalina 355 had won the 2011 midsized cruising boat of the year. Terry and Heidi named their boat *Nauti Boy*.

Terry took the cover off the mainsail and got ready to raise it. Heidi cast off the lines and they motored away from the dock. Terry found the direction of the wind and pulled on the halyard to raise the mainsail. He adjusted the trim and was beating to wind. He then pulled the line to pull the headsail out of the roller furling. Terry adjusted it, wound the sheet around the wench, and then cleated it off. They were making way in a nice 10-knot breeze. They sailed for a few hours and practiced some sailing maneuvers. They had a lovely time taking their sailboat out for its maiden voyage.

As everyone else was either riding motorcycles or sailing in the open water, Sally was flying across the Atlantic Ocean. She was waiting on the pier as TJ came ashore in Naples, Italy. TJ dropped his bags and grabbed his wife, kissing her hard. It was evident to those surrounding them that they had missed each other immensely.

The next couple of days were wonderful for Sally and TJ. They explored Naples and Rome, feeling like they were on another honeymoon. TJ took Sally to a different restaurant for every meal, because she loved Italian food. Sally had said she would like to eat her way through Italy and TJ wanted to make that dream come true.

Unfortunately, all good things must come to an end. The ship had to deploy and, once again, Sally stood on the pier waving good-bye to TJ. Sally went back to Norfolk and TJ, on the USS George Bush, went to do naval exercises just off the Gulf of Sidra and Libya.

· · · · · · · · · · · ·

The USS George Bush made several stops at different ports of call on this deployment. TJ saw the sights of Cartagena, Spain, and the Kingdom of Bahrain. The sailors were treated to a food tasting and a grand tour of a Grand Mosque. Some sailors got to swim with dolphins, while others went fishing or to a water park. TJ would play sports, like softball or flag football, whenever he had the chance. Along with working hard, sailors also had the opportunity to play hard.

Chief Balorous told Frank to have his crew show up for morning muster. Normally, when the ship is out to sea, CTs do not have morning muster, because they are working at their stations. This must be something special.

Everyone went topside and got in line at attention. Lt. Commander Tom Brown came and inspected the Division. He told them how proud he was of the job they were doing. He then asked for Seaman Apprentice Martina Gonzales to come forward.

She stepped forward. He read that Martina Gonzales was promoted to Seaman. Lt. Commander Brown turned to Martina and shook her hand as he said, "Congratulations, Seaman Brown."

Frank shook Martina's hand as he teased her, "You better watch out. Your next promotion is Petty Officer Third Class and that's when we get to tack it on. You better be really nice to me or else…"

Martina went to her berthing to write a letter home to tell them her good news. She did not have her Seaman stripes yet, because the ship's store did not have any in stock. Frank offered Martina his stripes; she thanked him, but told him the male stripes were too big. A few days later, a female Petty Officer Third Class from the USS Ronald Reagan Battle Group heard about Martina not having her stripes yet and offered to send hers over. She would not need them since she had been promoted. Martina thanked her for being a good shipmate.

A few days later, the Commanding Officer of the USS Ronald Reagan called an all hands meeting and inspection in the hanger deck. The CO addressed the crew and asked for CTN Petty Officer Second Class Frank Adams to come front and center. Puzzled, Frank went, but did not know what was going on. From the looks on their faces, neither did his Division Officer or Division Chief.

The Captain announced, "For those who don't know the story I will explain. On our last cruise, Petty Officer Adams did a heroic thing while in port in Perth, Western Australia. While Frank was coming back to the ship to stand duty, a Fremantle law enforcement officer was shot and lay dying. Petty Officer Adams used his Naval Training and treated the law enforcement officer for a sucking chest wound. He did this while the shooter was still in the area taking shots at them. The reason for this announcement is because the Prime Minister of Australia wants Petty Officer Adams to come back to Perth to be honored and awarded the Australian Conspicuous Service Cross.

"This medal is awarded for outstanding devotion to duty in the exceptional skills and judgment in a non-warlike condition. The Government of Australia will pay for his and his parent's expenses for the trip. The presentation will be in December. So, on behalf of the

Officers and crew of the USS Ronald Reagan, I congratulate you, Petty Officer Adams, on earning the Conspicuous Service Cross."

All the people at the meeting cheered for Frank and wanted to shake the hand of a real hero. Frank felt like he shook the hand of every person onboard the ship by the time he made it back to his berthing. After emailing his parents, he called Sue on Skype. He told her everything about the medal and the trip to Australia. She was excited for Frank and proud of the honor he would receive. They talked for quite a while before Frank told her he had an idea and wanted to know what she thought about it.

"I thought that since I'm going to be in Australia anyway and since the government is picking up the check for all of that, why don't we just plan our wedding around the ceremony?" asked Frank.

There was silence on the other end of the phone for a minute. "What do you think? Can we even plan a wedding that quickly?" he asked.

Sue answered, "You know, I think I might be able to pull it off with my mother's help if I start right away. Are you sure about this?"

"I'm sure, but it will have to be pretty small. Do you mind?"

Sue responded, "The only ones who have to be there are you and me. Anyone else is icing on the cake."

They agreed to get married at King's Park near where they first kissed. They talked for a while longer about the wedding plans and Sue made lists of the special things they each wanted included. Sue said she would Skype Frank in the next couple of days to let him know what she had worked out.

The USS Ronald Reagan stopped for ports of call in Guam and also Hong Kong before its final port of call in Pearl Harbor. The sailors manned the rails in their dress white uniforms as they went past the USS Arizona Memorial. Before leaving to head back to San Diego, several of the crew's family members boarded the ship for the Tiger Cruise. This is a special cruise for the dependents of the crewmembers. To come aboard, you have to be cleared by the State Department and the Department of the Navy, but everything checked out for Sue. She packed her bags and flew to Hawaii to be part of this cruise.

Sue took guided tours around different parts of the ship. She could not be with Frank all the time, because he was working. Other Tigers were able to go into their sponsor's work area, but Frank's area was classified Top Secret.

The whole Tiger Cruise went well and everyone enjoyed their time onboard. The Air Wing put on a great air show for those onboard. Sue and the rest of the Tigers were very impressed. The Commanding Officer even had a Steel Deck Day, which is a picnic up on the flight deck. The ships Culinary Specialists cooked steaks, hamburgers, hotdogs, baked beans, cake, and had fresh fruit. Far too soon, it was over and the ship pulled into San Diego.

This time there was no one waiting for Frank. He would be going home for one week and then flying back to the ship. Sue's parents, Henry and Emily Poxon, were in Pennsylvania at Sam and Hope's house. They were planning on going to Shanksville, PA for the 10th anniversary of the 9-11-01 attacks. Frank had e-mailed his parents and said he was on his way home, but did not know exactly when he would arrive. He wanted to surprise everyone.

Frank helped check in the two new crewmembers coming aboard, so it was late afternoon before he picked up his leave papers. He checked off the ship and he and Sue drove to a hotel near the airport. They flew out early the next morning to Harrisburg.

When they arrived at Frank's parent's home, Sue got the video camera ready to record the surprise homecoming, but no one was there. Frank drove over to Joey D's and no one was there either. Finally, Frank pulled out his cell phone and called Todd's home.

Bobbie Jo told him that they had all gone to Shanksville a couple of days earlier than scheduled. She also told him, "All the hotels are booked up and they had to stay in a hotel in Bedford, about twenty miles from Shanksville. They're staying at the Omni Bedford Springs Resort." She gave him the phone number and Frank called to see if they had any available rooms.

Everyone was in the lobby talking when Frank snuck in and said, "Attention on Deck!"

Hope screamed and ran to Frank. People in the lobby were looking at Frank in his dress white uniform. Sam walked over to his son and hugged him. Frank cried, "Dad, you're walking!"

Frank and Sue were so happy for Sam. Sam said he guessed Frank was not the only one who could surprise people. He told them he could walk up to half a mile now, but for anything further he still needed the wheelchair. He had been working hard in therapy and would be good as new in a few more months.

There were hugs going around the room as everyone greeted Frank and Sue.

They had a wonderful time together and the ceremony at the crash site was filled with people. They all called the people on the flight the first heroes of the War on Terrorism. Frank said to Sue's parents, "Now, this has come full circle. I went to your memorial at King's Park for your War on Terrorism and now you came to ours."

When everyone went back to Shade Gap, they worked long and hard on the wedding plans. Sammy told them he was able to take leave to come to the awards ceremony and also stay for the wedding. Joey D and Kelly, as well as Mark and Paula, were coming. Other than family and these longtime friends, Frank was able to invite only a few of his friends from the ship.

The date of the award ceremony would be Monday, December 19th. Sue said, "I thought of something I want to do for the wedding. There is a 12-hour time difference between Perth and Shade Gap. I thought that we could get married at King's Park like we planned, but do it on Sunday, January 1st. We could have it all timed out that the preacher would say you may kiss the bride exactly at noon, which will be midnight, New Year's Eve back in the States. That way, for the rest of our lives when we kiss each other on New Year's Eve at midnight, it will also be our anniversary. What do you think?"

"I think it's a great idea," Frank said.

• • • • • • • • • • •

The last liberty port for the USS George Bush was Marseilles, France. The French people treated the sailors well and they had a good time. Once the ship left port, the Commanding Officer said over the ship's intercom system how proud he was of the crew for their work over the last seven months. He was also proud of the way the crew had acted ashore at each of the ports they stopped in. The CO said that this crew was the best he had ever had the privileged to command or work with during his naval career. He said, "Men and women of the USS George Bush, I know that the man this ship is named after is very proud of you and will be seeing you and the ship in the future. He also sent word that he loves our ship's motto, *Freedom at Work*."

For the last two days of the deployment, they cleaned the USS George Bush top to bottom until every corner gleamed. The ship's TV station would normally shut down at 2200 hours. The last night at sea, they had an all-night showing. Sailors were restless and some found it hard to get any sleep. It had been a long seven and a half months.

The ship passed the Chesapeake Bay Bridge Tunnel and a small aircraft pulling a banner behind it was noticed by everyone. It said, *Welcome Home USS George Bush Battle Group*!

Sailors were now able to pick up their favorite radio stations and the ship's TV was able to broadcast local TV stations. The TV stations showed the crowd that was gathering on the Norfolk Naval Base Piers for all of the ships. It was an exciting time for all!

Sally was standing by the fence with Terry and Heidi holding up signs for TJ. They had gotten there a couple of hours before the ship was to arrive. It was an anxious time for everyone on the pier waiting for their loved ones. It would be a long wait; there were over 5,000 crew members onboard and it would take a long time to disembark.

Everyone was wearing coats because it was a cold, damp December day. The family members did not seem to mind the cold, but the sailors were returning from warmer weather and the cold would be a shock for them.

Sally said to Terry, "Isn't it great to see all these American and Navy flags all over the pier? It makes one proud to be an American!"

The media was everywhere snapping still photographs and also interviewing families waiting for their loved ones. Later sailors would go to You Tube and look at all the videos that were posted on it.

Finally, Sally saw TJ in his dress blue uniform with his sea bag over his back, carrying some roses. She went running to him and the hugging and kissing commenced. When TJ had hugged and kissed his wife and his mother over and over, Terry reminded them they would have all the time in the world to hug him later.

They all left the base and looked for somewhere to eat. TJ said, "I don't care where we eat lunch, just as long as it's a place where I can have a milk shake. I haven't had one in over eight months!"

· · · · · · · · · · ·

Frank, with his family and shipmates, all arrived at Perth airport. They had one day to relax before the award ceremony. The next day, the media was there to cover the ceremonial event and the law enforcement officer whose life was saved finally got to meet Frank. He gratefully shook Frank's hand and his wife told Frank how grateful she was for his bravery in the face of great personal danger. Mick, Sue's brother, came to the ceremony along with some of his shipmates from the HMAS Arunta. Mick was awarded the same medal for helping Frank and chasing after the gunman.

For the next few days, everyone toured the western coast of Australia while Sue and her family showed them the sights. Sam and Joey D wanted to rent Harley-Davidson Sportsters to see how they would each fare on a bike. They chose the Sportster because it is the most lightweight of the Harley line. They were not confident they could hold up big bikes. Everyone else in the wedding party, besides Martina, could also ride motorcycles, so they all rented bikes and took a long ride along the Western Australia coastline. Martina rode on the back of Hunter's bike, who was one of Frank's friends. It was her first time on a motorcycle and she loved it!

When they got back from their ride, Sue got a phone call from Rose. She said she had finally found a way to make it there for the wedding; she would be there in a few days. Sue was overwhelmed and started to cry.

At that moment, someone tapped Sue on the shoulder. Sue turned around and it was Rose! Sue hugged her and they jumped up and down. It had been over a year since they had seen each other. Rose told her that Dugan had gotten his act together and they were doing okay now. She said that Dugan had been promoted to Petty Officer Third Class and they would soon be living in the Navy Base housing. Sue was so happy for her friend.

They all gathered in the River District near the yacht club to watch the New Year's Eve fireworks. Everyone had a good time, but since the next day would be busy, they turned in early to get a good night's sleep.

The wedding the next day was beautiful in its simplicity. God had favored them with a glorious day for the outdoor ceremony. Frank and his bride, Sue, stood under an arch covered in golden wattle and white roses. Sue looked beautiful in her tea length white dress. She was radiant as she listened to Frank pledge to bind his life to hers forever. Sue had thought she would be nervous, but as she slipped the ring on Frank's finger, her voice rung out with clarity, "I give you my hand, my heart, and my love, for all eternity whatever life may bring us."

The preacher read I Corinthians 13 and then pronounced them man and wife. At precisely noon, he told Frank to kiss his bride.

CHARLIE RESPONSE
CHAPTER NINETEEN

It was the third week of January when the USS Ronald Reagan began its trip to the Puget Sound Naval Shipyard in Bremerton, Washington. To save the Navy and sailors traveling expense, the Navy loaded some of the sailor's cars on the flight deck and into the hanger bay for the trip. Sailors already had their housing set up before they got up to Bremerton. When the ship got there, they waited for their cars and then went to their new homes. They would be staying there for a year.

Sue and Frank really noticed the cold, damp weather, since they were used to the weather in Australia and San Diego. They would have to dress warmly for the next few months.

Since Frank was a Second Class Petty Officer, he easily got into base housing. They moved into a two bedroom, two bathroom apartment. Frank found a local discount furniture store and they outfitted their new home.

While in Washington, the Cryptologic Technicians could not do their cryptologic work, so most went to school or helped with the painting and different odd jobs in the shipyard. Frank had been enrolled for two years with the American Military University, taking online courses. He was going for dual majors, a BS in Intelligence Collections and a BS in Intelligence Analysis. These majors would help advance his career as a cryptologic technician.

Frank was assigned to be in charge of the Fire Watch Division over the welders. Most of the time, it was a boring job with not much to do, so he would bring his college work along with him. He found out that he was getting a lot of his class work done ahead of time and he started taking additional classes.

Sue was working part time at a local hospital as a nurse. She became close friends with Martina, who spent a lot of time missing her boyfriend, Jose. Sue told her she should save up some money and on a three day weekend fly down to San Diego and visit Jose. Frank was glad that Sue had made a good friend so quickly.

· · · · · · · · · · · ·

Frank flew to Washington D.C. and met up with his parents, while Sue stayed behind to work at the hospital. He, his family, and their friends were attending an awards ceremony with Mark and Paula. The President of the United States was awarding their late son, Lt. Luke Brown, who had been killed in action, the Medal of Honor and they were accepting on his behalf.

Sammy was being presented the Navy Cross for his actions on this same day. He pinned his medal on his chest, along with the countless other medals he had been awarded. Sammy was good at his chosen field.

That evening, Sammy told his parents he was thinking about taking his doctor's advice and leaving the Seal Team. His doctor told him he should take a medical discharge, but Sammy wanted the military to be his career. He said he was thinking about taking an assignment at the National Security Agency and wanted to know what they thought.

Sam said it sounded like a good opportunity and told him no matter what he decided, they would always be proud of him. Sammy told them he was told he is a Chief Petty Officer selectee. Hopefully, in just a few months he would be promoted. Sam, Hope, and Frank all congratulated him.

Sammy took Frank aside and said, "Can I talk to you in private?" They went down the hallway and he continued, "They want me to be Division Chief of a section at the agency. I'll get to pick some of my supervisors. I know you're up for re-enlistment and I'd like to offer you one of the Petty Officer positions. It could mean a promotion for you in the near future."

Sammy told him the position was with NSA's Combat Cryptologic Special Operations Group, also known as the Mobile Cryptologic Support Facilities Van. They would go out in the field and provide support to the Special Forces, but they wouldn't have to go through the Seal Team's BUDDS training, He told Frank that he would be a supervisor on one of the three NSA MCSF teams. Frank said he'd have to talk it over with his Sue, but was fairly positive she would go along with it. Sammy told him that he would have to re-enlist for four more years and the assignment would be at least three years at Ft Meade, MD. They would be only a two and a half hour drive to their parent's home in Shade Gap, PA.

They talked further about the assignment and Frank told Sammy his recent worries about the government heading towards a reduction in the armed forces. He was worried the military would be reduced so much that terrorist forces, both outside and inside the country, would take control.

Sammy was thoughtful a moment and then said, "That's why we need to be inside the NSA and get all the training and information they offer. We can ward off any terrorist or socialist take over by getting the word out. We both took an oath to support and defend the Constitution of the United States of America. We need to keep that oath in any way we can; I think this is the answer for both of us."

•••••••••••

Memorial Day weekend, Joey D and Sam each rented a Harley-Davidson Trike to ride in the Rolling Thunder Parade in Washington, DC. Hope and Kelly went with them and they met up with Terry and Heidi, Mark and Paula, as well as TJ and Sally who were also going on the ride. Everyone enjoyed the time there. Again, they saw the Lone Marine, who was there to salute everyone as they rode through.

They bought their ride pins and even stopped at the Harley Owners Group stand to purchase more pins. They talked to fellow veterans of all the different wars and met disabled veterans that rode in the parade. It was a great time for everyone who attended.

Back in the state of Washington, Frank had issues with re-enlisting. He talked with his parents, with Sue, with Sammy, with his shipmates, and with the officers in his Chain of Command. He said he wanted to make the Navy his career, but he had fears about the direction the country was heading under the current administration.

Finally, Frank and Sue came to the conclusion that Frank would do more good in the NSA than as a civilian. And so Frank took the oath and signed up for another four years of active duty.

The first week of June saw Frank and Sue busy packing for their transfer across the country. They loaded all of their belongings into the largest U-Haul trailer and set off. The Navy paid for everything and gave Frank seven days to drive across the country. He would not be charged any leave for the travel days; however, Frank also took an additional seven days of leave. They decided to make it an adventure, so that Sue would get her first glimpse of the entire country.

Driving across the country was more of a vacation than a moving trip. They took pictures and visited the tourist sights. They saw Mount Rushmore and also Crazy Horse carved into the mountain. They stopped in Sturgis, SD, where the world famous motorcycle rally was held. Sue was surprised such a small town could hold the half million people that attended. They visited Little Big Horn where General Custer made his last stand. They went to Yellowstone National Park, where they both were amazed by God's handiwork. Sue was excited to be seeing some of the sights of America.

Sammy was already stationed at Ft. Meade by the time his brother and sister in-law arrived. He had the Base Housing Office hold a townhouse for Frank and Sue. It would only be a two mile drive for Frank to get to work. Sammy stayed in his room in the Navy barracks since he was still single.

Sammy showed Frank and Sue the way to their new home and helped move their things in. It had taken them seven days to drive across the country and two days to move their furniture in and unpack.

Sammy showed Frank the barracks and the Quarter Deck where he was to check in. He showed him the Navy Personnel Office where he was to turn in his medical, dental, and personnel records. Frank met the Commanding Officer, Executive Officer, and the Command Master Chief. He was told he would supervise the seamen that were assigned to take care of the grounds. He would report to work at the Quarter Deck at 0700 and get off at 1530. He would do this job until his Top Secret SCI Clearance came to the NSA and then he would be transferred over to the Agency.

Sammy said, "I already told the softball coach that you would be playing. We're more than half way through the season, but our centerfielder got hurt and we lost two other players due to transfers. Our coach said he was going to bring some players up from one of the other 2 NSGA (Naval Security Group Activity) teams. I told him you play outfield, had a great arm, and could track down balls in the outfield. I said you had a great bat and you played on the USS Ronald Reagan softball team. We have a game tomorrow and practice tonight."

While Frank was getting acquainted with Ft. Meade, TJ and the USS George Bush were heading out again for just a couple of months. They went off the coast of Maine and Former President George H.W. Bush came out to the ship to look it over. He also was there for a promotion ceremony and the crewmembers of the USS George Bush were excited to see the namesake of their ship.

Many of the crew had not even been born when he was president and had only read about him in their history books. He casually greeted many of them with a handshake and a big smile. He treated them like they were part of his family and made them all feel comfortable with him. The sailors came away with even more pride in their ship.

It took about a month for Frank to get his clearance to go inside the NSA Building number 3. Frank and Sammy met for lunch inside the NSA building. Sammy told him that he thought they were going to win the base softball championship. Sammy said, "Brother, you're the missing link we needed to win."

Frank responded, "We have a good team. We'll see how good after tonight's championship games."

Sammy said, "We need to win both games of the double hitter in order to win the championship. If we lose the first game, we won't even get to play a second game. So winning the first game is the key to victory."

Sammy and Frank were called into the Director of NSA's (DIRNSA) office. They were told to get ready for deployment sometime between ten to fourteen days from then. They were told they would receive their orders at Andrews Air Force Base and the mission was classified Top Secret. They both wondered what kind of mission it would be and where they would be going.

Sammy came to the softball game with Petty Officer Second Class Sara Jean Murphy. Frank asked his brother who she was and Sammy said, "We met in the barracks playing pool and throwing darts. I invited her to come watch us play the base championship tonight. Some others are also coming to cheer us on to victory."

NSGA won the first game 28 to 21. Slow pitch softball normally has high scores. They were playing with a restrictive flight ball, which does not travel as far when it is hit. These balls are designed to restrict home runs, but strong hitters can still drive them over the fence for a homerun with a solid hit. When swinging for the long ball, the coach would yell at them to "Lift and separate."

During the second game, NSGA was the home team, so they batted last. They went into the last inning behind 38 to 36. With one out and a man on first, Sammy hit a double to make it second and third with only one out. Sammy thought the runner might have scored, but you do not take the chance in sending the runner and take away the big inning.

The next batter was walked in, hoping for a double play to end the game. Frank came up with the bases loaded and only one out. Sammy yelled from second, "Come on, brother! A base hit ties the game!"

With a one ball, two strike count Frank drove the ball to left center. Sammy yelled to the guy on third, "Tag up! Tag up!"

Then they noticed the ball going over the fence for the game winning homerun—a Grand Slam! That made the winning score 40 to 38. Everyone was jumping and screaming! The Commanding Officer was there and came over to shake Frank's hand. Sue ran to him and hugged and kissed him. With a smug smile, Sammy told the coach, "See, I told you my brother was a good player."

The coach said, "I have us signed up to play in the Naval District of Washington DC Softball Tournament. We'll see how good we are then."

They were told that game was the following weekend. Sammy could not tell him there was a good chance he and Frank would not be there because of an NSA assignment. They went back to the barracks and had a big party. The Commanding Officer called for ten pizzas to be delivered for the celebration.

After eating some pizza, Frank and Sue went back to their new home. Sue called her parents on skype and told them that Frank was the superstar of the game. Sue said she liked Ft. Meade more than she liked being stationed in Washington. She said it was as hot as it was in Australia. "Today, it was 34 degrees!" (Celsius)

She said that she and Frank were planning a weekend trip to Ocean City, Maryland. It would be nice to finally be able to see the Atlantic Ocean. They talked for a while longer about the plans they had and the job interview Sue had for a flight nurse position. Her father told her they were planning on coming for a visit at Christmastime and Sue said she would have a hard time waiting. She missed her family a lot. It was a good thing she had both Frank and the Navy Wives to help her along.

A week later, Hope and Sam drove to Ft. Meade to be with Sue while Sammy and Frank were away. The brothers, unfortunately, did not get to play in the upcoming game. Sue and her guests were watching Fox News and heard the reports of some disturbing occurrences in Libya. They worried that Frank and Sammy were over there; unfortunately because of the nature of Frank's job, Sue did not know where he was. She would just have to trust the Lord to take care of him.

Todd took his dad to #1 Cycle Center to look at the new models for 2013. He found a bike that he wanted and called Bobbie Jo, who told him to buy it if he wanted it. He told the salesgirl to ring it up and also to order a backrest for it.

Todd saw Joey D walking around and around a bike, inspecting every detail on it. Todd walked over and asked Joey D what he thought. "Do you think you could hold it up?" he asked.

"Well, I'm thinking I won't have to. I'm planning to have a sidecar put on; it should help carry some of the weight for me," said Joey D. Todd took a step back and looked more closely at the motorcycle. He nodded his head as he decided that was probably a pretty good idea.

Joey D flagged down the salesman working with him and said he had made up his mind. He ordered the 110th Limited Edition Electra Glide Ultra Limited with the custom painted sidecar with stereo speakers and intercom. The salesman informed him it would take a week before the sidecar came in. Joey D said he would wait to pick up the motorcycle until the sidecar was ready.

They both loaded up on 110th anniversary shirts and souvenirs. On the way home, Joey D called Kelly and told her about the motorcycle he had just ordered. She said she would be happy to ride in the sidecar and it would probably be safer for both of them.

· · · · · · · · · · · ·

About a week later, after he picked up his motorcycle, Joey D called Sam to come over. He had not told Sam about his bike yet, because he wanted to surprise him. However, Joey D was the one who was surprised when he looked out the garage door to see both Sam and Sammy pull up on new Harleys.

"Wow, look at these beautiful bikes!" he exclaimed. Sammy was riding a Fat Boy Lo and Sam was on a 110th Limited Edition Tri Glide Ultra Classic. They joked about the fact they had each bought new bikes at the same time, but kept it secret from the other. Joey D sat on Sam's motorcycle, which was a trike and said that he had not even thought about this option. It was a good way to go; Sam and Kelly would be more stable on a trike.

Sam joked, "I guess we're truly old geezers now, you with a sidecar and me with a trike." They all laughed, but Sammy reminded them they were not old, they were crippled.

Soledad and Fiona called Sally to tell her that they had decided to take the riders safety courses and get their motorcycles licenses. Sally exclaimed, "Sole, you were the one saying how crazy I was for riding!"

"I know, but I've been riding a lot and I love it. I discovered with the proper training, riding a motorcycle can be safe. I figured if I was going to ride, I should get my own bike—the first step to that is getting my license."

Sally was excited for Soledad and Fiona, "I can't wait to be able to ride with you!"

Soledad got quiet and then said, "By the way, TJ's friend, Doug, did something to me that I think you should know about."

"WHAT?"

Soledad let silence hang between them for a moment and then she started giggling, "He asked me to marry him. We're getting married when he comes back from his next deployment."

Sally was excited and congratulated her sister. "Hey, no fair! You can't keep secrets like that from me—I'm your sister!"

Then Fiona got on the phone and told Sally that she had also gotten engaged. She said she was marrying Lt. Jg. Bruce Bair. Sally was equally excited for Fiona.

Later, when she told TJ about the two couples, she said, "I guess it's the magic of riding a Harley-Davidson that gets couples together."

. . . .

Joey D and Kelly decided to take their new bike out for a ride. Kelly rode in the sidecar and told Joey D from the intercom that she was comfortable and she liked it. She asked her husband if he was comfortable with the bike.

"I love being back in the saddle again. I want to put my feet down at stops though. I also love having reverse. It makes it so much easier to back up."

They were riding to the Belleville Sale. As they got closer, Kelly could tell Joey D was having some anxiety. "You know, we don't have to go the whole way. If you're getting nervous, we can turn around."

Joey D responded, "No, I need to face my fears. If I don't, I'll never get past them."

They arrived at the Belleville Sale parking lot and got off the bike to walk around. Kelly searched for two familiar faces and finally found them. Joey D and Kelly were happy to see Jacob and Rebecca and greeted them with hugs. Kelly said, "Look at him! Little Daniel is really growing fast! How old is he now?"

"Eight months old today! He's such a good baby," answered Rebecca. While the women talked, the men went over to look at Joey D's new bike. Jacob proclaimed it the prettiest set of wheels he had ever seen.

Joey D said, "You'll have to see my new pontoon boat too. It's bigger than the last one I had. Are you and your family doing anything this Friday or Saturday? We could take it out on the lake then."

Jacob said he would have to check with the rest of the family, but he was reasonably sure they could come. The four of them walked over to say hello to Jeb and Sarah. They were talking to their good friend from the fire department, Jackie. Jacob mentioned that the Daniels' had invited them to the lake on the weekend. Jeb said they would be able to go, if they could find a ride from a neighbor. Jackie mentioned she had a full sized van and would be happy to take them out there and then pick them up later. Joey D said there was no need to make the drive twice; Jackie should consider herself invited as well. They all agreed to meet at 11 a.m. on Saturday.

Early Saturday morning, Kelly cooked chicken at her home and brought it along for lunch out on the lake. She also brought potato salad, hamburgers, and hot dogs. They had a couple cases of soda pop and also jugs of ice tea for drinks.

Everyone admired the new pontoon boat. Joey D had ordered this one with all the options; it was more of a party boat. It had three tubes with lifting strakes, so the boat would go faster and handle better. There was an island bar with bar stools, refrigerator, sink, and a rail mounted grill.

Joey D took the cover off the boat and loaded all the food into the fridge. As everyone came onboard, he was playing with the stereo. He said, "In the Navy, we had a breakaway song. Every time we left the dock or came into the dock, we would play this song over the loud speakers. In keeping with my naval background, I also have a breakaway song. It's a song by Little Big Town called *Pontoon*."

Jackie commented, "You couldn't have picked a more appropriate song."

The song played over the stereo speakers as they motored past the docks and into the no wake zone. They turned right and headed toward the bridge and onto the dam's overlook.

After a couple of hours on the water, Joey D motored close to the shore of an island and dropped anchor. Kelly lit the grill and soon the smell of juicy burgers was wafting through the air. As they ate lunch, little Daniel rolled around the deck in his walker, getting bites of food from everyone. Rebecca said, "This really is the perfect boat for families with children. Just look at the way Daniel can go everywhere on the boat. Also, I've noticed how many people the boat can hold. It's the perfect boat for a family gathering."

"That's what I thought too," agreed Joey D. "I would never have any other kind of boat. Other kinds of boats just don't have this kind of room."

When everyone had filled up on good food, Joey D pulled up the anchor and they leisurely rode around the lake some more. He explained to Jacob how they had used nature's barriers of ridges and cliffs to build the lake. When they flooded the lake, abandoned houses and farms were buried below hundreds of feet of water. With a good sonar device, you could still make out some of the houses.

In the heat of the day, Joey D pulled out his ski tube to pull behind the boat. Once the ski tube was pumped up and the towline was attached, he got out a life vest for the people who were going to ride. Jacob was the first to ride and he loved it. It had been a long time since he had that much fun. Later, when Jeb took a turn, Jacob stood at the edge of the boat in amazement. Jeb was such a hardworking man and Jacob was hard put to remember the last time he had seen his father so carefree.

As the pontoon pulled back into the docks, Joey D again played his boat's breakaway song, *Pontoon*. Everyone thanked the Daniels and they talked about getting together again. Rebecca invited Kelly and Joey D for dinner in a couple of weeks and they said they would look forward to it. Everyone helped as the boat was put into its slip and the cover was replaced. They said their good-byes as they walked up the pier. Kelly climbed into the sidecar, Joey D got on his motorcycle, and they pulled away. Jackie followed them in her van until she had to turn toward Belleville.

• • • • • • • • • •

Todd helped Joey D hook up the motorcycle trailer to the pickup truck. Sam, Joey D, and the Admiral all loaded their bikes into the trailer. The Daniels and their entire family, along with the Adams, the Browns, the Millers, and the Morgans, were all taking a vacation to Florida together. The Admiral had a few speaking engagements scheduled for when they were down there and he and Cindy would be flying down. They would meet them and he would get his bike off Joey D's trailer then.

They were going to spend a full week at Disney World's Animal Kingdom. The Admiral and his wife would leave Animal Kingdom after two days to give his speeches at McDill Air Force Base. The others would have fun at the attractions in the area while he was gone.

Before they set out on their adventure, they all joined hands as Joey D led them in prayer. Then they traveled down the road with the motorcycles in front and Joey D's truck in the back, along with Rich and Tracy's minivan.

The next day, they were at Jacksonville Naval Base, where they picked up the Admiral and Cindy. One the way to Orlando, they detoured into Daytona to spend a short time seeing the sights there. They took the time to ride on Daytona's famous Loop, which is on every motorcyclist's to do list. After taking a break at Daytona Beach, they got back on the road.

When they arrived in Orlando, they checked into their rooms and then went exploring. Everyone enjoyed seeing all the animals running free. Sue was like a little kid running around trying to pet the animals.

Peggy Sue could not believe the grownups wanted to take the next day to relax. She was closer than she had ever been to seeing Mickey and Minnie and she had a hard time waiting. When they finally were getting ready to go to the Magic Kingdom, Peggy Sue was the first one ready. "I'm finally going to Disney World!" She was so happy.

When they arrived at the Magic Kingdom and saw Cinderella's Castle, it seemed that Sue was just as excited as the kids. They saw Mickey Mouse and the kids ran up to him. Peggy Sue told him, "I've waited my whole life to see you."

Joey D pulled aside a Disney employee and asked him to take a group photo with all of their cameras. The young man said he would be delighted to. Mickey was frantically waving his arms and in a few seconds they were surprised when Minnie joined them for their pictures too.

They had a great day at the Magic Kingdom. The kids went to bed very tired, but very happy that night. Whenever they were not having fun in one or another amusement park, the kids were generally found outside at the pool. Joseph made a friend named Skylar and they played together all the time. On Saturday evening, Joseph told Skylar that since they were traveling and did not know where to go to church, they were having Bible study in one of their rooms the next morning. Skylar said he had never been to church before.

Joseph looked shocked, "How do you learn about Jesus Christ?"

Skylar gasped, "You just said a bad word!"

Joseph explained that when you are talking about God, Jesus Christ was not a bad word. He asked Skylar if he knew Jesus Christ. When Skylar said he did not, Joseph told him about God and invited him to meet with them the next morning.

The following morning Joseph introduced his friend and for the first time Skylar learned about Jesus Christ. After the Bible study, everyone left for their day's activities. That evening, Skylar asked Joseph what it would take for him to be saved. Joseph told him to say the sinner's prayer and ask Jesus into his heart. So Joseph led him in prayer to ask forgiveness of his sins and Skylar asked Jesus into his heart. For the next few days after that, Skylar and Joseph would meet and Joseph would tell him stories about Jesus and the miracles He did while on the earth. Skylar's biggest question was why the people wanted to kill him. Joseph told him he did not know the answer to that question, but Jesus rose from the dead and is alive in Heaven with God.

When they went to Sea World, everyone loved the show. Of course, Joey D had his grandchildren sit in the front row with Frank and Sue. When the killer whale did its performance, he splashed everyone in the first few rows. No one seemed to mind getting wet though, since it was a humid day in the mid-90s. Of course, Joey D laughed that he caused them all to get soaked.

They all loved the water rides at Blizzard Beach and Typhoon Lagoon—even the adults were having a good time. Since the temperature was in the high 90s with high humidity, the water rides were the perfect place to be. Sally told TJ that she wished that her dad would not have left for Tampa so soon, because he would be having fun too.

Everyone loved the roller coasters and the water rides at Universal Studios. That evening they went on City Walk and saw all the sights there. They all had dinner reservations at Hard Rock Café. They bought t-shirts and some other souvenirs.

Everyone was having such a great time that they did not want to leave Orlando, unfortunately they had to. It was time to go to Tampa and meet up with Sally's parents. Before they left, Skylar's mom came over and said, "I want to thank you for teaching Skylar about Jesus Christ. Our family has decided that when we get home, we're going to find a church and start going. You people have touched us." Joseph and Skylar exchanged addresses and phone numbers. Joseph was pretty happy; he did not realize it yet, but he had made a lifelong friend.

After they found the Admiral and Cindy, they headed south towards Fort Myers. They rode over the Sky Way Bridge, south of St. Petersburg. Those who were on the motorcycles did not like the steepness of the bridge. Some of them did not know what to expect because they had not been on this bridge before and a late morning breeze was blowing.

They went into Sarasota so they could see The Kiss statue again at the marina, but when they arrived, it was not there. They found out that it had been shipped to New York City to be refurbished. After that, it would be going to San Diego. They were sad they had missed out seeing it.

They arrived in Ft. Myers and rode down McGregor Blvd. Everyone commented on how beautiful it was with the twin rows of towering palm trees. They went by the Winter Estates of Thomas Edison and Henry Ford. They all agreed that they would visit there before they left. Sally just about sprained her neck trying to see all the beautiful old houses that lined both sides of the boulevard.

Finally, they rolled up in front of the Pink Shell Resort. Everyone checked into their rooms and commented how much they all loved the view. They unloaded their baggage and went to eat their evening meal at Pinchers Crab Shack. When they got back to the hotel, they walked out onto the sand at Bowditch Point and watched the sunset.

For the next few days, they spent their time sightseeing and enjoying the area. They went to Harley-Davidson of Ft. Myers and signed up to do a charity ride for a fallen motorcyclist.

While they were exploring Sanibel Island, they went to the Ding Darling Wildlife Refuge and a few gift shops. They really liked Mango Bay, but their favorite was Jerry's. They liked seeing the exotic birds in the courtyard.

They went across the small bridge and visited Captiva Island, as well. They went to the South Seas Resort, which cost over a billion dollars to build. On the way back, they stopped at Doc Ford's Restaurant. Doc Ford is a character in a local author's series of books. The author, Randy Wayne Wright, owns Doc Ford's Restaurant. Some of the group bought some of his books that the cashier suggested.

The Admiral said to Cindy, "You know, this would be a great place to retire. I really love it down here." Everyone else agreed. Joey D and Sam said they were talking to a local man and he said the housing market was a buyer's market right now. He told them about an open house in Gulf Harbour Yacht and Country Club. He also told them there are many foreclosed properties for sale.

They decided to visit the open house and were impressed by what they saw. Todd, Tracy, and their families played on the beach as the others went to the open house and checked out the area. Afterwards, they went to downtown Ft. Myers by the riverfront. They saw the high-rise condos there, as well as the Ft. Myers Yacht Club and the Royal Palm Yacht Club. Cindy said, "James, you should be welcomed in either of these yacht clubs."

Heidi said to Terry, "I really wouldn't mind spending our winters down here. I've been thinking about retiring from the agency and this looks like a swell place to retire to." Terry agreed with her.

Then Joey D said, "I really wouldn't mind spending from January to April here and then maybe some in the summer. I would like to be away from the cold, but I still want to stay up north in the mountains, too."

"As long as I can see my grandchildren, I would be okay with it. I know we have enough in the bank to buy a place, but I want to think about it a little bit first," said Kelly. Sam and Hope agreed with Kelly.

Mark looked at his wife and said, "I think we're both ready to retire. Our bills are paid, we could sail the boat down here and live on it or get a condo with a dock for the boat." The group decided they had quite a bit to think about and should not jump into anything too quickly.

When it was time to go back home up north, everyone agreed they had a wonderful time. This was one of the best trips they had ever taken. Hope looked around at their group and was amazed at how much it had grown. It occurred to her that from now on it would keep getting larger and larger. They were one extra-large family; some related by blood, some by marriage, and some by choice. No matter how they were connected, Hope loved and thanked God for each and every one of them.

The ride up north was uneventful. Everyone talked over the CB radios. Most of the talk was centered on living near the Gulf of Mexico over the winters. They made it to Kingsland, Georgia, by sunset and decided to spend the night there. Soledad and Fiona came over to meet them.

Kelly said, "This sunset is pretty, but it's nothing like the sunsets we saw at Ft. Myers Beach."

Cindy agreed, "James and I have traveled the world in his 30 plus years in the Navy and I say those were some of the prettiest sunsets I've ever seen! The ride from Bonita Springs through Lovers Key State Park and onto Times Square at Ft. Myers Beach at sunset was just amazing." Everyone else agreed with her.

The next morning, they went to Kings Bay Submarine Base. They could not see the submarines, but they could look around the base. The Admiral said he could get clearance for everyone to go to the docks where the subs were, but everyone agreed that they should be on the road before the afternoon thunderstorm came.

The Admiral's bike was loaded into the trailer, because he and Cindy stayed behind to visit with Soledad. They talked a lot about the plans that Soledad and Fiona had for their double weddings. It was going to be beautiful. Deciding on the date had been easy; both girls thought the idea of a wedding on 12-12-12 was spectacular. Saying good-bye was especially hard for Cindy. She hated not being there to help Soledad with the wedding plans, but they had to go home.

After being home for a few days, Kelly and Hope got together and made a power point presentation of their trip to show at Westminster Woods. Since Sam and Joey D had spent so much time there, the girls tried to give back in every way they could. Hope would quite often bake several batches of cookies to take them. She also volunteered to give the ladies manicures or play games with the gentlemen whenever she could. Kelly would play church hymns on the piano a couple times a week while they were having their lunches.

Whenever any of them went on a trip, the girls would turn the photos into a slide show for the residents. They appreciated it so much; it was nice seeing a broader view of the world than what they saw every day from their own small windows.

Sue posted her favorite pictures of the trip to Facebook so her family back in Australia could see them. When she spoke to her parents, she told them, "Mom and Dad, you have to go to Disney at least once in your lifetime! I know you think it's for kids, but it's fun for everyone, trust me. It's my favorite place! I really enjoyed Florida!"

In the fall, they went on their motorcycles to Benzette, Pennsylvania, to see the elk. It was mating season and the elk would come down from the mountains and roam all over the place. People would come from long distances to see them and hear them bugle. They even saw the elk standing in yards in town with people around them taking pictures. When the animals got annoyed with the people, they would just slowly walk away. Sue exclaimed, "Wow! They're so big and graceful. This is great. Thank you so much for bringing me here." It had become obvious to everyone that Sue was a great lover of wildlife. She was always excited to see wild animals in their natural habitats. Joey D told her that they come here a couple times a year to see the elk.

The elk were out in the early morning and late evening, so the rest of the day the group went riding. The roads around Benzette were a motorcyclist's paradise, twisting and turning in every direction. Everywhere Sue looked was the glorious handiwork of God known as autumn. Showy fall colors and clear blue skies marked the most beautiful of the seasons. "This is the prettiest thing I've ever seen. All the maple, oak, and white ash trees in full color are like a brilliant painting by God Himself. Absolutely magnificent!" burst out Sue, trying to take it all in.

· · · · · · · · · · · ·

Saturday, October 13, 2012, was the Navy's 237th birthday. All over the world, the naval bases would throw Navy Day Balls. Everyone was excited to go to the ball at the closest naval base to them. Sammy took his girlfriend, Petty Officer Sara Jean Murphy, and they met up with Frank and Sue.

The men looked so handsome in their dinner dress blues; but when the girls came out in their formal evening gowns, Frank let out a long, low whistle that made Sue blush. The Navy Day Ball was a big deal. They heard a few speeches and several toasts were given. For dinner they were served prime rib. Sue and Sara Jean rolled their eyes at each other because it was so delicious.

After dinner, cake was served; but first came the cake cutting ceremony. It was tradition that the oldest and the youngest sailors at the ball would hold a ceremonial officer's sword and cut the cake. The oldest would feed a bite to the youngest and then the youngest would feed a bite to the oldest. After that, the cake was served to all those in attendance.

Throughout the evening, photographers would take pictures and all throughout the evening there were gift drawings. Sue's name was drawn and she won a gift card to Hess's Gas Station. She stood and said, "I want to thank you for this; but since the base is running a bus to drive sailors home if they have imbibed too much, I would like to donate this to put gas into that bus." She was given a loud round of applause and Frank was proud of her for her gesture.

Finally, a deejay started to play music for them to dance to. Sammy told Frank, "Watching all the high ranking officers trying to learn to line dance has made my day."

They went home late and they were exhausted, but they all had a memorable evening.

Then next morning, Frank received a phone call from Sue's father, Henry. "Frankie, my boy, how is everything going?" Frank assured him they were doing great.

"Well, the reason I'm calling is about your stock we invested in. Remember? Of course, you do. Anyway, we bought stock from Google for a little under $100 per share and if we act quickly and sell right now, that stock is worth $800 per share. That means your $100,000 investment could pay off in a big way, like $800,000!"

Henry advised him that if he wanted to sell, they needed to do it right now; if it fell, it would fall fast. Frank decided to sell enough that he could put $600,000 in the bank and he would decide what to do about the rest later.

Frank handed Sue the phone and told her that he had to go to the Personnel Office and report his earnings, so they did not think he was selling classified documents. He kissed her and said they would go out and celebrate later.

Sue lifted the phone and said, "Daddy, I always knew you would take care of Frank. I've always had faith in you."

• • • • • • • • • • •

The Adams went to Frank and Sue's home for Thanksgiving. Sue did a first rate job on dinner with Hope and Sara Jane helping in the kitchen. After dinner, Emily called to see how Sue's first American Thanksgiving had gone. Sue put her parents on speakerphone so everyone could talk to them too.

Sam told Henry about a trip they were planning to the 110th birthday party for Harley-Davidson in Milwaukee. Henry said since he was an Australian H.O.G. member, he would plan to go along too. Frank yelled in the background that he heard Kid Rock would be performing at the Buffalo Chip campground. Sam told Henry that the whole group was on board to go; they had been hoping he and Emily would be able to come too. Sam offered to make the hotel reservations for everyone and told Henry he could not wait to tell everyone he was coming.

A few days later, TJ was talking with other officers that served with him on the USS George Bush about Harley-Davidson bash. Several others were planning to make the trip if they could. TJ thought it would be cool to have a group of sailors ride to Milwaukee together. Sally was waiting for him on her bike and he said he had to go, but they would talk more about it later.

As Frank walked over to his bike, he thought about the trip they were planning to Milwaukee. He also thought about another motorcycle trip which ended tragically, now far in the past. Not only had his loved ones all recovered physically, but also, mentally and spiritually. Bones had healed, fears had healed, and faith, though never completely lost, was restored. Frank said a quick prayer of thanks for the everlasting faithfulness of his Savior.

"You ready?"

Frank threw his leg over the seat of his bike, "Ready? Yeah, for just about anything."

They started to head off base, but before they got there, TJ noticed a Volvo semi-truck parked by a building. At first he did not think anything about it; but as he noticed men with hoods over their faces carrying large boxes out and putting them in the truck, it crossed his mind that his dad had been hit by a Volvo a couple of years ago.

He motioned to Sally to follow him and he circled the block. By the time they got back around, the truck was loaded up and starting to move. TJ yelled at the truck to stop, but the driver steered the 18 wheeler towards TJ and Sally to hit them. They quickly maneuvered around the truck.

Sally immediately retrieved her cellphone and called the authorities on base. By this time, an alarm was sounding from the building where the truck had been parked. As Sally reported what they had seen, she was told that someone in one of the storage buildings reported being robbed at gun point. She told them the make and model of the truck.

TJ said they were going to track down the truck. He told Sally to stay behind, but she told him she was a naval officer too and she did not take orders from him.

TJ found the truck heading west on I-64 towards the Hampton Bay Bridge Tunnel. By this time, the Navy had contacted the Virginia State Police and the Norfolk Police. The Virginia State Police set up a rolling roadblock on I-64. The Volvo was caught in traffic and saw police cars coming from behind, so the driver bumped cars out of his way and caused a major pile up. It was so bad that emergency response vehicles could not get through. TJ and Sally were able to get through traffic by lane splitting on their bikes.

The Volvo smashed through the rolling roadblock and three State Police cars were wrecked. The Volvo had no one in front of him at this point and it sped up to get away. TJ and Sally were going over 90 mph on their motorcycles when they caught up with the semi-truck. That is when TJ saw the man hanging out the passenger side window, pointing a large gun at them. They swerved to the other side of the lane as the man started shooting wildly.

Virginia State Police had a helicopter in the air within seconds heading to the scene. The Virginia State Police asked for help from the US Navy.

Meanwhile, the Admiral had contacted the President to inform him that two nuclear missiles had been stolen. The President asked if they had any drone aircraft available. "Yes, Mr. President, we do."

TJ and Sally came up on the wreckage of the 18-wheeler. The drone fired two gunshots and had taken out the truck. Wreckage was everywhere. TJ noticed a person running toward the woods. He went after him and caught the driver of the semi. TJ had him in an arm bar when Sally got there. He told Sally to get the string out of her jacket hood and tie up his hands. As she worked on getting the string loose, the man tried to run away, but TJ caught him.

The man grabbed a fallen tree branch and swung it at TJ's head; Sally placed a well-aimed kick to the side of his knee. It snapped—he was not going to run anymore. Sally let her husband tie the driver's hands together as she called 911 to let them know they had the driver in custody.

TJ searched for the man's wallet and found his driver's license. He was from Canada.

"So, Hugh, how do you pronounce your last name?"

CPSIA information can be obtained at www.ICGtesting.com
Printed in the USA
BVOW10s1416301113

337768BV00006B/10/P

9 781630 730031